THE CALL OF MCCALL

THE CALL OF MCCALL

GREGORY J. LALIRE

FIVE STAR
A part of Gale, a Cengage Company

LIBRARY OF CONGRESS CATALOGING-IN-PUBLICATION DATA

Names: Lalire, Gregory, author.
Title: The call of McCall / Gregory J. Lalire.
Description: First Edition. | Waterville, Maine : Five Star, a part of Gale, a Cengage Company, 2022. | Identifiers: LCCN 2022000083 | ISBN 9781432892722 (hardcover)
Classification: LCC PS3612.A54323 C35 2022 | DDC 813/.6—dc23
LC record available at https://lccn.loc.gov/2022000083

First Edition. First Printing: July 2022
Find us on Facebook—https://www.facebook.com/FiveStarCengage
Visit our website—http://www.gale.cengage.com/fivestar
Contact Five Star Publishing at FiveStar@cengage.com

Printed in Mexico
Print Number : 1   Print Year : 2022

In memory of Wild Bill Hickok biographer
Joseph G. Rosa (1932–2015)

INTRODUCTION

Call me McCall. No, not Jack McCall. Zach's the name. Jack's my younger half brother . . . or was. Jack's long dead. Long live Zach, full name Zacharias "Wild Child" McCall. Seldom, though, has anyone called me Zacharias. I acquired the Wild Child label early on, but it had far more to do with my rocky parentage and questionable upbringing than my behavior. It stuck with me, never mind that I haven't been a child in a crow's age and have been *mild* for as long as I can remember. I suppose it beats being called "Bastard McCall," which is what Little Jack called me plenty of times after we got to know each other.

It's a well-known fact that Jack McCall shot Wild Bill Hickok dead during a card game in Deadwood, Dakota Territory, fourteen years ago. Most people today aren't sure why he did it. More than a few still think it was out of revenge because Hickok killed his brother back in Kansas. Sure, I've been in Kansas. Even rubbed elbows with Wild Bill in Hays City and Abilene. But here I am alive and kicking in the booming copper mining town of Butte, Montana, home to 10,723 people and just four living trees—the rest having been removed to provide timber for mine tunnels, wood for new houses, and fuel for the smelter, or because they died from the sulfurous and arsenical smoke that is sometimes so thick I lose my way walking from my boarding-house down Iron Street and through the warehouse district to my job clerking at the Butte Hardware Co. Still, I am never late for work. Back in 1876, Deadwood was a boomtown, too—named for all the dead trees found in its gold-laden gulch—and even wilder than Butte. Not that I've done any mining in either place. I'm simply a hardware man, a mild one at that.

Truth be known, Little Jack had no full, legitimate brother—only three sisters. Those four were raised in Louisville, Kentucky. We had the same daddy, Fat Jack McCall, but I was raised as the Wild Child in a tavern-cum-brothel down in Boonesborough, and Fat Jack was barely involved. I never met Little Jack till the second-to-last year of the Civil War, and even those times he was at my disposal I didn't have much use for that cussed hobbledehoy. Not long after the war ended, he got drummed out of the family home at age fifteen and showed up at the Daniel's Den with his tail between his legs and his nose out of joint. He was looking for me, having heard about my shady home from Fat Jack. My half brother wasn't much, let me tell you, a scrawny, cross-eyed young rebel turned lickspittle whose broken nose was compliments of our daddy. He was desperate for a big brother. He dropped to his knees, kissed my shoes, and whimpered like a beaten dog. I got him back on his feet and to hold his head up, and then I couldn't get rid of him. He became rather full of himself. "Call me Little Jack," he demanded. "That's what I want to be called. You can see I ain't fat and I ain't never gonna be fat. So don't think of me as fat. But don't you ever think of me as *too little,* only as your *brother!*"

Sometimes I managed that. Mostly, though, I thought of him as only half a brother. Those times, I might call him "Crooked Nose Jack," which certainly fit. He got to hating that second nickname, just as I got to dislike being called "Wild Child" or "Bastard McCall." And it stayed that way right up to the day they hanged him.

—Zach McCall, August 1890, Butte, Montana

CHAPTER ONE:
OLD KENTUCKY HOMES

I was born in Boonesborough in the spring of 1845, the same year a Kentucky delegation that included Fat Jack McCall dug up the remains of Daniel and Rebecca Boone in Missouri and reburied the couple in our state capital, Frankfort. Daniel Boone, who died in 1820, was big even in death all over Kentucky and was an unrivaled giant in Boonesborough, which he had founded a month before the Revolutionary War started in far-off New England. Not that I'm related in any way to the Boone family, but Daniel was Fat Jack's hero, and I saw my first light in an upstairs room at the Daniel's Den, the same place I was conceived. The stone-and-brick building, a combination tavern and brothel, sat comfortably on Boonesborough's main thoroughfare. It had no known connection with the Boone family either but was a popular stopping-off place for travelers such as my daddy, who was based in Louisville, represented a number of distilleries between there and Lexington, and sold quality bourbon whiskey to establishments as far off as Pike County. My earliest memory is of me lying on the kitchen floor of the Daniel's Den cradling a bottle that didn't contain a drop of milk. For years I wasn't sure which of the working girls upstairs gave birth to me. I thought I had five or six mamas to go along with my visiting daddy, whose constant alcohol breath somehow comforted me.

The truth was, as I found out by accident when I was eight, my actual mother was known at the Daniel's Den and for miles around as "Virginia Reel," and, soon after naming me Zacharias (for the father of John the Baptist of biblical fame), she ran off in early spring 1846 with a passing stranger to Independence, Missouri. From there they joined the Donner Party—he one of the few bachelors, she the only unmarried lady—and set out in a wagon train bound for California. That pioneering group is well known to this day because they spent the winter of 1846–47 snowbound in the Sierra Nevada, where some of them resorted to cannibalism to survive. I wasn't one to ask questions or say much at all during my early years, but I always had my ears open, and Fat Jack was a talker when he got flushed on either bourbon whiskey or the lesser corn whiskey (not that I ever learned the difference). When I was nine or ten, I overheard him mesmerizing one of the newly hired girls at the Daniel's Den with secondhand tales of the Donner Party, and my mother's name came up again. "Truth be known, sugar, none of us knows exactly what happened to dear Virginia Reel on that unpleasant trip, but my best guess is our pioneering prostitute was one of the first ones eaten."

Fat Jack enjoyed being a traveling whiskey salesman to the hilt. He loved his drink—but never drank up his profits—and he loved his free-spirited ladies. Most of the Daniel's Den's female workers fell into that category, and they loved him back—in part because he was a free spender downstairs in the tavern and up stairs in the color-coded rooms but also because he treated each one as if she were a queen. I can't vouch for him treating his actual wife back in Louisville so well. All I know is he didn't mind being on the road and was never in a rush to get home.

He never spoke much about Mrs. McCall, and all he said about his three pampered daughters was that they were as fragile as china-head dolls and just as useless. He had more to say about his son Jack, calling him a lazy mama's boy with discomfiting eyes who could, if the moment struck him, be as ornery as a honey badger and show a stubborn streak as conspicuous as the Cumberland Gap. "That boy's worse than a china-head doll; he's a tiny weather-beaten rag doll who'll be the death of me yet," Fat Jack once told Belle Bragg, his most obliging upstairs girl and my favorite mother figure. "Considering vexatious Little Jack and his three fussy little sisters, none of whom even seem like my own flesh and blood, I got to say Zach is the apple of my eye." I heard Belle's reply, too: "You betcha, lover-honey. I was fond of poor old Virginia Reel all to pieces, and with you being a tied-up Louisville family man and all, least I can do is take heed of young bastard Zach for you till he's halfway grow'd up."

Being around Belle Bragg and the other gals, the hard-drinking patrons, and the Daniel's Den's predatory owner Angus Doyle got me grown up mighty fast. The first thing I learned to read were the labels on whiskey and medicinal bottles before graduating to *The National Police Gazette* and parts of *Uncle Tom's Cabin*. I saw more stockings, petticoats, and chemises by age twelve than a washerwoman sees in a lifetime. Angus Doyle put me to work by age seven, sweeping floors, washing glasses, fetching water, bringing hot and cold packs to his "doves of the roost," and emptying spittoons and chamber pots. The tavern customers were a diverse lot—some married, others far from it; some taking the time to pat me on the head, others knocking me over in their rush to get to a bed; some arriving wearing money belts, others showing up with just enough coin to leave flat broke; some owning land and slaves, others admitting to being abolitionists from Ohio; some regulars, others one-timers, but only one who I called Daddy. Fat Jack McCall, a king at the Daniel's Den whenever he paid a visit, treated me like a prince destined to inherit his throne. I never found his long absences peculiar, and it never bothered me that I got all my education in the home tavern, most of it thanks to the forbearance of Belle

Bragg and Daniel's Den long-time customer Robert "Raccoon" Gentry, who happened to be a learned circuit-riding preacher. After all, that was the only life I knew.

When I turned sixteen, on the eve of the Civil War, Fat Jack stayed over an extra day at the tavern to tell me the facts of life as he knew them, which didn't differ terribly much from the ones I had been picking up upstairs from the fallen Southern belles. That night I cornered him at the bar where he was building up courage to talk freely to his oldest son. He finally acknowledged what I had suspected for eight years—that Virginia Reel was my actual mother. He insisted that *we* shouldn't blame her for running off the way she did since she was white and free and unencumbered.

"What about me?" I asked. It was past my bedtime, and I was delaying his bedtime, too, but I was looking for some answers.

"What about you? You were just a baby."

"I know, Daddy. Didn't that make me a . . . what do you call it, an encumbrance?"

"Not at all. Virginia totally lacked motherly instincts. She knew there were plenty of other gals around here who weren't going anywhere and would feed and shelter you till manhood. Besides, you were my responsibility, Zach, and still are. I paid to have you, you might say, and I'm still paying for your upkeep. I don't mind, mind you. You can stand on your own two feet. One day you might even make your father proud. At worst, I can't see you ever being a major disappointment to your daddy, unlike some sons who sure enough are that."

"Like the one in Louisville?"

"Yeah. How many do you think there are?"

"I wouldn't know. I don't even know that one's name."

"No reason to. He's eleven years young, clings to his mother's skirt tails, tells me nothing but tall tales, is mean enough to hang cats and rats by *their* tails, and turns tail and runs whenever he feels threatened by anything or anyone."

"Including you?"

"Especially me. He's the nervous type. Wouldn't surprise me if he turned into a nancy-boy."

"Nancy his mother's name?"

"No, and no need for you to know her name either or give her a moment's thought. My wife is pious, delicate, submissive, and unquestioning and bores me to tears. Enough said. She is making the three girls in her own image, while she allows Little Jack to question every damn thing I ever say and *never* submit to my requests or obey my wishes. Nothing I can do, and I've tried; Lord knows I've tried. He's a namby-pamby, and I can't beat it out of him."

"Jack is his name, too, huh, my little half brother?"

"Look, that just slipped out. He has nothing to do with you. He isn't anything like you."

"I'm no namby-pamby, that's for certain. Maybe he'll grow out of it."

"Not likely. He's growing into it."

"You don't beat me."

"You don't give me cause. You aren't gonna start now, are you?"

"Not if you don't start something. I'm sixteen. I won't stand to be beaten by you or anyone else. I told Angus Doyle the same."

"Bully for you. You're a real McCall, Zach."

"Thanks, Daddy. I don't mind at all being your bastard son."

"Good boy, nearly a man. Maybe next time I'll buy you your first drink."

"Right. So far, all my other drinks have been free, you know, on the house for services rendered to old man Doyle."

"Yeah. Angus ain't all the time a bastard, no offense intended."

"I think of the mama I never knew from time to time, you know?"

"Suppose that's natural. But you ain't had it so bad, have you, what with Belle and the others?"

"No, sir. It's just, sometimes I picture one of them Donner people taking a bite out of her. Don't wish that fate on anyone, let alone my own mother."

"Life is hard, Zach, not that you need me to tell you that."

"Would you have married her—I mean, if you weren't already married?"

"Virginia Reel wasn't the marrying kind. A man couldn't tell her what to do. She was as rebellious as the Southern Democrats. She wanted to paint her face, so she painted it. She sure never bored me. Had a mind of her own, she did—never learned the secret of obedience. I don't blame her one bit for taking off with that mule man to see California. Let me tell you, boy, it wasn't to settle down with him or to get rich. That was three whole years before the Gold Rush. I figure Virginia just felt like dipping her bare feet into the Pacific Ocean."

"But she never got there. Some sorry starving son of a bitch ate her."

"Sad but true, Son. But don't you go believing like Preacher Raccoon that she died for her sins. Forty others in the Donner Party died, too, including the very young and very righteous."

"You got to leave tomorrow, Daddy?"

"At the crack of dawn, first thing, or second thing anyway. But I'll pass this way again on my return from Pike County. I always do."

"You sure do like the ladies, don't you, Daddy?"

"Nothing wrong with that, is there?"

"Not in my mind, but I'm not your son in Louisville, let

alone your wife?"

"She might suspect my road trips aren't all business, but she doesn't ask questions. I'm a damn good provider. That's what matters most to them; that makes me a good family man."

"Even though you beat Little Jack? But not your daughters and wife, right?"

"Of course not. The McCall females are dwarf cinquefoils—delicate flowers. Little Jack is like purple cudweed."

"Belle hasn't taught me the names of all the plants yet."

"Cudweed isn't necessarily plug ugly, but it is almost always objectionable. You know I wouldn't strike Little Jack if he wasn't so . . . so obstinate."

"I don't think Belle taught me that word either."

"It means he keeps acting like a little shit, if you'll pardon my French."

"No problem. I hear a lot of *French* here at the Daniel's Den."

Beauregard the bartender brought around another bottle of bourbon whiskey, but Fat Jack put a hand over the top of his glass and said, "No more, Beau. It's bedtime."

Beauregard glanced at me with his one good eye (a mean drunk had poked his other one with a knife, as I had witnessed at age eight) and smirked. He knew of a couple occasions in which I had drunk enough corn whiskey to get sick. He had never personally been the one to pour me a drink, said it was against the rules, but I wasn't sure if it was the preacher or Daddy who had laid down that particular rule. "Past bedtime, I'd say," Beauregard said as he picked up the empty glass and wiped the wet ring off the bar top.

"You like Belle Bragg best?" I asked after Beauregard had bowed to Daddy and shuffled off to another customer.

"How 'bout heading off to bed now, Zach," Fat Jack said. "You'll have to get up plenty early if you aim to bid me farewell tomorrow."

"What has she got that your wife in Louisville doesn't?"

"Damn. What a question to ask at bedtime. You're sixteen going on twenty-one."

"How 'bout an answer, Daddy?"

"Fine. I'll tell you." But now he did want another drink, and he waved Beauregard over to pour it. He gulped every drop, and his next words came out slightly slurred. "Hannah—all right, now you know her name—and Belle are as different as a plowhorse from a racehorse. Belle is a lot the way Virginia Reel was, as free as the wind, as wild as the Missouri River, and as inviting as the mouth of Mammoth Cave. Did I just say that? Pardon me, boy, but I must be three sheets to the wind. I'll have to tell you about Mammoth Cave sometime."

"I know what *inviting* is. I reckon your wife, your Hannah, is just too tame."

"Smart boy. We understand each other. A man needs a home with a domesticated lady to run it, but there are times a man needs to run off and get his other needs met."

"And Belle Bragg obliges real good in her Red Room."

"You got that right. She's my wild woman, and you are my wild child."

"Except I'm not a child anymore, and Belle isn't my real mother."

"Sure. Still, I'm your daddy and always will be. I raised you right by not trying to raise you or taking you home to Louisville and allowing Hannah to get her smothering lily-white hands on you. Let me tell you—and I meant to tell you this years ago—there's plenty worse things to be than Wild Child McCall."

"Remind me to thank you someday."

"It's a blessing, believe me. You have no idea what she's done to Little Jack."

"Maybe one day I'll see for myself."

"Don't make a point of it. Best you forget all about the little shit and the other Louisville McCalls. Now, we really should go upstairs and turn in, Zach. But hold on one minute. I almost forgot. I've been meaning to lay a bit of advice on you about the ladies that is sure to come in handy most anywhere you go in this world."

"Shoot, if you must."

"Females of the species ain't naturally as pious, delicate, submissive, and unquestioning as most of the male population demands them to be."

"You don't think I already learned that at the Daniel's Den?"

"Maybe, but there's a second part to it. What you got to do is go against the grain, boy, and put smiles on their faces by listening to their deepest, darkest secrets, letting them be who they want to be, and doing unto them as you would have them do unto you."

"Got it. Thanks, Daddy. Good night. And say good night to Belle for me."

"You got it, Wild Child."

Chapter Two:
A Confederate Spy

Fat Jack did stop back at the Daniel's Den on his return trip from Pike County to his Louisville home, but he didn't even stay the night. The Civil War had started with the bombardment of Fort Sumter down in South Carolina, and he knew his beloved Kentucky, as a border state, would be right in the middle of it. He figured spilling blood would be the same as spilling good whiskey—a terrible waste. He professed his love for the Union, even if it was imperfect, saying he believed in freedom as much as the Northerners did, but not to the extent they should be allowed to freely deprive good citizens of the South of their property, namely slaves. He was anxious to get the lay of the land in Lexington and Louisville and let Kentuckians know that the best course of action to achieve peace and security in these troubled times was through full-fledged neutrality.

"All I'm saying, Wild Child, is don't do anything too wild," he advised me before departing Boonesborough in his whiskey wagon. "Don't go picking up a musket and marching off to fight for either side just to prove yourself a man. The horrors of war are real. Sometimes the best way to reconcile differences is by compromise. Look no farther than Henry Clay, the pride of Kentucky. His son was killed down Mexico way in '47, and Henry worked his britches off making sure we wouldn't get in another damn war, a far costlier one at that. A pillar of the Lexington community and the best damned statesman who ever went to Washington, old Henry played a mean game of poker and was known to raise a whiskey glass or two hundred. He was against war for sure, but nobody ever said Henry Clay wasn't a *man*."

"Trouble is he died eight years ago and there is war now—one that's a hell of a lot closer than Mexico," I said. "How can we stay out of it? I say if South Carolina or any other state wants to leave this here Union, they should be free to do so."

"You been listening to Beauregard, who is trying to make amends for being the black sheep of his Virginia slaveholding family, and those fallen Southern belles they got around here putting on airs for their warlike Southern gentlemen frequenters."

I started pacing because I had been listening to everyone and didn't know what to think. My feet began to feel as if they were made of clay, so I sat down.

Fat Jack patted my head and continued. "A couple years ago, Kentucky-born Abe Lincoln said, 'A house divided against itself cannot stand.' Abe's no doubt right, but I say there can be a house standing up north, another house standing down south, and our Kentucky log cabin standing smack dab in the middle on our neutral path."

"Angus Doyle wholeheartedly supports President Lincoln and the Northern cause. He makes no bones about that. He claims it's in Kentucky's best economic interest, meaning his own. What does he need with slaves? He has Beauregard and me."

"I thought you were happy here at the Daniel's Den, son?"

"Well, Daddy, let's just say I'm not so unhappy I'd want to shoot a Yankee, not even Doyle."

"Good boy. I'll be seeing you down the road. Remember: neutrality is the word."

It was easy to remember for a while. The state legislature

agreed with Fat Jack and declared Kentucky would take no part in the Civil War, Lincoln tolerated neutrality so as not to lose the state to the Confederacy ("I think to lose Kentucky is to lose the whole game," the president said), and I didn't view myself as a natural-born fighter. Things changed in late summer 1861. The neutrality was too fragile to last, with both sides violating it, and I could no longer tolerate Angus Doyle's bossing me around and giving me little more than room and board for my services. On September 18, the legislature declared neutrality formally over, and Kentucky entered the war on the Union side. At dawn less than a week later, still only sixteen, I stole one of Angus Doyle's riding horses and galloped away from the tavern after a tearful parting (which did include one lengthy, smothering kiss) with Belle Bragg, who had come out of her Red Room to see me off. No, I wasn't planning on enlisting in any bloody army. It was my intention to look up my father in Louisville because he hadn't returned to the Den since his "neutrality" speech.

"Don't blame you for skedaddling, lover-honey," Belle had said through her tears and yawns, though calling me a lover-honey was a pronounced exaggeration (perhaps my father was on her half-awake mind; Daddy and I did have the same well-defined jawlines and well-cut noses, plus I had started growing a beard like his). "Angus can be such an ass sometimes. He never appreciated what he had in you all these years; it was like having his own eunuch to do the dirty work and protect his harem."

My tears instantly stopped running. This was clearly another pronounced exaggeration, but in the opposite direction. "What do you mean by eunuch?" I snapped.

"Shush—you'll wake somebody. It was a poor choice of words on my part."

"I'll say it was," I shouted, crossing my arms and lifting my well-defined jawline.

That's when she uncrossed my arms and gave me the smothering kiss to quiet me down, which in turn gave me second thoughts about leaving.

"It's a sad day, but it's for the best," Belle said as she backed out of my arms. "Give my regards to your daddy. If Fat Jack's not been too hampered by the war troubles, ask him to come down and see me some time. I'm not too proud to request the king's company again."

I would have delivered the message, but I wasn't at that time able to locate the McCall residence in Louisville. I was stopped by federal troops who were flooding the city. Some suspected me of being a Southern sympathizer or a spy and wanted to boot me clear out of the state, and the others tried to muster me into the Union Army. I must have looked much older than I was. I became disoriented, and in the confusion, my horse (well, Angus Doyle's horse) ran off. Not liking the treatment given me on the street, I hid out in an alley for several hours and then slipped into an inviting tavern (being at home in such places) with a young man—that is to say, only slightly older than me—who couldn't stop whistling "Dixie." He and a couple other fellows were willing to share their drinks with a stranger, and that unparalleled amount of whiskey consumption got me in a fighting mood. I dropped my glass and made two fists, which I waved about until I passed out. It turned out these fellows were anti-Union State Guardsmen whose weapons had been taken away from them by the military board. They must have carried me out of that tavern, but soon enough I was on my own two feet walking with them all the way to Tennessee. We were leaving Kentucky to fight for the Confederacy.

Just below the state line I was readily accepted as man enough to fight and got my quick training at Camp Boone before heading north again. I was one of 1,300 Confederate soldiers who helped Kentucky-born Brigadier General Simon Bolivar Buckner occupy Bowling Green, which in November became the capital of the provisional Confederate government of Kentucky. We only stayed until February 1862 because General Ulysses S. Grant was in the neighborhood. During the withdrawal, we were blowing up some bridges on the Barren River so his Union forces couldn't use them when a premature explosion near crippled me. I was left behind—not sure if it was intentional or not—and eventually got a ride in a farmer's wagon back to Bowling Green, where I turned seventeen and spent the next nine months recovering from my ankle wounds. I wasn't what you'd call a die-hard Rebel, but the Yankees found me, made me their prisoner, and treated me so bad that I vowed vengeance.

Thing was, the bluecoats paroled me, which meant I couldn't return to the military of the Confederacy in any capacity. At that point I became a civilian spy by accident. One day I slipped into a tent in search of something—medicine or whiskey—to ease the pain in my ankles, and it turned out to be the tent of Colonel John Hunt Morgan, known as the Thunderbolt of the South. Impressed that I had gotten by his staff unseen, that my face showed youthful innocence (I was still trying to grow that beard), and that I possessed an inner eagerness to pay back those damned Yankees, the colonel declared, "Son of the South, I like the cut of your jib."

My main job was to stir up pro-Southern sentiments in Kentucky and gather information for the colonel. Indeed, when Morgan rode into my home state in July 1862, many admiring citizens openly welcomed him and his nine hundred handpicked Confederate cavalrymen. The raiders swept through the state winning assorted skirmishes, some of which I witnessed, and striking fear in the hearts of Kentucky's Union military government and its supporters. "They are having a stampede in

Kentucky!" President Lincoln cried from the White House. I felt I had done my job, and Morgan did, too. He took me to Knoxville, which was then controlled by the Confederates but whose citizens were divided in their loyalties. It was my job to report to Morgan any pockets of strong Unionists. Not that I saw much of him. On December 11, 1862, he was promoted to brigadier general, and three days later he married Mattie Ready, the daughter of a politician.

I myself met my share of fair ladies in Knoxville, some for the North, some for the South. Their political persuasions didn't matter to me; despite my friendship with General Morgan, I was adaptable to whatever ways they wanted to persuade me, short of marrying them, that is, since I was too young for that sort of thing. Too shy to talk most of the time, I listened to them (as Fat Jack had advised me to do), and one or two suggested that I was the first male of any age to ever truly do that. On occasion I put smiles on their faces, sometimes even intentionally. They did all they could to make my ankles feel better. During this pliant period, I stopped missing Belle Bragg and got over my homesickness for the Daniel's Den. It was strange that I had to leave there and the state of Kentucky to uncover some—but certainly not all—of the deeper mysteries of womanhood.

By the summer of 1863 when I was all of eighteen, a certain trouble had arisen with one enticing belle intent on me making an honest woman of her, since she had a two year old at home named Jeb (after the Virginia cavalry general J. E. B. Stuart) who needed a daddy (the real one had never married her and then had gotten himself killed at Shiloh). I admitted to Frances Clayton that I was a bastard myself but told her I grew up just fine without a mother and only seeing my Daddy McCall every two months or so when he traveled my way on whiskey business. She wouldn't buy it. She wanted better for little Jeb—and was damn insistent about it. Lucky for me, I could defer immediate living arrangements with Frances and Jeb by leaving town with Morgan, who was planning another raid of Kentucky and again wanted my services as a civilian spy. That was as close to becoming a rogue as I ever was, before or since. Miss Frances couldn't complain, not when she was of the opinion that General John Hunt Morgan was nearly as handsome and heroic and loyal to the Confederacy as General James Ewell Brown Stuart.

Plenty of folks in Kentucky again welcomed Morgan and his cavalrymen with open arms. His superiors wanted him to cause enough havoc in the state to divert Union troops and resources from operations elsewhere. After I provided the general with some valuable information about a small Union garrison at Lebanon, Kentucky, Morgan surprised and captured it. In the last successful charge, his younger brother Thomas fell to federal bullets. Despite his sorrow at the loss of a brother (I told him I knew exactly how he felt even though I had not yet met my half brother), Morgan patted me on the back and told me I was just like Thomas (when Thomas was alive, of course) and that nothing would stop *us* now. When Morgan headed northward toward Louisville, I gladly went along, hoping to catch Fat Jack there and perhaps even get my first glimpse at the rest of the McCall family. No such luck. South of the city, Morgan suddenly turned his men to the northwest and headed for the Ohio River. He confided in me that it was his long-held desire to bring the terror of war to Indiana and Ohio just as General Robert E. Lee was doing over in Pennsylvania. I couldn't say no when the general asked me to ride along with him and then requested I proceed ahead on a secret mission into Indiana to see if the Copperheads there would support his impending raid.

I located the Copperhead leader in Indiana, but he wasn't inclined to aid Morgan. In fact, this fellow definitely did not like the cut of my jib and notified some Union boys, who chased me down to the Ohio River, where I had no choice but to swim across under gunfire. Back in Kentucky I wanted to try to locate kin in Louisville again, but my sense of loyalty to Morgan was too strong, so I wandered around till I found him. Indeed, he was chomping at the bit to be fed information. I told him about all those able-bodied Indiana men forming militia companies and organizing their state's defense. Morgan shrugged, gave me a friendly tap on the cheek, and then plunged ahead with me right behind him in case I could be of further spying service. After doing some burning and looting in a few Indiana towns and with federal soldiers in pursuit, Morgan boldly continued on into Ohio, destroying bridges, railroads, and government stores. The Ohioans had been aroused and put up strong resistance. Union gunboats kept Morgan from crossing the river to the relative safety of Kentucky. Morgan reversed course and got as far north as the village of Salineville. It was there on July 25 I was arrested as a suspicious character while pretending to be a young Union businessman looking to relocate to northeastern Ohio. Near Salineville the next day, the outnumbered Confederates got whipped, ending Morgan's Raid. The elusive Morgan himself was caught at last and jailed in a place misnamed Wellsville, where who should he find simmering in the next cell but me.

Morgan expected to be taken to a prisoner-of-war camp, and indeed many of his men ended up in the Camp Douglas stockade in Chicago. The authorities, though, had heard that captured Union officers were placed in Southern prisons, so they decided to treat the general the same way, sticking him in the recently constructed Ohio Penitentiary in Columbus. I was labeled a notorious Confederate spy and tossed in the same primitive facility. It wasn't long before I came up with a plan that Morgan readily approved—one that would get us the hell out of that joint before Christmas. It was daring, all right, but really quite simple. Morgan, a half-dozen of his captains, and I tunneled from an air shaft under our cells to the prison yard, emerged like moles, and scaled the walls like monkeys. We immediately headed south, looking to hop a railroad car to get across the Ohio River. Only two of us got caught, and one wasn't me, because Morgan shot two of our closest pursuers, and I shot a third while aggravating my right ankle by stepping into a gopher hole. We missed catching a train but managed to purloin a boat previously used by the Underground Railroad to help slaves escape into the free states. While under fire from shore, I rowed like the devil, and Morgan sat in back giving me the necessary directions and encouragement.

"That sure was close," I told the general once our feet were planted on Kentucky soil, my right one not so firmly because that ankle was still throbbing.

"We've lived to fight another day," Morgan said. "We'll head on to Tennessee and resume these intoxicating activities."

"You, not me, sir. I aim to find me a Kentucky tavern and drink enough to forget this war. I'm no soldier."

"But not a bad spy at all, and an excellent tunnel digger."

"Thank you, General. But I'll be looking for a new line of work."

"Good luck, Zach. You did good for a young man whose heart wasn't in it."

"But the rest of me sure was. My ankles are worn out. My hands are still shaking as much as my knees. And my head's spinning. I killed that fellow back there. Got him in the stomach. It was too easy, too bloody easy."

"A blue belly. You did good. And don't you ever forget it, friend. Farewell."

"You, too, General. Peace be with you."

It was a ridiculous thing to say, what with a civil war going strong and him being a feared Rebel raider, but Morgan merely tugged on his pointed beard and tipped his rakish hat to show his respect to his civilian friend, yours truly. "Till we meet again," he said.

But, of course we didn't. Morgan was closer to a court martial than a commendation for his flashy northern raid because he had disobeyed his specific orders *not* to cross the Ohio. He went to Richmond to plead his case and eventually was given another command in eastern Tennessee. He went back to raiding in Kentucky but without his old vim and vigor, and then he decided to attack the Union forces that now had the upper hand in Knoxville. In early September 1864 he was spending the night at the Greenville, Tennessee, home of one of his wife's distant relatives when Union soldiers surrounded the house in an attempt to capture him. Morgan was trying to surrender when an itchy-fingered Union private shot him in the back and shouted, "I have killed the damned horse thief."

When I learned of Morgan's death, I felt worse than I had when I was wounded or when I was thrown in prison as a Confederate spy or even when I shot (and almost certainly killed) that man to keep from being recaptured. John Hunt Morgan was an army general, an important man—that was obvious to everyone, no matter which side of the Ohio River you lived on—yet he had treated me as a friend, if not a younger brother. No man had ever done that before. I reckon I was wracked with guilt because I hadn't been in Knoxville spying on the Union forces for him and could have maybe warned him to get out of Greenville before the blue bellies moved in for the kill. At the time of his death, I was in Louisville, Kentucky, where I was nursing my old war wounds (both ankles) and bottles of Fat Jack's whiskey, as I had decided at age nineteen to become *neutral* and sit out the rest of the war with the McCall family.

CHAPTER THREE:
TWO BROTHERS

It was necessary for me to lay low in late June 1864 when I arrived in Louisville. Union General William Tecumseh Sherman's brother-in-law, Hugh Ewing, served as the military commander of the city. But the real problem was General Stephen G. Burbridge, who had fought against John Hunt Morgan and now, as the big blue belly in Kentucky, was charged with weeding out Confederate guerrillas. In early July, President Lincoln declared martial law in the state, which meant Burbridge had ultimate rule. Eleven days later, the Butcher of Kentucky issued Order No. 59, which stated, "Whenever an unarmed Union citizen is murdered, four guerrillas will be selected from the prison and publicly shot to death at the most convenient place near the scene of the outrages." I had no wish to commit murder or any other outrages, but as a former Confederate soldier and spy who had ridden with Morgan, I didn't dare show myself on the streets of Louisville during the Butcher's reign of terror. My safe haven was the attic of the McCall house not far from the Gait House, on the northeast corner of Second and Main Streets, where U. S. Grant and other Union generals had met in March to plan the scorched-earth campaign known as Sherman's March to the Sea.

I had not been unanimously welcomed at the home of my father's legitimate family. Fat Jack had genuine concern for me, but he was more concerned about me interacting in his home life, which he had made as separate from his life on the road as

Massachusetts is from Mississippi. He had good reason. His wife, Hannah, was on the surface a genteel, milky-white Kentucky woman, but she possessed a mean streak wider than the Missouri River. She had not known about Fat Jack's bastard son—me—until I showed up one rainy July day with hat in hand, looking for handouts and protection. Little Jack was off in the alleyways playing Rebel soldier by himself. The three girls were in their room playing dolls (china-head dolls, I assumed). Fat Jack was out somewhere trying to drum up whiskey business at one of the local saloons and likely wouldn't be home until the evening meal. Hannah's good manners as the lady of the house lasted about five minutes, right up until I revealed my true identity.

She allowed me to wait without offering me a chair or a drink of any kind. The three sisters soon ventured down the stairs and curtseyed in well-trained fashion, but this time it did not please their mother. The tallest girl, twelve-year-old Emily, offered her hand as if she meant for me to kiss it the way a true gentleman might. I didn't get the chance to try that out because Hannah stepped between us and sent all three daughters into the kitchen to drink cold lemonade.

"Don't go near them; don't tell them anything," Hannah warned me when they were gone, and to emphasize the point she kicked me in my aching right shin. Being well bred she automatically apologized for her clumsiness but then said, without a hint of a smile, "Everyone will have to watch their step in this household."

I kept thinking Little Jack would show up at any moment, and I would finally get to meet my half brother, but an hour passed without any sign of him. I felt about as welcome as a rabid dog, but Hannah did finally direct me to sit in an armless chair in the corner of the parlor. It was Fat Jack who returned first, and he was in a bad mood because nobody in town was buying his good whiskey. Hannah's mood was worse. She came out of the kitchen, where she had no doubt been guarding the girls, waving an iron skillet. Husband and wife were arguing about me even before Fat Jack could spot me in the corner. I sat frozen, wondering if this was a regular occurrence or if Hannah was now delivering pieces of her mind that had lain dormant or suppressed for years of marriage. Things took a turn for the worse right before my eyes. With something close to a Rebel yell, Hannah charged her husband and crowned him with an iron skillet before he could defend his position.

Fat Jack went down hard, but seeing him laid out on the parlor rug didn't make me rush to his side. Instead, I held my own head and warily eyed the skillet in Hannah's hands. But she ignored me and just stood over her husband, the skillet lowered like a smoking rifle no longer needed.

"There's no room here for one of your bastards," she told Fat Jack when he woke up and immediately reached for the back of his head.

"For land's sake, woman!" cried Fat Jack. "How many do you think there are?"

"All I know, Mr. Jack McCall, is there is one too many in *my* home, you bastard."

I jumped clear out of my chair when she used that word again and might even have said "Yes, ma'am" before I realized she was actually addressing her husband.

"Thanks for nothing," said Fat Jack, rubbing the bump I thought I could see even at a distance. "Did you have to hit me so hard in the head?"

"Yes, I did," Hannah said without hesitation, and then she hurried off to the kitchen. I wanted to say something to my father but couldn't even manage to clear my throat. I could hear Hannah talking to the girls, probably telling them to have some cornbread with their lemonade. She returned, thankfully without the skillet. She carried a damp cloth and several bandages. She knelt beside Fat Jack, cradled his head, wiped the wounded area with the cloth, and then applied a bandage that seemed mighty large for one bump. "There," she said, standing up and wiping her hands on the front of her dress. "All better now."

Fat Jack McCall looked as if he were recovering from some dreadful Civil War wound—a sight that no doubt would cause their neighbors to treat the McCalls with more respect than when they viewed the man of the house as nothing more than a whiskey salesman hell-bent on neutrality and profits. Fat Jack seemed to be struggling with his response. He did manage to push himself up to a sitting position on the rug.

"You have behaved badly," she told him. "Don't make things worse."

"Me?" Fat Jack then saw me in the corner, standing like a soldier at attention, and waved me over to him. He nodded to me, and I helped him stand and shuffle to a chair. Once he was reasonably comfortable, he sat back and let out a long sigh—the kind President Lincoln no doubt frequently issued in the White House. "What do you expect me to do?" he asked.

I thought the question was directed at me, so I quickly mentioned how I was his own flesh and blood, wasn't even twenty yet, and my ankles hurt. I didn't tell him they had been injured while serving John Hunt Morgan, if not the South, in the war, because he had warned me about the dangers of involvement in the "brother vs. brother" conflict and because I wasn't certain where he stood now. He wasn't listening to me anyway. His wife was talking at the same time. When she enunciated the word "obligation," Fat Jack bolted upright in the chair. "What are you saying, woman?" he demanded to know.

She eagerly repeated herself, telling her husband exactly what she expected him to do now. "One night under *our* family's roof is enough," she insisted. "Give him a bottle or two of your precious whiskey, if you must. But show him to the door come morning and tell him to hit the road—to skedaddle to wherever he came from, to return to the trollop who bore him."

"His mother isn't around—dead! The place he was raised is in far-off Boonesborough and owned by a die-hard Yankee not inclined to show mercy." Fat Jack snorted with every third word, his face reddening. But then he hung his head, his eyes downcast. "The wild child doesn't have anywhere else to turn," he added in a distressed whisper.

"Well, damn him and damn you . . ."

"All right. I be damned. But the truth is, Little Jack acts like a bastard more so than any natural child. And I'd rather turn out *our* son than send Zach into the clutches of Burbridge."

"How dare you say such a thing about our curly-haired baby boy! It isn't natural!"

Grumbling under his breath, Fat Jack accidentally bit his tongue so hard that he forgot for a moment about his sore head and pressed his knuckles to his closed mouth. It was for the best. Hannah looked ready to fetch the skillet.

I already had an idea why Fat Jack had said that about Little Jack, and I would learn more because the curly-haired baby boy soon marched through the front door whistling "Dixie." Fat Jack, no doubt realizing there was no point trying to hide the truth with me standing in the middle of his Louisville parlor, introduced us as brothers, which caused Hannah McCall to throw up her hands and retreat into the kitchen. We shook hands, and Little Jack seemed to squeeze with all his strength as if that might impress me.

"What a grand surprise," he said, still trying to squeeze but losing his grip. "I . . . I . . . I always wished I had me a brother. Where you been all my life?"

"Around, but not around here," I said, pulling my hand away.

"Lately, I've been soldiering some."

"No foolin'? That's grand! I'm fourteen going on fifteen. I'll be doing the same in a year or two if General Lee keeps up the good fight."

"Let's hope not. There's been enough killing."

"How many you killed, brother?"

"Even one is one too many. There's no glory in that."

"There is if they's Yankees. You were trying to kill blue bellies, right?"

"Look, kid. I don't want to talk about it."

"Right. Burbridge or one of his damn Yankee spies might be listening."

We were silent for a while, sizing each other up. Little Jack was small, all right, the top of his head barely as high as my Adam's apple, but he was no baby, and his hair wasn't all that curly. When he looked up, it was discomfiting at first because he didn't look at me straight on; his brown eyes were slightly crossed and restless. He reached up and touched my head, as if trying to figure out my exact height.

"I figure to be as big as you one day," he said, and then he began asking me more questions about the war. I was glad when we were called in for the evening meal, not wanting to think about the war and not having eaten regular for weeks. There was plenty on the table to devour—pan-fried chicken, black-eyed peas, mustard greens, and, yes, cornbread—and Little Jack matched Fat Jack bite for bite. I tried to show some restraint, not filling my mouth too fast and not talking with my mouth full, but Hannah scowled at me the whole time anyway from the other side of the table, where she sat with her three manner-minding daughters.

During the meal, Little Jack and the girls talked a bit too freely to please Mrs. McCall. When Little Jack prattled on about putting on a gray uniform and going off to help Robert E. Lee, eight-year-old Sarah, who did have impressive blonde curls, suggested that her brother was actually a "fraidy-cat" who liked to bake bread with mother and play dolls with her when nobody was looking. Little Jack called her a brat and a liar and boasted that killing a Yankee wasn't any harder than killing a cat. That got the middle girl, ten-year-old Catherine, crying and repeating the word, "Minnie." The oldest girl, Emily, explained to me that two weeks ago her brother had hanged Minnie, the family tabby, by the tail, thrown stones at her, and finished her off with Papa's nasty old switch. Minnie was buried in the backyard in case I wanted her to show me the stone marker.

"It scratched and bit me," Little Jack explained. "Minnie was a monster."

Hannah McCall told everyone to hush and eat their black-eyed peas. Sarah quickly gulped down whatever food was in her dimpled mouth before adding, "I always liked Wyatt better. He was such a nice dog." I later learned that Fat Jack's old hunting hound used to growl steadily at Little Jack before somebody fed Wyatt pork laced with rat poison more than two years ago. Some things children just don't forget.

By the end of my first day with the McCall family, it had become abundantly clear that the house was loaded with tension and dissension and that my presence exacerbated the unsettling situation. Still, I was exhausted and glad to be allowed to share Little Jack's bed for the night. He kicked in his sleep, and many of the kicks found my sore ankles. I was about ready to go sleep on the floor when he started screaming. I shook his shoulder to wake him up and let him know he was having a nightmare. He told me he had been surrounded by blue-coated men with bayonets who intended to make a slave out of him. Since bluecoats were not in the business of enslaving, the dream made no sense to me until Little Jack admitted one of the fiercer men surrounding him sported the same short beard, Roman nose, and whiskey-wet lips as our father.

"You don't like your daddy much," I commented, which was a mistake, because I wanted to go back to sleep.

"Not much at all. About as much as I liked Wyatt."

"You mean the hound dog you poisoned?"

"Mother's more likely to poison Father than I am. She hates what he did. And she hates you because you are living proof of what Fat Jack did on the road."

"In the Daniel's Den, a drinking place that's also a brothel, down in Boonesborough. That's where I happened to grow up."

"Grand! What exactly is a brothel, Brother?"

I spent the next half hour telling him about the Daniel's Den and my modest existence there. He clung to every word, showing no signs of wanting to go back to sleep. Finally, I was too talked out to continue, turned my back on him, and made snoring sounds.

"Don't worry, Brother," he told me. "Mother isn't half as mean as Father is. She'll get used to you. I sure don't hate you just because you were born where you was. Being a wild child and then a Confederate soldier having all those adventures makes you kind of . . . I don't know, special."

"Well, I'm not. I need my sleep like anyone else."

"Sure, Brother, sure. But you'll stick around here now, won't you?"

"Not sure they'll let me. Daddy might, but not your mama."

"You can't hit a lady, but maybe you could give Father a sock in his fat jaw."

"What for? I wouldn't be here if not for him."

"Yeah, but he's awfully mean to me, and what can a little guy like me do about it? Give him a sock for me, would you?"

"I don't plan on socking anyone anytime soon. Go to sleep, Little Jack. Dream about something else."

In the morning I got a hot biscuit and scrambled eggs but a

cold shoulder from Hannah McCall and not so much as a "good morning" from Emily, Catherine, or Sarah.

"Maybe it's best that I leave now," I said after my belly was full.

"Yes, for the best all around," Hannah said. "If you don't know the way back to Boonesborough, my husband can give you directions."

Fat Jack stopped chewing, sighed, and closed his eyes.

"He can't go, Mother," said Little Jack, spitting egg.

"And why not? He has his own life to lead."

"What a life he's led! He has lived in a brothel and shot Yankees. He . . . he needs a rest. I don't want him to leave."

"You hush, Little Jack McCall," said Hannah, making her fork clink against her plate. "Your sisters can hear while they are chewing, you know? This is a family meal."

"Zach is family, isn't he?"

"No, he is not. If you're finished eating, you can go to your room."

"I'm not at all finished."

"Then don't talk with your mouth full. Sit and chew with your mouth closed."

"I won't!" Little Jack threw his napkin toward his mother (it landed in Catherine's plate instead), pushed back his chair so it screeched against the floor, and ran upstairs.

Hannah immediately excused the girls, who obeyed without objection and scurried off to their own rooms. She did not excuse me but ignored me and my feelings. "See what a terrible influence *your bastard* is on *my boy*!" she said, so coldly I shivered.

"*Your boy* killed Minnie, and I haven't forgotten what happened to my hunting dog," Fat Jack muttered. "And now that we're talking about him, I meant to say something earlier about several missing bottles of my best whiskey and one empty bottle

36

I discovered beneath Little Jack's bed."

"I'm well aware of it. I am here every day, Jack, so I know what's going on. Little Jack said Emily put the empty bottle under his bed to get him in trouble."

"And you believed him? The boy lies like Harriet Beecher Stowe. Do you honestly think your carefully trained Emily would allow whiskey to touch her soft, innocent lips?"

"Of course not! I'm sure she dumped out the whiskey instead of drinking it."

"And that somehow makes it better? Land's sake, Hannah, the children are enough to drive a man to drink."

"You've never needed an excuse to do that. I'll have you know Little Jack doesn't even like whiskey."

"It's an acquired taste."

"All this is beside the point at the moment," Hannah said, pounding a fist on the table, an action I most associated with Angus Doyle back at the Daniel's Den. "We're talking about . . . about . . . him." She pointed a finger at me as if lining up a musket shot. "He'll have to go."

"We'll see how it goes in the next few weeks."

"What? No. Absolutely not. He must leave today."

"That isn't being charitable, Hannah. Just look at him sitting quietly there, being seen but not heard. Why, his elbows aren't even on the table."

"Do *not* mock me, Jack McCall. He'll keep Little Jack awake with his horrible tales. And, heaven knows, Little Jack is prone to nightmares. I simply won't allow it!"

"Very well," Fat Jack said, rubbing his belly but then quickly raising the hand to touch his bandaged head. "It's settled, then."

"Oh?" said Hannah, arching one eyebrow at him.

"Damn right, dear. Zach sleeps in the attic tonight. End of discussion."

The attic was low ceilinged and cramped but still bigger than my closet-like Blue Room back at the Daniel's Den. It is where I spent that night and many nights afterward. Hannah McCall stayed away and warned her three daughters to never set foot in the attic, as if I were the boogeyman ready to eat the little darlings alive. I had no complaints, though. Little Jack brought me my meals and the only bottle of whiskey I needed (since I only sipped those times he carried on too long about the war and the glorious South). Without complaint he emptied my bedpan (or handed the bedpan off to a sister to finish the dirty job), brought downstairs my dirty clothes for his mothers and sisters to wash, and hauled up a tub and buckets of heated water so I could take baths on Wednesdays and Saturdays.

What he received from me in return were riveting, mostly true accounts of John Hunt Morgan's raids and untamed tales of gold, lust, and blood. Some of these were based on things I'd heard or exaggerations of personal experiences, while others came straight from the Bible, as told to me when I was a boy by Preacher Robert "Raccoon" Gentry. With those slightly crossed eyes, Little Jack looked up to me (and usually down at me, since he would hover at my attic bedside while I lay on my back half-asleep). Often, he let me know how much better it was to have a big brother than a mean father. He liked it most when I stirred his imagination by speaking of Western adventures and opportunities (for gold and lust, not necessarily for blood) that would be possible after the Rebels had won the war. (Even though I figured that was a long shot, I was playing along to ease any possible tension.)

On August 17, a bunch of Burbridge's bully boys invaded the McCall house. I thought they were after me, so I hid in a trunk with some of Hannah's old clothing, including her white wedding gown. But the bluecoats never came into the attic. Little Jack McCall steered them away by making accusations against his own father. The lad was highly convincing. Indeed, the intruders arrested Fat Jack, charging him with aiding and abetting the enemy by supplying them with vital information and selling liquor to Nathan Bedford Forrest's raiders, even though it was generally known that the Confederate general abstained from hard drink and that the elder Jack McCall had remained a devout neutral amid the uncivil bloodshed. Hannah McCall apparently was having another fight with her husband at the time (whether over me or not, I do not know) and didn't mind the Yankees hauling him off for a while. She had miscalculated. For four months Fat Jack seethed behind bars while I stayed largely confined but relatively happy in the attic, reading good books and an occasional Northern-leaning newspaper, eating regularly, and losing myself in city sights, sounds, and smells those few times I got the urge to go outside and visit the cruel, divided world.

Hannah McCall came to tolerate me in the house after it became clear I would stick to the attic and bore no malice toward her or her three young daughters. I might be the real Rebel bastard in her eyes, but I was behaving like a kitten, and that sure made me preferable to the Yankee bullies who had arrested her husband. Little Jack contended that his mother and the entire family were enjoying their time together without Father getting in anyone's hair. Hannah had no idea her own son was the informant who had caused Fat Jack to be locked up. I suppose I could have informed on the informant, but I didn't want to spoil a good thing, and anyway, I didn't really miss Fat Jack, having spent most of my youth without having a father around.

By January 1865 the Confederacy was falling apart, but Burbridge was continuing to execute alleged guerrillas. Fat Jack wasn't in danger of facing a firing squad, though the controlling Federals were allowing him to rot away in prison. I finally felt guilty enough about the situation to send a note to Burbridge saying how Fat Jack was a "damned Yankee bastard" who was getting what he deserved and how it pleased me that the "flag-waving abolitionist McCall family was suffering like hell in the absence of their blue-coated breadwinner." I signed the note "A Son of Dixie." Burbridge's minions returned to the house to assess the situation, and Hannah, by then desperate to get her man back even if it meant my hide, told them there was a Southern spy in the attic who had made himself at home and threatened to rape her young daughters and burn down the house if she didn't keep quiet about his presence.

They stormed the attic this time, but, fortunately, with the help of Little Jack, I escaped with no time to spare onto the roof and then high-tailed it out of town on a "borrowed" McCall family horse. Little Jack desperately wanted to come with me, but I told him he best rest in the bosom of his family so as not to arouse suspicion and that we could always meet again after the hostilities ended. I admit, I didn't actually believe we had any kind of future together. Despite all his kindnesses toward me, I found him a devious, tiresome bore, a boy largely lacking in integrity. I mean, how could that *unnatural* bastard do what he did to our mutual daddy!

CHAPTER FOUR:
AT WAR'S END

Kentucky Governor Thomas Bramlette, tired of watching Burbridge overstep his bounds as overseer of operations in Kentucky, dismissed him in February 1865, complaining to Secretary of War Edwin Stanton about the "unwarranted assumption of power by an imbecile commander." I welcomed that news, of course, but I had no wish to return to Louisville to see how my daddy and the other McCalls were faring. I was living well enough undercover yet out in the open in Lexington. I had gone there to visit the grave of my old commander, John Morgan Hunt. He was interred at the family plot of his brother-in-law, Brigadier General Basil Duke, who had assumed command of Morgan's forces. Duke had been sent recently to Virginia to help Confederate President Jefferson Davis in Richmond. But my connection to the Hunt and Duke families landed me a job as an assistant groundskeeper in the Lexington Cemetery, replacing a Kentuckian who bolted to the Deep South because of his unrelenting hatred for what his native state had become—a confused place where neither masters nor Negroes knew whether slavery existed or not.

As for me, I had never thought enough about that institution to fight for or against it, and now I had no fight left in me for anything. I was just happy at almost twenty years old to have a job that put food on the table and could keep me safe until the stupid war ended. Digging graves seemed more honorable to me than sending men to them. My aggrieved ankles were only aching on rainy days by then, but I went about my work limping like all get-out to let people know why I wasn't soldiering. When strangers inquired about my war record, I also pretended I was deaf or a mute or both.

I don't doubt that sitting out the last year of the war saved my life. My luck surely would have run out had I not found sanctuary in the Louisville McCall house and then in the Lexington Cemetery. Union soldiers from Kentucky outnumbered Confederate soldiers well over two to one, and one-third of all Kentucky soldiers—nearly fifty thousand men—died during the war from battle wounds, accidents, or disease. I was long past being a soldier by April 1865, but I developed a bad case of bronchitis that I attributed to all the grave dust I was breathing at the Lexington Cemetery. When I heard the news that General Robert E. Lee had surrendered at Appomattox Court House on the ninth, I was in my boardinghouse bed with a hacking cough that kept bringing up greenish mucus. I was neither happy nor sad, just plain sick. One doctor was treating me with doses of opium and another with quinine and mustard plasters. I thought them both quacks, and under their care the pain returned to both my ankles, but at least neither was a true "sawbones" who wanted to resort to amputation below my knees.

Five days after Lee officially turned over his sword, John Wilkes Booth assassinated President Lincoln in Washington's Ford Theatre. Unlike the woman who was nursing me in the boardinghouse and taking my last penny for her efforts, it was not an event I would have celebrated even had I been healthy. I even left my bed to shamble across town to West Main Street to say I was sorry to the Todd house, where Mary Todd once lived and later brought husband Abraham and their children. After all, Mr. Lincoln had ended the stupid war, not started it. The poor man didn't have much time to enjoy any peace.

Coughing for nearly two months nearly cost me my life. It did cost me my job at the cemetery, all my money, and my room at the boardinghouse. At least I was feeling well enough again by early June to "unmute myself" and tell several unsympathetic people in Lexington to go to hell before I footed it out of town. I suppose I could have left Lexington for the McCall house in Louisville and again sought my daddy's aid, but I wasn't so sure Fat Jack's prison time and family situation would have put him in a giving mood, and I knew Hannah wouldn't want me to set foot in the house again, let alone make myself at home in the attic. What's more, I had no desire for a reunion with my half brother now that I was free to go where I pleased and to spend my time with people of my own choosing.

Maybe all that opium did something to my brain, because I felt too drowsy, weak, and confused to strike out on my own from Kentucky and seek adventure and opportunities in the West. What I chose to do instead, and this seemed like a mistake at first, was to return to my roots, the place I was born and raised—the Daniel's Den in Boonesborough. The Civil War had diverted the attention of proud Kentuckians on both sides of the nation's great divide, and they all but forgot about a town that had been a center of settlement during the pioneer days and a scene of much action during the Revolutionary War. The now neglected village was on the road to disappearing. Even the memory of the great founder, Daniel Boone, had fallen into the shadow of not only the late Kentucky native son Abraham Lincoln but also all those freed black men (the state had not abolished slavery during the Civil War) now making their presence felt in society. The Daniel's Den itself was hanging on by the skin of the soiled doves' teeth, though the same old wooden, hand-lettered sign was hanging from a chain above the front door. When I arrived through the battered back door, the one I was supposed to use when I was a boy, the owner himself confronted me with a bloody butcher knife in hand.

"I know you," Angus Doyle shouted, waving the knife wildly as if shooing away flies, and there were plenty of those hovering over the side of beef carcass he was carving.

"Careful with that thing," I said. "I come in peace."

"You turned my best whore against me, stole my favorite riding horse, and ran amuck with that Rebel reprobate John Hunt Morgan. You're the Bastard McCall!"

I was impressed he remembered me and more than amazed that he had heard of my association with my late mentor Morgan. But I didn't speak again until he lowered the butcher knife.

"Good to see you, too, eh, Mr. Doyle," I said out of old habit, although I began recalling just what an arrogant ass Angus was, the epitome of the evil boss. "It's been awhile."

"Not long enough. I figured you got your head blown off, boy, dead like Morgan and the whole goddamned South."

"What happened here? I mean, the place doesn't look the same."

"Of course it don't, you goddamned idiot. The war is what happened. All but killed my business. A contingent of Morgan's men raided my place, drank or destroyed my last stock of whiskey, and took everything else they could lay their filthy hands on *without paying.*"

"I didn't know about that. I swear. They didn't hurt anyone, did they . . . I mean, the girls?"

"Damn the whores. Three-quarters of them left with Morgan's men . . . and they weren't forced. They became goddamned camp followers."

"Oh. What about Belle Bragg?"

"The dad-blamed bitch led the mutiny, and it started long before Morgan's raiders got here. It started with *you.* When she helped you get away with my horse, I naturally beat her. It was in my rights. But she pulled a pistol on me and told me if I touched her again, she'd shoot me in the tallywags. She meant it, so I stopped laying a hand on her. And how did she repay me? She demanded more coin and better working conditions, not only for herself but for all the other doves of the roost, not to mention my long-time bartender Beauregard. I must say Belle was the one strumpet I wished had followed Morgan's men the hell out of here. But she stayed, damn her hide, and it's a miracle I've stayed in business despite her. Beauregard left me—damn his rotten Robert E. Lee-loving soul—and, with my ebbing cash flow, I had to let go of my cook and all my domestic help. Of course, you were no longer around to do your duty around the Den, you ungrateful bastard. I haven't yet been able to celebrate the Union victory. It'll take a long time before this country is put back together, and the Den might never be. Damnation!"

I took his ranting in stride. I had become a peaceable man, and I'd been that way since long before the war's end. I took several deep breaths and suggested he do the same. When he went back to slicing the meat in a fashion calm enough not to chop off one of his fingers, I whispered the question I was dying to ask: "You mean to say, Mr. Doyle, Belle is still here?"

"It is so. So, what's it to you?"

"I remember her well. She interests me."

"Forget it. She doesn't work like she used to—not that way."

"Oh. What way does she work?"

"Like a queen bee. She's married now, you see, and overseeing all the precious soiled doves, making sure they are treated right and properly paid. She can be a royal pain. I mean, I shouldn't have to do my own cooking, bartending, and cleaning up? The thing is, though—and I hate like hell to admit this—I wouldn't have any whores anymore without her. She has that much influence over the flock. She calls herself Madam Raccoon."

"Madam Raccoon?"

"It is so. Remember that circuit-riding preacher Robert "Raccoon" Gentry, who came around regular to lecture us on the finer points of sin and to keep his spirits up?"

"Of course. How could I forget him? He got me to read books, and not just the Bible, and would quiz me on what I read whenever he came back to the Den. If not for him, I wouldn't know about the Trojan Horse, the cabin of Uncle Tom, or Fort William Henry."

"Only fort I know 'round here is Fort Boonesborough, founded in 1775 by Daniel and defended by him three years later during the siege led by Shawnee Chief Blackfish. If Daniel saw the way the Den is now, he'd turn over in his grave!"

"Right," I said, though the truth was, Daniel Boone had never seen the Daniel's Den in any condition. "Fort William Henry isn't around here, Mr. Doyle. It's way up near Canada in the northern wilderness of New York. The siege there was in 1757 during the French and Indian War, and after the British surrendered to the French, Huron Indians allied to the French killed and scalped the surrendering soldiers. It was a real massacre. Fenimore Cooper wrote about it in his novel *The Last of the Mohicans*. Frontier tales like that were exciting, even to a little shaver in Kentucky. That was my favorite book the preacher lent me to read. He knew so much about everything. I thought he was the smartest man alive. But he seemed kind of old even back then. He can't be the one who married Belle, can he?"

"It is so. Raccoon Gentry put an end to his own sinning ways by getting himself hitched to the pick of the Den's litter."

"That doesn't explain why Belle would agree to it."

"She was truly enamored of Fat Jack McCall, but the son of a bitch was a married man up in Louisville."

"Don't I know it. That's my daddy you are talking about."

"Almost forgot. But right you are—a son of a bitch and his bastard boy."

"Hey, he used to be your favorite patron, supplying whiskey the way he did. He used to get the royal treatment in the Den, like he was a traveling king or something."

"He must have been dethroned during the recent hostilities. Anyway, he completely stopped coming around once Morgan and the other lowdown Southern scoundrels—you included, boy—made the Kentucky roads unsafe for a traveling man. No more special whiskey for me, no more special bread and butter for Belle."

"The good whiskey ran out, I reckon. And Fat Jack was unfairly jailed for some time up in Louisville. It's hard to travel when you're behind bars."

"Whatever. I got my own worries. Belle figured he'd forgotten about her, and with you long gone with my horse, he didn't have a reason to stop by anymore."

"Well, he sure doesn't now, her marrying the preacher and all."

"Preacher Raccoon Gentry was her second choice for sure, but he was just what she was looking for—being book learned, generous, reliable, possessing a bankroll blessed by God, and *not all the time around* preaching to her like some men of his ilk. She knew she wouldn't tire so easily of a man who spent most of his time riding through the countryside spreading the gospel."

"Belle is happy being Madam Raccoon?"

"It is so. And Preacher Raccoon has no complaints I know of. But what about me? Does anyone think of me? Am I happy? No, sir, boy. Treating all the whores right isn't financially sound. To me, Belle is Madam Magpie."

"Magpie?"

"The thieving birds. Belle is robbing me blind, but what can I do? One would think Angus Doyle was her goddamn slave!

I'm all the time here suffering on account of the queen bee eating into my profits. Can't live with her but can't do business without her, not in old Boonesborough. You'd think things would be better with Robert E. Lee out of the way, but they sure ain't! I should pack what little of value is left here and haul my ass up North, 'cept I'm too old to start over."

"I'm sorry," I said, but I was already shuffling my feet toward the kitchen door, imagining the whiskey bar beyond it, the stairway with the black oak bannister, and especially two rooms at the top of the stairs—the Red Room once occupied by Belle and the little, dark Blue Room next to it where I had slept alone with all my dreams, proper and improper. "Mind if I look over the old place, Mr. Doyle? I have so many memories."

He stopped slicing beef and thrust the big knife into the cutting board. "What would make me happy," he said as he wiped his hands on the front of his shirt, "is for you to pay for the horse you took five years ago. You owe me."

I turned out my empty pockets just before I reached the door. "The war has been hard on all of us," I said. "I'm sorry." But I felt no sympathy for Angus Doyle. My father had paid him plenty for my sustenance, yet Angus had still worked me like a Southern dog around his place while otherwise leaving my upbringing to Belle and other charitable ladies in his employ. If anything, I thought he owed *me*. I wasn't sorry about the horse I had taken. I'd have rather taken another one than labor for this taskmaster again.

"Where do you think you're going, boy, without a penny in your pocket?"

"I'm not *your* boy, never was. Belle still occupy the Red Room?"

"It is so. Only the best for Madam Magpie. Despite what I told you about the queen bee, you're still figuring to get lucky, ain't you?"

"That *is not so*. You have no call to say that. You have a vile mind, Mr. Doyle."

"I haven't converted the Den into a church yet. Sleeping here ain't free either."

I said nothing, just started walking away again. But Angus wasn't finished. "Have it your way, bastard. You'll see."

"Yes, sir."

"I heard tell when her preacher husband is here, like now, she makes him sleep next door in the Blue Room, in your tiny old bed, in fact. Preacher Raccoon snores like the dickens."

"Oh. I'll knock first."

I was out of the kitchen now, giving a passing glance at the empty shot glasses on the bar, and then looking back to make sure Angus Doyle wasn't chasing me with knife in hand. I slowly climbed the staircase, each stair creaking despite my light steps, the worn-down banister wobbling under my unsteady hand. I went to the blue door of my old room first out of habit, but I didn't knock because I could hear from within the snorts and whistles of a resounding snorer. Next, I went to the Red Room door, which was actually yellow with a red plaque that read in fancy script, *Madam Raccoon*. I knocked three times. Nobody answered, but I heard squeaky bed springs, a groan, and then footsteps. When the door finally swung open, I had a lump in my throat and sweaty hands. I was anticipating Belle Bragg, perhaps in a state of undress, looking no worse for wear. Instead, I got Robert Raccoon Gentry, fully dressed in black, with a gray beard down to his belly and a Bible under his left arm. In his right hand he held out a box of large pills but quickly withdrew it. He looked about as surprised as I was.

"These aren't for you," he said. "I thought you were the man looking for a cure for the great pox." He leaned closer, scowling as he peered at me, the dark circles under his eyes that gave him his nickname expanding, his hawk-like nose threatening to poke me in the forehead. "But you are someone I have seen before. Perhaps a face in the crowd during one of my prayer meetings in western Kentucky? Do you know me? I am Robert Raccoon Gentry, preacher man. I dispense God's words for the spirit, Shakespeare's words for the mind, and Dr. Rush's bilious pills for the body."

"Has it really been that long? I've grown, changed some during the war, but . . ."

"Do I know you, young man?"

"We know each other from your sociable visits right here. You taught me a bit of Shakespeare and much more James Fenimore Cooper. I'm Zach."

"Praise the Lord. So you are. Zach McCall. Who else could you be? You haven't grow'd that much, and my eyes haven't grow'd that bad not to see the truth of the matter." He put aside the pill box and clasped hands with me. The Bible was between us for a while before it crashed to the floor. I picked it up for him. "God bless you, Wild Child."

"That's what they used to call me, all right."

"And now I reckon you're a man. Goodness gracious, you look like a man."

"I'm older, anyway. And not so wild, though I had me some wild times in the war."

"We all used to be younger and perhaps a little wilder. Haven't seen you in a month of Sundays, your daddy either. Heard Fat Jack McCall is still in the blessing business."

"Huh?"

"Dispensing good whiskey to needy men."

"Times were hard during the war. Business should be getting better now. Could be he'll come down this way again someday, maybe give Mr. Doyle a good deal."

"Heard that, too."

"But you said you haven't seen him."

"That's right, but I have myself a reliable source. Tell me, Wild Child—pardon me, I mean Zach—what brings you back to Boonesborough at this particular time?"

"The end of the war, I guess. This was my home, the only one I ever had." I looked past him to study the leaf patterns on the rose wallpaper because I felt a tear coming on.

"Suppose it could still be if you have a mind to stick. Things have changed here since you left. Tell me, Zach: did you happen to come back to see anyone in particular?"

"What? Well, it's good to see you, Raccoon . . . I mean, Mr. Gentry."

"Raccoon is fine. I know you didn't return to hear me preach to you again."

"You didn't preach that much, and it was never so bad. But I'd sure also like to see Belle . . . eh . . . your wife."

"You heard about the big event last year? Hard to believe. I thank the Lord every night she'd have me as her one and only living man. I know she was something special to your daddy and, well, some other Den regulars. But she's not knockin' boots with customers anymore, as the saying goes. She's above all that now . . . an angel reborn, you might say."

"Eh . . . congratulations. Madam Raccoon, right?"

"Sounds divine, doesn't it? We're just a couple of old raccoons, we are. You can catch her as soon as she gets back from the general store, Zach. We ran out of canned peaches—my favorite. She's good to me, bless her heart."

"I imagine. I mean, good." I quickly walked away from him and studied an unfamiliar painting on the wall showing five sheep—four white, one black—grazing in a valley below a small white church with a slightly crooked steeple.

"Madam Raccoon, the former Belle Bragg, painted it herself—her wedding present to me. She'll be glad to see you."

"I heard snoring in the room next door, my old room. I didn't figure that was her. Actually, I thought it was probably you."

"My reputation as a snorer precedes me. But *this* snorer is noticeably younger, someone you might have heard before."

"Oh? One of the other working girls?"

"Not a girl at all. He came here in hopes of seeing you, so I figured you might have heard about that and decided to come here yourself to see him."

"Huh? You've lost me."

"Don't want to have that, do we? He wants to see you—says he is dying to see you. Go on over and wake him. He won't mind."

"Who won't mind? Who's sleeping in my old bed?"

"Your brother Jack. He came down from Louisville last night in extreme distress. I assured him God feels his suffering and that a lament prayer would help him navigate his pain. But he dismissed me with these impious words, and I quote: 'I'm here to talk to my big brother, mister, not some unbelievable supreme being.' "

CHAPTER FIVE:
MY BROTHER'S KEEPER

I decided I wouldn't wake Little Jack right away. Nothing to do with him or his needs. I needed to let his presence sink in. He was out of context here in my hometown, in my boyhood residence, in my very room, by God! I sat down in the only chair to look at him, but it made my blood boil, even though his entire face was covered by a pillow. He was like Goldilocks of Three Bears' notoriety; as far as I was concerned, he had eaten my bowl of porridge, sat in my chair, and was now sleeping in my bed. I walked out and paced the hallway. Preacher Raccoon watched me as if he were keeping an eye on a devil's disciple. He reminded me that the lad was no stranger but a blood brother. "Half blood brother," I corrected him. The preacher looked like he wanted to say something more—like, *I never thought a bastard would be so particular*—but he, being basically a good man, held his tongue.

At the end of the hallway, near the window that looked out on a double-decker outhouse that had seen better days, I paused to mutter to myself about Little Jack. "Why are you here?" I said. I thought I was talking to myself, but the preacher heard me.

"It is the will of God," he said. "Your brother needs you, Zach."

"I don't need him," I said.

"You did once, I understand. He told me he showed you great hospitality when you came to the McCall house in

Louisville and protected you from the malicious Union forces."

"He feels I owe him?"

"He only said he had nobody else to turn to in his time of need."

"Maybe he should try God."

"Yes, you feel as I do. In the long run, putting your faith in God does everyone some good. But the young man is not yet ready to invite God into his heart. Right now, it's up to you, Zach."

"You saying you think I owe him?"

"There is something to be said for brotherly love even among divided brothers."

"Sure, he told you he helped me in Louisville during the war, but did he also tell you he told lies about our daddy that got Fat Jack locked up in a Yankee jail for four whole months?"

"No, he did not. He came here in dire need of rest. We didn't talk long."

"Not only that. He killed the family cat and I think Fat Jack's hunting dog, too. He clings to his mother at times but will lie to her just as he does to anyone else when it suits his purpose."

"The Bible says not to judge others or you, too, shall be judged. We must treat the sins of others with truth and love."

That caused me to pause for a moment because I did sometimes judge myself harshly for having killed a fellow human being, having fought for the wrong side in the late war, having hid out in the McCall attic, having allowed my daddy to stay in prison too long, and having possessed sinful thoughts about a variety of Kentucky and Tennessee women. But this wasn't about me; it was about Little Jack. "Something's not quite right upstairs with him," I said, pointing to my own head, which immediately began to ache.

"Why do you say that? Wasn't he kind to you?"

"Sure, but it wasn't like he was kind to be kind. He did it

because he wanted something from me."

"Such as?"

"Me. All of me. I can't explain it. He expects me to show him the way to fun and adventure and happiness or something. He says he hates Fat Jack."

"Yes. Everybody needs somebody. You disagree?"

"No, but I don't need him."

"What makes you so sure?"

"Look, Little Jack is a little guy with a big mouth. Daddy thinks so, too. One time he said Little Jack's mouth reminded him of the bellows of an accordion with a few screws missing so that it all the time produced sour notes. Of course, Fat Jack had been drinking quite a bit of whiskey at the time, but the point is, I may be a bastard, but I'm the favorite son."

"And that makes you feel better about yourself?"

"Huh? I thought we were talking about Little Jack."

"There's something you should know, and you'll see this for yourself when you look at him more closely. Little Jack, as you call him, arrived here with his nose out of joint . . . literally."

"What do you mean?"

"It was swelling and bleeding and bending noticeably to the left. I treated it best I could with a cold cloth and making sure he kept his head elevated, even when he went to bed. But his head won't stay up on the two pillows. It keeps slipping off to the side. And a pillow keeps falling over his face. He was kicking a lot, having nightmares. His breathing is agitated."

"I noticed. Poor boy. I suppose Belle felt sorry for him and let him sleep in my bed . . . I mean, what used to be my bed."

"I've slept in the Blue Room, too."

"Fine, preacher. I don't mind you sleeping in there."

"She feels sorry for him, and why not? She hates to see any human being getting abused. He has a broken nose, a black eye, sore ribs, and nothing but the clothes on his back."

"I guess I didn't notice all that. Wonder what he did."

"Nothing to deserve this, I'm sure. He's only fifteen."

"I was only sixteen when I went to war. And there were boys younger than me fighting. I saw some of them."

"Those aren't battle wounds on him."

"I know that. He tell you otherwise, the little liar?"

"He did not. He spoke the sad truth."

"Really? And what was that?"

"Your daddy beat the devil out of him, if you'll pardon my language."

I was still wondering what Little Jack had done to provoke Fat Jack, but I decided to drop the subject. I hadn't come back to the Daniel's Den to talk about my half brother. Out the window, I saw Belle Bragg put down a package and enter the outhouse on the lower level while tugging at the folds of her dress. Her black hair was piled on her head in a bun the size of a cannonball. In the old days, I remembered all that free-flowing hair dancing over her shoulders and extending halfway down her back.

"Your canned peaches have arrived," I told the preacher, but I turned away from the window as if to give Belle more privacy. "She was like a mother to me, you know?"

"She has a good heart," he said, tapping his own chest. "A heart of gold."

"I know," I said, recalling how she had loved my daddy so much during his visits that she stopped charging him for her professional services.

The preacher and I went into the Red Room to wait for her, him lying down again on the big bed leafing through his Bible, me standing by her dressing table counting the strands of hair in the stiff bristles of her wooden brush. Some of the strands were no longer black.

Belle must have spent a long time in the outhouse. It took

her forever to get upstairs. She immediately tossed her package on the red sheets, and the preacher, who had remained on the bed, quickly opened it up and kissed two cans of peaches at once.

"God bless you, Belle," he said, laying the cans on his belly and patting the empty space beside him in a manner I found excessively suggestive, especially for a preacher.

Fearing Belle might take her old husband up on his offer, I started to clear my throat, but Belle had turned her back to him and me and was walking toward the large closet. I knew that at the back of the closet behind the hanging dresses was a small secret door that led to the Blue Room where I used to sleep and where Little Jack McCall, he with the broken nose, was now snoring away.

"How's our little patient?" Belle asked from inside the closet.

"Sleeping like a baby," Preacher Raccoon said. "A baby with consumption."

"Don't even joke about such matters, Coony. Anyway, he isn't ill at all, just hurt."

"Of course, you're right, Madam Raccoon. With the help of the Lord, he'll be just fine."

I heard the rustle of clothing and the secret door opening, and then nothing for a long time. Finally, the door closed again, and Belle, glowing like something between a proud mother and a gaudy fallen angel, stepped out of the closet.

"Poor dear," she said. "I removed the pillow from his face and put it back under his head where it belongs. The boy is completely worn out. We'll let him sleep. When he gets hungry again, he'll awaken on his own. I'll ask one of the girls to make some pea soup. I had a good look at him, Coony. His face isn't as clean-cut as his father's, but, even behind the black and blue-ness, I can see he has his father's eyes. Of course, Fat Jack's eyes aren't the least bit crossed."

"Neither are mine," I said, stepping away from the shadows of her dressing table.

"For the Lord's sake!" Belle cried, putting her hands on her hips that started swaying. "Another McCall. Zach has come home, Coony."

"Indeed," said the preacher. "The Lord works in mysterious ways, eh, Madam Raccoon?"

"Damn right." Belle swayed right up to me and gave me a squeeze that was full bodied all right but didn't last as long as I anticipated. She broke it off to look over both my shoulders. "Your daddy isn't hiding someplace, too, is he?" she asked.

I assured her he wasn't, and it was hard to tell whether she was disappointed or relieved. The three of us all half lay and half sat on the red comforter, eating peaches directly from the can and waiting for Little Jack McCall to wake up. I talked about my time with Rebel raider John Hunt Morgan because Preacher Racoon asked about it, but I didn't say a word about shooting anyone.

"Your Morgan is gone, a lot of good men are gone, and so is the goddamned war," Belle said. "Good riddance. Men are meant to be lovers, not killers."

"Amen," said Preacher Raccoon. "A staggering number of bodies broken, and heaven knows how many human souls destroyed! Let us be thankful that Zach McCall, who went off to battle so young and innocent so many years ago, has safely returned to the fold."

"Tell us more about what you've been up to," said Belle, wiping a little peach juice that was running down my chin.

She took a much greater interest in my time doing nothing in the attic of the McCall home in Louisville. She thought it was wonderful that my little brother had looked after my welfare so diligently, but she mostly asked questions about our daddy. She wondered about his health, his whiskey business, how he behaved at "home," what his wife looked like, and how he treated her and the other family members. The preacher didn't seem to mind his wife going on so about her old special customer and love interest. He did open the second can of peaches, and feasted as if gluttony wasn't one of the seven deadly sins.

"Well," Belle persisted. "Does Jack let his temper get the better of him?"

"I never saw Fat Jack beat Hannah or their three girls," I said. "Or even Little Jack."

"But he does. The evidence is in the next room. He clearly thrashed the boy."

"They've always had their differences. I don't imagine the boy told you how he lied to the Yankee authorities, so they'd take away his father and stick him behind bars."

"I can't believe a son would do such a thing."

"This son wouldn't. Little Jack did. That's a fact."

"He told me that Jack—that is, your father—gave him that severe beating just because he was teaching his three sisters a game of cards that was popular with Southern soldiers when in their camps waiting to go kill and be killed. Five-card stud, I believe it is called."

"Northern soldiers played it, too," I said. "John Hunt Morgan once surprised a group of drunken bluecoats dealing it in Ohio. Some of them won't ever deal again. I never played it myself. It's a gambling game. Little Jack was probably only teaching them so he could win their dolls, colored hoops, and shiny marbles."

"You shouldn't covet your neighbors' belongings even when your neighbors are your sisters," said Preacher Raccoon.

"That doesn't justify a beating," said Belle. "A lot of coveting goes on in this house, but nobody ever gets beaten, not since I laid down the law to Angus Doyle. Your father was always respectful when he visited the Den. I can't understand it."

"There must have been more to it than Little Jack told you," I said. "I figure he's a natural born liar."

"Whatever happened up in Louisville, he did say his mother took his father's side, and his three sisters spoke out against him. He ran away from home not just because of the beating, but because the family was decidedly against him.

"So says Little Jack."

"But he views you as the family exception, Zach. He believes you are on his side. He came here to find you. Before he collapsed from exhaustion, he talked excitedly of your war record and your life at the Den. I would say in fact, Zach, that your brother idolizes you."

"Half brother. Tell me, Belle, who looks more like Fat Jack, me or him?"

Belle cupped my chin with a slightly sticky hand and examined my face like a doctor looking for spots. "Well, I'd say you look more like your mother, Virginia Reel," she finally said. "You have the same high cheekbones and almond-shaped eyes. Your brother—half brother—has his father's eyes but lacks his large nose and strong jaw. I have never seen his mother, of course. You describe her as looking delicate, even fragile. The boy with the crooked nose has a little of that, too. It's not an easy question to answer. You do have your father's jawline, Zach, and a big but not terribly big nose."

Belle pinched the skin under my chin hard enough for me to yelp, then pinched my nostrils shut a little too long for comfort. "You McCalls are all so adorable," she said, laughing.

Preacher Raccoon laughed considerably harder and then rubbed his dark eyes when tears began to form. "I know I look nothing like Jack McCall," he said, raising his chin and turning his head to give Belle and me a profile view. "I'm *not* a handsome man. I don't frighten my flock, but sometimes I set their babies bawling!"

"Looks aren't everything; you're a godly man, Coony," Belle Bragg said.

"I thank you for your kind words, Madam Raccoon."

"But speaking of Jack McCall, do you think he'll be coming down this way again, Zach?"

"If you mean to chase after Little Jack and bring him back home, I strongly doubt it. And he wouldn't come to see me. He doesn't know I'm here."

"Little Jack thinks his father will come and try to sell whiskey to Angus Doyle again. Not sure Angus could afford the good stuff anymore, though."

"I imagine Daddy also might want to see you again, Belle."

I glanced over at Preacher Raccoon and felt badly about saying it. He started choking as if he had swallowed a peach pit whole, though canned peaches didn't come with pits inside. Belle and I both slapped him on the back, and our hands touched. Somehow that was more invigorating than the hug she had given me when she noticed I had returned, and I began to appreciate more her recent hard pinching. The preacher stopped choking and issued another burst of laughter.

"I wouldn't blame him," he said, a little too seriously. "Fortunately, I'm not the jealous type, or I might say something that displeases him and get punched out like the boy."

"Fat Jack's not like that," I snapped, surprising myself. I guess I enjoyed being the *loyal* son. "In all the years he knew me—and he has known me longer than Little Jack—he never once struck me in the face."

"Nor has he ever slapped me or anyone else at the Den," said Belle, "though he must have wanted to slap Angus Doyle a time or two."

That made me want to plant a kiss on her face. "So, you— both of you—wouldn't mind if Fat Jack showed up here?"

"Not if he came in peace, with no intention of inflicting any more damage on the boy's poor nose and body," said Belle.

"Amen," Preacher Raccoon said. "The Civil War is over. Peace is here. Families have no reason any longer to be divided. It can't be father against son or brother against brother now. We are all one."

He was staring at me as he spoke, as if sensing my resentment toward my brother no matter how well Little Jack thought of me. It made no sense, of course. War wasn't the only reason for families to be divided.

"In any case," said Belle, patting her husband on a cheek that was puffed out from him sucking on too much peach all at once. "We're all a happy family here."

That didn't make much sense either, but I let it pass. A moment later, I heard the little secret door in the closet creak open and the rustling of hanging dresses before my half brother appeared in the Red Room. He looked ragged and disreputable, and though his nose was rather small, you couldn't miss it, red, swollen, and leaning hard to the left as it was. He saw me and began blinking rapidly. His eyes worked hard to latch on to me, ignoring the other two people in the room. Instantly, his crossed eyes and battered nose annoyed me.

"Zach!" he cried out.

"Crooked Nose Jack," I replied.

He wasn't offended. Maybe at that moment it sounded better than "Little Jack." He said, "You noticed" and clearly wanted to say more but became tongue tied and then red faced. He scurried across the room like a mouse, dropped to his knees beside the bed, and laid his head against my shinbones. It sounded like he was crying. Preacher Raccoon and Madam Raccoon reached out simultaneously to gently touch his hair. I crossed my arms.

"You came for me, brother," Jack said, his words partially muffled by hard bone. "I hate everyone in Louisville. I had to leave. I was at the end of my rope!"

"I had no idea you'd be here," I said, rather coldly, I must admit.

"Thank God I was, and that you found me."

"Amen," said Preacher Raccoon.

"You must be terribly hungry," Belle said to the boy, giving his head an extra pat. "Sorry, but we seem to be all out of peaches. How would you like a little pea soup?"

"Anything," Crooked Nose Jack said. "Anything at all. As long as I can share it with my brother."

I felt his wet tears running down my ankles, which somehow made them ache as if my old war wounds were acting up.

CHAPTER SIX:
THE DECISION OF 1865

Even though I had no use for Angus Doyle, or for that matter Crooked Nose Jack, I took a temporary position at the Den tending bar—that is, serving drinks but also washing dishes, sweeping the tavern floor, and showing disagreeable drunks to the door. My plan was to earn enough traveling money to make it to Missouri, where I hoped to settle down and start a new life. If that was good enough for Daniel Boone, it suited me fine. I made the mistake, during a weak moment after a fair amount of bad whiskey, of telling that to Belle Bragg, who thought it would be a good idea to share my plan with my half brother. She felt sorry for the boy, because no sooner had he recovered from the beating he had taken from our daddy in Louisville than he developed a bad cough that could be set off at any time by his simply breathing in and out in bed—yes, in my old bed in the Blue Room. He thrived on the attention of the Raccoon couple.

He got to stay in the Blue Room while I slept downstairs on a cot that I set up behind the bar each night after the tavern closed. The other upstairs rooms—Gold, Yellow, Pink, Purple, and Green—were occupied by the horizontal workers, a couple of whom were still around from the old days. Those rooms were off limits by my choice. Somehow those gals seemed like sisters to me. Besides, I was intent on saving my money. Sleeping on the big bed in the Red Room, where our daddy had once slept (when not otherwise busy) on his pre-Civil War visits, was naturally out of the question. Preacher Raccoon slept there when not driving his buggy around on the preaching circuit and when *not* snoring too loudly to bother Belle, who—at least most of the time—continued to seem like a mother to me. When she was bothered by her husband's sleep noises, he was very understanding about it—he seemed to accept the will of Belle even more than the will of God—and would take his blankets downstairs to sleep on the floor on the customers' side of the bar.

Hearing from Belle about my plan to go West lifted the spirits of Crooked Nose, since he assumed the plan included him going with me, but not enough to immediately lift him out of bed. I wondered how sick young Jack McCall really was. He had worked hard to please me when I was in the attic in Louisville, but he had no wish to be of any service to that mean-spirited old Union fanatic Angus Doyle. He conveniently developed his cough on the day he was supposed to start sweeping floors. He had heard about me getting sick while working at the Lexington Cemetery, and his cough sounded a lot like mine had. Of course, he couldn't blame his respiratory illness on grave dust, but he did attribute it to the cheap perfumes that the soiled doves (not counting Madam Raccoon) practically bathed in instead of clean water. Nevertheless, he readily accepted their sympathetic visits to his bedside.

He outdid me, too, by developing other symptoms— headaches, dizziness, nausea, fatigue, weakness, insomnia, numbness, shortness of breath, skin irritation, confusion, difficulty concentrating, and malaise. Preacher Raccoon, who acted in place of a real doctor, listened to his patient's complaints and, being a kind, trusting soul, believed every last one of them. If Belle felt any differently, she didn't say so. She liked having the boy in the next room so she could mother him and relive the old days when I was the boy in that room. Belle clearly thought me too old for mothering now, too much like all the other men who come to the Daniel's Den to get certain needs met. To feel more like a man or to forget what a man needed, I drank some when Angus Doyle wasn't looking, but I never acquired a real fondness for it. I wasn't going to waste my money actually buying whiskey.

And then the day came toward the end of June that Fat Jack McCall appeared at the door of the Den while I was polishing a spittoon. He brought a crate of whiskey that he sold to Angus Doyle at a cut-rate price since the owner was still complaining about fewer customers than before the war and insignificant post-war profits. But that was not the main reason Daddy had come. And neither was it to see his old mistress. Belle Bragg had sent word to Fat Jack in Louisville that she was happily married and that both his sons were in Boonesborough, one terribly sick (because of a new illness) and hurt (because of the old beating that had driven him out of the family home), and the other perhaps drinking more than he could handle but otherwise working hard and trying his best to save money. Fat Jack had come, and I had no reason not to believe him, to see about the welfare of his two sons.

I must report that Fat Jack's mission was a failure. Part of it was his own doing. Practically the first thing he said to his youngest son was this: "Get the hell out of that bed, boy. It's as clear as the Kentucky River that you're feigning illness just like you've done since you were a baby to get the undying sympathy of your mother." He also tried to justify the harsh punishment that had led to Little Jack's broken nose, black eyes, and sore ribs. "A father," Fat Jack insisted, "must do all he can to maintain a happy home no matter if it causes a little pain now and again."

Little Jack replied from the bed, "You're a big, fat pain, and the pain won't go away."

Fat Jack sighed and drank some of his own whiskey down at the bar. He told me he needed to show patience because the boy's mother didn't want her husband to return without Little Jack. Fat Jack quoted what Hannah McCall had said in Louisville: "You need to convince him that his place is with us. I know what a defiant, headstrong lad he has become, but I can't help but recall how he was once my sweet baby boy. I would never forgive myself or you if we gave up on him too soon and allowed him to wallow with the black sheep in a degenerate mockery of civilization." Yes, I was the black sheep, and the Daniel's Den was the lower civilization.

Fat Jack then went back upstairs to try again, with me trailing along because I believed it was probably best for Little Jack to return to Louisville—and definitely better for me. But Little Jack would have none of it. He looked daggers at Daddy, those crossed eyes like crossed swords.

Crooked Nose Jack spoke with quivering voice: "You go back and tell Mother her sweet baby boy is gone forever, that his nose and everything else will never be the same again. Further tell her that I won't be beaten down and dragged back to Louisville. You can't make me."

"You can't stay here, not in this place. You're not even sixteen."

Little Jack laughed in our daddy's face. "You let Wild Child grow up in this place."

"That was . . . different," Fat Jack said, but he grew silent. He turned to study me from head to toe and then turned back to Little Jack, scratching his head and looking puzzled all the while.

"Anyway," Little Jack said. And then he threw aside the pillow he was clutching, cast off his blankets, and sprang from the bed. He wobbled only slightly before scuttling over to me, standing as close to shoulder to shoulder as he could get, at least until he grew another six inches.

"Anyway, what?" Fat Jack asked.

"Anyway, I don't aim to stay here long. I'm going places."

"What places?"

"No matter to you. We got places in mind, Zach and me."

Daddy looked at me, and all I could do was shrug.

"Your mother won't like that, Little Jack. You still mean a lot to her and to your sisters and to . . . eh . . . me."

"You lie like a brothel rug!"

"Me?" Fat Jack's face reddened, as might be expected, and I saw at least one fist form at his side. "Who's the liar in the family? Who told Burbridge's bullies that I . . ."

He stopped when Preacher Raccoon and Madam Raccoon entered the Blue Room arm in arm. "We were napping next door," Belle said. "What's all the commotion?"

"Nothing," all three of us McCalls said at the same time.

A tense silence followed, until the preacher spoke, no doubt with the sincerest intentions. "I suggest we all come together, clasp hands, and pray for the forgiveness of each other and for God—that is, for the forgiveness of God."

That didn't happen. Crooked Nose Jack dared step toward our daddy and point a finger. "I'd rather clasp hands with Ulysses S. Grant, another whiskey tippler. You don't even apologize for what you've done to me. When you get me home, you're gonna punish me for running away. I wouldn't put it past you to take another crack at my nose. I know you, Father. You need to have your way, to lay down *your* law, to make me your slave!"

That was big talk for a fifteen year old. To his credit, Fat Jack didn't raise a fist. No doubt the presence of the preacher and Belle, if not me, had something to do with that. He rolled his eyes, sighed heavily, and stared at Little Jack's extended finger, which began to shake. "Slavery is now illegal in Kentucky," Fat Jack muttered.

"It's illegal everywhere, praise the Lord," Preacher Raccoon needlessly added. "We're all brothers now."

"At least two of us are," said Little Jack, taking two steps back from our daddy and then reaching high to put an awkward arm around my shoulders. "I'm gonna follow in Zach's footsteps now, and I'm pleased as punch about that." He rubbed his nose.

I stiffened and breathed hard through pursed lips but said nothing. "Punch" didn't seem like an appropriate word. I felt as if I were in the middle of something not of my own making, and that wasn't where I wanted to be.

"What if Zach wants to come back to Louisville with me and earn his livelihood?" Fat Jack asked. He tapped me on the chest, right over the heart. "You'd be welcome, Wild Child. You'd be able to call my house your home, and you could help your daddy sell the finest whiskey in the world up there, down here, and everywhere in Kentucky. How does that sound?"

Little Jack didn't give me the chance to answer, one way or another. "No!" he shouted. "Zach doesn't want to go to Louisville any more than I do. That would be as bad as slaving for Doyle downstairs! Besides, Mother hates him. We're going somewhere else. We got ourselves a plan. You have no idea."

"Is it such a big secret?" Belle asked. "Are all you McCalls going to up and leave us again?"

"Yes, do tell us," said Preacher Raccoon. "You shall be blessed wherever you go."

"Zach and me are gonna seek our own fortunes and adventure, preacher. We're gonna go far, farther than you can imagine. My brother and me are bound for the Wild West."

Our daddy, the good preacher, and his madam wife all looked at me to see if I shared my half brother's enthusiasm. Instead, I turned away, told them I had some thinking to do, and headed downstairs to the bar, where I did more drinking than thinking.

Not one drop went down smooth.

"That stuff ain't free, you know," Angus Doyle said as he came out of the kitchen wiping his hands on his blood-stained apron. He'd been butchering something out back, hopefully an animal. "I'm keeping a tally sheet."

"My daddy's going to bring you more of the good whiskey, and that'll bring your customers back," I said. "You should be thanking me."

"For what? You aren't your daddy or even your daddy's legitimate son. Fat Jack can only do so much. Boonesborough ain't what it used to be before the war. Too many drinkers are dead; too many have moved on. I can barely keep you on as a paid hand at the Den. I tell you, boy, things are bleak."

"There are still some . . . eh . . . nice women upstairs."

"Sure. Real ladies. I can't afford all those whores the queen bee is protecting. I tell you something else: you touch them, you pay. They work for me."

"For Belle, Madam Raccoon."

"I get my cut. This is my place. Madam Magpie works for me, just like you."

I was ready to punch him, steal another of his horses, and make my break, sans Crooked Nose Jack, but there wasn't nearly enough coin in my pocket, and I needed another shot of the bad house whiskey. "You'll change your tune mighty fast should I take up Daddy's offer to be his partner in the whiskey-selling business," I said, before the owner pulled the half-empty bottle away and I had to be content with licking the inside of my glass.

"That'll be the day," Angus said, as he stomped back toward the kitchen. "And you'd better watch yourself. I pay you to pour drinks for customers, not for that big mouth of yours."

For about ten seconds after the tyrant was out of sight, I considered rushing upstairs and taking Fat Jack up on his offer to prove Angus Doyle wrong. But I forgot all about it when an impressive figure of a man came rolling into Daniel's Den like a black rain cloud in a time of drought. Yes, he was a colored man. It turned out he was there to continue his one-man celebration of universal freedom that had been going on since General Lee's surrender at Appomattox Court House. He came right up to me, clapped me on the back without quite realizing his own strength, introduced himself as Jasper Washington, and began talking away as if he had known me for a lifetime. He had showed up because he once met the fair-minded Preacher Raccoon on the road and learned that owner Angus Doyle had been faithful to the Union cause throughout the war. But Jasper Washington didn't ask to see either man right away. He was mostly there for the drinking, whoring, and storytelling, not necessarily in that order. The first two activities cost money, the third was free.

It turned out that this extremely exuberant and enormous black-skinned man was a Kentucky native who had been freed long before the Civil War and starting in 1857 had attended Berea College, a small school founded by the Rev. John Gregg Fee that was open to both blacks and whites of either sex. In the aftermath of John Brown's 1859 raid on Harper's Ferry, Virginia, a mob of pro-slavery supporters raided the Kentucky college, temporarily closing it down and driving Fee's followers, including Jasper, out of the state. Fee had recently returned to Berea and was making sure the college lived up to his vision of freedom and education and its high-minded motto, "God has made of one blood all people of the Earth." Jasper had also gone back, but he hadn't stuck.

"Nobody was telling me I couldn't be there anymore, but I was telling just that to myself," he told me after talking me into opening a bottle of the good whiskey Fat Jack had brought from Louisville. "I was on the far side of twenty-five, and I didn't want to be cooped up with all those textbooks and the pedantic, righteous crowd. Besides, I already had more than enough education to do any work open to a black man in Kentucky. I thanked the good Reverend Fee for all he did for me but told him I had to flee, and before he could talk me out of it, I got the hell out of there."

"So here you are," I said, refilling his glass. "I never had much schooling myself, except what I got right here in the Den from . . . well, Preacher Raccoon and some of the . . . eh . . .working girls."

"Imagine that. You're one lucky son of a bitch."

"The preacher sure knows a lot."

"And I'm betting a good man, too, like the Reverend Fee. But I was thinking more about all those Den ladies, thank you. They surely taught you things you can't find in books."

"I suppose. I read some good books, too."

"And you prefer bacon and beans to beefsteak and oysters?"

"Huh?"

"Forget it, Zachary. I was funnin' you. Your mother is one of those Den ladies?"

"She was. She left when I was knee high to a grasshopper. I'm a bastard."

"And I'm a black bastard. Raised good but still a bastard. Let's drink to bastards all over Kentucky. Hell, let's make it all over the world. We're of one blood, Zachary."

"Sounds sublime. To bastards everywhere!" We clinked glasses. Daddy's whiskey went down smooth as honey this time.

"You are a gentleman and a scholar, Zachary."

"Nobody calls me Zachary. I don't think of myself as a Zachary. I'm just Zach."

"And I'm just Jasper."

"I got to tell you something, Mr. Washington. I fought for the South, or at least fought for a man who supported the South,

John Hunt Morgan. But I never had anything against you fellows."

"You mean us distinguished college men?"

"Exactly."

"I offer a toast, no, toasts . . . plural. I toast your papa for bringing us this outstanding refreshment, to the papa I never knew but who acted free when he wasn't, to our mothers for giving us life and shelter for however briefly, to your Preacher Raccoon for teaching you right from wrong, to my Reverend Fee for having unusual vision and devoting his energies to improving the lots of former slaves, to your Den ladies and the beauteous lasses I have known, and to my boon companion Wild Bill, who I have the misfortune of being separated from at the moment—but not for much longer."

"Wild Bill?"

"William Hickok. He was born James Butler Hickok. I call him Bill. He got *wild* during the war. When I was in exile from Kentucky, he was scouting and spying against the Confederates. I was passing through Springfield, Missouri, where he and a fellow Bill and fellow scout name of Cody were having a jolly good time. Hickok, raised right by an abolitionist father, stood up for me when I was attacked by a trio of ruffians who objected to a colored man being free enough to drink heartily and admire the turn of a lady's ankle. Together Wild Bill and I walloped the three louts and sent them packing. He and Cody then let me in on their bacchanal, which lasted another week. I fully intend to head back to Springfield to look up my good friend . . . as soon as I've gotten my fill here, of course. I'm expected."

"Wild Bill, huh? Somebody here nicknamed me Wild Child long ago. What a coincidence. Now, you know two Wilds."

Jasper Washington clapped my back again, causing whiskey to spill from the glass at my lips. "Don't think I'll ever mistake you two Wild gentlemen for each other."

"No matter, Mr. Washington. I don't mind drinking to a Union loyalist like him." I located Jasper's glass with some difficulty, offered a toast to everyone in the world named "Wild," and then we clinked glasses again.

"That's mighty magnanimous of you, Wild Child. No, that doesn't sound right. I'm looking right at you, but the name doesn't fit."

"Right, I'm a man now."

"And how wild you are remains to be seen."

"I might be no Wild Child, but I'm no Mild Man! I'm a . . ." As I fumbled to think of a more appropriate nickname to give myself, I accidentally dropped my glass and then couldn't quite pick it up as it spun on the bar top. I'd gone far beyond my limit for any kind of whiskey.

"I'll call you Zach. But you better stop calling me Mr. Washington. Makes me think first of President George, and he wore a white wig. Besides, I'm only a half-dozen years older than you and I'm blacker than Kentucky coal in case you didn't notice. Jasper will be fine. Better yet, call me Wash. That's what Wild Bill calls me. Since you drank to my Wild Bill, I suppose I should drink to your John Hunt Morgan. Hard to do, though, Zach. That Rebel bought and sold slaves. Of course, Morgan is dead, so maybe I can toast to that."

I finally recovered my glass, but our toasting and drinking came to an abrupt halt when Angus Doyle emerged from the kitchen on the run, waving his arms as if surrounded by a swarm of bees. He went right to me, his active hands fluttering in my face.

"What in the hell do you think you're doing, boy?" he shouted, yanking the glass out of my hand and sliding it down the bar so I couldn't reach it. "You're not only drinking when you shouldn't be drinking, but you're drinking the quality whiskey."

"Yes, but with a customer," I said.

"That's me," said Jasper Washington, holding his glass off to the side in case Angus tried to grab it.

Angus tilted his head as he looked up at the dark-skinned face, seeming to study the frizzy hair before focusing on the large mouth that was doing the consuming.

"No," Angus said, shaking his head and waving a single finger in front of Jasper's nose. "I won't have this. You'll scare away the other customers."

"What other customers? My money's good. I aim to spend plenty, Mr. Proprietor, down here and upstairs."

"The hell you will. We don't have any Negro whores here. You best go get your horizontal refreshments with a big fat mammy in Lexington or Louisville."

"My mistake. I had heard you were all for the North and freeing the slaves during the country's recent troubles."

"You heard right. I've always supported my country staying whole. I don't mind you colored folks being free, but you be free outside of the Daniel's Den or I'll . . . I'll throw you out."

"You will?"

Angus Doyle ran his eyes over the wide-shouldered, barrel-chested body before him and couldn't hide his awe. His face grew paler, and he took one full step back. It was as if he had come face to face with Black Mountain, the highest peak in the commonwealth of Kentucky.

"Zach here will," the owner corrected himself. "That's his job."

I didn't say a word or move an inch in any direction.

"Get on with it, McCall," Angus ordered, without taking his eyes off the unwanted customer. "I want this black bastard out of here."

"Well?" Jasper said.

"Well, I quit," I said. "We bastards stick together."

CHAPTER SEVEN:
GO WEST, YOUNG MEN, GO WEST

There was no long goodbye. Time was part of the reason. Angus Doyle produced a shotgun and waved it around like an American flag while giving Jasper Washington ten minutes to vamoose the Daniel's Den. Because Angus wanted my daddy to supply him with the good whiskey again at a good price, he gave me twenty-four hours to settle whatever affairs I had there and even handed me some back pay, though most of it was in useless Confederate money. Jasper Washington said he could have bent the shotgun barrel over the owner's fat head but that it was damn hard being a free man behind bars. He would wait for me with his walking boots on at the big-leaf magnolia tree on the edge of town.

I needed only about an hour, not twenty-four. I felt I should say goodbye to Daddy and tell him I wasn't joining him in the whiskey-selling business, so I trudged up those stairs, recognizing the squeak on each step. The Red Room door was wide open. Inside, Fat Jack was engaged in an argument with Crooked Nose Jack over their past and future differences. Preacher Raccoon was acting as a sort of referee while Madam Racoon, who I would always think of as Belle Bragg, served as a vocal spectator.

"See you all later," I said, deciding not to mention the confrontation with Angus Doyle or my new friend Jasper Washington, or my rejection of the McCall whiskey-selling business.

"Where you off to, brother?" Crooked Nose Jack asked.

I flinched and then gave him a shrug that I hoped didn't look too dismissive. "Just outside for a little walk," I said, trying too hard to sound both casual and truthful.

"Wait. I'll come with you."

"No, no. You still got things to work out here."

"No, I don't. I . . ."

"Yes, *we* do," Fat Jack said, his face as red as Belle's surprisingly decorous dress. Daddy looked ready to give his full-blood son another sock in the nose. I wouldn't say my relationship with Fat Jack was ever close, but who wanted to be *that* close. It was probably a blessing he hadn't taken me into the bosom of his Louisville family. I, even though more mild than wild then and now, no doubt would have socked Little Jack myself a time or two.

"There's nothing that can't be worked out," Belle said, stretching out her arms like a bird opening its wings. She simultaneously patted the two Jacks on their backs, which caused them to recoil as if bitten by a copperhead. I'm sure if she had maintained her touch, they both would have adjusted to it plenty fast. But she withdrew her hands, clapped them politely as if she had seen a not particularly entertaining stage play, and then blew me a kiss.

"Amen to that," said Preacher Raccoon. "Madam Raccoon and I are most fond of you, Little Jack, but it's in your best interests to reach a peace with your father and go home with him to your loving mother and sisters anxiously waiting for you in Louisville."

"No!" Crooked Nose Jack screamed, crossing his arms. "There ain't been much loving up there lately."

"Bull," shouted Fat Jack. "Your mother's been coddling you since the day you were born, you ungrateful son of a . . ." He cut himself short, perhaps because the preacher was wagging a finger at him. In a whisper he said, "In a day or two we'll leave here together."

"When I leave here . . ." said Crooked Nose Jack, pausing to hitch up his britches, "it'll be with my brother, and we'll be heading out West for great adventure. I keep telling you that, but you don't listen."

"I hear, Little Jack, and what I hear is pure foolishness. You got a safe, warm home in the city. Out there is nothing but savages and wilderness and danger. Tell him, Zach."

"We are westbound," said the rebellious son. "Tell him, Zach."

I pretended I didn't hear either of them or see Belle blow me a second kiss. But I got her message: that I was better off without either of the quarreling McCalls. I spun around and walked out of the Red Room. "See you all later," I repeated as I headed for the stairs, but I didn't figure on seeing any of them for a long time.

"Certainly," called out Preacher Raccoon. "When you get back, Wild Child, we'll all have a nice family meal together and thank the Lord for this reuniting."

I thought what a curious thing that was for him to say, but it did cause me a slight hesitation. Belle had mentioned the "family" thing earlier. The more I thought about it now, the more sense it made. Fat Jack was my daddy, Little Jack was my half brother, Belle Bragg was the closest thing I had to a mother, and the preacher himself was like a friendly uncle. It didn't make me change my mind, though. I was ready to leave *my family* all behind.

Downstairs, Angus Doyle was waiting for me with that shotgun again in hand. He didn't need to point it at me. I assured him I was leaving now and had said nothing bad about him to Fat Jack that might jeopardize any future whiskey transactions. Angus grunted and pointed the barrel toward the front door. "So leave, you . . . you ungrateful bastard," he said.

"Who needs you."

I didn't much object to being called a bastard, but it vexed me to be tagged "ungrateful," the same way Fat Jack had labeled Little Jack. Maybe Angus Doyle had let me grow up in the Den, but he hadn't had much of a hand in my upbringing except to teach me the meaning of unrewarded work. He was unkind, but he knew that without me telling him. I just flashed a half smile at his ugly mug and ambled toward the door.

"And don't get the notion to steal one of my horses this time," he shouted at my back. "I got my eye and my gun on you."

"Right. Long live the South!"

I wasn't sure why I said that. I was about to abandon the South. There were some things at the Daniel's Den that I would miss and that would stick in my head for as long as I lived. But I was certain I could forget him soon enough once I was outside that door.

True to his word, Jasper Washington was waiting for me under the large magnolia and wasn't even acting impatient about it. He was lounging on the ground, his square black head resting on the tree trunk, his thumbs twiddling on his massive chest, his left foot planted on the ground, the other foot crossed high up over his left knee.

"This is how the plantation owners used to do it," he said. "Do I look like one?"

"Not exactly," I said. "Do I, standing here over you?"

"Not hardly. That's why I'm letting you come with me."

"Right. Even though I fought alongside John Morgan Hunt."

"Just in case some steadfast Southern gentlemen stop us, you tell them you once owned me and treated me so good that this big old colored boy couldn't help but stick to you like stink on a skunk. That might make for easier going through this part of the country. Got it?"

"Yes, sir."

We followed Kentucky roads running west to Hickman on the Mississippi River, sometimes on foot, sometimes catching rides on farm wagons. All the while Jasper Washington pretended to be my loyal servant even though my money soon ran out, and we relied on the wad of greenbacks he kept in a hidden pocket sewed inside his trousers in case we ran into highwaymen. He said that while it took a lot of brains to get by in the white man's world, he had earned most of that money using his prodigious body. As a free black man during the Civil War, he explained, he had risked his life wrestling black bears in the backwoods and back taverns of Ohio, Indiana, and Illinois under the auspices of a white confidence man named Harry Hellerman. The danger lessened and the profits increased once he and Hellerman had fully tamed a willing opponent. Jasper, as massive as he was, would have been no match for a 350-pound bear in the wilds. But Victor the bear was so well trained that he would give a good fight without living up to his name. He always allowed his two-legged opponent to throw him and be victorious, except in the rare instances when the locals wagered whatever cash they had on the underdog, the man. Harry Hellerman always found a way to make a killing, and Jasper did all right, too, while staying in one piece.

Nevertheless, when Jasper removed his clothes for the first time on our travels to immerse himself in what he called "the blessed Father of the Waters," I saw scars running up and down his legs and claw marks crisscrossing his back. He plunged into the Mississippi and was strong enough to swim against the current for five minutes.

"I'm glad you're on my side," I told him when he finally climbed onto the bank and on all fours shook himself dry like a dog, or even a bear, I reckon.

He laughed when he saw me staring in wonderment.

"Victor was a good soul at heart," Jasper said as he swatted himself on the back with a river birch branch to get the circulation going. "Never once scratched my face. From the neck up I'm as beautiful as ever, unmarked by Southern man or Mr. Hellerman's beast."

I handed him his shirt, long johns, and trousers as if I was *his* servant. "So, what happened to him?"

"Victor or Mr. Hellerman?"

"Well, both."

"I was with them in Darke County, Ohio, when I heard the war was over. I decided to quit wrestling on the spot and head back to Kentucky to see if Berea College could be the place for me again—you know, to rest my battered body and do some brain work. But the war and all that bear wrestling had changed me. My mind couldn't sit still anymore."

"Yes, you told me that before, but what about Victor and . . ."

"I'm getting to it. I was saying my goodbyes up in Darke County when the two of them turned primitive on me. Mr. Hellerman told me I was an ungrateful black bastard and that I had no right to leave him, while Victor growled like he didn't even know me."

"I reckon we all seem ungrateful to someone."

"There's a lot of truth in those words. Anyway, Mr. Hellerman said there was even more money to be made now that the war was over. I bowed to him but told him he couldn't change my mind. I was leaving no matter what. So, Mr. Hellerman told Victor to use his jaws, claws, whatever to stop me from going. Victor had the sense not to obey his master. That infuriated Mr. Hellerman, who proceeded to beat Victor with a horse whip. It was a major thrashing. No slave should be treated that way. When I tried to grab the whip, Mr. Hellerman started in on whipping me. Victor didn't take kindly to either of us getting flogged, so that old bear bit his master's head off . . . well, not literally, but he did take half the old bear baiter's face clear off."

"That's awful," I said, thinking of not only the man's half face but also the savage whipping. "What did you do?"

"A lynch-minded mob was headed in our direction. Yes, it was a northern mob, but I figured they might blame me as much as the bear for what happened to Mr. Hellerman. I ran and kept on running until I reached the Ohio River, at which point I dove in and began swimming. Isn't that a lark? I was a darky taking the old Underground Railroad in the opposite direction. I swum clear across the river and was resting up in Clarksburg, Kentucky, a few days later when I read in the newspaper that a wild and dangerous bear had been shot twenty-one times and a disfigured itinerant tradesman was somehow hanging on for dear life but was not expected to make it one more night in Darke County."

"That's awful, Wash," I said again because I couldn't think of anything else to say on the subject. That was the first time I called him Wash instead of Mr. Washington or Jasper.

"I don't hate Harry Hellerman, though. He and Victor made me a lot of spending money. Mr. Hellerman was a pretty fair card player, too—taught me all there is to know about the odds in poker and how to spot a cheat, him being one himself. He was a greedy, gambling son of a bitch confidence man all right, but unlike a lot of white folks, he didn't pretend to be something more than he was."

I handed Jasper his bowler and his bandana, and we strolled back to our boardinghouse in the center of Hickman. We planned to spend one last night in Kentucky and then cross the Mississippi (on a flatboat ferry, not swimming) in the morning. Parked out front was a horse and buggy that looked familiar. On one seat was a lone leather-bound Holy Bible, on the other an almost empty bottle of good Kentucky whiskey and a cracked wooden sign with hand lettering in red paint that read clearly enough, *THE DANIEL'S DEN*. There could only be one of those.

"Hey, Zach," Jasper said, fondling the bottle. "There are a couple of swallows left."

"I can't believe it," I said, picking up the Bible. "That's Preacher Raccoon's rig."

"The devil-dodger back in Boonesborough who married your mother?"

"Not my actual mother, not the one who ran off to California but got eaten along the way."

"I know. He married the one with the pile of black hair and fetching stare—Madam Raccoon."

"Yes. Belle Bragg. She married the circuit-riding preacher because my daddy was already married up in Louisville."

"All right, that's fine. But what's the preacher doing way out here at the very end of Kentucky? Has he expanded his gospelizing or you think he deserted his madam?"

"He wouldn't be fool enough to leave Belle even if God told him to."

"I suppose Hickman has souls that need saving like any other place in this cotton-pickin' country."

He took one long pull on the bottle, and no swallows were left for me. But I didn't care. On the inside of the Bible cover, I read this inscription:

TO ROBERT GENTRY, THE KINDEST MAN I KNOW. THANK YOU FOR UNDERSTANDING. CHILDREN ARE INDEED A BLESSING FROM THE LORD, WHO MAKES NO DISTINCTION BETWEEN A HUMAN LIFE BORN IN MARRIAGE OR A HUMAN LIFE BORN OUT OF WEDLOCK. MAY GOD AND MY LOVE BE WITH YOU ALWAYS—BELLE BRAGG, MAY 12, 1865.

"And this is his," I said, waving the Bible in Jasper's face as if I were a prosecutor presenting damning evidence to a jury of my peers. "Belle gives him Bibles as presents. She gave this one to him, I'm sure."

Jasper read the inscription aloud. "Sounds like the madam is saying it's all right to be a bastard like us, Zach. I reckon she had you on her mind when she wrote it to him?"

"I'm not sure. Could be Preacher Raccoon was a bastard himself at birth."

"Too bad I never got to meet Belle. I did meet the preacher once on the road, and it sure looks like I'll be meeting him again soon enough. I'm not exactly zealous about that, but at least, as I recall, he wasn't one of those ardent Rebel reverends who claimed God favored the Confederates and slavery."

"Of course not. As far as I know, he mostly left God out of the Civil War. You think he might have trailed us all the way out here, Wash?"

"Seems that way, but I can't imagine why. Only a runaway slave or maybe a runaway son would be chased this far. You sure you aren't the son of a preacher man instead of a whiskey drummer?"

"Positive. All I can think of is he's brought bad news from the Den, like Angus Doyle kicking him and Belle out or Fat Jack and Crooked Nose Jack murdering each other."

"Stop fretting, Zach. Only one way to know what brought him to Hickman. Let's go find your man of the cloth and ask him."

We entered the clapboard boardinghouse, me carrying the inscribed Bible, Jasper carrying the empty whiskey bottle. We got no farther than the hallway when the fastidious housekeeper dashed toward us in an agitated state. She ignored the large black man and addressed me.

"I couldn't keep him out, Mr. McCall," she said, wringing

her large hands. "He's in your room right now, sir. He says he knows you, but I'm not at all certain he does. I suspect he might prove troublesome. He laid himself right down on your bed, if you please, with his boots on, no less. He patted your feather pillow and said something . . . well, something rather indecent that I would rather not repeat. I must say, sir, I'm beside myself."

Jasper Washington tried to control his laughter but failed. "That's some preacher you know," he said to me, slapping my back, clearly forgetting his place in front of the housekeeper. "Boots on the bed. Indecent suggestion to this clearly respectable lady. I guess that's what to expect from a preacher married to a madam and living in a den of iniquity. No wonder we found this bottle near empty in his buggy."

The housekeeper gave a disapproving glance at the bottle Jasper was holding, still not looking directly at him. I stepped around my friend since I knew I couldn't budge him or bring myself to censure him.

"Don't worry, miss," I said. "Everything will be fine. I'm quite sure I know the gentleman in my room. He's a man of . . . well, a good man. See this Bible I'm holding? It belongs to him. What you've said about him sounds totally out of character. Perhaps you misunderstood him or he was exhausted from a long trip and didn't quite know what he was saying. I'm sure the old gentleman meant you no offense."

"I will *not* be made sport of, sir," the housekeeper persisted. "He neither acts nor looks like a gentleman and he is certainly *not* old. With his contorted nose, roving eyes, and rude manners, I suspect he's a ne'er-do-well, perhaps a loafer or even a rowdy."

Jasper saw fit to laugh again. I was ready to scold him now, but when I turned toward him, he looked so jolly that I just shrugged. Although the housekeeper's words had me confused,

I again tried to reassure her that nobody wanted to make sport of her.

"What about your colored man?" she said. "Order him to stop laughing."

That made Jasper laugh so hard that he accidentally slapped a knee with the bottle.

"Look, miss, did the gentle—the not-so-old fellow in my room give a name?"

"He didn't bother to introduce himself. He was far too rude for that."

There was nothing else to do but go upstairs and see for myself who was lying on my bed. I took the stairs two at a time, and Jasper stayed right at my heels. He was quick for such a large, jolly man.

I hesitated for only a second before flinging open the door to my room. Once inside, I could only gawk. Jasper, breathing down my neck, stopped laughing.

"So, there you are!" said the young man on the bed, squeezing my pillow so hard that several feathers flew out and floated about the room. "You shouldn't of oughta run out like that. Brothers should stick close together."

CHAPTER EIGHT: ERUPTION IN NEW MADRID

Crooked Nose Jack did his best to make me feel guilty about leaving him behind in Boonesborough. It didn't work. I wanted to leave him behind again. He admitted to stealing fifty dollars from Belle Bragg and three bottles of whiskey from Fat Jack while they slept (he said together in the Red Room while Preacher Raccoon snored on the floor downstairs, but I say he was lying) and then knocking Preacher Raccoon over the head with the Daniel's Den hardwood sign before taking his rig. Talk about ungrateful. Belle and the preacher had shown unusual kindness toward him, and Daddy had been trying to bring the boy back into the bosom of his family. Little Jack only viewed it as everyone conspiring against him.

What's more, Little Jack kept talking out of both sides of his mouth about brotherly love, as if he had read every single reference to it in Preacher Raccoon's Bible and truly believed such love was the greatest virtue a man could possess. "It is because I have so much brotherly love that I am ready to forgive you, brother, for skedaddling." To top it all off, he wanted me to dismiss Jasper Washington not only from the boardinghouse but also from my life but didn't dare say so in front of the large black man who had wrestled bears. I didn't have to say anything, though. Jasper Washington made it easy on him.

"I'll leave you two brothers to thrash out your family matters," he said with a grin that suggested he was above it all. "The Civil War still divides you people."

When my friend was gone, Jack demanded a straight answer on why a brother would desert a brother and rub elbows with a colored man. I mentioned the Civil War again, reminding him how brother had fought against brother in Kentucky and elsewhere and that the enslavement of black folks was a major bone of contention. He replied that I had fought Yankees unrelated to me during the war until I gave up all fighting and moved into the McCall attic, where we two brothers hadn't fought even once. I couldn't argue with that. How could you fight with someone who was waiting on you hand and foot? Instead, I reminded him once more of something else.

"Fact is, Crooked Nose Jack, you are *only* my half brother," I said. "There isn't anything in Preacher Raccoon's Bible about half-brotherly love, is there?"

"That book don't tell you everything there is to know about everything," he replied. "Sometimes you just know things yourself."

I couldn't argue with that either, so I tried a different approach. "I was thinking what's best for you, Little Jack. I can't offer you food or shelter or anything. You have a mother and a father and three sisters in a fine Kentucky home. I'm an outsider. I don't have a right to interfere with your family of six, which has gotten along all these years without me and in five out of the six cases without even knowing I existed."

"But you do exist, and the family doesn't get along that well. You might be the number seven McCall, but you're the one I'm closest to, the one I get along with most. I don't need a fine Kentucky home. I can rough it as good as anyone, and I want to rough it with you."

Crooked Nose Jack broke down at that point and began sobbing as if I had told him his family had been struck down by cholera.

"You . . . you mean the world to me . . ." he managed to get out before he licked tears from his lips and struggled to regain his composure. Meanwhile, I twiddled my thumbs and tried to recall anyone in trousers putting on such an unmanly display. I was unsuccessful. Among the gentler sex, the Den working girls included, I recalled only one who had carried on so—an Ohio farmer's wife upset because the horses of John Hunt Morgan's raiders had trampled her rose garden.

Jack wiped his eyes with one shirtsleeve, his crooked nose with the other, and was able to continue. "I was good to you in the Louisville attic, wasn't I? I brought you food and water and kept my mother out of your hair? When I made it down to Boonesborough, I was sickly and couldn't do much. But now, I can be good to you again, really I can." He let his shoulders droop, making himself appear even shorter than he already was. I thought he might actually drop to his knees and kiss my feet. But he suddenly rose up on his toes, swiped at his eyes as if bothered by flies, and tilted his head to the side like a puppy who has heard an unfamiliar command. "You said we'd go west together—you promised!"

"I mentioned I might head out there, but I never promised I'd take you with me," I said.

"Instead, you took that monstrous colored man." He looked at the door warily as if he expected Jasper Washington to come bursting back into the room. "That don't seem like a natural thing for a white man to do 'less the darky is a slave, and there ain't no more of them around, least ways not legal."

"Jasper Washington happens to be my good friend."

"But I'm your brother. No darky can be your brother."

"Who knows. Fat Jack got around. We could both have a handful of half-Negro brothers running around the state of Kentucky."

Little Jack had to think about that one for a while. He paced the room, muttering some, and then stopped by the only window and parted the yellow curtain. It happened to face west. I wasn't sure of the view from there, but I imagined he was seeing the sun going down.

"You got to take me with you," he said, opening the window. For a moment I thought he might jump out. "You want me to turn around and beg, I will. I can't go home again, and I can't go it alone . . . not out there. I ain't got the . . . the experience, you might say. You do, brother. You fought alongside John Hunt Morgan against the Yankees. You shot a man. You know how to handle danger. You know how to survive in a dangerous world."

He paused as if he expected me to vigorously nod. Instead, I shook my head. I wasn't going west to face danger, to shoot anyone again, or to prove anything. Fact was, I just wanted to get away from Kentucky and start over. Survival anywhere was often just a matter of luck. And as for knowing how to survive in a dangerous world, I knew I didn't know half as much about it as Jasper Washington did.

Little Jack sniffled and continued. "I know danger is lurking out there behind every bush, every boulder, every corner on the far side of the Mississippi—savages ready to take your scalp, road agents who'd just as soon kill you as look at you and then rob you blind, and hungry wolves and bears ready to tear you apart and make their next meal out of you."

He was actually frightening me some, but I kept a steady voice, talking sensibly. "There's no danger if you go back home, Crooked Nose Jack. There's peace in the East now and in your daddy's heart."

"But he's your daddy, too, and you had no trouble leaving him behind along with all the rest."

"I'm older than you," was all I managed to say.

"Look, there is danger like I said, but I don't mind some danger, not if I'm *not* alone. You see, Brother, I ache for adventure. Where else to find it except on the western frontier?

90

With you leading the way, I won't be afraid. You'd protect me. I know you would. A brother has got to look after a brother."

I started to mention the half brother thing again, but I didn't feel up to it anymore. Maybe he was getting to me. Nobody had ever said they needed me before. He had made it by himself all the way from Boonesborough to Hickman, but that didn't mean he didn't need me. He had been desperate to catch up with me. It seemed rather big of Crooked Nose Jack to admit he couldn't go it alone on the wild side of the Mississippi River.

"You don't even know where I'm going, where we're going— Jasper and me."

"West. It don't matter exactly where as long as I'm with you. I got the double buggy . . . room for you and me . . . but not for three people. Anyway, Washington is big enough to be two people all by himself. And there's only the one tired horse pulling."

"We'd manage. You could sit on his lap."

"I would never . . . oh, you're joking. But I'm serious. It ought to be just me and you."

"Look, Jack, I'm going with Jasper. Anyway, it's *not* even your buggy."

"He'd have to get a horse or mule or something or else walk behind us."

"Jasper and I got this far without Preacher Racoon's buggy. We don't need it."

"I suppose we can take turns—two riding, one walking. Yes, that'll work. Washington's muscle could be useful if there's trouble out there. He's powerful, I'll give him that. It's true he really fought bears?"

"At least one I know of, name of Victor."

"It's all settled then, Zach. Tomorrow we'll cross the river together. Neither of us will have to be alone out there. Jasper can come along."

"Seeing as he's the one leading me, that goes without saying."

"All right. All right. But why is someone like him going west, anyway? He running away from the law or something like that?"

"No more than I am. He has a friend in Springfield, Missouri, he aims to look up."

"White or colored?"

"White, I imagine. His name is Wild Bill Hickok. What difference is it to you, Little Jack?"

"No difference really. Don't matter if he's black or white or even a redskin. Really, it don't."

"I'd like to believe you, but . . ."

"Any friend of my brother's friend is a friend of mine."

"Oh, there's one more thing you should know. Wild Bill Hickok fought for the North. He's a Yankee all the way."

"Well, that's OK, too. He can't be as mean as Angus Doyle."

"I just wouldn't try to cross Wild Bill or Wash, if I were you."

"No, sir, Brother. I ain't of a mind to do that. Whew! I'm just glad everything is settled."

I didn't think anything was settled yet. I wanted my half brother to do the right thing, which was to return the buggy and Bible to Preacher Raccoon. I couldn't make him go back, of course, but I was confident Jasper Washington could. Trouble was, Jasper wasn't interested in flexing his muscles. "Don't much care for the kid tagging along," he said, "but he is kin to you, and that buggy of his surely does appeal to me and my tired feet."

I brought up the fact that it was a rather light, two-person carriage, but Jasper shrugged that off. I then reminded him that the buggy belonged to somebody else, somebody who needed it badly in his line of work—spreading the gospel. "The gospel's been spread for hundreds of years now, and it hasn't yet done a lick of good for any of us dark-skinned folks," he said, patting me on the back as if he were unaware that beneath all the dirt and grit my face was white. "It'll do us good to ride that carriage into Springfield like we were somebody. I aim to play stud poker, drink cheap whiskey, take a twirl with a pretty girl or two, and hash over old times with Wild Bill."

Crooked Nose Jack had used up the fifty dollars he stole from Belle Bragg, but we said he could stay with us in our boardinghouse room. I even offered to flip a coin to see which McCall got to share the bed with Jasper (there was no fitting three) and which got the floor. Jack wasn't interested. He chose to sleep out in the buggy, saying one of the suspicious characters he saw in town might try to steal it, even though the housekeeper boldly suggested that the only suspicious characters in Hickman were Jasper, Jack, and me. It was plain to see that Jack was afraid Jasper and I would make off with the already once-stolen buggy in the middle of the night, leaving him behind again.

In the morning we—Crooked Nose Jack still resting in the buggy—ferried across the Mississippi in a flatboat, and I must say on the other side I took a deep breath, and the air seemed more sun-sweetened, invigorating, and soul-sustaining. On the frontier side, the buggy labored on rough roads no matter who was driving or riding and who was on foot bringing up the rear. Jack and I ended up doing most of the walking, because Jasper said he needed to give directions west, his boots were too tight, and he was too proud to be treated like a lowly slave forced to eat the dust of two white men. His arguments were shaky, but then he was far bigger than us, and I didn't hold it against him.

That evening we arrived in New Madrid, Missouri, where the earth quaked a thousand times back in 1811 and 1812 and where the cotton plantations on the fertile floodplain were in turmoil because the once enslaved laborers were looking for new lives after emancipation. The citizens of New Madrid welcomed Crooked Nose Jack and me at first, seeing as we were

Kentucky boys who had supported the South (me by joining up with John Hunt Morgan, Jack by belittling Jayhawkers, Union soldiers such as General U. S. Grant, and Yankee businessmen such as Angus Doyle of Boonesborough, as well as shamelessly boasting how if he'd been a couple years older he would have joined the noble Rebel fight against Northern aggression and beaten the tar out of them damned Yankees). But then they saw that the enormous black fellow was far from subservient; in fact, he appeared to be the head of our small party, the money man, and downright insolent. A half-dozen of the more sensitive New Madrid citizens took offense at the dark stranger but didn't seem to want to start anything until they were joined by six others of the same sort.

"Case you boys aren't up on your recent history," Jasper began, before pausing, not because he was fearful but because he wanted to look directly into the eyes of all twelve, "you had a constitutional convention early last year and an ordinance that stated all of the slaves in Missouri were immediately emancipated without compensation to their owners. As for me personally, I've never been a slave anywhere, and I'm just visiting your fair state to reunite with one of your finer citizens who was a spy and a scout, on the *right* side, during the recent rebellion."

"We don't care if you're here to see Governor Thomas Clement Fletcher himself," said the most vocal member of the unwelcoming committee. "We don't want troublemakers like you stirring up our darkies."

"It's you boys who are unwanted and are being encouraged to leave the state. Haven't you heard about the Ironclad Oath? Every one of you who supported the Confederacy has been disenfranchised in Missouri and lost your right to hold office or practice a profession, not that any of you look capable of holding even a low office or practicing anything but stupidity."

"Them is fighting words," the man said, but instead of stepping forward, he stepped back and looked toward others to take up the cause. A loud shuffling of feet followed, accompanied by some serious muttering. "You ain't got a vote on anything in Missouri," he added when it seemed like more words were needed. "You get your black ass back across the river to Kentucky or wherever else you come from. You ain't nothing but an interloper."

"Interloper, huh? That's a mighty big word, mister. Your black mammy *learn* you it?"

It wasn't much of a fight. Only half of the rabble-rousers moved in on Jasper, and the punches they threw were largely wild and ineffective. That made Jasper laugh until one of those Southern boys began flogging him in the head with a hickory stick. That made my friend mad. He caught the stick, snapped it in two, and then, in bearlike fashion, squeezed the breath out of the fellow. Most of the others just watched with nervous feet, except for a skinny, long-bearded man in a gray slouch hat who produced a bludgeon and intended to strike Jasper from behind until I grabbed the raised weapon from him, tossed it aside, and punched him below his hollow belly. He doubled over and dropped to his knees. I immediately raised my fists to fend off his friends, who no doubt saw me as an easier target than Jasper. Nobody touched me, though, because the sheriff arrived and fired his pistol once in the air. No doubt most of the mob had heard their share of gunshots before, but they all froze in place. Not Crooked Nose Jack, though. He picked up the bludgeon, tiptoed up to the kneeling man, and crowned him with it. Nobody noticed but me.

The sheriff dispersed the mob before he realized two men were down. The one finally caught his breath, caught sight of Jasper hovering nearby, and hightailed it even though the sheriff called him by name. The other one wasn't getting up. The sheriff asked what had caused the lump on the man's head, but Jasper and I only shrugged, and Little Jack offered an innocent smile as he held the bludgeon behind his back. The sheriff announced that the Radical Republicans had got him elected, and he was all for giving black men their equal rights whether they deserved them or not. He then ordered Jasper to carry the unconscious man to the doctor's office. The fellow had a cracked skull, and the sheriff threatened to arrest Jasper and me (Jack had slipped away to wait for us in the buggy) before he decided it would be better for New Madrid's peace and our health if we left town.

Jasper had nothing against the sheriff, so we pushed on in the dark toward Springfield. Jasper, no doubt pleased with the fight's outcome, even volunteered to take the first walk.

"I saw what you did," I whispered to Little Jack once we were clear of the town limits with me at the reins.

"What did he do?" asked Jasper, who was walking fast enough to stay at the side of the buggy instead of behind it.

"I participated," Jack said, holding the bludgeon proudly in the air.

"Did you now? On my side, I take it? You were trying to protect me from that poor white trash? Maybe I should thank you, Little Jack."

"No need. I just did what I had to do."

"Why?" I asked.

"Just did, Brother. I missed out on the Civil War. I needed to hit someone awfully bad."

"You did good," said Jasper. "We all did good. Just like Wild Bill and me that time back in Springfield when those three ruffians attacked me for no other reason than I was a colored man enjoying himself."

There was a long silence, though I could almost hear Jack's thoughts churning.

"What I did back there in New Madrid don't make me a

Yankee lover," Crooked Nose Jack said at last, finally lowering the pilfered bludgeon.

CHAPTER NINE:
SPRINGFIELD SENSATION

We were no farther along than Poplar Bluff when we had to deal with a loose wheel, and at West Plains, we needed to replace a broken axle. Clearly the buggy wasn't meant to operate on such questionable roads. At Hartsville, the other wheel snapped off in a gigantic rut we named "Mammoth Cave." The next morning, we took the blacksmith's best offer for the buggy, minus the tired horse. We traded Preacher Racoon's vehicle for a mule named Devil, so named because he was red, although his disposition wasn't so great either. We traveled on, still with two riding (one on Devil, the other on the nameless horse) and one walking. The mule, who moved at his own pace, objected to Crooked Nose Jack rapping his sides with the bludgeon and refused to carry him at all. And the old horse wasn't up to handling Jasper's weight on its back. Our progress was slow to say the least. At Walnut Forest, the old horse up and died. Not having the tools to dig a grave, we covered it with leaves and brush. Jack blamed Jasper for killing his horse, even though the horse actually belonged to the preacher, of course. Jasper didn't apologize, but he did say a little prayer over the dead horse, which he said was more than the slaves got who were worked to death on Southern plantations.

The last ten miles to Springfield, Jasper sat Devil, while us McCalls walked behind. Crooked Nose Jack cursed the rider and the mule equally the whole way. Still, Jasper didn't exactly ride in style into Springfield. A group of local long-haired men in dirty buckskins, with apparently nothing to do but wait for the arrival of strangers, greeted our struggling, exhausted party with mocking laughter. I thought Jasper might take offense, but he wasn't dumb—all the members of the welcoming committee wore revolvers about their persons. When Jasper laughed with them, that was the end of it. Those men didn't seem to object to Jasper's presence. They were certainly more kindly disposed toward him than they were to former Rebels, which I admitted to being and which Little Jack claimed to have been despite his fuzzy cheeks.

"Looking at you two goosecaps, it ain't no wonder the South lost," said one of them.

First thing Jasper did in Springfield was get a bath and a shave. We McCalls didn't have the price for either (and Crooked Nose Jack wasn't shaving yet anyway), so we stabled Devil and waited on a bench in the town square, both of us as wide eyed as children on Christmas morning. Most folks passing by—and there were plenty of them, almost all male—didn't appear to be clean-shaven or clean in anyway. It was difficult to tell the difference between the settlers and our fellow adventurers but much easier to identify which ex-soldiers were Union men and which were Confederates, since the former still favored blue and the latter gray. Jack had trouble sitting still. He took a couple turns around the square to look at the storefronts after I promised to stay put and not desert him in the strange town.

"I like it," Little Jack announced after his first turn. "I love it," he said after the second.

"That was quick," I said.

"How can you just sit there, Brother? I thought you was the Wild Child."

"This bench fits me."

"Springfield's not too big like Louisville and not too small like Boonesborough. It's an exciting place, lots of saloons and such. The men look ready for a fight with gun, knife, or fist. The women look ready for . . . you know. I saw a couple of them sportin' women. One of them even talked to me, asked if I was lost. She wore a dress as red as the sun, and she was all over as smooth and rounded as the Appalachians."

"We saw plenty such women at the Daniel's Den," I said, although it was true that while growing up there, I often didn't dwell on what profession Belle Bragg and her associates pursued. "And Angus Doyle was always ready to let loose with both barrels of his shotgun if he didn't like your looks."

"It ain't the same. Springfield is the West."

"I reckon, but there's a lot more West to the west of us."

"I know that. I got top marks in geography. But right now, we're right here. The rest can wait. Come on, Brother, let's go see more of this western town. We're free as the wind; nobody's telling us what we should or shouldn't do. Nothing at all to hold us back. I'm ripe for adventure. There's entertainment all around us. How 'bout it, Zach?"

"I told Jasper I'd wait for him in the square. Besides, the kind of entertainment you want costs money, and that's something neither of us has got."

"I got a hankering for cards—faro, I believe you call it. I heard that's the way to make some money."

"That's the way to lose your shirt. Jasper told me it's also called 'bucking the tiger' or 'twisting the tiger's tail.' That should tell you something."

"All right, then, we'll play that other gambling game. I already know poker."

"I'm only slightly acquainted with it."

"But it's better, right, for winning more money?"

"I doubt it. Jasper said it is also called the bluffing game, or just plain bluff. It takes a lot of nerve to play, not to mention a stake to start with."

"All right then. There'll be time later. We'll wait for your colored man."

Jasper showed up looking distinguished in a new red bib shirt, his curly hair cut close, his chin whiskers trim, his skin glistening and perfumed, his new black boots as shiny as his face. He still wore the same old wool trousers, but they had been washed and the wrinkles pressed out of them. Crooked Nose Jack grumbled and then snorted when Jasper leaned in close to ask us to sniff his neck.

"Can't go find Wild Bill looking like one of the bummers who infest this city," Jasper said. "Follow me, boys."

We did, but Jack whispered a complaint to me—that our well-dressed associate must have spent his last penny on himself or else was carrying far more money than he had ever let on.

"Quit your lamenting," I told him. "I got a feeling Jasper is leading us to places where there'll be more excitement than you know what to do with."

"Nothing I can't handle, Brother."

It wasn't hard finding Wild Bill Hickok. He had been frequenting Springfield's gambling establishments for almost a month, and the fact was he stood out like a bejeweled thumb. He was six feet, supple, and broad shouldered with long, auburn locks and pale-yellow mustache, buckskin coat and leggings, broad-brimmed hat, and two Navy Colts with butts forward in his open-top holster. We went to two saloons where he had been seen earlier in the day at card tables. We were directed to Oak Hall, the working home of several professional gamblers. When we arrived, Hickok laid his cards face down on the table and leaned back in his chair so that it pressed against the back wall.

"You got me again, Dave," he said. "It's like you were out to get me."

The man across from him kept his poker face and slowly folded his hands on the table as if he were about to pray. "It's nothing personal, Bill. Your cards weren't hard to read, not after you twirled your mustache."

"How much I owe you?"

The man called Dave Tutt stood up and smiled. He wore a black frock coat that he quickly buttoned up, but not before I saw he was wearing two pistols waist high, just like Hickok, except Wild Bill wore his pair outside his buckskin coat.

"Nothing at the moment. Don't want to pluck your feathers just yet. It's your turn to buy the drinks, friend."

The two gamblers moved to the bar, where the bartender was already filling two glasses for them. Jasper tried not to make his new boots squeak as he walked up behind them. He was about to tap one of Hickok's broad shoulders when Wild Bill spun around with one pistol jabbing into Jasper's belly and the other pressed to Jasper's groin.

"Damn," said Jasper, but he was grinning. "You haven't slowed down. How'd you know?"

"New boots, Wash?" Hickok asked, smiling out of one side of his mouth. "I mighta plugged you. You were taking a mighty big chance."

"I don't think so. You wouldn't shoot a man who isn't heeled, would you, Bill?"

"Wasn't sure you'd ever get your mangy hide back to Springfield," Hickok said, but he didn't withdraw his six-guns. "Let me feast my eyes on you, Wash. Why, you don't look mangy at all. Even smell nice. You must have grown some, too, while you were away."

"Just big enough for wrestling bears. But even the bears are too tame back East."

"Well, welcome to Springfield. We got everything you want and everything you don't want right here."

"We got a Springfield in Kentucky, too, but it's too domesticated for me. Davy Crockett once said he was half horse, half alligator, and a little attached with snapping turtle and that he could lick any man in Kentucky. Well, I'm half bear, half panther, and a little attached with you, Wild Bill. I catawamptiously chewed up the beatingest men in Kentucky. Now I aim to see if there be any human being I can't lick in Missouri."

"I'd put my money on you anytime against man or beast."

Hickok's smile spread to the other side of his mouth. But the Dave fellow frowned and quickly opened his coat to make his own six-guns more readily available. Even when Wild Bill finally holstered his pair of Colts, Dave's hands still fluttered at his waist like butterflies. Only when Wild Bill slapped Jasper Washington on the back did Dave drop his hands to the bar and fondle his empty glass. The barkeep gave him a prompt refill. Hickok introduced the two men, and Jasper started to extend his hand, but Tutt just nodded as he studied his drink.

"Crockett was known to exaggerate," Wild Bill said. "His last words at the Alamo were, 'There must be a million Mexicans out there ready to tear down these walls.' "

"Anyway, there were enough Mexicans to do the job, weren't there?" said Jasper.

"That's 'cause you and me and Cody weren't there."

"Damn right, and I wouldn't have needed a gun. I'd have held off Santa Anna's army with my bare hands."

"You know, Wash, I missed you. You exaggerate as good as Crockett."

"Could be, but I'm a Negro, so it doesn't amuse anyone. But to answer your question. The boots are new, it's true, but I say you couldn't possibly have heard me walking up behind you. I'm half bear and half panther, but I know how to walk quiet despite my sheer bulk. I've been known to stalk a full-blown bear or the buxom daughter of a sharecropper."

"You got me there, Wash," Hickok admitted. He pointed to the mirror above the back bar, and all three of them looked up to see themselves. Crooked Nose Jack and I moved in closer to have a look, too. The barkeep didn't look, but he nodded his head as if he had seen it all before and had put up the mirror specifically so customers could watch for possible back shooters. "Even a half-blind man could see you coming," added Hickok. "I swear, Wash, you've grown wider than a side-wheel steamboat."

"Who's exaggerating now?" Jasper asked.

Hickok chuckled, and then the two men crossed arms to pat each other on the back. I was content to just listen, but Jack moved closer still, no doubt impatient to have himself recognized. Finally, he cleared his young throat like a sick frog.

This time it was gambler Dave who spun around. He kept hold of his glass with his left hand, but his right one now held a large six-shooter. It was pointed at Jack, but in a flash was redirected toward me, no doubt because I was bigger and looked like the more serious threat, though neither of us was armed.

"Who the hell are you two?" Dave Tutt spit out, sounding as if he were doing us a favor by asking that question instead of shooting first.

"The gambling McCall brothers," said Jack.

"Never heard of you." Dave kept his six-shooter pointed at my belly.

"Friends," I said, gulping.

"They're with me," Jasper said. "This is the first time they've crossed the Mississippi."

"And it might be the last time if they should cross me. The young one don't look at me straight."

"His eyes don't work quite right," I explained. "He's a little bit cross-eyed."

"That's like being a little bit in the family way."

"Little Jack McCall is all right, even if he's never forgiven Robert E. Lee for surrendering," Jasper said.

The gambler lowered his six-shooter and stuck it back under his coat. "Can't blame a man for feeling that way."

"Thank you, Mr. Tutt," Jack said. "Some people just don't understand."

"Little Jack, is it? I was born Davis Tutt in Arkansas. Some call me Dave, friends call me Little Dave. That doesn't diminish me any. But you're no bigger than a jackrabbit and mighty young, Little Jack. Where's your daddy?"

"Fat Jack's at his old Kentucky home where he belongs," Jack said. "I'm here to gamble."

"I see. Poker happens to be my game."

"Me, too." He extended his hand, and Dave Tutt took it, but just for a second.

"No squeezing, Little Jack," said Tutt, wiggling his fingers to make sure they all worked properly. "My hands are my livelihood."

"I understand, Mr. Tutt. I'm just honored to meet you. No need to shake on it."

"Forget what I said earlier about your eyes and your height. You're all right, Little Jack."

"Thanks, Mr. Tutt. May I call you Little Dave? Seems fitting since I'm Little Jack."

"Why the hell not. A gambler can never have too many friends."

"That's a good one, Little Dave. I saw you take Wild Bill Hickok over there."

"At cards, sonny," said Hickok. "Only at cards."

Wild Bill, Little Dave, and Jasper Washington shared a good laugh. I was glad to see that my half brother was getting along so well with the two much older men. I hoped it would last.

"What about your brother?" Dave Tutt said, suddenly turning to me. "You come to Springfield for the poker, too—Big Jack, is it?"

"No, sir," I said. "I'm not a Jack at all. I'm a Zach. We're half brothers. Truth is, I'm no card player. I figure cards can only lead to trouble." Tutt was glaring at me, so I quickly added, "What I mean is, it could get me into trouble since I don't know how to play."

"Most men don't, at least not well. It's a good game, but bad cards have led to many a good fight. I'm a professional. I deal with these and shoot with these when necessary." Tutt held up his hands in case I wanted to examine them. I didn't, but Crooked Nose Jack did. "It can be dangerous, boys. Many a man would love to break my hands to get the advantage on me."

"That's awful," said Little Jack. "What kind of man would do such a thing?"

"A bad man. They come cheap out here. I know you like poker, Little Jack, but my advice to you and your brother is to head back to your Kentucky farm where it's much safer."

"We ain't no farm boys," Jack snapped. "And I aim to gamble even if my brother ain't."

"Suit yourself. You have spirit, Little Jack, and I'm nobody's keeper. Seeing as you are new to Springfield, though, I'll buy you and your brother a drink, but only one round. That's a little rule I have."

"Forget it, Little Dave," Hickok said, stretching a long arm over Tutt's shoulders; his other arm was resting easy on Jasper Washington's right shoulder. "I'm buying for the whole gang."

It turned out that Dave Tutt and Hickok had been acquainted for some time and had more in common than a love of gambling and the propensity for strapping on two shooting irons for more firepower. They had both served as scouts and spies during the recent war, though on opposite sides, and were considered dashing and dauntless battle-tested men. Wild Bill was born in Homer, Illinois, and came from an abolitionist family, which naturally made him a Union man like his friend Bill Cody. Tutt came from Yellville, Arkansas, and served the Confederacy, but he easily enough left the Lost Cause behind to find a gold mine on the gambling tables of Springfield. I, of course, was happy to forget the Confederacy, too, but other than that I didn't feel comfortable with Mr. Tutt any more than I did with Mr. Hickok. They both seemed exceptional. And my time serving with John Hunt Morgan had *not* made me their kind of man.

Little Jack, wanting to learn Tutt's secret to making big money at cards, made a nuisance of himself the rest of that long night, hanging on to Little Dave's coattails and peppering him with questions that the gambler mostly waved off. To get Tutt to think more favorably of him, he made up some wild stories about undermining Union officials in Louisville and exaggerated my role as a spy and scout with John Hunt Morgan. "J.H. had nerve, but he couldn't have done what he did without my brother first proceeding ahead to get the lay of the land," Crooked Nose Jack boasted. I wasn't sure what Tutt believed. He made one or two comments about Morgan and asked one question that had nothing to do with raiding.

"John Hunt was by most accounts a gambler who didn't know his own limitations at cards and indisputably a Lothario without limits," said Tutt, talking more into his whiskey glass than to me. "You ever meet that bastard child he fathered with some slave woman? Didn't he call the boy Samuel Morgan or was it Stuart Morgan? No, Sidney Morgan—that was the bastard's name."

"I wouldn't know," I said. "I mean, we were plenty close for a while, and I was loyal to him, but I didn't stick with him to the end, and he didn't share all his little secrets with me."

"It wasn't much of a secret. He more than owned up to it. Talk was, he was half-proud of his slave boy. But no matter. John Hunt Morgan is long dead, and who the hell knows where

Sidney Morgan is now. Wouldn't surprise me if he was the first dark-skinned mayor of Lexington, Kentucky, overseeing a free colored school in Nashville, or operating a coal mining and manufacturing company in Knoxville."

"You got a problem with any of that?" Jasper Washington asked, getting in Tutt's face.

"Just speculating, big fellow. Any damn thing's possible back there with the carpetbaggers controlling the southern cities."

"Well, I for one hope this Sidney Morgan has amounted to something. I happen to be a black bastard myself . . . a pure one, no white blood mixed in."

Tutt took no obvious offense. His eyes stayed on his whiskey.

Little Jack, who treasured the "Little" part of his name after meeting Little Dave Tutt, squeezed past Jasper to stand at the bar next to the professional gambler. "Did you know, Little Dave, that Zach here is also a bastard, the Bastard McCall . . . fortunately, no slaves involved? As for me, I'm the legitimate son of a genuine Kentucky gentleman with a Southern belle wife and . . ."

"Wonderful, I'm sure. That doesn't mean all that much to a man from Arkansas."

"I've never been there, Little Dave, but I bet it's a grand place, and maybe someday you can show it to me."

"You know something, you're starting to get on my nerves, kid. I like you fine, but no need for you to get too familiar. I allow my old friends to call me Little Dave, and I said you could, but I'm not so sure it sounds right coming from you."

"Sure. I understand. You want me to call you Mr. Tutt? Not a problem. You want me to earn your respect. Sure, sure. I'll do it, Mr. Tutt."

"No. That's worse. Tell me, what the hell happened to your nose anyway? I figure you must have gotten on somebody else's nerves, and he up and planted a sockdolager on your sniffer."

"Little Jack is also Crooked Nose Jack," I volunteered. "That genuine Kentucky gentleman married to the Southern belle did that to him—our daddy."

Jack folded his arms and glared at me, his crossed eyes making him look downright malicious. "All I was saying, Little Dave, Mr. Tutt, is that the McCalls are from Kentucky, which should have gone from neutrality to the Confederacy, and you are from Arkansas, a Confederate state. That gives us something else in common. Now, Wild Bill, Mr. Hickok, isn't from the South at all. But still, we all left where we were from to come out West for the freedom, the adventure, and the gambling."

"I have no intention of doing any gambling," I told everybody.

"All right, damn it, all right," Jack yelled. "You know something, Zach. Sometimes you don't say a word when something needs to be said, and other times you can't keep your bone box shut!"

I turned quiet. He had never shown that much anger toward me before, not even when I left him behind at the Daniel's Den and headed west with Jasper. I suppose I was huffing and puffing myself. I had punched my first man back in New Madrid, Missouri, in support of Jasper Washington, and I was ready to punch again in support of myself even if Cross-Eyed Jack was only fifteen and trusted me *not* to be mean like our daddy. Dave Tutt and Jasper Washington watched us out of the corners of their eyes, both seemingly amused, perhaps even hoping to watch the McCalls brawl.

"Come on now," said Wild Bill, the only one who wanted to play peacemaker. "You two brothers shake hands." Hickok took Jack's right hand, then my right hand, united them, and shook them as if he were pumping a well handle. "Now, isn't that better, *y'all*? I'll buy another round. We may fight before this night's through, but let's not make it a fight with each other."

We didn't end up fighting anyone that night. Jack drank more than he ever had in his young life and passed out. I stayed quiet, and the whiskey started to make me feel sick. I began to question myself, wondering what the heck I would be doing in the West if I wasn't going to gamble. Wild Bill, Jasper, and Little Dave took turns buying rounds and kept drinking long into the night, talking about narrow escapes in the Civil War and from certain women with marital designs on them. I think one of those women mentioned was Dave's sister, who apparently had come to Springfield to make eyes at Wild Bill. It was all amiable conversation, though, even after the trio of tongues stopped forming the correct words. At some point, I found a back corner of Oak Hall and fell asleep on the floor. It felt right even if my head didn't. Who needed a spring bed and a soft pillow when you were a free man of adventure in the Wild West?

CHAPTER TEN:
JACK GETS A STAKE

Crooked Nose Jack's badgering of Dave Tutt paid off that July. Tutt finally got over his reluctance and taught the young man numerous things—how to play serious stud and draw poker, how to play the odds, how to keep your face and mannerisms from giving your hand away, and how to beat a cheat at his own game. How much Jack actually grasped is debatable, but he was eager to put the Tutt teachings to the test. To get himself a stake, Jack sold Devil the mule for fifteen dollars, which he quickly lost in one hand that same night when he relied too heavily on two high pairs—kings and queens—and a card sharp showed he had the third deuce.

"I'm certain he cheated," Jack complained to his teacher, who was observing from the bar, "but what could I do? I know that son of a bitch has a bulge in his vest where he carries some sort of a firearm, and I still don't own a gun. I'm starting to feel plumb naked when I sit down at the table."

"His name is Joe Riggs," said Tutt. "He doesn't cheat unless he has to, and he doesn't have to going up against a greenhorn like you."

"Greenhorn? What's that?"

"Exactly my point. You don't know everything there is to know. You were too sure of yourself, Jack McCall. You raised again when you should have called. Royalty doesn't always win out in the game of poker. It was clear as the nose on your face that Riggs had his three of a kind. Chalk it up to profit and loss."

"I hate losing, especially to him."

"Everybody hates losing. Hickok hates losing to me."

"But you and Hickok are friends, right? Joe Rigg isn't my friend."

"Not usually wise to sit down at a poker table with your friends."

"That's what my brother's colored man Jasper Washington says, too."

"From what I've seen, Jasper Washington ain't nobody's man but his own. I won't sit down with him, but not because he's a friend and not because he's blacker than pitch. He knows too much, enough to be a sharper. That means a cheat."

"I know. I know. Like Joe Riggs."

"Best not call Riggs that to his face, kid. Unless you can handle a pistol better than you can five cards, you'll be a dead man soon enough if you ever try to pull one on the likes of him. Anyone would tell you, you're too young for this serious game of skill and chicanery."

"But you ain't saying that, are you, Little Dave?"

"All I'm saying, Little Jack, is you might consider spending your money on biscuits and beans. At least grub will keep you alive to see your sixteenth birthday."

"What money? I'm cleaned out."

"Grab a broom. Saloon needs a good sweep. Wash glasses. They pay you for that."

"I didn't come West to work that way."

"Rob a bank."

"I couldn't do that. Can't you lend me a little, Mr. Tutt? I promise to do better."

"You bet you will, if you use your own hard-earned money."

"I thought you were my friend."

"Sure, I'm your friend, Little Jack. That's exactly why I'm telling you this."

Crooked Nose Jack didn't press the issue. He paid a visit to Jasper Washington, who was in one of the shadowy saloons winning regularly against amateurs who played looser the more they drank. Jack had learned not to come to me. It had little to do with our near fight at Oak Hall. It was more because I'd become too respectable and careful with my hard-earned money. I had taken a job at one of the livery stables, mostly feeding and shoveling, because I figured it was safer being around horses than their owners until something better came along. I didn't like sleeping with the horses, though, and I needed all I earned to pay for our room and meals at the Lyon House. Jack also knew I was still sore at him for taking Devil out of the stable and selling the mule without consulting Jasper or me.

After he watched Jasper rake in a sizable pot, Little Jack quietly asked for a handout, but the other players heard him, and they all laughed. One of them suggested that Jasper be a good "darky daddy" and give his adoptive son a Liberty dime to buy a glass of milk. Because Jasper was winning big, he didn't feel it was the time to teach the other players better manners. When he asked what Jack would use the money for, the laughter continued, so Jack stormed out.

While stamping through the town square, Jack told himself those laughing gamblers were lucky he didn't own a gun, because he might have blasted a couple of them along with Jasper Washington, who not only was too black but also was too lucky. Jack had no wish to blast his teacher, though, only to prove to Little Dave Tutt he could hold his own at any poker table. He sat on a bench to think things through, something he didn't often do. He decided that picking up a broom to sweep a saloon floor was as out of the question as picking up a gun to rob a local bank. Instead, he sought out Wild Bill Hickok, who was made of stern stuff but not stone and just might take pity on a penniless fellow from the East. After all, Wild Bill had previously bought him several drinks and hadn't questioned him about his age, where he was from, his Southern leanings, the assassination of President Lincoln, or anything else.

At one of the gambling halls he found Hickok with his back up against the wall and in the middle of a losing streak, so Jack showed a little patience, hovering as close to the table as he dared but not saying a word. Trouble was, Hickok kept losing. When Jack couldn't stand all that folding a moment longer, he tried his luck, stepping forward and asking Wild Bill for the loan of two or three dollars. Nobody laughed at that table, and Hickok didn't ask why Jack needed the money. Maybe the big man hadn't even heard because he just sat there stone faced shuffling and reshuffling the cards.

Jack finally spoke again: "Two dollars would do me just fine, Mr. Hickok." Wild Bill slammed the pack of cards onto the table and asked the man next to him to cut. Jack had jumped back and now had to step forward again. But Wild Bill was in no mood to be generous. He leaned back in his chair and told Jack to beat a hasty retreat because his bad luck was worsening. Jack could see Hickok's two holstered Colts now, and he imagined Wild Bill's lightning draw and deadly aim. He backed slowly away, finally turning and running. He left the gambling hall mad—but not fighting mad, of course—at not only Hickok but also Jasper, Joe Riggs, every other gambler in Springfield, me over at the stables, and even our daddy in Louisville (for never teaching him how to play poker and never approving of it once Little Jack learned the game on his own).

Crooked Nose Jack didn't give a second thought to what he did next. He ran through the town square and down the east side of South Street, one block to the three-story Lyon House.

He wanted to get to our room before I finished my stable work for the day. He knew I kept my money in a bottom drawer tucked under my only other shirt. It wasn't much, nine dollars and fifty cents, and he took it all, stuffing it in his boot before racing out onto the street in search of another poker game. I got to the Lyon House a half hour later and went right to my stash because I intended to buy Jasper a flat-brimmed, tall-crowned Stetson as a birthday present. It was the least I could do since it was his money and leadership that had gotten us this far west. When I opened the drawer and saw nothing under my second shirt, I immediately searched the other drawers and the bed and the floor under the bed. It made me angry, of course, and for a minute I cursed the lawlessness in Missouri. Nothing like this had ever happened to me back in Kentucky, not even in the Daniel's Den with its money-hungry owner and working girls and its share of disreputable customers.

"I was robbed!" I told the clerk at the desk downstairs. "All my money is gone!"

"Oh, well, sir, you've paid a week in advance," he replied.

"You're missing the point. It was hidden in my room. Somebody came up there and—"

"I assure you, sir, nobody has been in your room except for your brother."

"Are you suggesting . . ." I cut myself off. He was only suggesting what I was thinking.

It wasn't hard for Crooked Nose Jack to find a poker table with an open chair, and greedy men eager to take his—rather, my—money. One of those other gamblers was Joe Riggs again, but that didn't scare off Jack. He had something to prove to Little Dave, Wild Bill, Jasper, and every other gambling man in town—that it would cost you plenty if you took Little Jack Mc-Call lightly. I tracked him down but didn't approach him since, as angry as I was, I wasn't about to call him a little thief in front of those other players. Jasper and Wild Bill happened to be together at the bar, Jasper buying on account of his being a winner again that night while Bill had lost the entire roll he was carrying. I joined them but not to drink. I was cutting back after getting my stable job. I asked about Jack, and they told me he was defying the odds and had already quadrupled his investment in chips.

"It can't last, can it?" I asked.

"Nothing in this world lasts forever," Wild Bill said. "Your brother is doing all right, a hell of a lot better than I did tonight."

"With my money."

"He doesn't know enough to know how lucky he is," Hickok said. "At least I didn't lose to your brother tonight. Only thing worse would be to lose to your sister."

"I don't have a sister, Mr. Hickok. In fact, I don't have a brother—only him, a half brother."

"Nice of you to stake him anyway. Looks like it'll pay off."

"I didn't."

"Bill and I sure didn't," said Jasper. "I heard even Tutt turned him down. Wonder where he got the money to play."

He stole it from me, the little looter. That's what I thought, but I decided not to divulge that information, especially since Wild Bill and Jasper didn't seem all that fond of him in the first place. For another thing, he appeared to be winning; and for a third thing, it would have embarrassed me to have them know Crooked Nose Jack was a sneak thief.

"Anyway, somebody did, and it's paying off," Jasper continued. "The cards have been right fine for me, too. Plenty of suckers here in Springfield. It's damn exciting. Surely by now you've been tempted to have a turn or two at the tables yourself. Let me tell you, Zach, it beats shoveling manure."

"Amen," said Hickok. "Even though I couldn't buy a pair, I'd just as soon go deaf, dumb, and blind as give up poker. For

Wash and me—and for Little Dave over there at the fancy green-clothed table—it's the same. Men like us breathe to gamble."

"But we don't gamble with a man like that," said Jasper, pointing toward the other table where my half brother was seated with three solemn men.

"You talking about Little Jack?" I asked.

"I said *man,* not boy. It is true I wouldn't want to take Little Jack's money. But I was remarking about that slicked-up Puke across from him with the waxy cheeks, tobacco-stained mustache, and bear grease in his hair."

"Joe Riggs," said Wild Bill. "He takes to losing worse than anyone I know."

"And he won't like losing to the kid," agreed Jasper.

"What'll we do?" I asked.

"Have a drink on me, Zach."

"No thanks, Wash. I have a mind to warn Jack."

"Forget about that. He'll find out soon enough about the Joe Riggses of the world."

Jasper and Wild Bill turned away to take care of their empty glasses on the bar. I moved a little closer to the table where Little Jack was the only one smiling. I felt I should at least watch. I was surprised when somebody else decided to watch, too, and a lot closer than I was doing. Dave Tutt stood up from the green-clothed table, told someone to cash him in, and crossed the room in a few long strides to take up a position directly behind the chair of Joe Riggs. There, he alternated between looking over Riggs's shoulder and gazing across the table to his student of the game, Jack McCall.

Jack just kept smiling and apparently winning, too. Riggs squirmed some and blew smoke, some of it rising right into Tutt's face. It didn't seem to bother Tutt, but Tutt was bothering Riggs, who twisted around in his chair and asked Little Dave to kindly plant himself elsewhere. Tutt just shook his head.

117

The game continued.

Riggs folded early on the next hand, then snuffed out his cigarette and tugged on his mustache. When he spoke again, he didn't address the other players but the man standing before him. "I advise you to watch your boy, not me. He can't be this lucky—and you and me both know he isn't this good."

Tutt still didn't speak, but Crooked Nose Jack did. "I'm winning fair and square, mister," Jack said to Riggs. That wasn't enough for my half brother. "Winning really big," he added, looking past Riggs now and flushed with pride. "I'm a fast learner, Mr. Tutt."

"Shut up and deal, kid," Riggs said. "And from the top."

"I don't know what you're talking about, mister," Jack said.

"The kid's right. He doesn't know how to cheat, Mr. Riggs. He's a greenhorn."

"I know full well you've shown him the ropes, Mr. Tutt."

"You casting aspersions in my direction, Mr. Riggs?"

"Not at all, Mr. Tutt. I'm just trying to figure out what you've been teaching him."

"For one thing, to watch out for you, Joe."

"Yeah, you do that, kid," said Riggs, shuffling the cards and staring at my half brother. "Get ready for another lesson, this one from Joseph L. Riggs."

But Jack kept winning, and Riggs, no doubt feeling too humiliated to think straight, forgot about the well-armed man standing behind him. Riggs reached into his vest and pulled out a six-shooter with a cut-down barrel and an ivory handle. He was in no hurry. He pointed the weapon across the table and accused Jack of palming an ace or some such forbidden act at a poker table. Jack dropped the cards as if they were burning coals and held up his arms as if he were being robbed at gunpoint.

"Don't shoot," Jack said, his eyes as wide as poker chips.

"Take my money."

Before Riggs could make another move, Dave Tutt swung out one of his long legs and kicked the customized Colt out of the accuser's hand. Riggs raised the bare hand and sucked blood off the knuckles. Tutt opened his coat and rubbed the handles of both his still holstered six-shooters.

"You knew the kid wasn't heeled," Tutt said.

"I wasn't aiming to shoot him," Riggs said. "Just to scare him. You had no call to interfere."

"You want to make something of it, Riggs?"

"I was just making a point."

"I'm making the only point that matters. Little Jack learned everything he knows from me, and I'm no cardsharp. I don't stand for anything underhanded. When you call him a cheat, it's like calling me a cheat. You understand, or do I need to make myself clearer?"

"I understand, but did you have to kick like some kind of wild Indian?"

"My boots are hard. My hands are soft."

Tutt showed him his hands, his livelihood. Something flashed in Riggs's eyes, like this was his one chance to pick his gun off the floor and end his further humiliation one way or another. But Tutt smiled as if he had just invited his fellow gambler to a dance. That seemed to unnerve Riggs.

"You bloodied my hand, Little Dave," Riggs finally said, showing the damage to Tutt.

"You'll deal again, Joe," Tutt said. "It could have been worse."

"It's getting late. I'm standing up now. 'Til next time, gentlemen." Riggs stood and tipped his hat to the two poker players not involved in what for Springfield was a minor scrape. He didn't look at either Tutt or Crooked Nose Jack as he departed the saloon.

"Anytime, Joe," Little Jack called out. He reached out with

both hands and hauled in the chips from the middle of the table. "Any objections?" he asked the two other players, who merely shook their heads and also got up to leave. "Your money's always good here," he added, no doubt oozing with confidence at having Little Dave Tutt standing up for him.

Red-faced Riggs had left without making any threats against Jack or bucking the odds by challenging two-gun Tutt to a duel. He had also left his short-barreled Colt on the saloon floor. Tutt told Jack to pick it up, and Jack obliged. My half brother weighed the weapon in one hand and then the other before holding it in the air by the trigger and presenting it to his benefactor the way a cat presents a dead mouse to its owner.

"Keep it, kid," Tutt said. "You're gonna need it."

CHAPTER ELEVEN:
THE POKER DISPUTE

Without actually admitting he got his poker stake by raiding my bottom drawer, Crooked Nose Jack paid me back with a few pennies of interest. He could afford it now. Still, he managed to harbor a silent grudge against me, Wild Bill Hickock, and Jasper Washington for not giving him a loan. Dave Tutt had also turned him down, but that fact Little Jack conveniently forgot, which was certainly easy to do since Little Dave had stepped in with a foot to disarm Joe Riggs. Little Jack followed Little Dave around the gambling halls like a dog that had a juicy bone but wanted more of them. They never sat at the same table but always plenty close, sometimes even back to back as if that allowed their good luck to rub off on each other. Both were on winning streaks, however modest. Little Jack's head got too big for his brown "General Lee model" slouch hat, but he wasn't about to go head to head at stud with Little Dave . . . at least not yet.

Before he headed out on the night of July 20 to find his tutor, I said my usual parting words, "Good luck, Jack, and be careful." His almost automatic response was, "Sleep well, Zach, and safe dreams." He had something else to add this time, his way of reminding me that while I was floundering in the livery stable muck, he had already made a name for himself in town: "We're Little Jack and Little Dave, an unbeatable combination. We're big, big men at all the Springfield gambling houses. And it's still two months before I even turn sixteen. Little Dave calls me *precopious*. That means really big for my age."

"I think he must have meant *precocious*. That means an advanced child."

"You better stop thinking of me in that way, Brother. No child could win the way I do. I get respect at the tables. I'm Little Jack, but I am big, really really . . ."

"Big!" I said, finishing his sentence for him. "That's even more reason to be careful."

"Stop fretting. You're like a mother hen."

And you're like a cockerel. That's what I thought but didn't say. Calling him an advanced child was enough for one night.

"I ain't worried," he assured me, patting the bulge in one of the pockets of his latest purchase, a fancy silk vest.

On my advice ("Nobody will shoot an unarmed kid"), he had gotten rid of Riggs's ivory-handled Colt right away, selling it to a gun trader. But the next day, possibly on the advice of Dave Tutt, he bought a .22-caliber Stevens tip-up derringer that he kept close to his heart every time he went out at night, which was every night. "A gambler at the very least needs a small, easily concealable handgun," Jack insisted. I wondered if Tutt was teaching him how to shoot, too, but Jack insisted he couldn't miss at what he called "close poker range." Was it any wonder I worried about him? He had the derringer, he had the vest, and his next goal was to use his poker winnings to buy the kind of black frock coat that Tutt wore.

"I aim to make a killing tonight," Crooked Nose Jack said as he left our hotel room, already in full strut. "It's practically a sure bet. It's in the cards!"

His use of the word "killing" stuck with me all evening, and not even *Uncle Tom's Cabin,* a pre-Civil War book I was re-reading because of my friendship with Jasper Washington, could hold my attention. I had killed someone once at a young age, and I didn't doubt that Crooked Nose Jack was capable of doing the same with that new derringer. The difference was, I had been a soldier and was determined never to kill again as a civilian, while Jack was a gambler who acted like he might pull a trigger at the drop of a hat anytime, anyplace. Life in Springfield had transformed Crooked Nose Jack; a frightened boy who didn't want me to leave him had turned into a young man puffed up with conceit who only tolerated me because I made the bed, never asked him for money, washed his shirts on occasion, and paid for my own two meals a day and my own hot bath water twice a week. He certainly didn't respect me for working in the livery stable "like a slave," as he put it.

I came to realize halfway through the evening—after my eyes had shut and *Uncle Tom's Cabin* had fallen off my lap onto the floor—that it really wasn't the possibility of Jack's killing someone that concerned me most. My far bigger worry was that someone would shoot Jack. Whether or not Jack had learned from Dave Tutt how to cheat at cards, Joe Riggs or someone of his ilk was liable to egg him into a fight and be quicker on the draw. I couldn't exactly be my half brother's keeper since I worked by day while he slept, and I slept at night when he played. But I sure was his worrier. Could Tutt save him next time there was trouble and every time after that, too? One thing I was certain of: a man's luck could change at any time, especially in an on-the-edge place like Springfield, and no winning streak could last forever.

It so happened that Jack found Tutt that night right there in the Lyon House, where we had our rented room. Little Dave was involved in a private poker game with four other players, one of whom was Wild Bill Hickok. Jasper Washington had been in the game earlier but had bowed out by the time Jack arrived. Besides Hickok, all the remaining men at the table were Southern boys. They hadn't objected to playing with a colored man in part because the dangerous Wild Bill was Jasper's friend but mostly because the color of Jasper's money was good, and he had been losing it with regularity.

Jasper hadn't lost every pot, though, so he took what money he had left from the Lyon game and moved down the street to one of the faro banks to "tempt the fickle goddess." The odds in faro should have been even, but the dealers "gaffed" the faro boxes and used various other methods to gain an advantage over the players. Jasper, like so many of the Springfield gamblers, failed to "tame the tiger." Later he told me that, being a black man in Missouri, he strongly believed an injustice had been committed again him because of his color, but he stopped short of complaining. For one thing, all the other faro losers were white. And for another, it wasn't only the house that was against him but most of the other gamblers, whether winners or not. He couldn't even afford one last drink, so he returned to the Lyon, where Hickok generously tossed him a few coins since the two friends always looked out for each other. That's what I heard, anyway. I was in my hotel room at the time, or rather down the hall taking a long two-bit bath to wash off the muck from the stable.

The rest of what I heard about that night was even more disturbing. Despite his generosity toward Jasper, Wild Bill was losing steadily in that Lyon House game. Once he was completely strapped, he turned to Jasper, but Jasper had left again for his drink. He then noticed Little Jack standing there looking over Tutt's shoulder.

"How 'bout the loan of a couple dollars, kid?" Hickock asked Jack. "I hate to ask you, but it's been one of those nights."

"I never deal into one of Little Dave's games," Jack replied.

"I didn't ask you to sit in. I need a loan 'til tomorrow."

"What makes you think tomorrow will be any different?"

"You've developed some kind of mouth since coming to town."

"I've been learning, all right. I've been learning who my

friends are. I haven't forgotten the time you denied me a loan."

Hickok pushed back his chair, causing it to scrape against the floor, which in turn caused Jack to jump. That made Wild Bill shrug and smile. "Don't be nervous, sonny," Hickok said. "I never bother to settle the hash with b'hoys green as unsunned pumpkins."

"Leave Little Jack out of this," said Tutt. "You best pony up or . . ."

"Or what, Tutt?" said Hickok.

"Or I'll give you a loan of forty dollars my own self—that is, if you aim to see another hand or two."

"Why, that's mighty munificent of you, Dave." Hickok took out his watch, a gold hunting-cased Waltham with a flashy chain and seal. "I got time for a few more." He laid the watch gently on the table. "My deal, right?"

The next few hands went Hickok's way, so he kept on playing and kept on winning, occasionally grinning at his watch, which he now saw as his good-luck charm. He kept raking in the money of the other four players and soon was able to pay Tutt back the forty dollars. Not liking the way things were going, Tutt suddenly demanded another thirty-five dollars that he said Wild Bill previously owed him. Hickok said he had already paid ten dollars to Tutt the other day at Oak Hall but would pay him another twenty-five dollars when he won the next hand.

Tutt threw down his cards and shook his head.

"You calling it quits for the night, Dave?"

Instead of answering, Tutt seized Hickok's watch off the card table and stood up abruptly, practically knocking over Jack.

"You aren't by any chance fixing to take that watch out of this room?"

"I am. You get it back when I get my thirty-five dollars."

Hickok now rose and looked ready to draw a six-shooter, maybe both of them. Tutt froze for a moment, but the other players didn't. They were all armed and friends of Tutt. Not even Hickok liked those odds. Tutt offered a gleeful chuckle and slowly walked out of the room. Hickok had never shot anyone in the back. The other card players then backed out of the room with their eyes on Wild Bill's hands. When Jack realized he was now alone in the room with Hickok, he dashed out like a frightened rabbit. But by the time Jack was in our third-floor room, he was too flushed with excitement to sleep, so he woke me to report everything that had happened during the Lyon House poker game. Four times he repeated how Tutt had gotten the best of the dangerous Wild Bill and put him in his place. I didn't believe it, but I didn't argue the point. I had to be in the stables early the next morning.

At the livery stable the next day, Tutt stopped by to make sure his horse had been fed an extra helping of grain in case he had to ride out of town in a hurry. I didn't question him about that or Hickok's watch, which I saw dangling from the pocket of Little Dave's vest. A minute later, Jack showed up with a silver watch dangling from his own vest. He had trailed his mentor to the livery. Jack held up his recently bought watch and announced it was noon, though neither Tutt nor me had asked.

"Cute, Little Jack," Tutt said, glancing at the silver watch as he brushed past him. "Now you can tell when it's time to buy your big brother dinner."

"Half brother," said Jack, making the correction that only I had previously made. "But I'm not here for that. I have a message for you from Jasper Washington."

"I don't care beans for anything that presumptuous son of a bitch has to say."

"Me neither. But what I mean is that Hickok gave Washington a message that Washington gave to me to give to you."

"What? So, the message is actually from Wild Bill himself?"

"That's right, Little Dave. And I memorized it. Hickok said,

126

'Tell Dave Tutt he shouldn't pack that watch across the square unless dead men can walk.' That would be the town square, and the watch would be the gold one you took from . . ."

"I know. I know."

"There's more. Hickok was just talking big. He's afraid to fight you."

"The hell he is. Talk sense."

"I am, honest. Here's the rest of his message to you: 'But also inform him that I am willing to pay him the full amount I owe him to settle the debt and get my watch back because I've borrowed money from him time and again without there being any kind of fuss.' See what I mean? Hickok doesn't want trouble."

"That makes us even. Neither do I."

"Of course not, Little Dave. But remember the first part of his message was a warning to you, almost like he was daring you."

"Maybe, but there was that second part."

"But that was only because he knows you're a match for him. That's right, isn't it, Little Dave? You are a match for him or anyone else with your pair of six-shooters, and Hickok knows that full well."

"Why don't you pipe down, Jack," I blurted out. "Neither man wants trouble. You're just making trouble."

"All I'm doing is delivering a message," he insisted. "You won't let Hickok take the watch from you, will you, Little Dave? Didn't you say you'd wear it all day?"

"If he didn't pay. Hickok said he would pay twenty-five dollars or the full thirty-five?"

"Does it matter? It could all be a trick to get you off your guard. He's looking for any advantage he can get. In the town square he'll make sure the sun is at his back and in your face."

"It's directly overhead," I said. "Let it lie, Jack."

But Jack wasn't about to stop. "The sun is already going

127

down." He pointed to his own silver watch instead of the sky. "You won't give him back his watch, will you, Little Dave? You won't let Hickok back you down. He already has this inflated reputation from shooting down young Southern boys during the war and for massacring the so-called McCanles Gang four years ago at Rock Creek Station in Nebraska Territory. Nobody knows the truth about what happened there. Next thing you know, he'll be spreading lies about how he struck absolute fear in the heart of a onetime brave soldier in the service of the Confederate States of America."

I started to again tell Jack to shut up, but Tutt interrupted me.

"Let your brother speak," Tutt told me, and I was in no position to argue with him. He had two guns. All I had was a pitchfork and a shovel.

"Thank you, Little Dave," Jack said. "My half brother tends to be bossy just because he's a little bit older—no matter that he's a bastard by birth."

"I'm a thinking man, and I got some more thinking to do on this matter," said Tutt, as if trying to convince himself. "But I'm also a doer, a man who gets things done. I got to back up what I told Wild Bill. It would shame me with everyone who knows me in Springfield if I didn't wear the watch when I enter the town square."

"Amen to that," Jack shouted.

"I'm upping the ante," Tutt muttered as he departed the stables. "Wild Bill will now have to pay me forty-five dollars to get his damn watch back. Call it interest."

"Do what you got to do, Little Dave. We're behind you all the way."

"We?" I said, but probably not loud enough for the well-armed gambler to hear.

Tutt kept walking at a good pace toward the center of town, not once looking back at the quarreling McCall brothers.

CHAPTER TWELVE:
THE SPRINGFIELD SHOOTOUT

My workday was done at the livery stable by 5:45 on the evening of July 21, 1865. I usually went straight back to the hotel room to wash up, change my shirt, and figure out how much I wanted to spend on the evening meal. Crooked Nose Jack was often still up there rubbing the sleep out of his eyes, laying out his evening gambling clothes, counting his greenbacks, handling his derringer in front of the mirror, and practicing his card shuffling and manipulations. And now he had that silver watch to fondle. But I knew he wouldn't be up there. I knew he wanted to be where the action was or figured to be—namely, the town square in Springfield, Missouri. Did I?

I don't think so. I was hoping there wouldn't be trouble. Dave Tutt didn't seem like such a bad egg as far as sporting men went. A man who didn't spurn a brazen Kentucky boy (Little Jack), protected that boy from a hardened gambler (Joe Riggs), and made sure his horse was getting the right amount of feed couldn't be a total good-for-nothing. As for Wild Bill Hickok, he was a little too flashy and commanding for my tastes, what with his piercing eyes, wide shoulders, narrow waist, shoulder-length auburn hair, straw-colored mustache, well-fitted buckskins, and of course those two intimidating Navy Colts worn butts forward in the holsters for, or so I was told, a reverse, or twist, draw. I had no wish to see such a draw firsthand. Still, while I kept my reasonable distance, I had nothing against him, and we had a mutual friend in Jasper Washington. I looked up to Jasper as much as any man I ever knew, and Hickok looked at Jasper straight on with a twinkle in his eye.

Anyway, unlike my half brother, I didn't want to see the two well-known gamblers have a showdown, certainly not over the loan of poker money and the seizure of a gold watch. It seemed pointless, especially when both men were sober, and the sun had yet to go down since matters had become unsettled between them at the Lyon House. I went to the town square anyway. Could be I actually thought I could make Tutt and Hickok overcome their well-nurtured pride and see reason or could counteract any provoking of the pair that Little Jack might be contemplating.

When I passed the courthouse and stepped into the square from the west, I saw Jack in the northwest corner, standing almost in a crouch behind the right shoulder of Tutt, who stood erect with his coat open so I could plainly see his two six-shooters. Little Dave was staring at the southeast corner where Hickok stood larger than life. The square was eighty yards by eighty yards, so I estimated the two gamblers were faced off about seventy-five yards apart. From that distance, Wild Bill might have been mistaken for an overdressed dandy with perfumed hair except for those two easily accessible Colts. Jack wasn't the only hanger-on or friend present. Quite the crowd had showed up to witness the expected confrontation. Nobody had even tried to keep it a secret. I saw Jasper Washington with his arms crossed no less than ten feet from Hickok, but, as big as Jasper was, I may have been the only one to even notice him. I spotted more than a few of Springfield's regular gamblers, including Joe Riggs, the man who had tried to provoke Jack into a fight until Tutt interceded. All the spectators but Jack and Jasper were well out of the line of fire, standing as still as box elder trees on a hot, windless evening. Tutt and Hickok were mighty oaks.

"Dave!" Hickok called out. "Don't cross that square with my watch!"

Tutt didn't lower his eyes to the gold watch hanging from his vest. He seemed to be at a loss for words, not paralyzed by fear, certainly, but perhaps stupefied. Jack, though, glanced at the silver watch hanging from his own vest and announced the time in a peculiar fashion. "Six o'clock, knights of the green cloth, and all ain't well!"

Tutt nodded now and shifted his position slightly, so he was facing Hickok side-on the way Southern gentlemen did it in duels of honor. It left Jack more exposed.

My tongue became untied without consulting me, and I blurted out a warning, not to the two duelists but to my half brother: "Get the hell out of the way, Jack! What if Hickok misses the mark?"

Jack tried to hold his ground, but his feet had their own notions and were plenty nervous.

"Don't worry, kid," Tutt whispered. "That won't happen."

"Huh?" said Jack, now several paces away from his mentor. "You don't think Hickok can miss you?"

"I don't think he'll get the chance to fire, not after I get him first."

"Sounds good, Little Dave. I like your confiden—"

Jack never completed the word. Tutt had no intention of moving closer to his opponent or delaying the inevitable. He drew one of his six-shooters and fired. But Wild Bill had been fully prepared and did the same. The shots sounded as one. Gun smoke formed clouds that temporarily blurred my view, but an evening breeze suddenly kicked up and soon cleared the smoke away from Tutt. He was clutching his chest.

"Goddamn!" said Jack. "He didn't miss."

Tutt glanced at my half brother as if he were half-witted. "You don't say, Little Jack." The words came out shaky, full of pain. Still grabbing the front of his vest, Tutt gasped as he stumbled past Jack and then past me. He made it as far as the courthouse porch, circled one of the columns like a drunk, and finally staggered back onto the street, where he fell dead. His weapon lay nearby in the dirt.

When I looked back to the southeast, Hickok was still standing, his Colt still out as if to challenge any of the late Tutt's friends in the crowd. None showed the slightest interest in making a play, which was no doubt wise or there would have been more dead men that evening. I just stood there myself, marveling at how far Hickok's shot had to travel.

The Greene County sheriff came over and began questioning Wild Bill. A highly agitated Jasper Washington stepped up as if to confront the lawman, but Hickok calmly holstered his deadly Colt and patted his friend on the back. When Jasper and Wild Bill exited the square, it was as if they were taking a pleasant stroll through a park. The sheriff didn't try to stop them. The spectators mostly began scurrying in the opposite direction, toward the courthouse, and I went with the flow. By the time I reached Tutt's body in the street, several persons, perhaps a doctor or two, were hovering over the dead man's chest. Jack stood nearby, holding tight to his silver watch with both hands and allowing a surprising amount of wetness—from both his eyes and his nose—to run freely down his face.

"You all right, Jack?" I asked, touching his shoulder.

"Hickok's ball took him right through the heart," Jack replied. "They ought to string that Yankee son of a bitch up."

"Looked like a fair fight to me, needless but fair. I am sorry it happened."

"You would take *his side*, you and the colored man."

"Both men fired and—"

"A good man is dead. Shot down by a . . . a . . ."

"By another good man. It's tragic—that's what it is."

"It's murder! I'd like to have Little Dave's gold watch to remember him by, but some thief seized it before I got to him."

"The watch belongs to Bill Hickok. You seem to forget that."

"I won't forget this. I won't forget my best friend dead. I won't forget what Hickok did or how Jasper Washington and you supported him. Not ever!"

"I imagine this gunfight won't be soon forgotten. But I wasn't supporting him, Jack. I was just hoping Wild Bill wouldn't shoot you by accident."

"Is that supposed to make everything all right?"

"I didn't say everything was all right. When someone gets killed, nothing is all right."

Joe Riggs suddenly appeared out of nowhere and touched Jack, somewhat less gently, on the other shoulder. "He was more than a friend to you," Riggs said, rubbing the stubble on his jutting chin. "He was your great protector. Well, you're on your own now, gambling boy."

"I ain't scared of you," Crooked Nose Jack said, dipping his shoulder to get away from Riggs's hand. "I ain't scared of any of Hickok's friends."

"I'm no friend of Wild Bill's. Fact is, I was kind of hoping they'd kill each other."

Jack seemed at a loss for words. He watched some men carry off the body of Little Dave Tutt. His eyes were red and swollen, but no more tears fell. Jack glared at Joe Riggs as if the older gambler were Fat Jack. My half brother was that angry. I tugged at his arm, hoping to pull him away from Riggs, but Jack wouldn't budge. "Well, they didn't," he finally said to Riggs. "Why don't you try taking a crack at Hickok and see how long you're still standing."

"You got a big mouth for a little gambling boy. Hickok can wait. You're too big for your boots. You're liable to end up like Tutt, dead as a busted straight."

If Riggs was trying to intimidate or frighten Jack, it didn't work. Jack stood on the toes of his boots so he could almost look Riggs right in the eye while his hands formed tight fists. He lifted his right hand and licked the knuckles, perhaps remembering how Little Dave had kicked the six-shooter out of Riggs's hand in the saloon. Riggs seemed mildly amused until Jack pulled his derringer from his vest and pointed it at Riggs's midsection. Riggs gasped as if he'd been socked in the stomach. Little Jack might be just a boy, but a boy with a gun could be just as dangerous as a man with a gun.

"Back off now, mister," Jack said. "I ain't no sure shot like Wild Bill Hickok, but I'm armed now, and at this range I can't miss your fat belly."

Riggs took him—or at least the derringer—seriously. He held up both hands and backed away, right into two gawking ladies. Riggs excused himself as he tipped his hat and quickly disappeared into the crowd.

Jack stayed angry for several days. He mostly holed up in our hotel room, cursing at the world as he played solitaire and practiced his draw with his derringer, which he kept under his pillow when sleeping. And he wasn't sleeping that well. Once or twice he woke up screaming. When awake, he stayed away from the gambling halls and saloons because he said he was in mourning for Mr. Tutt. Possibly he had come to his senses and didn't want to butt heads with Joe Riggs again, but I think he mainly wanted to avoid running into Wild Bill Hickok. Jack had favored a fight and had backed Tutt all the way, only to see Hickok prevail and prove beyond doubt his excellent marksmanship. While on the job at the livery stable I heard some lynch talk among Tutt's friends, and I'm almost certain Jack would have joined in had he known about it, since he no doubt figured only a revenge-minded mob could give Wild Bill his just deserts. I didn't tell him, though. I wasn't sure if I was still trying to protect Jack or I cared that much about Hickok.

Three days after the sensational shootout, lawmen finally arrested Hickok on orders of the nearby military authorities. But he was released on bail, put up in part by none other than Jasper Washington, who had acquired a bankroll again by overcoming stacked decks and rigged dealing boxes in faro games; winning large side bets on four-ball billiards, cock fighting, and horse races; and triumphing in a winner-take-all wrestling match with a brawny blacksmith ("not hardly as tough as a bear," said Jasper). The original charge against Hickok was murder, but it was soon reduced to manslaughter. If convicted, Hickok still faced years in prison.

The trial lasted three days in early August. Wild Bill's lawyer, Colonel John Phelps, was a former Union man, who found plenty of witnesses, including Jasper Washington, who stated that Hickok had tried to avoid the shootout and then had permitted Tutt to draw first. Nobody bothered to ask me to testify, but the prosecutor called Crooked Nose Jack to the stand, and he, without any encouragement, brought up the Civil War and the mistreatment of Southern men like Little Dave Tutt by Yankee dogs like Hickok. His words triggered some clapping from Tutt's friends until the judge threatened to clear the gallery from the courtroom. Jack then testified that Little Dave had never gone for his six-shooter but was only reaching for his gold watch to tell Hickok the time.

"That was Hickok's watch," Phelps told the jurors. "All the accused wanted was to get his watch back from the man who stole it. This may seem like a trivial matter, but Mr. Hickok, the reluctant duelist, honestly believed his life was in danger. The deceased was not really Hickok's enemy and may also have been reluctant to duel, that is until certain parties of the Rebel persuasion insisted that it was his duty to face the Northern aggressor to uphold Southern honor and manhood. In truth, the deceased was the actual aggressor. The most reliable witnesses we've heard from have stated that Mr. Tutt fired first, and we have seen exhibited here today his revolver with one chamber empty. David Tutt provoked the accused, and Mr. Hickok could not just stand there with his arms folded until it was too late to offer successful resistance. In short, gentlemen, the defendant would be entitled to defend himself whether he was in Springfield, Missouri, Boston, Massachusetts, or Montgomery, Alabama."

The jury didn't take long to reach a verdict, just ten minutes by some accounts. I was out of the courtroom at the time trying to soothe my parched throat at a horse trough nearest the courthouse steps. A roar came from inside that caused me to drop my hat in the trough and get a face full of Springfield water. I ran back up the steps without even recovering my hat. Once inside, I heard a scream that I thought belonged to a woman. But there were no women in the courtroom. Next, I heard a familiar voice rise above the din: "No, no, no! It wasn't self-defense! It was murder! Murder by a ruffian, a bully! There is no justice in the world, none at all—at least not in Missouri!"

Yes, Crooked Nose Jack had screamed and spoken. I couldn't image any other fifteen year old anywhere creating such a spectacle of himself. But it wasn't so easy as me saying Jack was just being Jack. Too many others in the town agreed with him that the not-guilty verdict was a failure in the justice system. For a while I started worrying more about Wild Bill's safety in Springfield than trying to keep Jack out of harm's way. Some of those Southern men who supported Tutt seemed capable of putting a slug in Hickok from ambush. But my fretting about the non-guilty duelist didn't last. Hickok got on a winning streak at the poker tables and continued to walk proudly down the streets of Springfield with his two Colts at the ready. What's more, his biggest supporter, Jasper Washington, got in the habit of following him around, always having Wild Bill's back.

CHAPTER THIRTEEN:
A LITTLE HORSE SENSE

After seeing Hickok go free, Crooked Nose Jack didn't speak to me for several days, which wasn't easy for him since we shared the same room and he had a big mouth. When he ran out of money, though, he got vocal again. He admitted that holding a grudge came natural to him but that it didn't feel right to bear malice toward his *only brother* for having supported the beguiling Hickok. I once again proclaimed my total neutrality during the Tutt-Hickok affair and that I would have supported Tutt's freedom had he survived the duel. I'm not sure Jack believed me, but he did give my upper arms friendly squeezes and then asked me for a loan. He needed money to get back to the poker table.

"I've mourned enough," he told me, his eyes not on me but on the drawer where I kept my small stash. "Why should I suffer any further? I'll let Little Dave rest in peace."

"And Hickok? You'll let him be?"

"Huh? Naturally. What did you think I'd do, pull my derringer on him?"

"Of course not. You aren't *that* stupid. I mean . . ."

"Two of your twenty-dollar gold pieces should do it. You know I'll pay you back."

I didn't know it, but I didn't say so. I suppose I was so glad he had asked for money instead of stealing it from me that I handed the coins over to him without a word.

"No lectures, big brother? No warnings at all?"

139

"Don't draw to an inside straight. I'm not sure what that means, but I heard Jasper Washington say it several times."

"Well, that's a general rule for poker players, but there are exceptions, especially when you have nerve. I wouldn't listen to the colored man too much, Zach. He happens to be a god-awful player."

"He's done all right. He made enough to bail out you know who and has made enough since then to make half the gamblers in Springfield jealous. The other day he brought to the stable a new black horse, one big enough to support a man of his size."

"The big bastard made wild side bets at the races and fights and broke a faro bank—it can't last. Nobody that bad stays lucky."

"You don't call me a bastard much anymore or hold onto your grudge against me, so why not let up on Jasper? After all, he's the one who got you and me to Springfield. He's our friend."

"His only friend is Hickok. He licks Wild Bill's boots, but back talks and spits at everyone else. He don't seem to understand that we're all white men, and he's darker than the coat of his horse."

It was a waste of my time trying to defend the manners and actions of either Wild Bill or Jasper to Jack. Not that I had a chance then. Jack was already out the door with my stake money.

"Be careful," I called out to him, more out of habit than anything else.

As it turned out, Jack wasn't careful at all, but his luck had turned. He walked into Ike Hoff's saloon and filled an empty chair at a poker table where none other than Joe Riggs was coming up big with every turn of the card. Riggs was doing too well to interrupt his streak by protesting against Jack sitting in without even being asked. But when Riggs showed a queen-high diamond flush and reached for the largest pot of the night, the newcomer, not able to keep a straight face, interrupted that movement by displaying five spades, ace high.

"I do believe my flush beats your flush," Jack declared. "Jack is back!"

Riggs, now flushed from forehead to Adam's apple, slapped the grin off Jack's face with one hand and at the same time yanked out his hideout revolver. It was a Model 1860 Colt .44 cartridge conversion with its barrel shortened to two and a half inches, identical to the one he had lost the day Dave Tutt disarmed him with a kick. Jack reached for his Stevens one-shot derringer as he had done so many times in our hotel room, but all his practice didn't pay off. The little hideout self-defense weapon slipped out of his hands, bounced off his knee, and landed on the floor. He quickly slid down to retrieve it, which was fortunate because Riggs fired high and only managed to take a nick out of Jack's left earlobe.

Riggs lined up a second shot but never got it off. Jasper Washington, fresh off winning a side bet at the billiard table in back of the saloon, happened to be walking past. Barely breaking stride, he reached out with a borrowed full-barreled Colt and used the butt to bash Riggs's skull—buffaloing, they call it. Riggs slumped over the table, out cold, and some of his friends had to pull him off before Jack could reel in the rest of his winning pot.

Jack pulled foot from the saloon after that, because someone called out to get the cheating white man and big colored man that did in Joe, and half the customers moved toward them with evil intent. There was no time for Jack, even if he was so inclined, to thank Jasper, whom he left behind to wrestle with five of Riggs's angry pals. Jasper, the great bear wrestler, held his own until the law arrived and fined him for disturbing the peace. A couple days later, thanks were made but through me as a friendly intermediary. Jasper just shrugged it off and commented, "I would have done the same for the son of Robert E. Lee or a dog."

Riggs was incapacitated for a while, but Jack still lay low, because he worried Joe's friends might be out for revenge, his gun only had the one shot, and he saw a piece of his left earlobe was missing whenever he looked in the mirror (which was often). Two weeks later, Riggs recovered enough from his head wound to offer a warning to Jack—again through me—to never show his face in Ike Hoff's saloon again.

Jack said to me, "Somebody ought to cut that Riggs down to size," but he had no intention of trying that himself. Word soon got around that Riggs had also threatened Jasper, telling him if he showed his black face in the town square on the very next Sunday morning, Riggs would shoot it off. That was enough for Jack to finally approach Jasper face to face behind the hotel and offer him some advice: "I know we've had our differences, my black friend, but I'm on your side this time. Don't let Joe Riggs get away with this. Even a colored man has his pride and don't take to getting humiliated. Come Sunday, you should take a stroll through the square, and if you see Riggs there, shoot him dead. He won't let you get close enough to wrestle that shortened Colt from him, and he for damn sure won't give you the first shot."

"It would altogether benefit you for me to do just that," Jasper replied. "With Riggs eliminated, you'd be able to play poker freely again in this town. It wouldn't do me any good, though. They'd lynch me for sure. But maybe that also sounds pretty good to you. I know you and Zach are only half brothers, but it still amazes me how different you two are. You got that low-down Southern mentality, and Zach is as fair-minded as any Kentucky-born man can be."

"We're *not* really so different down deep."

"If true, that would be a shame unless you were *more* like him down deep."

"Not sure what you mean. I never killed anyone like my brother did. I never ran out on him the way he ran out on me."

"Blame me for that if you want. I'm the one who took him West."

"I forgive you. That's forgotten now. We're together again, him and me. And I'm of a like mind with you when it comes to one Joe Riggs. He's a mean man."

"And you're just a boy. Why not find yourself a steadier, safer job, like Zach has."

"Look, Mr. Washington, if you're afraid to enter the square by yourself Sunday because Riggs has a reputation and you're not sure you can shoot straight, why not bring your friend Mr. Hickok along."

"Wild Bill has nothing against Riggs."

"He didn't have that much against Little Dave Tutt either, yet he shot him cold dead."

"Look, Jack . . . Little Jack if you prefer. I don't need the likes of you advising me to do something or not to do something else."

"I understand. No former slave wants to be told what to—"

"I never was a slave, and I'll *always* be your elder. Don't make me regret saving your life from Joe Riggs that time in Ike Hoff's saloon."

"That was a mighty fine thing you did, Mr. Washington, just like what I did back in New Madrid when I bludgeoned a man to save you."

"You did actually strike somebody that day, that's for sure. I almost forgot."

"That's all right. I forgive you. But the important thing now is *not* to forget about Joe Riggs. That mean man is threatening both of us. He's *our* problem."

"He's no problem to me. He's just another ex-Confederate

who hates to see my kind running free without asking his permission. They're as common as buffalo on the Plains."

"I know you don't normally carry a gun, Mr. Washington, but your friend Mr. Hickok carries two, and you could ask him to . . ."

"Quiet, Jack, and listen. The way I see it, you have four choices: face him yourself, stay holed up in your hotel room, give up gambling for the kind of job a boy should be doing, or get the hell out of Springfield and return to your mama and daddy in Kentucky. My advice to you is *do* the last; it's your best chance for growing up and living a long life."

"Never in a thousand years!"

"Then get a steady job. That's my second choice. I'm telling you this for your own good, and only because Zach McCall is my friend."

"I'm better than my brother!" Jack, with the flushed face of a Joe Riggs, called out without explanation. He might have drawn his derringer had he not strongly doubted he could smoothly pull that off before mighty Jasper took hold of him. Instead, he tugged at the earlobe that was missing a piece. When Jasper didn't say anything else right away, Crooked Nose also found himself at a loss for words. He spun around and ran all the way back to our hotel room, where he told me his version of their conversation and complained that my colored friend was trying to run him out of town.

Nothing happened that Sunday because neither Jasper nor Riggs showed up in the town square. Crooked Nose Jack sat there till dark waiting for the second sensational Springfield gunfight of the summer. He came back to our hotel room powerful disappointed. I myself had never expected it to take place. For one thing, Jasper was a formidable hand-to-hand fighter—a wrestler, actually—but no gunfighter, and he wasn't about to ask his best friend Wild Bill Hickok to fill in for him.

He confessed to me that on Sunday morning, for only the second or third time in his life, he had felt the urge to go to church, take a seat in the back pew and pray. He settled for sitting on the floor of an abandoned church that federal authorities had turned into a war hospital in 1861 and that had been battered by Confederate cannon balls two years later. "I'm not a-feared of Joe Riggs," Jasper told me. "But I'll meet him on my own terms." For whatever reason, Riggs had also avoided the town square that day. At the crack of dawn, he had showed up at the stable and rented a buggy, supposedly to go on a James River picnic with a genteel lady. But I was there after sunset when Riggs returned alone.

After that the two men continued to avoid each other while Crooked Nose Jack continued to avoid them both, and I continued to work in the stable. Yes, I was in a rut, but I became fond of most of the horses and was just glad to be working in peace for a regular wage instead of risking everything in the gambling parlors and worrying about someone wanting to do me harm for cheating, winning too much, or simply looking at them the wrong way. Being the stable man, I met most everyone that came to town, and one of them was a Colonel George Ward Nichols, a New Englander who had ridden with General William Tecumseh Sherman on his March to the Sea and had recently written a book about that scorched-earth campaign in Georgia. He was now a correspondent for *Harper's New Monthly Magazine* and was looking for a "dash-fire" story, by which he meant a manly tale (absolute truth not required) that would captivate Eastern readers and sell magazines.

"Tell me, stable boy, who would you say was the toughest man in town?" he asked me as he sized me up from manure-covered boots to hay-covered shirt to misshapen straw hat. "Don't go saying yourself. I'm dead serious. And don't point to some rigid hombre pushing up daisies in the local cemetery.

This man must be among the living. Understand?"

"I think so, mister," I said.

"Colonel," he said. "Well, speak up."

"I'm thinking on it, Colonel."

"Don't worry, boy. He a friend of yours? I don't mean him any harm. As a matter of record, I mean him a lot of good. I aim to write about him."

"Is that so, a writer? I read a lot of newspapers."

"Yes, a big-time writer. And I'm confident you know the man I'm thinking of. I've heard the stories but can't recall the handle he was given."

"Stories? About Jasper Washington?"

The colonel squinted hard at me and scratched his head. "Who?"

I repeated the name, but he looked at me the way I figured my daddy would if he caught me working in a Western stable—as if I were a prodigious disappointment.

"I mean in a man-to-man fight, Colonel, I don't know of any human being who could get the better of Jasper."

"Jasper, Jasper. Doesn't sound right."

"He's a powerful large man with a most fine physique. That's his horse over there—the big black one."

"Excellent. What else can you tell me about him?"

"He wrestled bears."

"Bears, you say? To the death? That would be an interesting angle. In the public square?"

"No, not here. Mostly back in Ohio, I think."

"Less interesting. Anyway, I believe I'm looking for a man killer, not a bear killer. Tell me, stable boy, does your toughest hombre use one of Colt's large Navy pistols?"

"Against the bears? No, no. That wouldn't be very tough, would it?"

"I suppose it wouldn't. But he has used a Colt against other men?"

"Could be. I doubt it. I don't know that he presently owns a gun."

"How can a man be in gunfights without a gun?"

"I didn't say Jasper was in any gunfights. He didn't go into the square to face Joe Riggs last Sunday, but then Joe Riggs didn't show up either. Riggs supposedly went on a picnic."

"I am beginning to doubt that this Jasper fellow is the man I'm looking for. What I heard was that the hombre fought for the North in the late War of the Rebellion."

"He wasn't a soldier, but he helped slaves get away."

"A strong abolitionist?"

"I'd say so, being a free Negro and all."

"What? Oh, never mind and never mind the one who went on the picnic. I want to know the toughest hombre in town with a six-gun. The one I heard stories about shot down at least two offensive fellows at Rock Creek Station over in Nebraska Territory and recently was involved in some kind of dramatic head-on shooting affair in your public square. Surely you know his name?"

"Yes, sir, Colonel. That would be Mr. Hickok. They call him Wild Bill."

"Excellent, and so shall I."

I told Colonel Nichols that his hombre wouldn't be hard to find; all he had to do was go to any saloon or gambling parlor and ask for Wild Bill. I thought nothing more about it until I was finishing up my day's work and Hickok himself appeared at the livery. He called for his horse, Black Nell, which wasn't quite as big as Jasper Washington's black horse. According to Jasper, Hickok had purchased the mare from the Union Army after shooting her Confederate rider off her back in an 1863 skirmish near Springfield.

"You fixing to go for a ride, Mr. Hickok?" I asked.

"No," he said. "I want you to bring Black Nell to Ike Hoff's."

"The saloon?"

"Just wait outside the door with Nell till I call for her."

I must have looked confused, because Wild Bill jabbed me in the Adam's apple. "No time to explain, young man. Just know that I've been relating some anecdotes to a magazine man, and I don't think he quite believes my one about Nell."

I wasn't done with work yet, but I told my taciturn white-haired boss I had a job to do for Hickok, and the old man grunted as usual but made no fuss. Soon I was dutifully holding the reins on Nell just outside the saloon—both of us had our ears perked up waiting for further instructions from Wild Bill Hickok. Almost right away, we heard his voice. He was talking to Nichols but loud enough to address the entire saloon crowd.

"I tell you, Colonel," Hickok was saying, "Black Nell has carried me along through many a tight place. Thanks to the careful training I gave her, she saved my life from the Rebs on at least three occasions. Let me show you just how obedient my trusty mount was and is to this very day."

"It's your show, Wild Bill," I heard Nichols say over the murmuring of the patrons.

What Hickok did next was whistle, barely loud enough for me to hear. Black Nell instantly pulled the reins right out of my hands and, on the run, passed through the doorway like a thirsty customer. I followed the horse inside in time to see an amazing feat. Hickok pointed to the billiards table in back, and without hesitation Nell went there and climbed onto the table, scattering the colorful numbered balls. The players and others gawked and gasped as the table groaned under the weight of the obedient four-legged animal. Meanwhile, Hickok awarded Nell with a sugar cube.

"I never would have believed it if I hadn't seen it with my

own eyes," Colonel Nichols exclaimed.

"My big horse can do that," said Jasper Washington, who was standing behind everyone else and no doubt hadn't been introduced to Nichols. "Only trouble is, he weighs so much he busts the table every time."

"You're a damn liar!" someone shouted. It was none other than Joe Riggs, standing with hands on his hips among his gambling friends. "You heard me, big man. No other horse in the world can do such a thing."

"You're right, Joe. Horses can't play billiards or poker or even faro."

"You heard me, Washington. I'm calling you a damn liar. I say you don't have now—and have never had in your miserable life—a horse that could climb on any kind of table."

"In this case, you're plumb right. But my big black beauty can dash better than a runaway slave and kick harder than a Missouri mule."

Riggs, seemingly confused that Jasper was agreeing with him, said nothing more. No fight ensued, mainly because it was still the Hickok and Nell show—Jasper wanted it that way. Wild Bill sprang onto his horse's back, caused Riggs and friends to scatter, and then galloped past the poker tables and out the door. Nichols and most of the others also made a hasty exit. I was one of the first ones out to avoid being trampled. Nell had jumped onto the street and kicked up dust, coming to an abrupt halt at some silent command from her rider. I saw Hickok swing his long legs out and leap gracefully to the ground, which reminded me of the way John Hunt Morgan used to dismount after a lightning quick raid.

"That's all, Nell," Wild Bill said. "Go get yourself some oats, girl."

The horse whinnied and bounded off down the street toward the livery stable. Being the diligent stable boy, I tailed her.

CHAPTER FOURTEEN:
THE OTHER SPRINGFIELD FIGHT

Colonel George Ward Nichols left town with more stories about Hickok's wartime feats of daring and Rock Creek Station exploits than any writer could shake a stick at, to go along with the grand details of the Springfield shootout with Little Dave Tutt and Black Nell's wonderful high-stepping performance in Ike Hoff's saloon. Not that the absolute truth mattered all that much to the colonel, who could embellish and sensationalize like the action novelist Ned Buntline. Hickok and the rest of us wouldn't find that out until early 1867, when Nichols's long article finally appeared in *Harper's New Monthly Magazine* and made Wild Bill a national sensation. Actually, Crooked Nose Jack—and I have to give him credit for this—had an inkling of what Nichols was up to during his short time in Springfield.

"Yankee writers are as bad as Yankee soldiers," Jack told me. "They'll lie and cheat and steal to get what they want. What that hack writer wants is to make Hickok bigger than Generals Grant, Sherman, and Sheridan, frontiersmen Davy Crockett, Daniel Boone, and Kit Carson, and abolitionist Harriet Beecher Stowe, all rolled into one larger than life American blueblood."

"I don't know about that. I'm sure Wild Bill impressed him the way he impresses everyone, but . . ."

"Not me. Hickok doesn't impress me, and neither does Nichols. One is a blowhard in buckskins, the other is a New Englander with a lying pen. I told him as much."

"You said that to Wild Bill?"

"Of course not. I don't have a death wish. I gave Nichols a piece of my mind before he took his Yankee pomposity out of town. I told him Hickok didn't do half the things he said he did during the war and at Rock Creek he didn't give the McCanles Gang a fighting chance."

"You don't know that."

"I know he was dead wrong to shoot Little Dave dead like that. I know Nichols wants to make Hickok a heroic, hand-some, homespun, fast-drawing, evil-punishing God of the West to please those East Coast readers and sell bloody magazines."

"And what did Nichols have to say about that?"

"He said great men like Hickok were sort of public property, and that little men like me were jealous weaklings who never amounted to anything."

"Nichols said that to your face?"

"Not in so many words. But he lumped me in with the dirty, greasy, no-account citizens of Springfield, saying—and I quote: 'The most marked characteristic of the inhabitants seems to be an indisposition to move, and their highest ambition to let their hair and beards grow.' "

"You still haven't been able to grow a real beard yet, Jack."

"Damn it, Zach. That's not the point! I'm a gambler like Hickok. I shuffle and deal cards at the poker table and put good money in the pot just like him. That's movement. I learned everything there is to know about the game, and I play to win. That's ambition! Anyway, Hickok's hair is longer than mine. I don't dress as fancy as him, but I dress well. And I'm every bit as clean as Wild Bill. Only man I know who bathes more than me is you."

"Yes, well, that's because I work in the stables. I don't want to smell like a horse."

"Why the hell not? I bet everyone in town thinks Black Nell smells better than you. And when Nichols prints his damned article, Black Nell will be more highly thought of than you ever will be, even if you live to be a hundred. No offense, Brother. I share a room with you. I'm glad you bathe."

More and more, Little Jack, who had once looked up to me and had even waited on me hand and foot for a time back in Louisville, was now treating his older brother like dirt. He was so full of himself, he probably thought that writer Nichols should have come to Springfield to see him. I wasn't sure where Jack had learned a word like *pomposity,* but it certainly fit him, which is what I said to myself on September 12. I had forgotten his birthday on the 11th, which was understandable since he was only my half brother, and I had no knowledge of him until well after he was born. But he censured me for my failure, adding: "It really shouldn't surprise me that you'd forget. You see me every day, yet you don't see me at all. You still think of me as that baby brother who was thrashed by our bully father and came running after you to the West. But that is *not me.* You think me unimportant, unnecessary, even though I have become a man about town, a man of the West. The truth is you need me more than I need you, Brother. You resent the fact I make easy money and made myself well known before I was sixteen while you labor your life away in nameless fashion amid the horse manure."

It was quite a speech, and I was quite determined *not* to give him a late birthday present. But on September 13 I did—a wedge-bladed razor with tortoiseshell handle inlaid with a crown emblem—even though he didn't yet need a razor and it cost me two and a half days' wages. He thanked me but saw fit to add a "better late than never." He took greater pleasure in what happened that same day politically.

Wild Bill Hickok, despite his gun-handling ability, his trick horse, and his boasts to Nichols, finished a distant second to Charles C. Moss in the five-man race for city marshal. The result stunned me but invigorated Jack, who despite barely knowing the eventual winner, had gone around town before the election carrying a homemade sign that read on the front, *Vote for Mr. Moss and a Hickok Loss!* and on the back, *Springfield will be the winner!* On the other hand, Jasper Washington had told every person he encountered that Hickok was the epitome of a lawman. Trouble was, only men were allowed to vote (women certainly seemed to favor Wild Bill) and most of them didn't like a dark-skinned gambler telling them what to do *and* had heard the rumor (Jack no doubt spread it) that, if elected, Hickok would appoint the faithful Jasper as his one and only deputy. It made no difference to Jack that Wild Bill had treated him decently enough or that Jasper had once saved his life. My half brother openly or otherwise wished the worst for Messieurs Hickok and Washington.

Despite his defeat, Hickok remained in Springfield another four months, probably to spite men like Crooked Nose Jack, not so much because they had supported Mr. Moss but because they were still wishing Dave Tutt had won last July's gunfight in the town square. Hickok continued to gamble, as did Jasper Washington, who had another run of luck in late September that allowed him to help fund Springfield's first colored school on October 1. In fact, he convinced me to quit the stables to teach those little (and some not so little) Negro boys reading and writing and sums. He told me it was a waste of my God-given abilities talking to and caring for other people's horses all day long when I was such a smart, caring people person. Nobody had ever called me such a thing before, so I couldn't possibly turn him down. He had me believing I had learned more than I thought I had from Preacher Raccoon, Belle Bragg, and the other scantily clad teachers back at the Daniel's Den. Anyway, none of the black lads told me different. "You be the only white man I ever know'd who asked us to learn something instead of told us to do something and who ain't never demanded we call him *sir*," said the oldest of the boys to show up at the makeshift school. "You musta sold your soul to Satan, and that old devil must be blacker than our Mr. Washington!"

Jasper Washington, who had attended Berea College in Kentucky for a time before turning away from all that stuffy indoor book learning, often sat in the back of the classroom observing the boys and me. He said it beat sitting in a stuffy saloon all day, and he forthwith would only engage in gambling at night or the very early morning. Although he didn't admit it, he must have wanted to make amends for never pushing education among his people back in Kentucky. He did admit he didn't have the knack for teaching anything but civil disobedience, though every day he insisted the boys recite the Berea motto: "God has made of one blood all people of the Earth."

Joe Riggs, for one, seemed like one of the Lord's exceptions. One morning after another night of losing at the poker table, drinking too much, and being intimidated by Wild Bill Hickok, he stumbled along South Street whooping and yelling for satisfaction from innocent bystanders. Everyone sidestepped him or ran, except Crooked Nose Jack McCall, who had a better idea than either fleeing or fighting.

"I know you," Riggs said, swaying like a sapling in the wind as he tried to focus his eyes on the potential human target. "You're the damn card cheat with the puny pistol."

"I only play fair and square, sir, and I left my derringer at home."

"Damn you, draw, and call me sir!"

"I just did, Mr. Riggs—that is, call you sir. And I can't draw since I am unarmed, sir."

"Not me. I'm loaded for bear."

"It's not me you *really* want, Mr. Riggs. I got lucky at poker, that's all. I'm but a cub. And you are the professional player.

You've already humbled me. Remember? You took a chink out of my left ear." Jack turned his head to give the drunk a better look, and Riggs peered like he was half-blind.

"I did that? Damn good shooting, I must say."

"Yes, sir. I bow to you." Jack only half bowed because Riggs was standing too close for a full one.

"But I hate you," Riggs blurted. "You're nothing but a little . . ."

"Right you are—Little Jack, a cub. You got bigger fish to fry. Who do you hate the most in all of Springfield?"

Riggs had his Colt out, but only to scratch his nose with the tip of the cut-down barrel. He brought the barrel up to his temple to ponder the question, but even in his drunken state he realized that wasn't too smart and quickly pointed the gun at Jack's chest. He was thinking hard, and the weapon got heavy, causing his gun hand to slowly sink. When the Colt got so low he would have shot his own foot off had he pulled the trigger, he came up with an answer. "Dave Tutt!" he shouted. "The miserable cardsharp kicked away my gun when I wanted to shoot somebody."

"True," said Jack, but he didn't mention he had been Riggs's intended target. "You can't shoot Little Dave. He's dead."

"Everyone knows that. Hickok shot him. I ain't no fan of Hickok, but he did kill Tutt. I got to give him that. I don't hate Hickok enough to shoot him."

"That's right. He shoots too well, anyway."

"You saying I'm afraid of Hickok? 'Cause if you are, then I'll . . ."

"I'm not saying that. I'm talking about the living man you hate worse than Hickok. Remember that other time you wanted to shoot someone, but he interfered and near caved in your skull with the butt of a gun? He embarrassed you in front of all your friends."

"Sure. I remember now. It was that big black bastard who shines Hickok's boots. I do hate . . . hey, hold on there. It was you I was trying to shoot that night. You look smaller."

"Right, but you already had shot me. You got my ear. No telling where you intended to put a second shot. But that's no matter now. What matters is that the big black bastard made you look bad."

"That's right. He should have let me shoot again."

"No, no. You're missing the point, Mr. Riggs."

"Think so? Well, right now at this distance, I couldn't miss hitting your cheating heart."

"Look, I don't cheat. But that's also beside the point. Don't you see? Shooting me down back then would have been as easy as flattening a bumblebee. And if you were to shoot me down, unarmed, right here in the street today, it would be like swatting a fly. There's no glory in that. It might even land you in Marshal Moss's calaboose. It's the big man you want."

"Moss ain't so big. Anyway, he has enough sense not to bother me and my pals when we're gambling. I voted for Jimmy Mays for marshal, but if it had only been Moss and Hickok running, you know I would have voted for Moss."

"Sure, but we're *not* talking about Hickok, Mays, or Moss here. Forget them all for now. You know the big man you want, the one who cracked your skull!"

"That's right, all right. I hate that big black bastard!"

"Enough to want to shoot him?"

"I'd put him in his place—six feet under."

"I don't doubt it. And it so happens I know where he is at this very moment, just down the street at that bloody school he started for little ignorant darkies so they can see the light and become big wiseacre darkies."

"Damn him. You know I've never shot at any man or beast who wasn't doing me wrong or trying to mind my personal business, and I never owned a slave in my life, but he ain't got no right."

"You bet, Joe. What are you going to do about it?"

"I'll show him. I'll show him . . . something."

"Do what you got to do, Joe."

Joe Riggs staggered in the wrong direction, so Jack turned him around and guided him along with the right amount of encouraging and discouraging words. The Negro classroom where I taught and the master Jasper Washington observed was in an outbuilding behind the Soldiers' Orphan Home, which housed orphans and half orphans of federal soldiers who had died in the Civil War and only released those old enough to fend for themselves. Jack pointed out the outbuilding's dilapidated door to Riggs and then retreated to visit the Yankee youngsters, as if that was his whole reason for being there.

When Riggs burst through the door, Jasper Washington, the school master, was dozing in the back behind a wood stove, hidden from the intruder's view. I was up front writing big words like *Freedom* and *Reconstruction* on the blackboard to give my students a little current events instruction, and the nine dark-skinned boys and two mulatto girls in attendance that day were seated on donated benches (we didn't have enough desks and chairs yet to go around). Most of them were suppressing giggles because I couldn't keep the chalk from squealing, and Jasper kept whistling through his nose. I was just putting the y on *Equality* when the back-shooter Riggs pulled the trigger.

The shot knocked the chalk out of my raised right hand without damaging a single fingernail. But that was an accident, not expert marksmanship. He was aiming for my back, or rather Jasper Washington's back, but in his drunken state, Riggs couldn't see how narrow his target was. His second shot also missed the mark, but it didn't miss me entirely, glancing (though in painful fashion) off my right shoulder blade. There was no third shot, because the second one woke Jasper, who immediately put Riggs in a bear hug, squeezing him until the gun fell free and then wrestling him to the ground and squeezing some more. Not one child fled the classroom. They held hands and formed a circle around the two fighting men as if it were some kind of game. It was no game and not much of a fight. In short order Jasper squeezed the life out of Mr. Joe Riggs.

The children let go of each other so they could clap for the school master, who knelt over his fallen opponent trying to listen for a heartbeat. I quickly dismissed class for the day and then collapsed on the floor. Nobody moved, until Jasper told the students to go, at which point they let out what sounded like a Rebel yell and ran off to play games or work in the fields or do whatever children did *after* school. Jasper himself could have fled, but he stayed put to assess my wound. I must have been only semiconscious when a crowd began pouring through the door, including white orphans and half orphans, their agitated custodians, gambler friends of the late Mr. Riggs, two saloon gals, workers from the brickyard and foundry, two physicians, one undertaker, a newspaperman from the *Missouri Weekly Patriot,* Mayor Benjamin Kite and three city councilmen, City Marshal Charles Moss, and, of course, Crooked Nose Jack McCall.

One doctor pushed away gawkers and knocked over an orphan to get to the dead body. "Riggs has blacked out," the doctor said but a moment later stated, "Correction. Riggs has breathed his last."

"Give me room," said the second doctor as he sidestepped the dead man and weaved through the crowd to reach me lying still below the blackboard. Once he was kneeling over me, he added, "Give this man room to breathe."

I lifted my head to see acquaintances of Riggs move in on Jasper with blood in their eyes, and then Marshal Moss move in on all of them while waving his arms like a man trying to flag down a train. Moving my head made me dizzy. A pain shot through my shoulder as if I had been hit by the slug all over again. I closed my eyes and gritted my teeth.

"Damn," said a voice, much higher than that of the doctor and whispering right into my left ear. "I can't say I'm displeased with what transpired here this morning—my worst enemy dead, a lesser one being fitted for a noose. But, believe me, Brother, I never suspected you might somehow get it."

I did get it, though. Last thing I focused on before blacking out was that crooked nose.

Chapter Fifteen:
Flight from Springfield

After the doctor was finished repairing my right shoulder to the best of his ability, I still couldn't raise my right hand high enough to write comfortably on the blackboard. But it didn't matter much. The school wouldn't reopen. Jasper Washington was sitting in Marshal Moss's jail cell, and the gunshots in the classroom had scared some of the parents enough to withdraw their children, even though the shooter, Joe Riggs, was dead. I had no teaching job anymore, and I couldn't get my old job back at the stables because my right arm was in a sling, and the owner had no sympathy for someone who would step away from manly work tending horses for a namby-pamby job learning darkies. So many people in this world have no interest in giving a fellow a second chance; they'd rather see you fall flat on your face.

Little Jack received no blame from anyone but me for his underhanded manipulating of the drunk Riggs that led to my wound, Riggs's getting squeezed to death, and Jasper's detention. The editor of the *Missouri Weekly Patriot* wrote that excessive drink, the unbearable sound of squealing chalk on a blackboard, and a colored carpetbagger bent on reconstructing Springfield were equally responsible for the "Dark Incident in a Primitive Classroom." My lack of funds prohibited me from breaking off with Jack and moving out of our shared hotel room. With Riggs out of the way, my half brother went back to gambling freely in all the usual places in Springfield, and he did well enough to keep us off the street. What's more, he began catering to my needs (providing food and rest to assist in my recovery) the way he had done that time during the war when I was holed up in the attic of the McCall home in Louisville. I suppose Jack felt a touch of regret for indirectly causing my wounded condition, though he never admitted that. He simply said brotherly love was something one could *not* cast aside when things got a little rough.

I withheld my gratitude. At any moment I expected him to say, *See how much you need me, Brother!* Whenever I even thought about thanking him for his caretaking, it caused my wounded shoulder to ache like the devil.

The way Riggs had died outraged certain citizens in Springfield enough for lynch talk to start in several of the saloons. Wild Bill Hickok squashed some of it by threatening to shoot it out in the town square with anyone intent on stringing up his good friend Jasper Washington. But the talk would have petered out anyway, not because folks felt any compassion for Jasper Washington, but because Joe Riggs had always been a mean drunk and a hard-nosed, take-no-prisoners gambler. Far more outrage had developed when the kinder, more generous Dave Tutt had met his match. Jasper lingered in jail, without bail, forgotten by the good and bad citizens, the press, and seemingly the entire justice system.

When I felt up to getting out of bed, I visited him in his cell to thank him for saving my life and to see if there was anything I could do. He asked how my wounds were healing up and told me I was his only visitor besides Wild Bill. He ended up thanking me for not turning my back on him the way the rest of Springfield had (Hickok being the only exception) just because he was a powerful black man behind bars accused of murdering a white man, even if the white man had been a son of a bitch who had more than earned his ticket to hell.

In December, Jasper finally got a preliminary hearing before the judge, who set the trial date for early in the new year. Jasper might have beaten the murder charge; he wouldn't have been able to claim self-defense, of course, but he could have claimed he was defending the life of a dedicated schoolteacher—me. I would have testified on his behalf. That, however, was a moot point. Three days before Christmas, Jasper Washington broke prison and made a clean getaway from Springfield. Crooked Nose Jack for one suspected inside assistance because the escape occurred the day after the "notorious" Hickok (as Jack called him) had spent several hours conferring with Marshal Charles Moss. Jack believed the two men had worked out a shady deal—Hickok wouldn't run again for marshal, and in turn the marshal would see to it that the prisoner got his freedom. I was sorry to see Jasper Washington leave town, but I was glad he was alive. I owed the man my life and wished I had been more thankful, though I wasn't so sure I was valuing my own life much during those months I was in the care of my half brother.

Considerable ill feeling rose in Greene County toward the Springfield police, but it only had a little to do with Jasper's easy escape. The people were accusing Moss and his men of arresting country folks for trivial offenses while allowing city bigwigs and gamblers who could afford to bribe the badge wearers to get away with everything just short of murder. In late January 1866, a scuffle broke out when police tried to arrest three drunks on South Street, and a policeman ended up shooting down one of them. Hickok witnessed the affray and even ran down one of the other drunks and locked him up. Because of the discontent with the police, some prominent citizens suggested that Hickok, who had demonstrated he could arrest inebriates without shooting them first, run against Moss in the next election. I suppose Hickok was tempted, but he was apparently true to that deal with the current marshal or else he just got a better offer. In any case, Wild Bill put Springfield behind him and moved to Fort Riley, Kansas, where he was appointed deputy U.S. marshal. He didn't come say goodbye, but who could blame him? I didn't feel worthy of being thought of, not even as an afterthought.

Jack was of course delighted by the turn of events—Joe Riggs dead, Jasper Washington jailed and then on the run, and now Hickok gone, too. Meanwhile, I finally got tired of living off my half brother. Even amid my self-deprecation, I couldn't bring myself to respect Jack. He had never properly thanked Jasper for saving his life from Riggs and then had tried to get Riggs to take Jasper's life. What could be more devious than that? Things hadn't turned out exactly as he'd planned, but still just fine for him. And bad for me.

But I was still alive, so I tried to become a working man again. Nothing worked out. I was turned down once more at the stables and then, because my shoulder never healed right, at the foundry, the plow factory, and the brickyard. I couldn't even find work as a teacher at one of the two public schools for white children because of my "reputation" (which was that of a man who got shot in a classroom full of coloreds), or at the *Patriot*, because, the editor told me, "A stable boy can't expect to be a newspaperman any more than a colored man can run for mayor."

All I wanted to do after my unsuccessful job search was run away. Still, I stayed for a while. The winter had about run its course when I finally told Crooked Nose Jack one night in our hotel room, "It's time I got out of Springfield." That was the same night I couldn't bring myself to raise a glass with him to toast his latest success at the poker table. Part of the reason was that such a simple act still caused pain in my right shoulder. That was my excuse to him, anyway. What I didn't tell him was that toasting him pained my brain far more.

"You mean like a vacation?" he asked. "A vacation from what, I wonder. You don't do anything, Zach."

"I'm going to do something. I'm going to leave this hotel room, this town . . . permanently."

"You must be joking, Brother. I'm doing great. I win when I get the cards, and I win when I only have a pair of deuces. I tell you, all my bluffs work. I'm on one of the best hot streaks of my life."

"Fine. I said it was time I left, not you."

"What the hell. You can't go anywhere. You don't own a horse and can't pay the stage fare to even reach the next town."

"I'll walk. I might not be able to lift my right arm, but I got two good legs, except for my ankles, of course. But they'll hold up."

"You're talking foolish, Zach. You know you really aren't the *Wild Child*. You know you can't go anywhere without me. Haven't I been taking good care of you here?"

"That's *not* the way it should be. A man should be able to take care of himself. In any case, he shouldn't have to rely on . . . you know, his little half brother."

"That's gratitude for you. When are you going to start appreciating me the way everyone else appreciates me?"

"Who would that be?"

"Everybody. I've made a name for myself in this town. I'm already bigger than Joe Riggs ever was."

"That's not saying much."

"Hell, if Little Dave Tutt were alive today, he'd be looking up to me or at least meeting me at eye level. They've started calling me 'Jack of Clubs' around the poker tables. That's a sign of respect, Brother. You want to do something? You want a job? I understand that. I'll ask around. I have some influence. You can be a swamper at one of the saloons or bordellos. You do have the experience from your days at the Daniel's Den."

I felt like slugging him, but my once strong right arm was now useless for such things, and I never did trust my left. Of course, the prospect of walking to some other town didn't suit me either; it made my weak ankles throb. I'd had them since the war, and they wouldn't let me forget it, especially when the weather was cold and damp. I lingered until early spring, washing dishes for assorted local establishments—at most of which cleanliness was *not* considered a virtue—to earn enough money to keep from being indebted to Jack. One brisk day in late March, I'd had enough of dirty plates and Jack's smugness, so I packed my knapsack and left Springfield on foot without telling Jack or the clerk at the Lyon House. I was pretty much aimless, but at least I headed mainly west.

I traveled seventeen miles that day, aching from ankles to head the whole time, before collapsing at a spring that flowed out of a cave in the middle of a small community called, fittingly enough, Cave Spring. As luck would have it, Captain Green B. Phillips stopped by the next morning for a drink and woke me up, since I was lying right next to his favorite drinking place. He wondered if I was running from the law or just down on my luck. I told him I had been living and working in Springfield, but the place just wasn't the same since my friends Jasper Washington and Bill Hickok left town. It turned out he also knew Hickok, calling him a real man of integrity, and had once met the black giant named Washington. Phillips had been a captain in the Enrolled Missouri Militia during the Civil War, defending Springfield from what he called the "Blasphemous Rebel Hordes." I elected not to tell him about my role with the Southern hero John Hunt Morgan. He asked my plans. I mentioned drinking lots of spring water and living off the land.

"Robberies and horse stealing have become everyday occurrences in southwest Missouri," he told me. "You plan to go that route, son?"

"No, sir, never stole anything," I said, conveniently forgetting how I had ridden off with one of Angus Doyle's horses and during the late war had pilfered a number of items up North in the name of Morgan the Rebel raider.

"I believe you, son. I got a farm two miles northeast of here, and there's more work to be done than I care to do myself these days. You come on home with me, and the wife will give you a hot meal."

Knowing I was *not* cut out to live off the land, legally or not, I went along with the captain. I spent nearly two months helping him out, feeding the chickens and hogs, grooming his prized horses, cleaning the stable stalls, painting his barn, hauling water from Cave Spring, washing dishes, and husking his corn. He and I were in the corncrib doing the latter one morning in late May when three Regulators, who had been hiding on the premises since daybreak, appeared with blood in their eyes and large six-shooters in their hands.

The Regulators were a band of men who had organized to handle, often by extreme means, the lawlessness in that part of Missouri. Even had Hickok been elected marshal in Springfield, it likely wouldn't have forestalled the area's crime wave. Outlaws were running rampant, and nobody was catching, let alone legally punishing, them. The Regulators often called their group the "Honest Men's League," but Captain Phillips questioned the honesty of some of these "destroying angels." The Regulators, in turn, were suspicious of the captain for his friendship with several suspected robbers, and possibly sharing in their profits. I never questioned the captain myself; he was paying me decent wages.

Anyway, the Regulator trio didn't give the captain and me much of a chance that day. Two of them poked their gun barrels through the cracks in the logs of the corncrib to keep us covered. The third one, wearing a sleeveless shirt that showed off his blacksmith arms, entered and ordered us outside. We obeyed. The other two Regulators each wore a long black coat with a red bandana over nose and mouth. The strong one, who left his face uncovered, demanded to know my name and why I happened to be there. I told him I was just a hired hand named Zach who was doing my chores and minding my own business.

"You mean Green business," he said accusingly to me while shoving Captain Phillips to the side. "Stealing horses."

The captain started to protest, for both our sakes I reckon, so the strong Regulator knocked him to the ground with one back-of-the-hand swat. Captain Phillips rose slowly to his knees and then stayed like that. Blood dripped from his lips. At that point, I decided I best not speak. But the man demanded I confess to my membership in an organized gang of road agents, so I began to apologize for *not* being one. That caused him to draw back his hand to swat me for my insolence, but the shorter of the other two other Regulators saved me from the nasty blow.

"Don't!" shouted the short Regulator, his voice higher pitched than one would expect from a masked man. "He's innocent!"

"How in the hell do you know that?" asked the strong one.

"I know him. He doesn't steal horses. He shovels their shit."

The voice was definitely familiar. I looked the short Regulator over, who struck me as being young. I hadn't seen the red bandana before, but I recognized the black coat. He wore it when he went to the poker tables.

"Crooked Nose Jack," I said, "is that really you under there?"

"Shut up," the young man replied.

And I did. There was no doubt it was him, but I knew it was best to drop the matter.

The strong Regulator didn't strike. Instead, he ordered me to lie face down on the ground and not to move a muscle if I didn't want to get my face blown off. I obeyed, but I kept my head turned to the side so I could see what happened next. It wasn't pretty. The strong one yanked Captain Phillips off his knees, wrapped a massive arm around him, and practically lifted him off the ground while directing him toward the front gate. The masked Regulator I couldn't identify tried to help out by rushing to the other side of the captain, but he wasn't needed. Jack hesitated and let out a long sigh before following. As he passed me, practically stepping on my face, he whispered, "You shouldn't be here, Brother."

I wanted to say the same thing to him. My lips did move, and I was drooling, but no words came out. I tasted wet clay.

"Nothing to be done," Jack continued. "In an executive session, they gave Green Phillips the death sentence. Just lie low. I'll assure them you're no sympathizer of the desperados. Once the sentence is carried out, nobody will come back for you. I'll make sure of it. I have influence. You can thank me later, Zach."

"Thank *you*?" I muttered, the two words sputtering from my soiled lips. And then I cursed him under my breath, but he had already marched off after his comrades.

The other two Regulators and their condemned man were still only about twenty feet ahead, moving slowly toward the gate. Beyond it was a large burr oak tree with a branch that looked noose worthy. Phillips surely knew what was in store for him. When the strong Regulator was adjusting his hold on him, the captain jerked free and started to run. In his panic he didn't see the hog that lay on the ground ahead of him without a care in the world. At the last second, Phillips tried to leap over the beast, but his back foot got caught on the hog's hindquarters. The captain stumbled and fell. He recovered quickly, but once he had regained his feet, two of the Regulators opened fire, and at least three slugs struck his back. This time the captain went down hard and didn't get back up. I saw the third Regulator, Crooked Nose Jack, fire his only shot, a late shot straight up in the air, before he sidestepped the lazy hog and then stepped gingerly over the dead man.

Chapter Sixteen:
The City of Kansas

I stayed on at the Phillips farm to help bury the captain and assist his widow, but my farming knowledge and skills were limited, and the Regulators were demanding other victims. Only a few days later over in the town of Walnut Grove, two men—whether they were actual thieves or not, I do not know—denounced the Regulator "assassins" for murdering Captain Phillips. The Regulators immediately went into executive session, passed a death sentence on the pair, captured them without a fight, and hanged them from a redbud tree a mile southwest of town. I was outraged over this lawlessness in the name of some warped notion of justice and even more so over the knowledge that my half brother was part of it all. As far as I was concerned, somebody ought to *regulate* Crooked Nose Jack McCall. But it wasn't going to be me.

My future looked bleak if I hung around in Regulator country. I figured sooner or later I'd be shot or hanged myself for just breathing the same air as the aggrieved and angry widow of Captain Phillips. If she had known how well acquainted I was with one of the Regulators, she might have shot me herself. I wished her the best of luck, accepted three carrots and two potatoes from the root cellar, and walked northwest all the way to the City of Kansas, as it was then called. I figured I was out of reach of the Regulators, including my half brother, so I sought out a job and a place to hang my hat in what was then a frontier town of less than four thousand.

It so happened that influential local leaders had gotten the support of the U.S. Congress and the Hannibal & St. Joseph Railroad to build a bridge across the Missouri River. I landed a job fetching food and drink and doing odd jobs for the three prominent civil leaders, who eventually brought in civil engineer Octave Chanute to do what was once considered impossible—bridge the "rapid, shifting, and ill-reputed Missouri." I might have been a common laborer working for common wages, but I felt as though I was part of something monumental and doing my small part to bridge to a brighter future. When George Ward Nichols's overstated article came out in *Harper's New Monthly Magazine,* making Wild Bill Hickok a household name across the nation, I couldn't keep myself from boasting to my fellow laborers and neighbors on the west side that this accomplished gun-toting celebrity had been a good friend of mine and that I had witnessed his amazing duel with Dave Tutt in Springfield's town square.

Everyone thought it was the whiskey talking (though I drank far more modestly than most working men I knew) or I was talking through my new straw hat; some even suggested that insanity must run deep in the McCall family. Few of my acquaintances in the City of Kansas doubted what the magazine claimed—that Hickok had killed dozens of men by jerking out a six-shooter faster than any other human and firing as calmly and accurately as an exhibition shooter aiming at nine-inch china plates from one hundred feet. But they *all* doubted me. "Why," one of them asked from point-blank range, "would this giant among men who shoots to kill with a large Colt and possesses the handsomest physique ever seen befriend a near cripple who doesn't even dare carry a derringer for fear he'd shoot off his foot?"

A lesser man might have let those kinds of questions vex him, but not me—at least not for long. My wounded right shoulder began to operate as good as new, and my much older ankle wounds didn't slow me down. I had kept my strong connection with Southern hero John Hunt Morgan a secret (no doubt they wouldn't have believed me anyway), and from now on these Kansans wouldn't hear me say another word about knowing Hickok. I told myself I didn't need fame and fortune or any ties to a man who was now furthering his legend in prairie land as a formidable deputy U.S. marshal and valuable scout for the U.S. Army during the Indian wars.

So it was that I darn near dismissed Wild Bill Hickok from my head, right along with Jasper Washington and everyone else I had ever known back in Kentucky, including all the other Mc-Calls, mother-substituting Belle Bragg, and her Bible-toting husband, Preacher Raccoon. Of course, it wasn't totally possible. Exorcising Crooked Nose Jack from my thoughts was the greatest challenge of all because my angry memories of him kept threatening to boil over like a pot of bad campfire coffee with the grounds floating to the top. Bad dreams (mostly about Captain Phillips's murder and me getting shot by Joe Riggs) and bad whiskey (if there was good whiskey anywhere in town, I never found it) occasionally disrupted my sleep and disturbed my nights at my lodgings next to the tracks, but I buried myself in my work every day. The months passed, none particularly distinct from any other. I wasn't going anywhere, but there was nowhere I wanted to go. I had my job to do and no greater purpose in life than that.

Octave Chanute himself took note of my diligence sometime in spring 1868 and rewarded me by making me an assistant to his personal assistant. I never let him down because I believed him to be a great man engaged in a great project. Workers would ultimately sink seven piers into the riverbed, and each time—though I only carried tools and messages for those workers and coffee and sugary cookies called "jumbles" for Mr. Chanute—I cheered the piers, my peers, and myself for advancing the cause of progress. On July 3, 1869, some forty thousand people, one of whom was me, lined the shores of the Missouri when the Hannibal Bridge, adorned with flags and other patriotic displays, officially opened. There were speeches, parades, and picnics, a banquet at the Broadway Hotel (I sat with my immediate boss just three tables away from Mr. Chanute), fireworks, and a hot-air balloon that crossed the river high in the sky.

Amid all the celebrating, I happened to cross paths with Mr. Chanute. That is to say, I approached him as he was drinking a glass of water at the podium. He could have ignored me easily enough. Instead, he graciously bent down from his place above me to thank me for all my hard work. I didn't mind that he accidentally spilled a few drops of water onto my carefully combed hair.

"You know, young man," he said, "thanks to *our* railroad swing bridge, the City of Kansas is destined to become a major hub of the cattle trade. It took two and a half years, but was well worth the effort to get connected with the rest of the nation, in particular the Chicago stockyards I designed before I came out here. From now on this place will boom! I hope you realize the significance of this day, young man, and the hand you had in making it all happen. You, eh . . . Frank, and all of my other little helpers have my heartfelt thanks."

"Thank you, sir, but I didn't do all that much except work hard every day no matter what," I said, not bothering to correct him for calling me Frank instead of Zach. "It's an honor to see your great design come to fruition."

"I'm sure it is, Frank my boy. Now I don't expect the Hannibal Bridge to be recognized as the Eighth Wonder of the World, but even I awaken each morning and look toward the river in wonderment."

"Yes, sir. I wonder if this will be the crowning achievement of your life or if even better things are in the works. I keep asking myself two questions, Mr. Chanute: 'What can top this?' and 'What is next?' "

He said nothing more to me because it was time for him to address the crowd again. That was fine with me, because I was addressing those two questions to myself more than to him. He straightened up, took one last sip of water, set the glass down, raised onto his toes, glanced at his notes, and began to thank various government and private bigwigs for making this glorious day possible. Little did I know that I would never talk to Octave Chanute again, even though he stayed on to design and construct the City of Kansas stockyards.

One of the out-of-towners who was there for the bridge-opening ceremony was none other than Jasper Washington. No, he hadn't been invited to the banquet, but afterward we literally bumped into each other outside the Broadway Hotel. After I picked myself off the street, he recognized me, and we greeted each other warmly. I reckon there's nobody I would have rather seen at that moment than him, since I was at loose ends what with the bridge being finished and my services no longer required by Mr. Chanute's assistant.

Since I last saw Jasper, he'd had more than his share of trouble. Evidence of that was the jagged scar across his forehead—not from wrestling a bear but from confronting a brawler who surprised him with a broken whiskey bottle in a Hays City, Kansas, saloon. I was sure his opponent looked worse. Jasper now considered himself a Kansas man, though he had no permanent residence. He had done some gambling with soldiers and assorted hangers-on out at Fort Riley and spent many long hours working for wagon master Lorenzo Butler Hickok and assisting Lorenzo's brother, Wild Bill, in recovering stolen government mules and horses. The whole time, he had avoided returning to Springfield, where he figured he was still a wanted man for eradicating Joe Riggs, and in fact hadn't set foot again anywhere in Missouri until learning of the new bridge.

"I'm glad you're alive," I told him after we'd caught up with each other for ten minutes. "That is to say, I'm glad you're here."

"And me you. You appear to be in one piece, Zach."

"Yes, sir. And your scar isn't that noticeable, Wash. You do look bigger than ever. I can hardly believe it. I wondered some about you."

"And me you. It's been ages. I thought you would have skedaddled back to Kentucky by now, what with you being such a sensitive soul and possessing—how should I say this?—a rather delicate constitution. Or maybe you've been waiting for the bridge to be built before heading east."

"You got me wrong. Just because you knocked me flat by accident, don't think I'm *that* delicate." I stood as tall as I could with chest puffed out, legs wide apart, and hands on my hips. Of course, there was no way *not* to feel puny standing next to Jasper. "No reason at all for me to return home. I mean the West is my home now. I'm doing right well right here."

"Mighty nice to hear. What about that brother of yours? He around?"

"Not here."

"I suppose he's around somewhere, though."

"Likely."

"Of course, one never knows. Everyone runs out of luck sooner or later. Life's a gamble, especially when you're a gambler. There's danger lurking behind every deal at the poker table, every roll of the dice, every spin of the wheel. Jack was caught up in a damn risky business, especially with that chip on his shoulder. Can't forget how no-account Joe Riggs was hell-bent on doing him harm."

I remembered how later on Riggs had meant to do Jasper harm, and how the gambling McCall would have been just as happy to see gambling Riggs kill gambling Washington as vice versa. But I couldn't bring myself—at least not at that moment—to talk badly about my half brother. As much as I detested things Crooked Nose Jack had done or tried to do, we did have some of the same blood. "I'll never forget how you took care of Joe Riggs for me," I finally said. "I can't thank you enough."

"You already thanked me plenty, Zach. Thing is, in case you haven't found this out living in the City of Kansas, the frontier is loaded with hard cases like Riggs."

"I've managed to avoid trouble."

"That's real fine, Zach. And Little Jack? He making out on his own hook?"

"I suppose. I know he doesn't need me, but last I heard he wasn't alone. He had these friends of sorts . . . Regulator friends. That was some time ago, of course."

"That right? That's bad company to fall into. It's not any husking bee those boys are promoting. They're vigilantes, lynch men. That's the worst kind. Just saying that word *lynch* sends a shiver up my spine and causes a fierce crick right up here." Jasper twisted his head and rubbed his stiffening neck.

"I know what you mean. I saw them kill a right fine fellow I was working for."

"No one man scares me. But a raving mob is something altogether different. You think a big old black bastard like me would have a fighting chance back there against the likes of them?"

I tried to shake my head and nod it at the same time. Finally, I just threw up my hands. I was thinking more of my half brother Jack than I was of my friend Jasper. What chance did Jack have if the Regulators had turned on him or, for that matter, if he had faced another Joe Riggs type? I didn't know if Jack was alive or dead, and for the last three years I had been trying to convince myself that I didn't care one way or the other.

"In just two months he'll be twenty," I suddenly uttered. "If he is . . . you know."

"And what are you? Twenty-three?"

"Twenty-four. I haven't thought about my age for some time. Last few years went by mighty fast."

"Both still pups. I'm pushing thirty at least. Not exactly sure when I was born, but I do know I was born free enough."

"Anyway, Jasper, I'm just glad you're here." I couldn't say that enough.

"Not for long. Wild Bill got back to Hays City from visiting his sick mother in Illinois. I'll be heading there directly."

"To Illinois?"

"What? I'm saying he's back in Hays, Kansas. That's where I'm bound."

"Oh. You're going to see Wild Bill Hickok?"

"And help him best I can."

"Hickok, the man who bested Dave Tutt fair and square, needs help?"

"Doesn't matter how gun skilled a man might be when back-shooters are out and about."

"Anyone in particular?"

"*Anyone* is right. Everybody is suspect, and he can't keep his back to a wall twenty-four hours a day."

"That bad, is it?"

"Nobody's liable to mistake Hays City for the City of Kansas, Zach. Like Bill often says, 'There's no law west of Hays City and very little of it in the town *improper.*' He speaks the gospel truth. It's been called the 'Sodom of the Plains.' What's more, Colonel Nichols did Bill a bad turn with that *Harper's Magazine* article."

"It made him considerably famous."

"It also made him more enemies than you can shake a six-shooter at. Most of those low-down dogs wouldn't dare meet him head on."

"Right, the back-shooters."

"And not just them. I'm sorry to say those colored troops of the 38th Infantry from nearby Fort Hays have been misbehaving when in town, adding to the overall anarchy. I'm all for universal freedom, and their place can't be in the cotton fields back on the plantations, but those black walk-a-heaps in blue should still *know their place*. They shouldn't be butting heads and exchanging flying elbows with those narrow-minded towns-folk."

"But Hickok always struck me as broad minded."

"That he is. You think I'd be his pal otherwise? I happen to be the best friend he has in the whole damn world, and that includes Buffalo Bill Cody. As his best friend I aim to make sure Wild Bill doesn't get attacked from behind in some saloon or get caught in a crossfire out on Main Street."

"Maybe he'd be better off someplace else."

"You won't get an argument from me. But that's his chosen headquarters, and he's not streaked by any man or any town. For a while he ran his own saloon on South Street so he could keep the roughs out and play a social game of cards without having to lay one of his six-shooters on the table. He's in and out of Hays doing scouting work and deputy work when not gambling, and I intend to have his back wherever he goes."

"I'm sure Bill appreciates having a good friend like you."

"And you're my friend, too, Zach McCall. It doesn't matter to me one lick that you haven't made any kind of name for yourself out West."

"That's mighty big of you, Jasper."

"Think nothing of it, pal. Say, when I leave to go see Bill

tomorrow, how's about you coming along with me? It'll do you good."

"You're leaving that soon?"

"Never can tell when Bill will need me. You're done with the bridge now, Zach. What's keeping you here in Missouri? The state of Kansas is full of possibilities."

"And violence, right?"

"Who'd want to harm a quiet fellow like you who minds his own business."

"I don't know. Sometimes you get shot by accident. And don't forget I did serve the South for a while when I was young."

"Still hard for me to believe you were ever a Rebel. But at least you don't feel the *need* to boast about having ridden side by side with John Hunt Morgan during his plundering of the North."

"It wasn't exactly like that, Jasper. I traveled in advance of his raids to scout things out, and then . . ."

"Forget about it. Morgan never got this far west to bother folks. And William Quantrill's massacre of the Jayhawks in Lawrence was six years ago. People do forget, at least some do. Anyway, Hays is 230 miles west of Lawrence and was born an end-of-track railroad town only two years ago. The present and future is all that counts out there."

"That far away, huh? That sounds like the real Wild West."

"Right. Plenty of habitual miscreants, white and black, inhabiting Hays, and wild red men skulking and sharpening their knives around the outskirts. Scare you, does it?"

"Not more than most any other place. Bad things can happen in the City of Kansas, too. I could have fallen off the uncompleted bridge and drowned. I could have been run over by a runaway whiskey wagon. I could have gotten food poisoning at the banquet. I could have . . ."

"I get your point, Zach. Danger is everywhere you look for it.

But no matter the dangers, the *real* West is also full of wide-open possibilities for adventure. I doubt you've had much of that lately, Wild Child."

I recoiled. I hadn't heard my nickname in years, and it startled me that Jasper remembered it. Calling me Wild Child would be like me calling him "Tiny."

"Maybe not," I said. "But I had a good job, and I made enough money to get by comfortably and honestly. That's something."

"Sure, it's something, but it's *not enough.* Life is more than just getting by day after day."

"I don't know. At least you live to tell about it."

"You came west with me after the war. You wanted something more then."

"I was young, and I needed to get away from Angus Doyle and the Devil's Den and, well, most everything else in Kentucky."

"By my book, you're still young. You don't have a job anymore, and, as far as I can tell, there's no female companion keeping you settled down. You left Kentucky behind. Why not do the same to Missouri?"

"What is there for me in the state of Kansas?"

"New opportunity, for one thing. You are not a child but, like I said, still young. You are not wild, but a part of you is wilder than you think. I'd say you need a good friend, too, one who is willing to reshuffle the deck, raise the ante, deal you out a new hand, make sure you don't fold too early, and gamble on your future."

"You mean you?"

"Who else?"

"I still don't play poker, you know."

"I'm speaking figuratively—learned that at Berea College."

"To stay or go? I don't know."

"Have I ever led you astray, pal?"

"I suppose Springfield wasn't too bad for either of us . . . for a while."

"Pack your knapsack, Zach. We'll move out tomorrow."

I couldn't think of any argument against it except fear of the unknown. I wasn't *so old* I couldn't brush that fear aside. "All right, Jasper. But before we go west again, I kind of want to do one last thing."

"Needing to burn a few bridges, perchance?"

"Huh? No. But I'd like to take a walk across the new bridge Octave Chanute built . . . you know, when the trains aren't running."

"Sounds doable. And then we'll ride west."

"I still don't own a horse. You have one?"

"Not here, but that's no problem at all. We'll take the train."

CHAPTER SEVENTEEN:
DAYS IN HAYS

Wild Bill Hickok was as solid a citizen as could be found in Hays City, having stepped into a lawless void and made his impressive presence felt. Yes, it truly was impressive, and not just on paper, as in that *Harper's* article. Law there in town and the surrounding area had been weak and fleeting (flight interested some of the badge wearers more than fight) until Hickok, at the request of a newly formed and not particularly powerful Vigilance Committee, became town marshal in July 1869 and then acting sheriff of Ellis County the following month. He was actually elected to the latter position; I know because I cast a couple of votes for him, and Jasper Washington managed to cast three with the help of the committee, which turned color blind and morally challenged to assure Wild Bill would win.

Hickok didn't disappoint, arresting rowdies left and right when nobody else would have dared and landing them safely in the log jail. Not that most stayed there for long, since no real court system was in place. Realizing that, Hickok soon adopted a different approach to dealing with lawbreakers. He invited them to leave town in one of three directions—on the next eastbound train, on the next westbound train, or to go north in the morning (north being where Boot Hill was situated). Holding down two law-enforcement positions as he did, Hickok didn't have much time to enjoy his favorite pastime—gambling—but he played vicariously through Jasper, who had the run of the tables as Wild Bill's unofficial assistant marshal and acting undersheriff.

Actually, about the time he won the election, Hickok sent a bad man north, which must have reinforced the committee's commitment to Wild Bill. An unpopular intoxicated rough from Missouri named Bill Mulvey was staggering from saloon to saloon shooting off his mouth and six-shooter. Handy with his weapon of choice, Mulvey managed to shoot up only mirrors and whiskey bottles and avoid putting a bullet in any innocent bystander. Learning that Hickok was on his way to send him packing out of town, he said that was all right by him because he intended "to kill that damned Yankee son of a bitch." When Hickok caught up with Mulvey and as coolly as ever instructed him to surrender his pistol, the Missouri man balked. The lawman chose to speak instead of immediately drawing his own Colt.

"Don't shoot him in the back, Wash, he's drunk," said Wild Bill, looking past Mulvey. The rowdy turned to glance over his shoulder, no doubt expecting to see an armed Jasper Washington standing there. But Jasper didn't carry a gun, and what's more, he wasn't even present, since at the time the cards were running good for him down the street at Tommy Drum's saloon. While Mulvey was briefly distracted, Wild Bill whipped out his own Colt and pulled the trigger, sending a fatal slug into Mulvey's head just back of the right ear. It wasn't exactly Hickok vs. Tutt in July 1865, but nobody blamed Wild Bill for using a ploy to keep the peace.

Jasper Washington told me he felt a little guilty not being there for Hickok on the night Mulvey threatened to kill Wild Bill. But since things worked out so well (with Wild Bill killing Mulvey instead), he wasn't going to kick himself over it. And Jasper kept on going to Drum's saloon regularly, not so much for the drinking and gambling but because he took a liking to the owner. Tommy Drum was the only saloon keeper in town who didn't drink, but he, of course, had nothing against any man who did. Jasper liked to hear the sober and fair-minded Drum talk about the important white men who had made their unofficial headquarters in his saloon—Wild Bill Hickok, naturally, along with Buffalo Bill Cody, General Phil Sheridan, and Lieutenant Colonel George Armstrong Custer—but also about the low-ranking black soldiers who had frequented his place for more than two years before they were recently reassigned to posts near the Mexican border.

"I heard those buffalo soldiers could be trouble," Jasper once said to Tommy Drum.

"Not for me," the saloon tender replied. "Soldiers are soldiers. Plenty of people around here felt otherwise. Those boys were hated, kicked around, and accused of being a threat to public safety for showing themselves here and drinking whiskey like all men have a right to do. But I can't blame them for getting crazy bored out at the fort and coming to town for entertainment. When they got mistreated 'cause of the color of their skin, they didn't just do an about-face, put on hangdog faces, and tiptoe back to Fort Hays. They were soldiers; they were willing to fight."

"Same as I'd do. Good for them. Too bad they didn't stay on. Wild Bill and I would have given them a fair shake."

"The United States Army doesn't exactly give enlisted men, black or white, a choice in such matters."

"Right. That's why I never joined up. I'd have fought the first man that ordered me around."

Jasper was particularly interested in hearing about the violent goings-on before he and I arrived by train in Hays City. Six months earlier, on January 6, 1869, three 38th Infantry soldiers from Fort Hays who had killed a Union Pacific watchman in front of Drum's saloon were seized from their cells by townsfolk with masks or darkened faces and strung up together on the railroad trestle west of town. Jasper liked to quote Tommy Drum as saying, "Hays City's high number of killings and savage beatings since '67 show a remarkable tolerance for violence—except when perpetrated by blacks." The triple lynching had enraged a white lieutenant enough to send black soldiers on a "raid" of Hays City in which they arrested fifty-one townsfolk and jailed them overnight at the fort guardhouse. The lieutenant threatened to close the saloons and livery stables and declare martial law, but it never happened. "Fortunately, calmer heads prevailed," Tommy Drum told Jasper. "If they had shut down my establishment, I'd have organized my most loyal customers, including Wild Bill, Buffalo Bill, and George Armstrong, and orchestrated an attack on the fort." In May 1869, though, black soldiers on the street and townspeople behind doors and windows exchanged four hundred shots in half an hour before white cavalrymen arrived to restore order. Amazingly, nobody suffered a serious wound on either side, but while that was happening, Hays vigilantes took their anger out on the small colored community—ordering every black family out of town and murdering two black barbers who, according to Drum, had never harmed a hair on anybody's head.

A couple of days after Wild Bill's silencing of Mulvey and Jasper's latest talk with Tommy Drum, a Southern gambler under the influence of corn liquor unwisely threatened Jasper: "Boy, you best get the hell out of town quick and join them colored bastards in blue sent to Apache Land or risk getting your black hide skinned alive by the good citizens of Kansas." Jasper immediately put the squeeze to the drunk and took most of the life out of him, though not entirely as he'd done to Joe Riggs back in Springfield. With three broken ribs and a possible collapsed lung, the misspoken gambler was in no condition to immediately take a train east or west but at least there was no trip north for him in the morning. For two days, he vowed vengeance from his sick bed. On the third day, though, after a short talking to by Hickok (who told him if he persisted in quarreling, "You must settle it with me"), he wisely chose instead to head south to Indian Territory where he figured he'd enjoy "fewer confounded coloreds and less high-handed white lawmen." He told me that himself, because on his way out of Hays City I was the one who saddled his horse at Walker's Livery, where I had landed a job thanks to my close association with Marshal/Sheriff Hickok.

In town Hickok took to wearing a Prince Albert frock coat instead of buckskins and carrying a sawed-off shotgun to complement his pair of Colts. He usually patrolled Hays by walking down the middle of the streets, looking straight ahead yet watching for any unusual movements, left or right, out of the corners of his eyes. Periodically, Hickok would do his patrolling on horseback, still sticking to the middle of the street with head held high but now able to command a greater presence, because old Black Nell was still a high stepper and wore a natural black coat that shined even after the sun went down.

"From this vantage point, I can better see any signs of trouble," he explained to me one day in early September after I had saddled Black Nell as usual and was looking up at Hickok's freshly scrubbed face. He was bathing every other day now, according to Jasper, and I was practically doing the same, though I didn't share that information with Wild Bill. I never scented my bath water either, but he smelled of lilac water like certain ladies did who I had known in my youth. There were similar lilac ladies in Hays, but they were seldom seen by day, certainly never at the livery, and my nightlife at the time was limited to trying to size up the moon or find the eighth star of the Big Dipper. My baths were taken to please only myself.

"You expecting trouble, Mr. Hickok?" I asked.

"I'm Wild Bill. There are those who want to kill Wild Bill. If someone is fool enough to hide out in the shadows waiting to jump me, I'll see him coming. I got the eyes of an eagle."

"I can see that, Mr. Hickok."

"Our mutual friend Jasper says I would make a fine peacock. What say you, Mr. McCall?"

He was teasing me because I couldn't get in the habit of calling him Wild Bill or even Bill to his face. It wasn't because I owed my job to him or felt he was a superior being to me— although those two things were true, of course. It was more because he inspired me to be polite just as I would be to any lady, of high standing or not. Yes, Bill Hickok was a real man, hard to fault as a physical model, yet he had a feminine quality to him, maybe because his skin glowed, his fine hair hung to his shoulders, his scent filled one's nostrils at short range, and his long fingers tended to flap like a butterfly's wings.

"I'd say you are more like a bird-of-paradise, Mr. Hickok. We don't see them here, of course, but they are said to be more colorful than even peacocks. I saw a painting of one in a book long ago."

"Sure. Why not! I don't mind being dazzling."

Even his laugh, which rumbled from deep in the chest, dazzled. I started to thank him for getting me the stable job, but he wasn't finished talking about himself and birds.

"And I'm sure you can plainly see I have a nose for sniffing out trouble, the nose of a hawk," he said, posing in profile till his nostrils flared. Black Nell's nostrils did the same.

"You bet, sir. I . . . What's the matter?"

In a flash the fingers of his left hand steadied, curled, and reached across his body to his right hip to yank the Colt holstered there. The blued octagonal barrel swung my way, and I felt myself shake like a dying man looking into the long, hooked beak of a vulture.

"Whoever you are, step out with your hands in the air," Hickok ordered. "At once."

His deadly weapon was now pointed over my left shoulder, but to play it safe I showed him the palms of my hands as I shuffled my feet, mostly sideways.

All was silent for what I thought was too long. I expected to hear a bang from either Hickok's Colt or the weapon I imagined was pointed at him from inside the livery. Finally, I heard nervous footsteps behind me and a high-pitched plea that caused a distant coyote to howl: "Don't shoot, Wild Bill. By God, you know me."

"Do I now? Your arms raised?"

"Raised right. My hands are empty, and so is my head. No bad thoughts at all. Not a single one, I swear. I'm an old friend."

"Says who? You look too young to be an old friend."

"It's me, Wild Bill. Jack."

"Jack who?"

I turned now, not believing my ears.

"Little Jack McCall. You know, eh . . . Zach's brother. I'm Jack."

Hickok did not lower his Colt. "Another McCall? I don't recall . . . Where'd you come from?"

"Springfield, Missouri, by way of Sedalia. I saw you . . . eh . . . shoot Little Dave Tutt."

"That was more than four years ago."

"It's not something I'll . . . we'll . . . ever forget."

"What brings you to Hays?"

"Steers. That is to say, a bunch of cowboys. You might catch a whiff of bovine on me. But I'm no cowboy. I'm a gambler like you, just like I was back in Springfield."

"I'm a lawman now. What were you doing skulking in that stall?"

"Wasn't skulking at all."

"You weren't aiming to surprise me, were you?"

"No, no. I wanted to surprise my brother here. Haven't seen him in years. I reckon you spoiled my surprise, Wild Bill." Crooked Nose Jack laughed from the teeth.

Hickok grunted but he did redirect his Colt, touching the end of the barrel to the brim of his hat before holstering the weapon.

"Did I spoil your surprise, Mr. McCall, Mr. Zach McCall?"

"Nope, Wild Bill," I replied, forgetting my place. "I'm as surprised as hell."

Hickok didn't stick around to hear more from Crooked Nose Jack. The lawman mounted gracefully, tipped his cap to me, and rode off on his evening patrol. I suppose I was relieved to see my half brother was still alive, but I soon wished I had business elsewhere. Of course, I didn't. This was my business— stable boy. Nothing I could do but shovel manure as I listened. He acted glad to see my familiar face, but I sensed he was looking down his crooked nose at me. I tried to get out that I'd been more gainfully employed in the City of Kansas for three years and was only lending a hand in Walker's Livery until somebody built another big bridge, but he didn't give me a chance. He was *telling*, not listening. I wasn't about to give him my undivided attention, though, no matter what exaggerations and lies he told.

He emphatically hailed his membership in the Honest Men's League and avoided the word Regulators, not because he was sensitive to the horrible visions that word triggered in me, but because he wanted to convince me the organization comprised nothing but good-deed doers. Besides dragging off my one-time employer Captain Phillips to be hanged, they had strung up at least three other horse and cattle thieves with the blessing of a Presbyterian minister, struck terror in countless other thieving hearts, and rendered Greene County as free from that kind of depredation as any place in the state. "Being a horse man yourself, I'm sure you can appreciate the work we did in your neighboring state and kind of wish you had a league of your own taking care of business here in Kansas," he told me, rather smugly. When not engaged in Honest Men's League activities, he was honestly dealing cards in Ike Hoff's saloon. He claimed he had won a fortune but lost it when three escaped felons— who somehow had avoided vigilante action—waylaid him right in the town square, just ten yards from where Wild Bill Hickok stood that fateful day he fired "the lucky shot heard 'round the world."

He said he would still have been in Springfield helping to mete out swift and cruel justice against criminals and working on making a new fortune had it not been for an outfit of cow pushers from Waco, Texas, who drove their longhorns through town on the Shawnee Trail. Their destination was 117 miles to the north in Sedalia, because the railroad had arrived there to ship the cattle to eastern markets. "The cowboys told me they wouldn't go on a spree until they reached their final Missouri destination," Jack told me. "That spree would include as many rounds of whiskey and games of chance as their wages would allow. I saw that combination as a golden opportunity to up my bankroll fast, so naturally I followed the boys and the beeves to Sedalia. You might say I rode drag, but far enough back to avoid most of the dust."

The drovers were within shouting distance of Sedalia when they received bad news. After seven hundred miles on the trail, they learned most of the population didn't welcome them. Earlier that year the Missouri House of Representatives had passed a bill prohibiting Texas cattle from entering the state. Texas fever, carried by healthy longhorns, had wiped out one too many Missouri cows. Lawmen and farmers drove off the drovers, but not without a fight that cost one Texan the immediate use of his left leg and another permanent use of his right arm. The outfit had no choice in the end but to take its business—two thousand head—west. Jack, not wanting to return to Springfield without a decent poker stake, continued to ride a distant drag. The first stop, the City of Kansas, had plenty to offer, but nothing for these men. Turned away again, they left the state of Missouri in late August, some of the outfit crossing the Missouri River on the Hannibal Bridge, completed with my assistance less than two months earlier. They were bound for Abilene, which had been welcoming longhorns ever since the Kansas Legislature had modified its own "prohibition" law two years earlier. Jack had come too far to turn back now.

In Abilene, buyers eagerly paid a good price for the herd and loaded the cattle for shipment by rail from Kansas. Meanwhile the cowboys had their spree, acting every bit like big spenders, which they were for a short time. Crooked Nose Jack won enough of their wages at the card tables to spend several nights at the surprisingly luxurious Drovers Cottage, which towered over the stockyards and every other building in town. It was there Jack learned from hotel owner J. W. Gore that there were gambling opportunities galore 118 miles further west in a town full of buffalo hunters, freighters, railroad workers, soldiers from the nearby fort, and occasional cowboys. "It was once as rough a hellhole as you'll find in Kansas," Jim Gore told him.

"*Once*, you say," replied Jack. "What happened? Did Regulators—that is to say, a vigilance committee—rise up to take control of the rowdies?"

"I believe there is such a committee there, but the rising up to take control was done by one man, a resolute lawman of some distinction."

"A great deal of distinction," volunteered Jim's wife, Lou Gore, who did the cooking at Drovers Cottage. "I've never seen a finer specimen of manhood in boots."

That lawman was of course Wild Bill Hickok, and the town Hays City. Jack had befriended some of the Texas cowboys who were also staying at the Drovers Cottage—the ones who hadn't lost their last silver dollar playing poker with him. And a couple of these men, knowing Jack had ten times as much spending coin as they did in total, asked him if he wanted to tag along with them to see the sights and seek new opportunities in Hays. Jack begged off until he picked up another bit of information from the Gores: Hays City had but one professional gambler of note, a bear-sized black man who went by the name of Washington and was only allowed to continue winning pots in town because he had the full support of the marshal.

In their absence, Jack had not grown any fonder of either Wild Bill Hickok or Jasper Washington, yet he headed west with the two Texans, even buying railroad tickets for all three of them. The Gores had never heard of me, of course, but Jack figured—and this he repeated over and over again in Walker's Livery—that, besides adding to a bankroll in a town that sounded like easy pickings, he was just liable to find his "long lost brother."

CHAPTER EIGHTEEN:
THE HAYS CODE

Crooked Nose Jack McCall, once I convinced him I did not live with the horses I tended at Walker's Livery, took a room next to mine at the Boggs boardinghouse. It was a good thing we had separate rooms because almost immediately we had a set-to. September 11 had come around again, and I had again forgotten his birthday. He still had the razor I'd given him four years ago, and he had more use for it now at age twenty to control the stubble on his chin. This time my belated present to him was a horseshoe with two rusty nails that my boss, Theodore Alexander Walker, claimed once belonged to a claybank ridden by George Armstrong Custer. Since Custer had been the celebrated Union "Boy General" during the Civil War, Jack took offense at this gift, which I had intended as a practical joke. It kept us from speaking to each other for an extra week.

Meanwhile, feeling too long like a fish out of water, Jack plunged into the Hays City saloon life, and by his own count there were thirty-seven establishments that specialized in drinking and gambling. For the most part, he avoided rubbing elbows at a bar or poker table with Jasper Washington, since he retained a strong resentment of this Negro who never was a slave, who had special status with Wild Bill Hickok, who was more than his match at five-card stud, and who had such a hold over me.

It's true that I was beholden to Jasper for saving my life back at Springfield, but it was more than that. I admired Jasper's strength and fearlessness, his intelligence and resolve, his assurance and self-confidence. Plus, besides the animals in the stable (mostly the horses but also the resident semi-tame yellow cat and a three-legged dog that visited once a day at dusk), he was the only one in town I considered a real friend instead of just an acquaintance or a stranger. Jack was jealous. It came out when he burst into my room and broke his vow of brotherly silence. He had been making the rounds that evening, and upon his staggering return he had several slips of his whiskey-wet tongue, calling Jasper "Hickok's fart catcher" and worse.

When I told him to close his bone box and get out, he screamed: "Damn it, Zach. We were separated all those years after you left Springfield, and we've had a few differences since I found you again, but I'm still your brother. When are you going to start acting like one? Must you keep acting like I'm your sworn enemy?"

"I'm not acting, not by a jugful. I hate it when you call Jasper names or say bad things about him."

"You act like *he's* your brother—a brute who is blacker than a moonless midnight. That can't be. It can never be. It ain't natural, going as it does against human nature. What's more, it ain't right!"

It made me wonder, not about big Jasper but about Little Jack. If I meant so much to my half brother, how had he managed to carry on for more than three years in Springfield after my departure? Had he missed me? Had he needed me? Had he looked for me? I didn't ask. Maybe being a full-fledged member of the Springfield saloon crowd and the Honest Men's League had been enough. I knew things weren't going terribly well for him in Hays City. At the card tables he had more downs than ups; making *another* fortune against the non-professionals wasn't going to be that easy. He had tried to join the local vigilance committee, but he wasn't wanted because of his association with Texas cowboys and other questionable characters. The most questionable was a Missouri-born ruffian named Samuel O. Strawhun, who had once been a member of a horse-stealing gang, had threatened the previous July to kill a member of the committee for ordering him to leave town, and had loudly opposed Wild Bill Hickok's right to be acting sheriff.

Things got worse for Jack—and Sam Strawhun lived down to his true nature—in the early morning hours of September 27 at John Bitter's Beer Saloon on Fort Street. Starting the evening before, Strawhun had invaded the place with a pack of his so-called wolves that included the two spree-minded Texas cowboys and the young gambler from Kentucky by way of Missouri. They were all guzzling beer and throwing the glasses into the street, intent on cleaning out the saloon. Hickok answered a call for help from owner John Bitter. Wild Bill's lawman code called for him to do his duty however unpleasant, to quiet disturbances firmly but calmly, to never back down when his authority was questioned, and to avoid starting or adding fuel to fights but to make a point of ending them.

In this instance—and I wasn't there but heard plenty about it later from Jack—Hickok scooped a couple of unbroken glasses off Fort Street, walked coolly inside, and set them down on the bar. When Strawhun objected to this simple act, Hickok objected to his objection. According to Jack, Strawhun stood his ground and suggested he just might throw the glasses out again, and Hickok replied, "Do, and they will carry you out." Strawhun then reached for a glass, not a gun, and Wild Bill shot him dead. Actually, Jack's exact words were, "The ironfisted son of a bitch shot Sam in the back of the head without having been given a chance for his life." Yes, Strawhun died from a head wound, but I didn't buy Jack's version, and neither did the coroner's jury, which ruled the killing was in self-defense, thus justifiable homicide. Jasper Washington was once more at Tommy Drum's when this shooting occurred, but he was never shy with an opinion, telling me, "Too much credit cannot be given to Wild Bill for his endeavor to rid this town of such dangerous characters as that Strawhun was."

It might be assumed that the people in Hays City and elsewhere in Ellis County viewed Hickok the way Crooked Nose Jack did or at least more so than how Jasper did. The acting (overreacting, in the opinion of Jack) sheriff lost the regular election in November to his official deputy, Peter Lanihan. His unofficial deputy, Jasper, who was finding it difficult to find townsfolk willing to sit at the poker table with a black professional, called the citizens ungrateful fools and suggested he and Hickok leave pronto for better horizons and less objectionable company (Tommy Drum and me being among the few exceptions). Hickok, though, agreed to finish out his term, which ran till year's end.

In the line of duty, he had already killed two bad men, but he had no reason to add a third. He did have to deal with one antagonist in December, a Southern fiend who earned a living by beating men to a pulp with his fists. He called himself Stonewall Patterson, and in the middle of Hays City he set up a ring, in which he provided free demonstrations of his boxing skills to anyone foolish enough to climb over the ropes. It was all a setup for his big money-earning show. In Drum's saloon he announced he wanted to fight the "toughest hombre on the frontier" and then challenged Hickok right to his face. Bets were made on the spot. Owner Tommy Drum put up a generous winner-take-all purse. Little Jack put his money on Stonewall, who had an advantage in size and a bigger advantage in the fact he would be battling Wild Bill with fists instead of pistols.

Now, as I've mentioned, Hickok was not a lawman who ever backed down against criminals, but Stonewall was a boxer with no record of lawbreaking outside the ring. Hickok said he was a busy peacekeeper who couldn't be bothered by such minor nuisances at the moment, though he hinted he might have cause to take action should the pugilist "create a disturbance by thrashing in a brawl some burly, well-dressed local poker-playing colored man." Stonewall located only one resident who fit that description, Jasper Washington, and immediately challenged him. This self-proclaimed champion of every state and territory between Louisiana and California stated that, all things being equal, except for skin color, Jasper didn't stand a gambler's chance of winning. "Anytime at all, General Slag," replied Jasper, who never wanted to let Wild Bill down. Stonewall wasn't sure if he should take offense at being addressed in that fashion, so he simply said, "The sooner the better, Sambo." Some of the bets were called off because of Washington's size, but others stuck with the experienced Stonewall since he claimed he hadn't been knocked down once in his many bare-fisted bouts, and, what's more, as he continued to emphasize, he was *the* white man.

Stonewall vs. Washington almost started on a street corner but was soon moved to the ring. No rules had been established. The "undefeated" Stonewall went into a boxer's crouch with fists raised, ready to take the measure of his opponent's "gorilla face." Those words fired from corner to corner were hurtful to Jasper, but that was the only hurt Stonewall was able to deliver. Washington gritted his teeth, pumped up his chest, tightened his belly, and moved in for the kill. Well, fortunately it wasn't actually a kill. The man who had once defeated bears weathered two ineffectual jabs by Stonewall before squeezing him into sudden submission. Cries of "foul" filled the air—yes, I heard them, having slipped away from the livery to watch the much anticipated ring action—and someone even suggested (I don't believe it was Jack) that the cheating colored man be strung up from the tall Osage orange tree on the east side of town. Hickok had not been so busy he couldn't watch the events unfolding from a room over Drum's saloon. He showed himself at a window and made a declaration: Stonewall Patterson would not be paid, and all bets were null and void because staged fights were illegal in Hays City proper. There were murmurs and muttering but nothing more. For one thing, Wild Bill flashed a sawed-off shotgun, and everyone knew who the law still was in Ellis County. I found out later there was no ordinance in the books that prohibited such a match, but Mr. Hickok had made his ruling and it stuck.

As planned, Wild Bill Hickok moved on to Topeka in the company of Jasper Washington in January 1870. I'm not sure anyone wanted to see them ever return except for me. Certainly, Crooked Nose Jack was pleased the pair had departed, although his gambling fortunes didn't improve much. At least twice I had to pay his rent at the Boggs boardinghouse. Although Hickok had been the lawman in charge for nearly half a year, Hays City saw thirteen murders in 1869, not counting, of course, his two deadly shots fired in self-defense. Wild Bill and Jasper traveled quite a bit in the first part of 1870 because Hickok had some old acquaintances he wanted to visit in Warrensburg and Jefferson City, Missouri. In the capital city, many legislators wanted to meet him, and one day, on invitation, his very presence enlivened the floor of the House. Jasper later told me that Bill had no strong desire at that time to return to Springfield, the site of the Tutt shooting that helped make him famous.

In July the gunfighter and the freestyle fighter were back in Hays City. Jasper said he had been missing me like a son, but as far as I knew he had no son, and he certainly wasn't old enough to be my daddy. I suspected the reason they had returned was because Mr. Hickok had some secret business as a deputy U.S. marshal. In any case, they soon ran into trouble with two cavalrymen, not a couple of returning buffalo soldiers but two pale-faced troopers of Lieutenant Colonel George A. Custer's 7th Cavalry.

A lot of wild tales have come down the pike about that saloon fight—discrepancies about the saloon's name, what triggered the confrontation, how many soldiers were involved, how many soldiers were killed, whether or not Wild Bill was wounded—but I was actually present. It happened at the ever-popular Drum's saloon on the evening of July 17. I was there by invitation of Jasper Washington, who insisted like a concerned father might that I begin to find more meaning to life (or at least more pleasure in life) than was possible dealing all day with the feed and waste products of stalled horses and associating mostly with a fat yellow cat and a crippled mutt. Jack McCall was also there that night because he had taken to fraternizing with certain Fort Hays soldiers willing to break free of their military chains on occasion. On the night in question, there were maybe half a dozen cavalrymen from Fort Hays circulating among the civilians. Crooked Nose Jack was drinking with troopers Jeremiah Lonergan and John Kite, who had left the fort without permission. I overheard Jack telling them how Jasper Washington had destroyed Stonewall Patterson the previous year, and Lonergan, the larger of the two privates, boasting how he could lick any two soldiers, black or white, at Fort Hays or any other fort in Kansas.

"This man is different," Jack said. "He's the beatingest ruffian around. He beats bears with his bare hands."

"Of all the lies I ever did hear, that beats the Dutch," said Lonergan.

"It's the truth, Jeremy. I swear on my mother's grave."

"And you've seen it?"

"Sure, I've seen the plot in Louisville, Kentucky, though maw ain't exactly dead yet as far as I know."

"You're plumb corned, McCall. I don't mean that. I mean,

have you seen this George Washington fellow take on a bear without benefit of a long rifle?"

"Jasper Washington's the darky's name. No, I haven't seen him do it in person, but my brother over there swears that . . ."

"Bull. I don't care beans what your brother says. Show me this bear killer and I'll go lick him."

"I never said he killed the bears, just beat them down some. But hold your horses, Jeremy, I'll locate the big son of a bitch, and you can ask him your own self about the bears."

Jack stood up and peered in every direction before getting dizzy and collapsing back in his chair. "I *am* corned," he admitted. "I reckon Jasper Washington ain't here, 'cause he'd be damn hard to miss if he was."

"If he even exists. I'm getting sick of your bunkum and balderdash, McCall."

"Hold on now, soldier. I see none other than the notorious Wild Bill Hickok right over there at the bar just itching to lay down the law even though he ain't the law here anymore."

"What of it? He don't bother me."

"You want to take on the toughest hombre in this here saloon and maybe the toughest on the whole frontier, if Colonel George Ward Nichols of *Harper's* is to be believed, then Wild Bill's your man. See him now—the tall one in the black hat with long rusty hair tumbling on the shoulders of his fancy imported coat? He may look like a dandy but he's the biggest toad in the puddle, leastways that's what he claims."

"That right? Well, I might go ahead and stake my own claim."

"Do it quick," said Private Kile. "Don't say nothing to him from here. Don't say nothing at all. Get to him before he can pull one of those Navies on you. He be a dead shot. He be the man who got Dave Tutt in the heart with a lone shot from two hundred paces. I'll be right behind you."

I knew two hundred paces was an exaggeration, and I could

have argued the point, which might have distracted the soldiers from their intended target. But I wasn't one to start trouble or redirect it, especially when one could never count on drunks to be reasonable or expect them to change their brassy tunes to peaceful hymns. I also knew Jasper Washington was in the saloon but out of sight, conversing in a back room with the closest thing Hays City had to a local historian—Tommy Drum. So, I could have rushed back there and told Jasper what was occurring out front. But I didn't want to get my friend involved. He was the physical match for any man alive, but those soldiers were armed and unpredictable, and ever since I was a lad growing up in the Daniel's Den I'd heard that famous quote about the revolver man Samuel Colt: "God created men; Colonel Colt made them equal." Anyway, I figured Wild Bill Hickok could take care of himself and that his pair of Colts made no two men his equal.

I watched in silence as Lonergan left his seat and moved toward the bar, more like a grazing cow than a charging bull. Kile stood up and stretched but didn't follow his fellow soldier until Wild Bill had finally turned his back to the room for a chat with the bartender. Lonergan saw his chance and sprang at Hickok, pinning his arms and pulling him over backward onto the sawdust-covered floor. While Lonergan was holding Hickok down, Kile closed in fast, drew his Remington New Model Army six-shooter, and bent low to stick the muzzle in Wild Bill's ear. I thought I could hear the click, but nothing happened. The gun had misfired or that surely would have ended the legend of Wild Bill Hickok.

Kile never got off a second shot. Hickok broke free of Lonergan's grip on his arm, freed his Colt, and fired a shot into Kile's right wrist. Wild Bill didn't wait to see if Kile could shoot with his left hand. Hickok's second shot struck Kile in the side, knocking him out of the fight. Meanwhile, Lonergan was holding on to Hickok for dear life. He wasn't strong enough to control his opponent. Hickok's third shot broke Lonergan's kneecap, causing the soldier to scream, release Wild Bill, and take hold of his own damaged leg. Jasper Washington had come a-running from the back room, but Hickok didn't see his friend, only the other four soldiers circling like hungry wolves. Wild Bill burst through the blue circle and did something out of character—he ran. He knocked over two spittoons but made it safely to the rear of the saloon, where he crashed through a window and kept on going despite the loss of his hat and all that broken glass poking at his Prince Albert coat.

"What the hell just happened?" said Crooked Nose Jack, but his jaw hung open after that. He made no move to assist the two wounded men lying in the sawdust. He made no move at all. Maybe the fight he had helped trigger in his own crafty way hadn't gone the way he wanted. Maybe he hadn't expected quite that much violence.

"Where's Wild Bill going off to in such a dad-blasted hurry?" Jasper asked.

Nobody was in any mood or condition to answer him except for me. I pulled my friend aside and provided details of the fight Hickok had put up, the results of which were two disabled soldiers, one looking near dead. I suggested Jasper stay out of it, and for a change he listened to my good advice. We both watched the other soldiers carry their wounded comrades from the scene of the battle. Lonergan would recover and resume duty, but Kyle would die the next day from his wounds, not acquired in the line of duty but, according to one soldier's report, "during a drunken row with anti-military town belligerents." Of course, the opposition had actually been just one civilian absolutely acting in self-defense. And when news of the double shooting reached the fort, a party of soldiers returned to Hays City and visited every drinking and gambling den, plus the town's several bordellos, but could not turn up the hated Hickok. Jasper and I couldn't find Wild Bill, either. We later learned he had spent the night lying low in Boot Hill armed with a Winchester rifle and one hundred rounds of ammunition.

It was around daybreak that my friend the three-legged dog located Hickok in the cemetery and brought a piece of Wild Bill's torn vest to me at Walker's Livery. I fetched Jasper, who hadn't slept all night because he was worried the soldiers might have found Wild Bill or that his noble gunfighter was dying somewhere from a gunshot wound I had failed to notice. When we finally reached Wild Bill, after going in several different directions to make sure we weren't followed, he was resting peacefully and unscathed behind an unmarked headstone.

"The odds were sure against me last night, weren't they, fellows?" he said. "That one cowardly soldier had me at point-blank range. I sure hope the guns of those 7th Cavalry boys work better next time they engage the Sioux."

"I'm damn sorry, Bill," Jasper said, kicking the headstone. "I wasn't there for you. I seem to be making a habit of that. It is the opposite of my intention."

"Forget it, Wash. Not even you can be everywhere at once."

"Actually, I was there, but I was in the back listening to Tommy Drum. He was telling me about the time he heard Libbie Custer describing this fine fellow, and it wasn't her husband George. Tommy quoted her as saying, 'Tall, lithe, and free in every motion, this picture of physical perfection swung himself lightly from his saddle, and with graceful, swaying step and well poised head approached me like he was about to ask me to dance right there on the Plains.' " Jasper suddenly turned to me. "You know who Mrs. Custer was talking about, Zach?"

I shook my head, wondering why Jasper could possibly have George Custer's wife on his mind at a time like this. I was thinking only about the Fort Hays soldiers who most likely were out again this morning looking for killer Hickok and his accomplices.

"This very fellow lying before you now," Jasper blurted out. "She was talking about our Wild Bill."

"Ah, forget about it, Wash," Hickok said as he stood, yawned, and rubbed his eyes. "Lib is awfully fond of her husband, too."

I quickly changed the subject, realizing that even with those two toughest hombres, Hickok and Washington, on our side, we would be no match for one hundred bluecoats from the fort. "You can't stay here, Mr. Hickok," I said. "I mean, none of us should stay here."

"The young man is right," Wild Bill said, picking his Winchester off the ground. "Or should I say *Mr. McCall*." Calling me a mister brought his deep laugh to the surface. "Anyway, fellows, time to put Hays in my dust."

He didn't go back to town for his personal belongings or for Black Nell, but he told me to take real good care of his old mount for him. He started walking the eight miles east to Big Creek station, where he would catch a ride on a Kansas Pacific train. Jasper shrugged and then followed. "I'm going to make damn sure you board that train in one piece, Bill," the big man vowed. "Soldiers could be anywhere."

I waved rather pathetically, but Hickok never looked back once. Jasper finally did when he reached the last gravestone at the eastern end of the cemetery. "See you down the road, Mr. McCall," he called out. "Beware of the 7th Cavalry."

I wasn't so sure about seeing either of them again. I hurried back to Walker's Livery to resume my job. I busied myself grooming Black Nell. I knew I was pretty much a nobody who had nothing to fear from either the soldiers or the townsfolk if I stayed. I hadn't spoken a single word at the boardinghouse to deceitful Crooked Nose Jack the night before, because of what he had tried to pull off at Drum's saloon. I didn't care if I spoke to him on this day either. It wasn't on account of Jack that I was staying on in Hays. But the fat yellow cat would expect food along with a few kind words, and I sure wanted to pet that three-legged dog.

CHAPTER NINETEEN:
WE ARE SEEN IN ABILENE

I know Wild Bill Hickok and Jasper Washington caught a train after the July 1870 shootout in Tommy Drum's saloon, but I don't know if it was eastbound or westbound or what they were up to in the ensuing eight months. I wasn't even sure they were still in Kansas. It must have been a quiet winter for Wild Bill because I never saw his name mentioned in the press. Not that I was reading many newspapers in those days since Hays City no longer had one, but I occasionally picked up out-of-town papers discarded or accidentally left behind at the livery or train station. I do know from word of mouth and my own two eyes that the army never preferred charges against him for killing Private Kile, that tensions between soldiers and townsfolk didn't disappear, and that Hays City's Boot Hill kept growing in population. It saddened me when Black Nell went to that big corral in the sky that fall. The gallant Civil War heroine's death was no fault of mine, since I fed and groomed her better than I did myself. It was a combination of old age and old war wounds, I figured. I hoped Wild Bill would figure the same when he found out sooner or later.

All this time I learned more than I really wanted to know about my half brother's activities either from him (often obvious lies) or from Tommy Drum, who kept him on as a faro dealer for a spell. Crooked Nose Jack made more money than he ever had in his life but kept losing it at the poker table due to reckless betting (Tommy's view) or pure bad luck (Jack's view). It all ended soon enough because Jack (yes, it wasn't only his nose that was crooked) took to running brace games in which he cheated anyone daring to buck the tiger at his table and each night would pocket too big a percentage of the house's take.

Tommy Drum had no choice but to give him the boot in October. The vigilance committee in turn would have banished Jack from town except Tommy himself recommended the young man get one last chance. It was me who had pleaded with the saloon owner to bend over backward for the McCall brothers in the name of our old mutual friend, Jasper Washington. Without steady work or much luck at stud poker, Jack gave up his room at the boardinghouse and moved in with me in the smaller room across the hall. He still managed to visit bordellos regularly until he became *persona non grata* at all of them for disorderly behavior, failure to pay, and the excessive use of single-lock handcuffs and a long leather cattle whip. I didn't ask questions, just paid Madam Mattie Wood enough hush money to keep him out of jail.

Yet, despite all of Little Jack's misdeeds, I couldn't bring myself to banish him from my room or my life. Maybe there had been a stretch after I left Springfield that he didn't need me, but he clearly needed me here in Hays City. He might have been growing up fast in the wild and woolly West, but not necessarily in the right direction. I was his rock—solid, steady, and stable—a good role model, if I do say so myself in retrospect. I suppose he climbed all over me at times, flattering me when he wanted something, ignoring me when he didn't. I took it, not always pleasantly but without ever trying to strangle him or inflict further damage to that nose our father had once rearranged with his fist. I didn't admit it at the time, but I reckon I needed Little Jack, too. He was my only connection to family, and I had begun to miss more than ever some of my unofficial family from the Daniel's Den days, especially mother figure Belle Bragg, as well as my real father, Fat Jack McCall of Louisville.

The highlight of the winter of 1870–71 for both me and Little Jack was meeting George Armstrong Custer. For Jack it happened at Tommy Drum's saloon, which Jack kept returning to even after Tommy fired him. The lieutenant colonel was there because he was writing his memoirs at the time and wanted to actually see the spot where the great Wild Bill had mortally wounded one of his cavalrymen and shot up the knee of another. Custer apparently didn't blame Hickok one bit.

While in Drum's saloon, Colonel Custer picked up some morsels of local history from the owner and made an impulse decision to sit in with the local card players for a friendly game. One of those players happened to be Jack, who had to hold his tongue when three of the other players started to gush over Custer's Civil War triumphs in the East against Rebels and his Indian wars victory over hostiles along the Washita River, south of Kansas. "He showed himself to be a damned Yankee," Jack told me when he got back to the boardinghouse. "He has a much too high opinion of his past performances on the battlefield and in high society sitting rooms. Like Hickok, he is engrossed by his own appearance. What's more, he is a bluffer, but I called him on that and won the largest pot of the evening." Whether the famous army officer actually lost badly and sorely in the game, as Jack claimed, is debatable, but no question Jack wasn't the big winner. He still had his shirt, but his pockets were empty.

My meeting with Colonel Custer was prearranged. Mr. Walker the livery owner sent me out to Fort Hays with a stallion—sixteen hands high, solid bay with black legs—that had caught the officer's eye. He made conversation—talking exclusively about himself—before trying to do a little horse trading. He complained that there wasn't enough activity to suit him, what with Sioux Chief Red Cloud now on a reservation and the free-roaming Sioux warriors attacking Crow and Shoshone Indians instead of white folks. Drilling his troops, hunting buffalo, and writing magazine articles as well as his memoirs just weren't enough. He was bored. "I aim to get that horse," he suddenly exclaimed. "This is a resolution, not the result of impulse, but taken after weeks of deliberation since my last visit to Hays City. This stallion will bring me new-found joy; I'll breathe freer galloping across the tall grass into the Smoky Hills. I'm not loath to say, riding this spirited animal is bound to lift my spirits, allowing me to respect my manhood more."

Mr. Walker had given me a minimum price to sell the stallion for and had warned me to watch out for Colonel Custer's silver tongue. Nevertheless, this great American hero practically made me believe it was my patriotic duty to give the horse away. I didn't do that, but I allowed Custer to talk me down so low that it shamed me to face Mr. Walker again. There was no avoiding it, though. What happened next at the livery made me *disrespect* my manhood more. Mr. Walker threatened to take the difference in price out of my wages, and when I protested meekly, he threatened to send me packing. In the end we reached a compromise: I would work for the same daily pay but an extra hour each day until spring.

I had my job, but it somehow wasn't enough anymore. While fulfilling my stable duties through rain, hail, snow, wind, and bitter cold, I became bored and restless. Perhaps it all stemmed from that one meeting I had with the energetic Colonel Custer. The dullness of my life in a frontier town wore on me like blankets of snow during that unusually severe winter. I still might not have done anything about it, if not for Crooked Nose Jack telling me it was time to move on. He'd been talking to some out-of-work cowboys who were hopping a freight train to Abilene, now by far the most active cow town in Kansas. It was the off season for trailing cattle, but they figured they could make friends with those who dealt in beeves while indulging in a little card play and a lot of convivial women. Jack reminded me he'd been in that town once before and said he should have stayed.

"I'm rarin' to go back," he told me one late February afternoon at Walker's Livery.

"You're no cowboy," I said.

"Hell, I know that. But Abilene is where the action is now. Those thirsty, trail-weary Texas cowboys can't play cards worth a lick. They don't know when the odds are against them and favoring a professional like me. They don't stand a chance—they're saps when it comes to stud."

"But not when it comes to six-shooters. Those wide-open towns can be big trouble."

"You can't hide from trouble your whole life, Brother. Trouble and the West go together like whiskey and saloons, horse shit and stables. Only safe place for a Kansas man is six feet under on Boot Hill less'n he's bothered by worms."

"I don't know about that. But I happened to read in an Abilene paper they had this city marshal, name of Tom Smith, who used only his powerful fists to put cowboy lawbreakers in their place, which was either jail or a road out of town. Everyone approved of Tom Smith's methods and the ordinance against carrying arms within city limits—that is, until last November when someone shot him in the chest and someone else clubbed him over the head with a gun and then severed the marshal's head with an ax."

"No worries. I'm sure they've found another marshal or two by now. Lawmen come and they go, as do professional gamblers. Let's go, Brother."

"I'm no more a gambler than I am a lawman."

"Sure enough, but I promise you they got horse shit and stables in Abilene, too."

I didn't agree to leave right then, nor even the next day when a member of the vigilance committee warned me that my brother's health was in jeopardy—for the vigilantes had heard one too many complaints from unhappy losers about Jack's marking cards and underhanded deals in every Hays City gambling establishment except for Tommy Drum's saloon. I was fairly certain the committee intended to banish him (which would also temporarily get Jack out of my hair) rather than hang him (a too permanent solution that would certainly leave me guilt ridden to the end of my own days).

Anyway, what convinced me to bolt from the livery to the station to catch the eastbound to Abilene the very next Saturday were a few harsh words spoken to me by my boss, Thomas Alexander Walker: "I never said much about it before, but it still bothers me how Hickok's horse died on your watch last year. And then yesterday afternoon you fell asleep on the job. Don't deny it, McCall. Right under your pointed nose, some cowboy made off with John Bittles's palomino and somebody else put that flea-bitten, three-legged mutt out of its misery by feeding it rat poison. And, by God, that tub-of-lard yellow cat must have consumed its share because I seen it crawl into the empty stall and curl up in the corner. Good riddance to the dog and cat, I say. But John Bittles wants money or my hide for losing his blessed horse."

I surely felt badly about the death of my canine and feline pals, and I wouldn't have put it past Mr. Walker to have done the poisoning himself. It was too bad someone had made off with the palomino, too, but horse theft wasn't exactly uncommon on the frontier. Without much trouble (or thought) I convinced myself that my boss was a son of a bitch; I only wondered why it had taken me so long to realize that. I had only one day's wages owed me at that point, and I felt friendless in Hays, so I said only two words in response to Mr. Walker's criticism: "Good riddance." I considered buying just one train ticket, but I couldn't quite bring myself to leave Crooked Nose Jack behind to deal with the sore losers and vigilantes. His bag was already packed, and anyway, going to Abilene was his idea.

And what a good idea it turned out to be for me—at least after a while. I was able to obtain a room for us at the three-story Drovers Cottage because expansion to a hundred rooms was well underway and most of them were unoccupied that time of year. The hotel was the center of Abilene's social and business life, and on our second day there we saw owner and town founder Joseph McCoy passing through the billiard room, although he was too busy to stop when Jack called out his name. His main cook, Lou Gore, did recognize Jack from his previous stay there, and as we feasted on extra-rare beef in the large dining room, she hinted that if Mr. McCoy was elected mayor as expected in the first municipal election on April 30, 1871, he would try to bring to Abilene "the finest specimen of manhood I've ever seen wearing boots."

"Seems I heard that imposing description before, Mrs. Gore," said Crooked Nose Jack with his mouth full. He turned to me and, with bits of beef spewing from a corner of it, added, "If not for Mr. Gore, you can bet she'd try to bring Hickok to her parlor whether McCoy is elected or not."

Mrs. Gore scurried off to the kitchen before I could question her about Wild Bill's whereabouts now or if she had any information about Hickok's friend Jasper Washington. After the meal, I walked over to Ed Gaylord's twin livery stables that could care for a hundred or more cow ponies, but the stalls were mostly as empty as the rooms at Drovers. Mr. Gaylord said he wasn't hiring until the spring cattle drives arrived from

Texas. I proceeded to the Alamo, where Crooked Nose Jack had gone to make himself known, intent as he was on improving his fortunes by a legitimate stroke of luck.

The Alamo was the most elaborate saloon in town, with long entrances on the west and east ends and in between a bar with polished brass fixtures and rails, the longest mirror I had ever seen behind the back bar, classically inspired paintings of nudes lining the walls, and gaming tables filling the entire floor space. Come summer the place would surely be packed with drovers, livestock commission men, cattle buyers, speculators, gamblers, vagabonds, and ladies who wanted a man to buy them a drink at the very least. Right now, though, I only saw what looked like a half-dozen businessmen, no doubt year-round residents, chatting as they sipped drinks and watched dealers turn over cards. I saw no sign of Jack, so I asked if anyone had seen a young man new to Abilene. Two of the card players laughed, glanced at me, and then laughed harder.

"A cross-eyed, twisted-nosed fellow off his head come in here an hour ago," volunteered the barkeep, who wore a string tie, white shirt, fancy red vest, and a spotless white apron—the best-dressed bartender I'd ever seen. "I had to show him to the door."

"What for?" I asked, amid more laughter. I made myself stop looking at the reclining nudes on the walls. But looking at myself in the big mirror made me feel even more uneasy about being there.

"He was bothering the regulars, disturbing their peace."

"How so?"

"By running off at the saucebox. He called himself the Jack of Clubs and boasted about all his triumphs as a knight of the green cloth. He invited himself to a private game without wit or wisdom, or even enough for openers or a short glass. He was out of his element. When the drives come, we tolerate the Texas rabble because they expend money along with all their bluster and unlawful acts. But no reason to welcome his sort in February."

I didn't like the barkeep's haughty tone and, without thinking it out, defended my half brother. "He's no Texan and isn't one to commit unlawful acts. He was born in Kentucky, lived in Springfield, Missouri, and we recently came over from Hays City."

"A friend of yours, is he? You cut from the same cloth? If so, come down that hallway with me, and I'll show you the same door."

"I haven't done anything."

"Haven't any money either, I'm betting. We have our own rules and regulations here at the Alamo, what with the marshal's office being vacant since fearless Tom Smith got the bullet and the ax last fall."

"I'm unarmed, I have money in my pocket, don't play cards, drink infrequently and moderately, and hail from Kentucky. I also call Wild Bill Hickok a friend. What do you think of that? Just wait till he comes to town as your next marshal. You'll sing a different tune."

The barkeep shut up and resized me as if to determine whether I was more important than he thought or else "off my head" like the earlier young stranger. The dealer stopped dealing and examined my face for the first time. Nobody was laughing at the card table. One of the players stood up and sauntered toward me, maintaining a poker face.

"There won't be a new marshal until we get a new mayor," he said. "What do you know about it?"

I didn't want to back down, but, being an honest man, I had no choice. "Not much. I . . . eh . . . overheard someone say something about it and . . ."

"Wild Bill Hickok isn't even in town or I would have heard

about it. Where is he?"

"Well, somewhere in Kansas, I suppose. I don't rightly know, mister."

"Doesn't surprise me. Are you even a friend of his?"

"We're well acquainted. I'm a better friend of his valuable deputy back in Hays City. His name is Jasper Washington, and he might be the strongest, fightingest man in Kansas."

"Never heard of him. They used to say the same thing around these parts about the late Marshal Smith. He could knock down a mule with a single punch."

"Jasper isn't so much a puncher. He wrestles and squeezes. Even against bears."

"Oh, sure. You must have had a snootful before you staggered into the Alamo."

"No, sir."

"All right, then where's this bear fighter now, still in Hays?"

"No. He left with Wild Bill. But I'm sure wherever Wild Bill is, Jasper is."

"I tell you what, sonny, why don't you walk out the way you came in, locate that other spinner of yarns, and the pair of you hit the trail in search of your imaginary pals."

"I happen to have no further business in here," I said, turning and hurrying out before the barkeep could show me to the door.

For the rest of the week Crooked Nose Jack borrowed more money from me than I cared to give him. He took it on down to the establishments on Texas Street where the whiskey and women were cheaper than at the Alamo and the card players less likely to object to strangers. He managed to get into several games and even win a handful of fair pots—without palming cards, he claimed, though I kept thinking a bullet would find him or he would land in jail, since Abilene had one of those even if it lacked a marshal. Meanwhile, the only job I could get was as a swamper at Shady Shane's saloon, and I was hired only because the owner, A. W. Shane, knew I wouldn't drink up his profits.

It seemed only a matter of time before Jack ran out of luck at the poker tables and Joseph "Cowboy" McCoy or the Gores booted us out of our room at Drovers Cottage. Jack and I periodically saw the slender, goateed McCoy patting backs as he passed through the hotel or waving and shaking hands as he strolled the streets. His great vision and tenacity had made Abilene "Queen of the Kansas Cow Towns," but now he wanted the people to show their gratitude by electing him mayor.

Realizing that the McCall brothers were there to stay and to vote, McCoy finally paused on the Drovers staircase—he was going up, we were going down—long enough for a brief chat. He told us he was born in Illinois, just like Wild Bill Hickok, and revealed that in 1861 his selling of a stockcar-load of mules, not cows, in Kentucky had been the financial break he needed to become a major dealer in livestock and "the Real McCoy" in Kansas. I wanted to ask about Wild Bill, but Jack quickly asserted that he was "the Real McCall"—a not so subtle poke at me—and then started in on how he had been raised in Louisville but knew from the time he was no taller than a tobacco plant that his "inexorable destiny" lay west of the Mississippi.

"Inexorable, huh?" McCoy said, stroking his goatee. "Like it a lot. A damn good word."

"Yes, sir," Jack said. "You know what else is inexorable—my inexorable wish to play a high-stakes poker game with the monied gentlemen in your Alamo saloon. I wonder if you might put in a word for . . ."

"It's not my Alamo, young man. I have been called brilliant in many ways, and I'm damn proud of what I've accomplished for the cattle industry and Abilene, but I must confess I have a tendency to be overconfident in my personal mastery over a deck of cards. It's best that I avoid the gambling tables."

"I understand, but it's not that way with me, sir. I'm a professional poker player. At the moment, I'm a little short, you know, moneywise. With a small stake, however, I know I'd break the bank at the Alamo."

"Good luck with that, young man. But while you're busy breaking the bank tomorrow, don't forget to take the time to vote—and remember the man you want for mayor *must be* the Real McCoy."

Joseph McCoy then tipped his Boss of the Plains hat at us and ascended the stairs quickly, his high-heeled boots clomping as if they too were eager to win over the voters.

CHAPTER TWENTY:
ABILENE'S NEW MARSHAL

As expected, the people of Abilene elected Joseph McCoy mayor on April 3, 1871, and, as Mrs. Gore predicted, the mayor wasted no time getting word to the man he wanted as his marshal, Wild Bill Hickok. Turns out Mr. Hickok was only sixty miles away, scouting some for the army out of Fort Harker. Eight days later, Hickok walked into McCoy's office, but he wasn't alone. Right behind him was Jasper Washington. "If you get me, you get him as my deputy," Hickok told the mayor. "Two legends for the price of one." As Jasper later told me, McCoy was wide-eyed at first and admitted that he'd known plenty of skilled black and Mexican cowboys pushing cattle through the years, but he'd not once seen a colored man wearing a badge west of the Mississippi. "He'll be your first, then, if I take the job," Wild Bill replied. "But first Jasper and I will need to look over your little town here and see if it suits us."

The pair took in the sights, taking special note of the Alamo on Cedar Street and all the other gambling opportunities offered by lesser establishments on Texas Street. When they arrived at Shane's saloon, I was trying to roll through the back door a four hundred-pound barrel of whiskey that Alan Shane had bought from a whiskey drummer, but my thoughts were of my father who had that same occupation back in Kentucky. "What would Fat Jack think if he saw me now?" I asked myself aloud because the job lent itself to muttering. It startled me to get an answer, and not even one from inside my head.

"He'd box your ears, boy, and tell you to quit your low-bred swamping in a no-account Western dive and get to drumming fine bourbon whiskey in your home state of Kentucky."

It was Jasper, of course. I nearly let the barrel roll back onto my foot, but he stopped it cold. With his muscle and my determination, we got the barrel into storage in record time while Mr. Shane and one dumbfounded drunkard watched. Then Jasper and I hugged as Mr. Hickok introduced himself to Mr. Shane by showing the proprietor one of the shiny Navy Colts. Mr. Shane was impressed, but no more than he was with Jasper's strength.

"Ten years ago, I'd have paid a pretty penny to buy me a brute like him," he commented.

"Ten years ago, that man would have wrung your Johnny Reb neck," Wild Bill said. "He happens to be my best friend in Kansas—hell, in the whole wide world."

"I sure as heck ain't gonna doubt your word on that, Mr. Hickok. The white boy ain't much with barrels, but he'll do. Don't need no muscle to sweep up, wash glasses, and clean out my three new spittoons."

"That boy happens to be a friend of my best friend. I promise you this: you won't have him long if I become marshal of this fair city."

"That right? Whatever you say, Mr. Hickok."

On April 15 Wild Bill Hickok did in fact become marshal of Abilene, with the city council unanimously approving Mayor McCoy's choice of "the squarest man I ever saw." The new marshal would receive $150 per month, collect twenty-five percent of any fine imposed in court, and be allowed to hire as many deputies as needed, starting with Jasper Washington. Even though Wild Bill hadn't asked for it, Deputy Washington would get a dollar a day. One of Jasper's principal responsibilities besides backing up the marshal was to keep an eye out for illegal activity at the numerous gambling tables. While watching out for cheaters, he would of course be allowed to supplement his salary with any poker winnings. The marshal stationed his deputy at the Alamo, where the pots were bigger, and spent most of his time there himself.

Further evidence of how much the mayor and council wanted Hickok came on April 19 when they approved of his second hire, yours truly at twenty-five dollars a month. My official title was "jailer." It wasn't a full-time occupation, but it was enough for me to immediately quit Shane's saloon. I didn't have to tell Wild Bill about Black Nell because he'd gotten word some time ago out at Fort Harker. He didn't hold the death of his favorite horse against me, simply saying, "Black Nell and I will meet again in the happy hunting ground to part no more."

The recently rebuilt jail wasn't large, but until the Texans came up the trail later in the spring, I didn't have many "guests." In fact, I often had the place to myself, since Marshal Hickok and Deputy Washington only showed up at the jail when they brought in drunken disturbers of the peace who needed to sleep it off till morning. But being bored beat pushing barrels and polishing spittoons. I got in the habit of putting my feet up and reading every issue of *The Abilene Chronicle* forward and backward and as much as I could take of the cheap, blood-and-thunder "yellow-backed" *Beadle's Dime Novels*.

The boredom ended soon enough. The first herd from Texas arrived on May 11, and by June there were ten times as many Texans as Kansans in and around Abilene. The council gave Marshal Hickok three more deputies to help enforce the ordinance against carrying firearms or other weapons within city limits and to patrol south of the railroad tracks, where so many wild cowboys were running loose that Jasper nicknamed that side of town Little Texas. Hickok didn't give up his gambling, but when out and about he made his presence felt, steel nerved and graceful as he walked in the middle of the city streets armed with a Winchester as well as those two ivory-handled Navy Colts. That he wouldn't hesitate to empty all three firearms at any parties who dared challenge his authority seemed abundantly clear. And if that wasn't enough of a deterrent, Deputy Washington sometimes broke away from the Alamo and followed in the same path as the marshal, flexing his massive muscles and looking larger than life. Most nights the jail was overcrowded, not only with stumbling drunks but with hard cases who had to be forcefully relieved of their pistols and Bowie knives (thankfully not part of a jailer's job). In early June, two such men wounded each other in a shootout, and Jasper arrested both. He carried to the jail the one with a leg wound while herding the other one in like a strayed steer. They received their medical attention behind bars.

One of the troublemakers to come up the Abilene Cattle Trail was eighteen-year-old John Wesley Hardin, who had apparently killed in Texas and again on the trail north. He arrived in Abilene with no immediate plans and spent much of his time in the Bull's Head saloon, where he met one of the owners, Ben Thompson, and Crooked Nose Jack on the same night. That was Jack's usual destination each evening, because the cards were often good to him there, and he took a liking to Thompson, who was born in England but became a Texan who fought for the Confederacy. Thompson had no love for Hickok, claiming that the Yankee scout turned marshal had it in for all Southern boys. Jack, of course, could never bring himself to like the man who had killed Dave Tutt and, in Jack's own words, made him feel as worthless as "a piddling amount of refuse." It didn't matter to Jack that Wild Bill had always been agreeable to me—a Kentucky boy who had served with the notorious Rebel raider John Hunt Morgan—and had recently hired me as his jailer.

Aware of John Wesley Hardin's reputation as a killer, Ben Thompson for days sullied the reputation of Wild Bill Hickok in front of the two young men—hard-nosed Hardin and Crooked Nosed Jack. It seemed to be Thompson's wish that Hardin would get angry enough at the Yankee marshal that he'd pick a fight and then best him in a gunfight. Although he didn't actually admit it to me, Jack no doubt wholeheartedly approved; in fact, it was the kind of scheme he was capable of working up himself.

"First off, no matter what you might have heard, I never killed a man who didn't need killing," Hardin said after listening to the Bull's Head co-owner for nearly a week.

"I never said a word about murder," Thompson replied. "But now that you mention it, Wes, wouldn't Abilene be a better place for all us Texans if the marshal was somehow removed from office permanently?"

"Secondly, I am not doing anybody's fighting just now except my own. If Bill needs killing, why don't you kill him yourself."

"I'd rather get someone else to do it."

"You got the wrong man for that kind of work. What about our little friend here? What say you, Jack McCall, you up to giving it a try?"

"Me? I . . . I'm no killer. I mean, I'm not saying you are, Mr. Hardin. But you have experience, right? As for me, I've never shot a single person in my entire life. I don't even own a gun, and . . ."

"Not true, Jackie boy," said Thompson. "You told me the other night you carry a derringer in your coat pocket in case one of the losing cowboys at the poker table takes exception to you winning so regular."

Jack patted his pockets. "Right. I forgot. It's very small. And the fact is I would only use it in self-defense."

"You think? I'm not sure you could even fire that thing at a prairie dog."

"Leave him alone, Ben," said Hardin. "A puny pea shooter like that wouldn't be worth a hill of beans against Hickok."

"I'm sure you're right, Wes. No offense, Jackie boy, but this is a job for a big man with a big gun."

"Not this man," said Hardin, and just like that he walked out of the Bull's Head.

Some days later young John Wesley did meet the thirty-four-year-old Wild Bill face to face on the street. I'm not sure which street. Little Jack wasn't present, but he heard about it from Hardin and told the story to me one hot summer night in our room at Drovers Cottage. How much truth was there to the tale? I figured not much. The boastful Hardin had reason to lie, and Jack was capable of inventing or exaggerating something to make Hickok look bad.

Like Wild Bill, John Wesley wore two six-shooters, but only a lawman was permitted to go about town armed. Hickok supposedly drew one of his Colts, said "This has gone far enough," and demanded that the young gunman surrender his weapons. Hardin presented his two six-shooters butt forward to Wild Bill and then rolled them over in his hands so they were fully cocked with the muzzles in the peace officer's face. At that point, Wild Bill supposedly said, "You are the gamest and quickest boy I ever saw," and the two gunfighters put away their guns, went into a saloon to share drinks, and became friendly. I doubted the marshal could have fallen for Hardin's trick, which Jasper later told me was known as the "border roll." Hickok never said a word about the alleged incident to anyone, not even to his best friend. "I didn't bring it up myself," Jasper told me. "Bill had enough on his mind without hearing that hogwash. I know the young lout Hardin didn't wear his guns in town. He wasn't fool enough to defy a legend."

Hardin, though, kept his guns close while staying at the

American House Hotel that summer. The story has been told that late one night he shot and killed either a fellow boarder for snoring too loudly in the next room or an intruder intent on doing him in with a dirk. No matter which way it was done, Hardin supposedly panicked upon hearing Hickok arrive at the hotel to investigate the shooting and, without taking the time to put on his pants, jumped out a back window and fled Abilene for good. Many years later, Jasper Washington set me straight on the last part of that oft repeated Hardin tale.

"It was me, not Bill, who scared young lout Hardin off," Jasper revealed. "I actually heard the shots fired. I was in the front lobby at the time checking up on a hotel guest who had stayed for three nights and then slipped away on the fourth night without paying his bill. I raced to the scene and caught young lout Hardin with a smoking six-shooter and no pants. I told him he was under arrest. He pointed the six-shooter at my chest and said he thought otherwise. He claimed he'd killed his first darky back in Polk County, Texas, at age fifteen, and he felt it was high time he killed another, especially a big, overbearing one wearing a badge. I told him I was unarmed, but that didn't matter to him one lick. He raised that six-shooter so the muzzle was pointed directly between my eyes.

"I then asked him if the *border roll* was the same as the *road agent's spin* and wondered if he might provide a quick demonstration. That made him grin. He wasn't quite dumb enough to show me, but it did give him pause to think. And during his pause, I made my move. I wrestled that six-shooter out of his hand, took hold of his middle, and squeezed like the devil till he cried for mercy. Being a sworn deputy, not a killer, I released him. Now I have to say, young lout Hardin had quick hands, but he made no attempt to pick his six-shooter off the floor. He'd had enough of this big bad darky. Instead, he demonstrated just how nimble footed he was—you know, racing to the window and crashing right through the way he did."

Did any other gunfighters blow into town that summer with a notion of taking on Wild Bill Hickok? I'm not sure, but if they did, they found reason to seek easier targets elsewhere. Rumor had it that five members of the James-Younger Gang, including brothers Frank and Jesse James and Cole Younger, showed up between bank robberies and used aliases to check into Drovers Cottage. I never saw them; that is, I don't think I did. Drovers was a noisy, crowded place that time of year, and practically every cowboy type I ran into looked a mite suspicious. Crooked Nose Jack heard the rumors at some point and began searching for these "fellow supporters of the Southern cause" and badgering desk clerk Charles Gross, who remained mum on the matter. Finally, Jack had to give up because he had more pressing matters at hand.

Gamblers and prostitutes kept flocking to Abilene, and Jack naturally dealt with both. It was no longer easy pickings at the poker tables for Jack because the new card sharps were as intent as he was at separating cowboys from their hard-earned money, and many of them were better at it. Wild Bill and his deputies were under instruction of the city council to arrest crooked gamblers and "to close up all dead and brace gambling games." Since the jail was small and overcrowded, the marshal often chose to run the offenders out of town. Because of pressure from decent citizens, the sinning ladies were moved en masse from Texas Street a quarter mile south and east to a new sporting district known as the Devil's Addition. The Texas cowboys didn't object; they could find the willing women easily enough, and the city lawmen were not such a bother in the new fenced-in location.

Even when he fared poorly at stud poker, Jack would try to keep enough money in his pocket to support a late-night visit to the Devil's Addition. On many a night he failed to return to our room at Drovers. In particular I remember July 31, because on that day he and I attended Agnes Lake Thatcher's "Hippo-Olympiad and Mammoth Circus," and that much older widow woman attracted his attention because, as he stated, he wanted for a change to be with "a really respectable and experienced member of the opposite sex, and this one not only had been wed to a circus clown but also had walked tightropes and tamed lions." I suspect Mrs. Thatcher reminded him a little of his mother back in Louisville (though Hannah McCall only had to tame Fat Jack), but I didn't say that to him, since he planned to go right up to her after the show and invite her to supper at Drovers and drinks at the Alamo. Needless to say, she turned him down flat—too young, too small, too cross-eyed, too boastful, too much *unlike* Wild Bill Hickok. Marshal Hickok was also in attendance that day in case anyone, human or beast, should disturb the peace at the traveling tent show. I can't say for certain whether or not she had her eye on the dashing avowed bachelor, who though younger than her was, of course, much closer to her own age than the kid with the crooked nose. I do know they would cross paths again and that on March 5, 1876, in Cheyenne, Wyoming Territory, Wild Bill and Agnes would marry.

On the same day he was rejected by Agnes Thatcher, despondent Jack drank alone most of the evening and then staggered out to the Devil's Addition, where he created a scene. He apparently took offense when laughed at by his chosen lady for the evening, slapped her around some, and refused to pay for getting such "poor service." Deputy Washington happened to be out there at the time, whether on official duty or not I cannot say, and he pushed and sometimes carried Jack on the long trek to the Abilene jail. Jack, according to Jasper, protested and cursed the whole way but did so with even more passion when he recognized the jailer who was locking him up for the night—me.

"You can't arrest me, Bastard McCall," Jack said to me during his ranting. "Blood is thicker than wa . . . wa . . . whatever."

"I'm not arresting you," I replied. "I'm simply placing you behind bars."

"If you aren't arresting me, I'm a free man. Freemen can't be confined against their will."

"That's what I've always said," said Jasper Washington. "But you are being confined because I arrested you."

"You!" Jack shook his fists and accidentally hit himself in the head with both. "You're nothing but a . . . a black bastard."

"Deputy black bastard to you, Little Jack. No matter what you call me, it doesn't change anything. Consider yourself arrested."

"What for? There's no law against hitting a whore who cheats you."

"There's a city ordinance against carrying firearms within city limits. And you were carrying this." Jasper held up Jack's derringer, which Jack squinted at without showing any signs of recognition. "Yes, it belongs to you. You were carrying it in the pocket of your coat."

"But you carried me into town. I didn't come voluntarily."

"The Devil's Addition is part of Abilene. The ordinance goes for out there, too."

"Well, you can go to hell. The both of you can. This whole bloody town is a goddamned circus!"

I listened to Jack carry on past midnight before the other part-time jailer, Mike Williams, showed up and I retired to Drovers Cottage where I could sleep in peace. At least, I thought I would. But I tossed, turned, and tortured myself with feelings of guilt all night. It didn't matter that I believed Crooked Nose Jack deserved to be scorned, I just didn't like other people doing it. I kept thinking as a jailer brother I could have done more to keep him out of trouble in this clamorous city. Three different times I reached the conclusion I should be there in the Abilene jail with him, even if on the other side of the bars. And three times I changed my mind and shouted to the thin walls, "To hell with him!" But that only made me more awake.

Wild Bill had released Jack and all the other drunks by the time I arrived late at the jailhouse the next morning. Hickok told me he wasn't one to play favorites and that my brother wasn't worthy of sympathy. But the marshal quickly added that he had always been loyal to his friends and that I was a friend of his best friend. Besides, he was fed up with the city council at the moment. He had been ordered to suppress all dance houses and to arrest any proprietors who persisted in these operations after notification. That didn't sit well with him. What would be next, suppressing all gambling establishments? The council members were also considering reducing the police force by half, mainly because so many undesirables had left Abilene for towns "still catering to sinful humanity" and because both the "safety prospects" and "moral status" of Abilene, even on Texas Street, had risen immeasurably since the brothels were relocated.

In early September the order came through from the city council that Marshal Hickok must immediately dismiss two of his assistants, "by reason that their services are no longer needed." Wild Bill at least put his foot partially down, saying, "I shall abide, gentlemen, but I *will* be keeping trusty Deputy Washington and conscientious Jailer McCall, that is, unless you intend to dismiss your marshal." They did not.

CHAPTER TWENTY-ONE:
A FEW GOODBYES

Wild Bill had more than lived up to the expectations of Mayor McCoy and the city council. The law-abiding citizens of Abilene, according to one commentator, had thought it best "to fight the devil with his own weapons," and that strategy had proved successful. The formidable two-gun Hickok and his deputies had brought law and order during the city's biggest cattle season yet. Nearly half of Abilene's annual budget was going toward law enforcement, though. Some of the local big bugs questioned that kind of spending at the end of September 1871 when not only most of the Texas cowboys started to leave town but also many of the gamblers and prostitutes who had bled them dry.

Marshal Hickok probably didn't mind seeing anyone depart by train or otherwise except perhaps Mrs. Agnes Lake, who had taken her popular Hippo-Olympiad to St. Louis after its run in Abilene. Not that he would say anything to his part-time jailer, but he was also close mouthed about the state of his heart around his favorite deputy. "I get the feeling that sometimes Bill is silently wishing that circus lady had lingered longer so that they could get better acquainted," Jasper Washington told me one day when my only duty was to sweep out the jail. "But other times I think he's relieved she's not around so he can play poker and sip whiskey in peace at the Alamo. It's not always easy reading Bill. Mostly he be soft spoken and pleasant, but on occasions he's altogether humps and grumps. Once after he lost half a week's salary in a peaceful poker game, he took me aside and grumbled, 'I'll be damned if tonight I ain't missing John Wesley Hardin.' "

Crooked Nose Jack was probably missing all the Texans who played reckless poker, and he might have missed Mrs. Lake, too, even though he once referred to her as "that old hag master of the trained animals" and another time as "all business and none fun," and a third time as "Hickok's Hippo-Harlot." He never thanked Wild Bill for letting him out of jail that one time and not fining him for carrying a gun within city limits. Jack never even asked for his derringer back since he wasn't talking to the man who took it, Jasper Washington, and saw no need to defend himself when his only games were penny-ante and, as he admitted to me in one of his weaker moments, "I don't win enough to buy spit." Actually, it was hard for him to get a game of any kind because the city council had ordered Hickok to shut down most of the gambling dens and brothels.

Ben Thompson, the Texan who had tried to convince Hardin to fight Hickok, had gone back home and not returned, but Phil Coe, his former partner in the Bull's Head, seemed to share his resentment of the marshal. Exactly why, I'm not sure. Could be it was because at six foot four and 225 pounds, Coe was the biggest Texan of them all and felt the weight of that Southern state's considerable pride resting on his shoulders. After Wild Bill had warned him about a Bull's Head dealer suspected of dealing crooked, Coe had muttered to Jasper Washington how he couldn't stomach "little law dogs in Kansas poking their snouts in my business." Hickok wasn't exactly little, at six foot, broad shouldered, and narrow at the hip, but Coe was thick all over. "Even more so in the head than stomach," said Deputy Washington, who was an inch taller than Coe and weighed a whopping 260 pounds, mostly heavy muscle.

Another time, Coe and Hickok nearly butted heads over a prostitute who, according to what the big Texan had heard, was providing favors to him at a fair rate but to Wild Bill for free at gunpoint. Coe accused the marshal of meddling in areas he didn't belong and abusing the power of his office and of his fabled pistols. His accusation was based on mere rumor, one I suspect was started by Little Jack while still recovering from the Agnes Thatcher Lake rejection, and Wild Bill refused to discuss anything so outlandish. "You being sober as a judge, Coe, those are fighting words," the marshal said. "And I don't need my Colts to teach you some manners."

Jasper stepped in before the two opponents could come to blows, poked Coe in the belly, and said matter-of-factly, "Everybody knows you're no match for the marshal when it comes to pistols, and if it's hand-to-hand fighting you're after, you'll have to go through me to get to him." That stopped the big Texan in his tracks. He swallowed his pride and backed away from the slightly bigger Kentuckian turned Kansan, probably having also heard the rumors of how Jasper had outwrestled bears and put the squeeze on John Wesley Hardin.

That wasn't the end of it, though, not by a long shot. That very next night, Crooked Nose Jack was among a group at the Bull's Head that heard Coe say he wasn't afraid of Hickok and would get him "before the frost." Jack didn't find that threat, possibly induced by alcohol, real or at least uttered in earnest. It amused him. "I reckon," he told me, "Coe is just trying to fill the boots of Ben Thompson as headman of the Hickok Haters Club." It was left unsaid by either of us that Jack himself was a full-blown member.

It turned out there were plenty more Texans besides Phil Coe still in town that fall, most planning to attend the Dickinson County Fair. Heavy rains had flooded the grounds on October 5, though, so about sundown fifty of them decided to make their own entertainment elsewhere. They started their spree at the Applejack Saloon and then proceeded to other drinking establishments on Texas Street. It wasn't enough to be drinking among themselves; the Texans hauled citizens off the street and made them "stand treats." One of them was me.

I happened to be out and about because I wasn't needed at the jail. Nobody had been locked up for days, and when Marshal Hickok went for supper at his favorite boardinghouse, he told me I may as well leave, too. Not that he had invited me to dine with him—that was something Deputy Washington did on occasion, but never the marshal, who must have figured giving me the easy jailer job was more than enough. I went to Drovers Cottage to see if Little Jack was hungry, but he wasn't there, so I ate alone in the dining room, not wanting to go back out in the rain. I treated myself to a rare steak for no reason other than the hectic cattle season had ended, and I was safe and dry.

Midway through the meal, though, I started to think of this mangy street dog that I called Jesse James on account of the large black splotch on his face that resembled a robber's mask. I had seen him getting kicked around some on Texas Street and had fed him bits of jerky and bacon and such because he seemed to need me, just like that three-legged mutt had back in Hays City. I left plenty of meat on the steak bone before wrapping it up and braving the rain to give Jesse James a real treat for a change. I soon enough found the dog, or rather he followed his nose to find me, and then the Texans discovered me in an alley watching Jesse tear into that valuable bone. The dog growled a warning at the cowboys, but when they lifted me onto the shoulders of the sturdiest one and took me inside the Alamo to buy them drinks, Jesse simply turned his head and continued to feast.

Mike Williams, the former part-time jailer and a far better friend of Wild Bill Hickok's than I was, was standing at the other end of the bar when a half-dozen cowboys had me lay my money down before the barkeep to buy rounds for everybody.

There wasn't nearly enough, so the cowboys started some unpleasant talk. "Another miserly Kansas farmer," said the one whose shoulders I came in on. "They dig holes in their cornfields to plant their greenbacks." A short cowboy wearing a mustache that resembled a longhorn's horns took hold of my arms and stood on his toes to peer up at my face. "This ain't no farmer, boys," he declared. "He was the deputy with the keys when Hickok tossed me in the calaboose last summer for disturbing his goddamn peace." That bit of news caused all six of the Texans to start poking and shoving me, and they didn't let up when I spoke the truth: "I was only the jailer, fellows. No hard feelings."

Williams, who wasn't even that anymore, left his spot at the bar and moved toward the cowboys and me. "You all right, Mc-Call?" he asked, which surprised me since we'd exchanged only a few words those summer evenings when we crossed paths—me leaving the jail for home, him arriving for night watch.

One of the cowboys answered for me: "He's standing treat and needs help. Good of you to volunteer, mister." Two others tried to grab Williams, but he slipped between them and dashed toward the front doorway, pausing only long enough to call back, "The marshal won't like this." One unsteady cowboy tried too late to stop him, but only succeeded in tripping over a spittoon and falling headfirst into a table leg. That knocked him out cold, and so much mocking laughter followed that I thought I could also slip away. I didn't get far. The Texan who dragged me back to the bar shouted into my ear, "Not so fast, jailer. We'll put you in jail, but not till you buy another round. And if Hickok shows up, we'll stick him in his own jail, too."

I didn't have the money or the inclination for another round, but that didn't stop the cowboys from demanding the barkeep keep filling their glasses and mine. I don't doubt that Mike Williams went to notify the marshal about trouble brewing in the

233

Alamo, but Wild Bill certainly let it brew at first, perhaps because Williams informed him that nobody appeared to be violating the gun ordinance. There's no telling how long the cowboys would have detained me at the bar had we not all heard a shot fired just outside the saloon. The Texans filed out the front door, some with drinks still in hand. I headed for the rear, but stopped when Hickok, who must also have heard the shot, came through the back door and without a glance at me continued to the front of the saloon, where he pushed his way through the glass doors. Curiosity got the best of me, and I followed him as far as those doors and peered out at the commotion on Cedar Street.

The Texans from the Alamo had joined the rest of their crowd in the middle of the street, dimly lit by kerosene streetlamps. Closer to me with hands on his hips was Wild Bill, surveying the cowboys but then turning his full attention to Phil Coe, who had a revolver out. It wasn't smoking, but it may as well have been. Upon seeing the marshal's steady frown, Coe lowered his six-shooter and shrugged. The cowboys in the middle of the street stopped milling about. I still only saw whiskey glasses in hands, but I knew some of them must be armed. With the steady gaze of coyotes, they stared at the two large men faced off before them. The rain had stopped, but drops fell from the brims of several hats. I knew something had to give, but I didn't know who would make the first move—Coe, one of the cowboys, or Hickok.

Wild Bill wiped his mouth with the back of his right hand, then lowered the hand quickly so both the left and right one hovered at his belt buckle.

"Who fired that shot?" Hickok asked.

"How many of the boys you figure are heeled?" replied Coe.

"I asked you direct. I want a straight answer."

"Don't get your dander up, marshal. It was *only* me and *only* one shot."

"One is all it takes in the city."

"If one goes absolutely by the book. I wasn't shooting at anyone. I got forty or fifty witnesses right here."

"You shot at something. Maybe you thought you saw the moon. But I don't see a moon shining through those clouds."

"Could be I shot it down."

"Tell me straight, Coe."

"Sure, marshal. If you must know, I took a shot at a stray dog that was looking at me funny."

Alarmed, I pushed open the glass door for a better look, but I didn't step out. Maybe Coe and Hickok saw me out of the corners of their eyes, maybe not. If they did, they knew I was no threat. I wanted to shout out: *What dog? Where is he?* But there was no need. A dog came racing around the corner from Texas Street and, like a bank robber, fled down Cedar Street, managing to get around or through one hundred bowlegs. "Thank God," I said. "Jesse James lives."

Hickok tilted his head in my direction. Maybe he believed the infamous Missouri outlaw was in town to test him the way John Wesley Hardin had. Or maybe he wondered what kind of man would be thanking the Lord at a time like this. Coe saw his opportunity. I saw the jerk of his gun and heard two shots, but it was actually four shots heard as two. One of Coe's bullets hit the ground at the marshal's feet and the other put a hole in the tail of his coat. Hickok's two shots—one from each Colt—were on the mark, both striking Coe in the belly.

As Coe went down, I saw two blurs come around the same corner that Jesse James had. Wild Bill saw them, too, and better than I did. The smaller of the two shadowy figures moved first into Hickok's line of fire. The face wasn't clear, but the pistol carried like a torch was. As quick as thought, the marshal fired.

The man went down fast, and the second, larger figure leaped at the last second to clear the body and then came to a dead stop. Hickok did not fire again. The second man was not armed, and what's more was now easily identified. Like all the cowboys in the street, Deputy Jasper Washington looked sober and paralyzed.

Wild Bill, with his two raised Colts feeling about in the night air like an insect's antennae, addressed the crowd, "If any of you want the balance of these pills, come and get them." Nobody said a word. "Now every one of you mount his pony and ride for his camp and do it damn quick," he added.

The cowboys might still have been stunned, but they all moved down the street. A handful carried off Coe, whose hands pressed against his stomach as if trying to plug the two bullet holes. The doctors couldn't do much for him, but he would hold on in agony for three days before dying. Jasper also moved, but took only a few steps back before he realized that Hickok's *every one of you* order didn't actually include him. The deputy struggled to get any words out. He tried to apologize at first, but then abruptly damned himself for getting there too late.

"I should have been here," he said. "I was having a late supper with . . . It doesn't matter why, goddamn it. What's the use of a famous marshal like you having a big black deputy if that deputy can't get his big black rump where it ought to be! I heard the gunfire, just like Mike Williams did, and we both came running. I knew it *must be* more than cowboys shooting at streetlamps. I never been one for hurrying my feet, but I stayed right on his tail, and I . . ."

"Whose tail?" Wild Bill asked.

It was me who answered. Along with a horse doctor, who was desperately trying to find one vital sign in the dead man, I knelt over the former part-time night jailer who never had said more than a few words to me but for some reason had stuck up for me that very evening in the Alamo. I was weeping so patheti-cally someone might have thought my mother had just died. Still, I paused long enough to utter, "It's Mike Williams—killed, Bill." I almost always said Mr. Hickok or Marshal Hickok, but this was no time for formality.

My words didn't register with Wild Bill at first. He was in a stupor. Jasper had to guide the marshal's hands so the pair of deadly Colts could be holstered. The legendary Hickok had killed before, but never a friend. "On the bright side, you didn't shoot me, too, though I must have made a large and tempting target running at you that way," said Jasper, but his attempt at humor didn't register with the marshal. Jasper began patting his best friend on the back, but gently as if afraid he might ac-cidentally crack the marshal's spine. When I felt a hand on my own back, my entire body jerked forward and my nose flattened against the chest of the dead man. I quickly straightened and turned. It was only Crooked Nose Jack.

"Land's sake," he said. "Hickok did this?"

My eyes dried fast. "Quiet. He feels awful."

"He can't feel anything now, Zach. He's dead."

"I mean Bill . . . Marshal Hickok."

"How many does that make now for Wild Bill? I've lost count."

"Not that many. Not as many as people say. Anyway, it was an accident, a terrible accident."

"Whatever it was, I'm damn disappointed. I was in the Bull's Head. That's where I thought all the action would be tonight."

Wild Bill suddenly snorted and stamped his foot like a wild stallion. He came right up to us without a word, scooped up Mike Williams, carried him into the Alamo, and laid him gently on the billiard table as if putting a baby into a crib. He didn't linger. He marched right back out, tears galloping down his face. Jasper tried to speak to him again, but Hickock brushed right past his deputy and then marched down the empty street swinging his elbows from side to side as if there were people trying to block his path. Jasper, Jack, and I followed him to the Bull's Head, where he found a couple people to knock aside on his way to the bar.

"A bottle," he demanded from the barkeep. "Leave it, and you leave. Everyone get the hell out! Can't a man *ever* drink in peace?"

"Let's go," Jack said. "It's over."

"I don't think so," I said. "Not for Wild Bill."

"He doesn't mean me," Jasper said, stepping well inside the saloon before hesitating.

"You too, deputy," said Hickok, looking into the mirror over the bar to see who was behind him. "I want the Bull's Head clear."

"I'm staying with you," Jasper said. "I want to help."

"You want to help, take care of Mike."

"It's too late," Jack said. "Mike Williams is dead."

Now Wild Bill did turn and shot Jack a look halfway between contempt and revulsion. "You still here?" he asked, grinding each word out through pinched lips.

I started to pull Jack away, but there was no need. He was backing up faster than I could pull.

Jasper held his ground in the middle of the saloon, but in a rare display of nervousness began apologizing for being there or not being there—it wasn't clear.

"He has a wife who is ill in the City of Kansas," Wild Bill said, his voice now just above a whisper. "He was going to go back to her on a late train tonight anyway. Now he'll just have to be shipped home in a casket."

"Right," said the deputy. "I'll see about the casket."

And life went on for us, the living in Abilene, but the place would never be the same. Marshal Hickok tried to carry on as usual after the double shooting. Outwardly he appeared like his old self, but now he was never on patrol without a shotgun in hand. He received death threats in letters from Texas. One writer said straight out that, even with Coe murdered, the marshal would still get it "before the frost." Another insisted that only a trip to the gallows could tame a "blood thirsty wretch like Wild Bill." Plenty of locals still supported their top lawman, enough so Jasper Washington was able to get contributions toward buying Hickok a specially engraved watch. I contributed to Jasper's cause, but Crooked Nose Jack did not (he claimed Jasper never asked him to). The six-pointed star on the back came with the legend *Marshal Abilene, Kansas.* Also inscribed were these words: *J. B. Hickok from His Friends, October 26, 1871.* Jasper told me he decided not to use the marshal's common nickname, Wild Bill, because he wanted it to be a "distinguished gift of dignity."

Jasper finally got to prove he was a good friend indeed before winter. Maybe most of us had no idea how tormented Mr. Hickok was over the accidental shooting of Mike Williams and disturbed by the hateful mail. But Jasper knew. He saw how that shotgun sometimes shook in the marshal's hands for no reason and how Wild Bill would nervously look at his watch every other minute as if he expected his time would be up at any second. In late November, Jasper finally talked his friend into getting away from Abilene for a short rest. Hickok thought of heading east to the City of Kansas to visit Mike Williams's gravesite, but then realized he wasn't prepared to face the widow just yet. He decided on traveling north to Topeka. Of course, Jasper insisted on going with Wild Bill to ensure the peacefulness of that short rest. It was a good thing he did.

On the platform at the depot in Abilene, Jasper overheard a tall Texan tell his three compadres, "Wild Bill is going on this train." Later, he watched them board. When they sat directly behind the two lawmen, Jasper knew it wasn't by chance. Upon

Jasper's suggestion, he and the marshal changed seats after the train had gone five miles, but then the suspicious-looking quartet did the same. When Jasper convinced Wild Bill he would be able to sleep better at the rear of the rear car, they moved once again. The Texans followed. On two of them, Jasper spotted guns not quite hidden under overcoats. To him, their murderous intentions were clear. Nevertheless, when the train was some ten miles from Topeka, Jasper left Wild Bill with his eyes at least half-closed in the back seat and walked boldly up to the Texans even though he still wasn't carrying a gun himself.

"You boys are disturbing the marshal's peace," he told them.

"The marshal?" said the tallest of the four. "Is that who it is?"

"What's your destination, boys?"

"We aim to stop in Topeka."

"That won't do at all. You've been hounding the marshal. You can't stop at Topeka, that is, if you know what's good for you."

The Texan looked over the enormous size of the deputy who had closed to within a couple feet and then glanced down the aisle where the seated Hickok must have winked or scratched a hip in his half sleep. The tall Texan nodded. "None of us have seen St. Louis," he said. "I might propose to the boys we stop there."

And the other three must have concurred, because after Jasper and Wild Bill climbed off at Topeka, they never saw the Texans again.

The marshal did get his rest, but it didn't help his future outlook in Abilene. In early December, after some debate, the city council members listened to the growing number of farmers in the area and decided to ban the cattle trade. They would notify all interested parties in Texas that the inhabitants of Dickinson County would "no longer submit to the evils of the trade." First, there was another order of business. On December

13 the mayor and the council discharged J. B. Hickok "for the reason the city is no longer in need of his services" and added that "all of his deputies be stopped from doing duty." A new man was immediately appointed city marshal at half Hickok's salary.

His eight months in office were over, but Hickok remained in Abilene to the end of the year as he negotiated with the council for not only his last month's salary but that of Deputy Washington and Jailer McCall. Jasper said Wild Bill was offered the position of marshal in Newton, Kansas, but turned it down because he had no intention of becoming a professional peace officer and had a strong hankering "to get away from it all." I never did get a full last month's salary, but Hickok generously gave me ten dollars out of his own pocket before he left. And I received another ten dollars along with a ton of well wishes and promises to meet again from Jasper Washington, the only one in Abilene who wouldn't allow Wild Bill to get away from him.

CHAPTER TWENTY-TWO:
ENTERTAINMENT IN ELLSWORTH

After Abilene quit the cattle trade, it became considerably quieter everywhere, including the jail, where I no longer worked, and Drovers Cottage, where I no longer lived. I suppose young men who farmed instead of cowboyed caused trouble from time to time and landed in jail, but that was no concern of mine. I went from being a jailer to a clerk at the Great Western Store. Crooked Nose Jack teased me about that, saying being a store clerk in Abilene in 1872 was no different than being a store clerk in any hick farming community east of the Mississippi. He shouldn't have complained much, because his winnings were less than moderate in the few gambling opportunities he found, and my salary was what kept a roof over our heads at a boardinghouse where prostitutes once plied their trade. We had lost our second-story room at Drovers Cottage when the Gores, with no drovers in sight, decided to only make use of the first floor. Not long after that, the couple shut it down entirely and tore down nearly half of it to rebuild sixty miles down the tracks at Ellsworth, which had become Kansas's new longhorn metropolis.

"I hate to say it," Jack said in late March for maybe the fortieth time, "but there ain't no future in Abilene."

"That's not what the *Abilene Weekly Chronicle* says. It says we can now have 'a substantial, prosperous, and moral town.' I know business is still good at the Great Western."

"Great, my ass. Seed, overalls, and farm implements." Jack

yawned, once naturally and twice more on purpose. "You may as well bury me out on the lone prairie with a Great Western shovel."

"It's not so bad. Abilene's a steady place now with permanent citizens and permanent growth. Beats being a town where business flourished only for three or four months when the cowboys were here and then fell flat the rest of the year."

"Quit quoting the damn *Chronicle*. Don't you ever get tired of reading about how nothing is happening?" Jack snatched the newspaper out of my hands and was about to toss it aside when a word or two must have caught his eye. "Listen to this, Zach: The writer says right here, 'Anyone who likes bad whiskey, bad women, and glories in deviltry in general, must go elsewhere to find such things.' He should have added *good poker*. That can't be found here either. They should change the name of Texas Street to Kansas Farm Road."

"I'm happy to have full-time employment. You should try it sometime."

"I should try the poker tables in Ellsworth. The gamblers and harlots have all flocked there. I hear it calling me."

"Well, it's not calling me. Mr. Hickok didn't become marshal there. I don't know where he and Jasper wandered off to, but I doubt it is there, so I have no interest in Ellsworth. The paper says that . . ."

"No self-important Wild Bill and no black lackey wearing badges. All the better."

"Jasper isn't a lackey. He's Hickok's friend."

"Sure. If I never call the bluff of either of them again, that's too damn soon."

In June 1872 we were both in Ellsworth, Kansas. You might say that Crooked Nose Jack wore me down with his pestering. He simply refused to go without me, maybe out of brotherly love but more likely because I was the one to fall back on whenever his monetary resources grew low. I held out and onto my job as long as I could. But then one evening on the last day of spring somebody used a key to get into the Great Western Store and rifled the hidden cash box. I was suspected of being an accomplice because my store key and a button from my shirt were discovered on the floor, I knew where the cash box was hidden under the counter, and my half brother Jack had appeared that same night at one of his frowned-upon, backroom poker games flashing greenbacks and betting far too much.

A policeman and my boss greeted me at the store when I reported as usual to work the next morning. I was fired, and the only reason I wasn't arrested was because I had an alibi. At the time of the robbery I was playing checkers with the boarding-house owner, a nimble-fingered almost old maid who just loved saying "crown me," and knew I was the only member of the male species willing to give her a game. Jack hadn't turned up, and a lawman who looked more like a lifetime bank clerk than a Wild Bill warned me to let him know the next time I saw my brother or face the full force of the law. Of course, I didn't comply. Jack showed up two days later during my evening visit to the outhouse. In one hand he held a duffel bag; in the other, two train tickets to Ellsworth, some sixty-five miles farther west.

We were again the guests of Jim and Lou Gore at the Drovers Cottage, relocated from Abilene to Ellsworth's South Main Street. We took a third-story nicely furnished room, one of eighty-four, and enjoyed superb meals in a dining room that comfortably seated one hundred. This luxury was made possible by the money Little Jack stole from the Great Western store in Abilene. It was something we didn't talk about, and I didn't allow my guilt over the matter to stop me from sleeping and eating well at the new Drovers. The Gores and everyone else in Ellsworth seemed blissfully unaware that the McCall brothers had hopped a night train out of Abilene and could never show their faces in that town again. Not that there was any reason to go back. I didn't need to find employment again right away because Jack was making the most of the unlimited gambling opportunities in a bustling cowtown in which he counted seventy-five other professional gamblers and knew which ones to avoid. He sat in on games where he went up against tall, longhaired Texas herders and other unsuspecting prey. He won something virtually every night that summer. Whether he needed to resort to sharp tricks, I didn't ask, because the money kept rolling in, and nobody pulled a gun on him or anything like that.

"A hell of a town," Jack said on a July night when he came back late with whiskey on his breath and told me about the record-sized pot he had just won. "One thousand head of people and a hundred thousand head of cattle—a profitable ratio for a gambling man."

"Maybe we should put some of the money in the D. W. Powers & Co. bank."

"And out of the thousand, there are only about two dozen of the terribly moral crowd." He poked me in the chest and then flicked the finger under my chin to make sure he knew where I stood, even though I was still lying on my side in bed. "It's *my* money."

"It was just a thought."

"Beeves going for as much as twenty-two dollars. Lots of money to be made before the drovers go home. You ever thank me for talking you into coming here to El Dorado, Kansas?"

"It wasn't talk that got me here. It was robbery."

"It was worth it to get to Ellsworth. Show a little gratitude, Zach. We're living like kings, are we not?"

"I suppose." He was living like a king. I was just a hanger-on in the king's court. More and more I was feeling like a court jester, one who didn't even have to provide entertainment.

"Suppose? I do everything for you here except blow your nose."

"You could let me sleep."

"Damn it, Zach. We got it made, best we've ever had it. One of the good losers at my table tonight handed me a pamphlet that spells it all out. It states flat out there's no better place on Earth for the moo beasts to get to on account of we're blessed with top-of-the-line Kansas Pacific shipping facilities, surrounded by abundant grass and water, and free from the petty annoyances of settlers who complain about longhorns trespassing upon cultivated fields." Jack fished in his pockets for the pamphlet but couldn't find it. "I reckon I misplaced it, but that's the *only* thing I lost tonight."

I made a snoring sound though I was now wide awake. "It can't last forever," I muttered. "Look what happened in Abilene."

"You got a way of putting a damper on everything, Zach. Some Wild Child you are."

"Never did like being called that. And right now, I'm feeling like I'm Worthless in Ellsworth."

"Don't worry, Brother, I won't throw you out onto the street."

I hung my head, couldn't even look him in the eye.

"I think I know what you need, Brother. It's what every king needs—a queen! And don't be so damn moral about it. I can introduce you to Josie Bell, the queen of Kansas whoredom."

"The copper-haired lady you say cost you a pretty penny the other night?"

"It's my money, Brother. Madam Bell is worth every penny, pretty or ugly. You'll be hooked, and she won't throw you back. What you got to lose?"

"Belle spelled with two *e*'s?"

"What? Just one. Thinking of your mother again, eh?"

"Belle Bragg wasn't my mother. She was . . ."

"I know, I know, our father's paramour, the queen of the Daniel's Den whoredom."

"Don't speak ill of Belle."

"She is what she is, Zach . . . or was. Some of them types don't last long."

"She will. Belle takes care of herself. What's more, she's decent. She took care of me after Virginia Reel ran off to the West with some stranger."

"Like you did many years later, except your mother departed with a white man, and you left with Jasper Washington."

I ignored that comment. I didn't miss the mother I never knew, and lately I hadn't been thinking much about my friend Jasper or where he might be. But I was missing Belle more than ever. She wouldn't let me wallow in self-pity or whatever I was wallowing in these days in Ellsworth. I wondered if she was still at the Daniel's Den pleasing her husband, Robert "Raccoon" Gentry, and looking after Angus Doyle's ladies.

"Belle raised me right," I muttered. "Now let me sleep."

"You find fault in how Hannah McCall raised me, you bastard?"

I figured it was the whiskey talking, so I said nothing.

"What the hell is wrong with me? I mean, what the hell is wrong with *you* to think something is wrong with me? I mean, really. Am I not my brother's keeper?"

I turned my back to him and clutched my pillow tight to my head.

"There were times in Louisville, I may as well have been a dead critter, the way she picked at me like a buzzard." He plopped onto the bed. "You'll never know!"

"I saw a little of that when I was there during the war and . . ."

"She ain't your mother. You ain't got the right to talk against her. Only I can."

"Sorry. I . . ."

"She hated you for invading our so-called happy home. Every day you, the misbegotten son, reminded her of Fat Jack's big mistake."

"I stayed in the attic, out of the way."

"She never missed an opportunity to disparage me for taking care of your every need up there. Sort of what I'm doing now, eh, Bastard McCall?"

That didn't deserve an answer. He was right, but he had no right to make such a point of it. After all, I'd supported him plenty of times when he was down on his luck.

"I bet she's still pampering my three wretched sisters, dressing them in lace and trying to turn them into proper Southern belles—an impossible task, let me tell you. As for me, she wanted a milksop for a son, not a full-grown man. If she'd gotten her way, she'd have put me in a dress—as if having three damn daughters wasn't enough already. Nobody ever accused the old lady of being fair minded."

"Fat Jack never did. Sometimes I heard him complaining about his wife to Belle Bragg and some of the other ladies at the Daniel's Den."

"Whores, you mean, nothing but whores. I don't blame him for leaving Louisville on his whiskey-selling trips any chance he got so he could get away from my mother and sisters and pay for all those whores. Fat Jack never treated me right, though. Never. I was his son, his only actual legitimate son, but he acted half the time like I was dirt. Look what he did to me with his fists, for God's sake! The evidence never goes away. He gave me the crooked nose of an old witch."

I turned myself over so I was facing him again. He tried to stand up but couldn't manage it and sat back down on the edge of the bed.

"It gives you character," I suggested.

"When it comes down to brass tacks," he said, glaring at me,

"Fat Jack's a fat bastard."

"But not like me, right?"

"Hell, no." He tapped my cheek a little too hard. "You're a legitimate bastard. Our father is strictly self-made."

"He was usually all right by me. At least you can't blame him for your crossed eyes."

"What?" He tried to look at me straight, which wasn't possible. "They're only a little crossed, you goddamn legitimate bastard."

"Sorry. I realize nobody's perfect. My ears stick out a little."

"A lot, Brother, a lot. Not that it'll matter to Josie Bell. My eyes don't bother her one bit. For that matter, she calls this beak of mine 'manly.' " He reached up to touch the tip of his nose but missed and poked himself in the left eye. "She's a queen in her profession for damn sure, but she's no different from any other wagtail in one respect: the only thing that counts is cash on the barrelhead. I'm not uncharitable when it comes to Josie, so don't let me stand in your way. In fact, I'll loan you a few bucks so you can call on her. It'll do you a world of good, Brother."

By summer's end I had not paid for Madam Bell to undress or even addressed her or any of Ellsworth's collection of sporting girls. But I did meet Lucinda, the daughter of one of the men in the Powers banker family, one late September afternoon when I had decided to finally stop living off Little Jack (he had started breaking even more than winning at the gambling dens) and seek a job at Nagle's livery stable. I told the boss man I needed work because sitting around all the time had started to stick in my craw. He was unsympathetic and flat out said no.

"I have experience in this field," I assured Mr. Nagle.

"Outstanding," said a young chestnut-haired lady whom I had never laid eyes on before. Mr. Nagle nodded to her and quickly took the reins of her horse, also a chestnut. By the look of the lady's wind-blown hair and dusty riding dress, I figured she had been out galloping in the pastures favored by Texas steers. She looked me over just as completely. "I like a young man with experience," she said, "especially when he comes with kind eyes, high cheekbones, a strong jaw, and a fine Roman nose."

I kind of lowered my head in embarrassment, but she must have thought I was bowing to her because she murmured with approval and gently touched the top of my head as if laying a crown on top. "Forgive my forwardness, sir," she said. "But how often do you go riding? Do you wager on your races, or do you mount up simply for the pleasure of a ride in the country, as yours truly has a habit of doing?"

"Well, I . . . don't actually ride, you know, as much as I'd like."

"Who does? Excuse me, but my name is Lucinda Powers. My father runs the biggest bank in town, though last I heard it was Ellsworth's only legitimate bank. We do all the Kansas-Pacific banking business. I am free most days, except once or twice a month when I do a little bookkeeping for Daddy, and every night that I'm not out dancing."

"Oh, I see," I said, but I didn't really see. "Dancing, huh?"

Mr. Nagle had returned and seemed content to chew on a piece of straw and observe us. That made me even more uneasy.

"I haven't seen you at any of the dances," Miss Powers said. "You do dance, don't you?"

"Sure. You know how it goes, when I'm not too busy."

"Busy with business?"

"Not terribly. I mean, I am usually free myself, except of course when I am occupied."

"Naturally. You ride and you dance and you have your own business—how stupendous! Your name, sir, if I might be so bold as to inquire?"

"Me? Zach McCall is what they call me."

"You have some other name?"

"No. That's all there is to it. I'm just plain old Zach to most everyone."

"Not so old, plain old Zach. And so modest."

Mr. Nagle shook his head. Actually, he had been shaking it for some time. I didn't have a job or a horse. I had never in my life asked a woman to dance, though back at the Daniel's Den when I was a boy Belle Bragg and other horizontal ladies used to get a hoot out of getting off their backs and swinging me around or even sweeping me off my little feet.

"If you aren't too occupied on Saturday night, Zach McCall, the Ellsworth Dancing Club has been running a series of dances at Drovers Cottage twice a month. The next one is Saturday night. Sometimes we dance till morning."

I nodded and shuffled my feet. "Yes, I heard—that is to say, I live there." From my room on the third floor I had often heard the music playing below but had never sought to be part of the merriment.

"I am certain several of the gentlemen from Texas plan to attend," she continued.

"Oh. But I'm not from Texas."

"I could tell that right off. You don't smell like a cow."

I wasn't sure if she was teasing me or not, but I was glad I had taken a bath and shaved that morning to impress Mr. Nagle, not a girl.

"Perhaps I didn't make myself perfectly clear, Mr. McCall," she said. "I wish to have a steadfast escort to these dances whom I can count on in case of any, shall we say, rude behavior. The gentlemen from Texas choose to add whiskey to the punch, and the next thing you know, they're acting like anything but gentlemen."

I wasn't sure why she assumed I always acted like a gentleman or that I even knew how a gentleman should act, but I decided to behave as one now.

"Yes, Miss Powers," I said. I even thought about gently lifting her hand and kissing the back of it, as I must have seen some drunk do back at the Den. But Lucinda Powers had her hands on her hips, and I didn't want to disturb either of those. "You have nothing to fear," I assured her, though she looked plenty self-assured. "I am at your service. What I mean is, you can count on me."

"I knew I could the minute I saw you. You have the look of a man who knows how to treat a lady . . . and, if need be, to provide protection."

I was already counting myself out, but I crossed my arms and said, "You bet."

"You can pick me up at ten minutes to eight on Saturday. The Powers house is the brick one with the green shutters at the east end of town. I'll tell Daddy you are expected. He's had a devil of a time keeping those boisterous cowboys away from our door, even with a shotgun. Until Saturday, Mr. McCall, or should I say *plain old* Zach?"

"Until Saturday, Miss Powers."

I became transfixed watching her riding dress ride her full backside as she walked away. And when she was out of sight, I kept staring at the space she had occupied until Mr. Nagle nudged me with a sharp elbow.

"She'd be some catch for any man, her father being the big banker man and all," he said. "But on horseback I don't figure any man can catch her. She rides like the wind."

"I don't plan to try."

"Gonna try to win her on the dance floor, then? They say she can dance all night."

"Who is *they*?"

"The Texas boys."

"Oh."

"She must see something in you, McCall, is it? No offense, but I don't get it."

"I don't either. I mean, I'm *not* Wild Bill Hickok, but I'm not nobody. I was bred in Kentucky."

"But now you're burnt toast in Kansas." Mr. Nagle tossed his head and whinnied like one of the occupants of his stable.

"Whatever I am now, I'm hoping to be working for you tomorrow, sir. I don't ride horses much, but I know them and . . ."

"You figure, Miss Lucinda Powers will be impressed with a stable hand, do you?"

"I didn't even know she'd be here. I came here for a job."

"Sorry, son. It's the end of the season. Only got some Texas stragglers around now. But you come back and see me next June when the drovers return. That is, if you aren't too busy dancing."

I felt like making him eat that straw dangling from his fat lip, but I just walked away, for I suddenly had no wish to tend to any horses, with one possible exception.

The odds were clearly against a romance blossoming, considering who she was, who her father was, and what I was *not*. But such odds-defying happenings do happen, and when they do, they often can't be explained. I won't even try to explain why Lucinda Powers took to me, for the simple reason I never truly figured it out. Only for a short while could I hide the fact that I was a mediocre rider at best and had never owned a horse in my life. She found my deception adorable because, at least in her eyes, it showed how much I desperately wanted to please her.

My lack of dancing ability didn't add to my adorability, but she was forgiving since her nimbleness on the dance floor allowed her to avoid my plodding feet, and I readily agreed to intense private dance lessons in the drawing room of the Powers's spacious brick home. Those lessons brought us closer together, you might say, and soon enough we were flying about the Drovers Cottage dance floor and were the talk of the Ellsworth Dancing Club. My lack of spending money was no problem at all. She had plenty to spend, and she spent enough on both of *us* to make Little Jack jealous. Her banker father wasn't an obstacle to our happiness because he realized his daughter's choices for finding an upstanding male companion in Ellsworth were limited. Mr. Powers didn't put an arm around my shoulders and call me "son," but he didn't reject me, either. In the words of Lucinda, "At least Pappy Powers knows I'm *not* dancing regular with a cowboy, gambler, or other miscreant."

The relationship between Lucinda and me was severely challenged on September 26, 1872. That evening, instead of another dance at the Drovers, a ball was held on the corner of Lincoln at the redbrick Grand Central, said to be the grandest and costliest hotel west of the Missouri, not counting two in Topeka. Lucinda bought me a Sunday suit for the occasion, and that irritated Crooked Nose Jack, who attended alone and wearing a well-worn jacket that needed elbow patches. Jack hadn't been able to avoid the other professional gamblers forever and had recently lost a record pot to a traveling card sharp who called himself the "Kansas City Kid" even though he was gray at the temples. This old Kid was also at the dance. He cut in to dance once with Lucinda, which seemed to please her. I thought nothing of it because Jack soon cut in on him, and the Kid and I went off into a corner and had a nice chat about none other than Wild Bill Hickok.

It turned out that Wild Bill had spent most of the summer in the City of Kansas gambling in various saloons and betting at the racetracks. Hickok had also acted in late August as a master of ceremonies for a show featuring Sac and Fox Indians engaged in a "Grand Buffalo Hunt." The Kid had attended and told me that, while the action seemed "realistic enough for city folk," the audience reaction had been mixed. Some fellows who had once hunted buffalo on the Texas Panhandle jumped out of their seats and began waving their hats and hollering that the whole thing was a sham. When they approached the stage, they were held back by Bill and his brawny companion. That bit of information, of course, particularly intrigued me.

"By any chance did this brawny companion of Mr. Hickok have dark skin?" I asked.

"Black as the devil's hat."

"Jasper! I know him."

"That right? You know some interesting people." He pointed across the dance floor.

"You mean Jack McCall, who you nearly cleaned out the other night? He happens to be my brother, well, half brother, but I don't play poker."

"I don't mean him at all. I'm talking about the lady in the red dress. Said her name was Lucinda."

"Right, Lucinda Powers. Excellent dancer."

"Excellent form. Matchless. Like a spirited filly. I intend to dance with her again. No objections?"

"No. It's a free . . . eh, dance floor."

"Glad to hear it. We'll see if your half brother is just as obliging."

As the Kansas City Kid walked away, I called out to him. "You know if Jasper is still in the City of Kansas—that is to say, Jasper Washington and Wild Bill Hickok?"

"No idea about the colored colossus," the Kid said over his shoulder as he kept walking. "Bill might be, but I'm not sure. His luck was running out, and he talked about finally heading back to Springfield to visit friends from the war."

The Kansas City Kid stopped in his tracks halfway to Jack

and Lucinda, who had stopped dancing. Two lanky, long-haired fellows who could only have been Texas cowboys had them surrounded with their widespread stances and long, active arms. One was pawing Lucinda. The other was pushing Jack. I was trying to make sense of it all when Jack took a swing at one of the Texans, hitting him in the jaw but to little effect. That Texan quickly responded, knocking Jack to the floor and then jumping on him to punch some more. Meanwhile, the other cowboy began swinging Lucinda around so hard that her feet started flailing three feet in the air. I took one step toward them but then froze. The Kansas City Kid played it differently. He ran to the scene and grabbed the offending cowboy from behind, which freed Lucinda. While he kept a lock on the Texan's arms, Lucinda started kicking the bad dancer in the shins, to the delight of the crowd. Meanwhile, although I was probably the only one to notice, the other Texas cowboy stopped wrestling Jack and, like a gentleman, helped him to his feet.

I couldn't quite digest what I was seeing, and what happened next was even more bewildering. Jack and his newfound friend from Texas walked up to the bandstand together, having reached some kind of understanding, and in piercing voices demanded that the band play "Dixie." Other dancers protested, and shouting followed. The Texan pulled his pistol and fired a wild shot that might have ricocheted off one of the brass instruments before striking an innocent dancer in the right calf. Only then did Lucinda stop kicking and the Kid release her target. The commotion continued in and around the bandstand, but after awhile I turned my attention to the punch-bowl table at the other side of the room. The best female rider and dancer in Ellsworth and the Kid from the City of Kansas stood next to the punch bowl but even closer to each other. Neither of them was drinking punch. It would have been impossible, what with their lips pressed together the way they were.

CHAPTER TWENTY-THREE: GOING TO THE CITY OF KANSAS

The days grew short and the nights grew long in Ellsworth. I never attended another dance, with or without Lucinda Powers. I slipped back into my stagnation, spending most of my time brooding in my third-story room at the Drovers. I truly believed I was brokenhearted, since the banker's daughter was my first love—not counting, of course, the come-and-go crushes on much older, infinitely more experienced working girls back at the Daniel's Den or the wartime flirtations with Southern belles like Frances Clayton in Knoxville, Tennessee. My eyes and ears in town, Crooked Nose Jack, let me know each time he saw Lucinda and the Kansas City Kid carrying on about town and even clipped a short item from a December *Ellsworth Reporter* that read: "Our celebrated high-stakes visitor known far and wide across our state as the Kansas City Kid has again extended his presence in our fair city at least through New Year's as he continues to keep company with Miss Lucinda Powers, the most vivacious member of the prominent Powers banking family. The father of the belle of the ball was quite ill but is better now."

It was enough to get me to stop reading the local paper. That was a good thing, because I later learned that misdeeds by Jack McCall earned him three mentions of arrest in the *Reporter* (although once he was only referred to as "the cross-eyed gambler previously headquartered at the Ellsworth Billiard Saloon"). It seems Crooked Nose Jack had been emboldened by three hard-drinking Texans who had stayed on to help tend the cattle wintering over in the region. One of them was the fellow he had tangled with and then befriended at the Grand Central ballroom—Jim "Rowdy" Favor.

Once, Jack and Rowdy were arrested on a Sunday for trying to again force "Dixie" on innocent citizens, in this case the congregation at the Holy Apostles Episcopal Church. Next, all four were arrested for entering the Ellsworth Billiard Saloon, breaking up the establishment with cue sticks, and forcing out into the street anyone who refused to drink with them and denounce six detested men—General George Armstrong Custer, General Nelson Appleton Miles, General Winfield Scott Hancock, General Phil Sheridan, William F. Cody, and James B. Hickok. Finally, Jack was arrested alone when a policeman asked Josie Bell to pay a fine as a madam and Jack aggressively protested that the hard-earned money he had just paid her with *must not* be turned over to a "lousy law dog too lazy to catch a real crook." I heard about these arrests from Jack himself, and, though his jail time was the bare minimum, he expressed the anger of a man who had been sentenced to life in prison. He vowed vengeance.

"I'm going to leave my mark on this damned town before we leave," he told me the day he was let out of jail so he wouldn't have to spend Christmas Day behind bars.

"We're leaving?" I said, not much caring if I stayed or went and much too used to such talk from Jack. I was lying in bed trying to carve a horse out of a piece of cottonwood with a knife I had borrowed from him. Carving this particular piece had been my main occupation for three weeks. I had some peculiar notion I'd give it to Lucinda Powers as a Christmas gift to show her I had no hard feelings toward her just because she had reached the obvious conclusion that the Kansas City Kid was a better man than me. Trouble was twofold—I still resented that so-called Kid like hell, and my horse looked more like a buffalo that had jumped off a cliff and crippled itself.

"You got any objection?"

"None I can think of. Where we headed?"

"City of Kansas."

"How come?"

"That's where Rowdy and I aim to go. You got something against the City of Kansas?"

I shrugged. I had helped build a bridge there. I had been somebody there, or nearly so. I only had something against the Kansas City Kid, and he was in Ellsworth for an extended stay.

"We'll go by train, of course."

"That costs money. Nobody's paying me for carving. And your luck hasn't been running too good since the Kansas City Kid won that huge pot from you."

"Never mind that. I hate the son of a bitch as much as you do, but nothing to be done about him. But there's something I can do about moving on. I'll have the train fare tonight. We leave at dawn. Call it my Christmas present to you, Brother."

"All right. I have one for you, too, Jack." Before starting on the wooden horse, I had gotten overly ambitious and tried to carve a Colt 1851 Navy revolver for him, but after doing a little too much cutting and trimming, it more closely resembled a derringer.

"Aren't you going to ask me how I'm going to get the money tonight?"

"I hadn't planned to. My guess would be by keeping an ace up your sleeve."

"Nothing that crude. I don't even aim to play cards tonight."

"All right, you raised my curiosity. What do you aim to do?"

"Never mind. It'll all get done. Rowdy and I have plans."

There would be no further discussion. Jack took his wooden gun, jabbed me in the chest, took his knife back, and told me,

"Be ready!" on his way out the door. My younger half brother was taking charge of our lives, but I didn't protest. I packed my few belongings, including my present for my lost love, and lay back in bed with my boots on.

I only learned what had transpired that night while on the eastbound train to the City of Kansas on Christmas Day. In short, Crooked Nose Jack took money out of the D. W. Powers & Co. bank without ever having put any in. The Powers family was holding an after-hours Christmas Eve party in the bank when Rowdy Favor, full of padding and dressed up to resemble the jolly, heavyset Santa Claus illustrated by Thomas Nast in an 1863 copy of *Harper's Weekly,* appeared with a sack in hand. By prior agreement with D. W. Powers himself, Rowdy's Santa had arrived to surprise the party guests. From the sack he pulled a bigger surprise—a real Army Colt. He left the door open for Little Jack, who wore an oversized brown coat that made him look far bigger than he was, as well as a bulky black mask that had cow horns attached to it in lieu of a reindeer's antlers. Jack admitted to me that touch was the Texas cowboy's idea of a little joke. He said the only gun he brought to the party was the wooden one I gave him for Christmas.

The two robbers didn't even request the safe be opened. They filled the sack with enough cash and other goodies (including champagne from New York and homemade gingerbread men) to meet their needs. They found the cash in various drawers, on countertops, and on the persons of many in the bank party, which included D. W. Powers; three of his trusted employees; two of his nephews involved in the family business; his daughter and part-time accountant, Lucinda; and the man she may or may not have been engaged to, the Kansas City Kid. The only partygoer who tried to act heroic was the Kid, and when he charged like a bull, Rowdy Favor was forced to buffalo him—that is, smash Lucinda's paramour over the head with the butt of his Colt.

I must confess that in the passenger car, when I heard of this violent act at the bank, I was not horrified. In fact, I smiled and thought more highly of Rowdy. The Kansas City Kid might have been a better man than me, but, still, he had stolen my girl. His getting bashed on his officious noggin that way felt nearly like retribution. Rowdy told me he hadn't hit the Kid hard enough to do any permanent damage, though he figured it had taken most of the starch out of him. That was good enough for me. I also took a certain pleasure in knowing that Lucinda and her moneyed Powers family were forced to give up some of their riches. No great harm done, I told myself, for they could certainly afford it.

What's more, I couldn't help but admire how the Texan and the Kentuckian, cleverly disguised as Santa and a misdirected reindeer respectively, had pulled off the robbery without being recognized or becoming suspects. We saw a policeman at the train station early that morning, seemingly checking on who was leaving town, but when Jack casually told him we were going to the City of Kansas to play poker with Wild Bill Hickok, the officer not only believed him but also wished us luck. Not that I completely disregarded the fact a serious crime had been committed back at Ellsworth, or that by departing with Rowdy, Jack, and the loot, I was showing myself to be as guilty as they were. But if I was going to feel guilty, it would have to be another day. Leaving Ellsworth felt like I was finally waking up from a long, dreamless sleep. What's more, I was really hoping we'd find Mr. Hickok in the City of Kansas—not to play poker with, of course, but just to know he was present and that Jasper Washington must be close at hand.

It took only a question or two at one of the big town's saloons to find out we had missed Wild Bill by less than a week. The City of Kansas, Missouri, now had a population of thirty-two thousand, but even so it wasn't a place where a man of Hickok's stature could blend in with the crowd and escape notice. His stature had only grown since leaving Abilene and giving up the lawman business, because newspapers and dime novelists like Ned Buntline continued to write about him as an occasional scout, occasional actor, frequent gambler, and fearless killer of men. What they said about him was even true on occasion. But false tales abounded, such as the one that said Wild Bill Hickok had gone to Nebraska and murdered three Sioux Indians for no apparent reason except to keep his hand in the killing game. It turned out the man behind the murders was a scoundrel named William Kress, who carried the moniker "Wild Bill of the Blue River."

A couple days after our arrival, we learned from the local sporting crowd that the "original" Wild Bill had actually gone to Springfield, Missouri. "Figures," said Crooked Nose Jack. "Bad men are known to return to the scenes of their crimes." My half brother was, of course, rewriting history in his unusual head, since everyone else knew Hickok had shot Dave Tutt fair and square in 1865. He found a believer in Rowdy, who asked Jack a hundred questions about that celebrated gunfight and swore he'd have sacrificed his left eye and his non-shooting hand to have been an eyewitness like Jack.

"I was there, too," I said, as we stood at the bar in Borders Saloon on 3rd Street. Rowdy and Jack had been buying each other rounds of whiskey and ignoring me. "I saw it all on the town square, and it came down to one thing: Wild Bill being the steadier, more accurate shot."

"Says you," said Rowdy. "I prefer to believe the eyewitness from Kentucky. You damn Yankees always stick together."

"You're mistaken. I happen to also be from Kentucky. It was a greatly divided state during the war."

"Bunch of namby-pambies straddling the fence. Nothing like Texas."

"Your own governor, Sam Houston, was against the Confederacy."

"We got rid of Sam soon enough. You looking to pick a fight with a Texas cowboy? If so, I'm your man." Rowdy lunged toward me, either to attack or just because he no longer was able to stay completely upright. Jack stepped between us, spilling his drink when Rowdy crashed into him.

"My brother's all right, pal," Jack insisted as he staggered some. "He rode alongside the one and only Thunderbolt, the illustrious raider John Hunt Morgan, during the War for Southern Independence."

Rowdy stared at me through bloodshot eyes, trying to make sense of that incredible statement. No doubt to him I neither looked nor acted like someone capable of raiding anything more than a root cellar.

"As for me, Mr. Cow Puncher . . ." Jack was waving like the flag over the Old State Capitol in Frankfort and needed to steady himself by taking hold of Rowdy's left shoulder. "As for yours truly, I never was one on the fence. Sure, I was far too young to join the noble cause, but, by Jefferson Davis, I'd have bagged me a passel of Yankees anyway if not for Mother McCall locking me in the closet for my own damn good."

Rowdy studied the hand on his shoulder as if trying to determine whether he liked it there or not. "You're all right for a couple of Kentucky boys," he finally admitted. "I heard tell that John H. Morgan wasn't a bad fighter, practically worthy of mention in the same breath as the generals from the great state of Texas—Benjamin McCulloch, Walter Payne Lane, Albert Sidney Johnston, John Bell Hood, Lawrence Sullivan Ross . . ." He interrupted what figured to be a long list to whistle "Dixie," but his lips didn't cooperate, so he poured whiskey into Jack's empty glass and then his own glass, even though it was already full.

"Save your breath, Lone Star," said a husky voice that was as easy for me to recognize as my own. "Some of them conspicuous Rebs might have met a bit of success while the South was losing its War for Slavery, but none of them ever had to cross swords with James Butler Hickok, the incomparable Wild Bill."

"Man alive!" shouted Jack. "Where in tarnation did you come from?"

"Same as you, Jack—my old Kentucky home. Nice to see you McCall boys are still respiring."

"You ain't the same as him or me," said Rowdy, spitting out his words. "Not by a long shot. Who do you think you are? And who the hell invited you to this party?"

My reunion with Jasper Washington was delayed because Rowdy didn't wait for an answer. He drained his glass and then took a swing at Jasper with the glass still in his hand. Rowdy's fist connected with Jasper's jaw, and there was a cracking sound. The punch clearly hurt Rowdy far more than it did Jasper, whose head didn't budge. The Texan howled like a lone wolf because the whiskey glass broke in his hand, and because the hand itself broke against the big man's unforgiving jawbone. Rowdy alternated between cursing and moaning as he swayed back and forth until he leaned too far to his left and started to fall over. Jasper caught him and could have easily enough squeezed the life out of him. Instead, he took out a handkerchief and wrapped it around the Texan's bleeding, broken hand.

Misinterpreting that kindness toward his pal as a threat, Crooked Nose Jack snatched a bottle away from the bartender, snuck up behind Jasper, and smashed it down on my friend's head. Jasper's knees buckled, and I finally did something: I tried to catch the big man by darting in front of him and holding my hands palms up. I may as well have been standing in the middle of a storm trying to stop a lightning bolt. I went down on my back, and when Jasper came down on top of me, he brought Rowdy with him, which created a three-man stack on the floor. Jack, who was largely responsible for creating the pile up, laughingly described what he saw as "a choice cut of Texas beef sandwiched between two slices of Kentucky-bred bastards, the white slice on the bottom, the black one on top." He thought himself quite clever, but I told him he was a fool as I struggled to get out from under Rowdy and Jasper. I'd been hearing remarks about being bred in Kentucky all my life.

"Better watch out when Jasper regains his senses," I advised Jack after finally getting free of Rowdy. "Jasper doesn't take to being manhandled by anyone. He'll make you pay for using that bottle on him."

And Jasper did so in the following weeks, but it was nothing done physically. Jasper didn't lay a finger on Jack. Instead, he followed him around from poker table to poker table at the numerous gaming houses and saloons in the city with one purpose in mind—to beat Jack at his own game, five-card stud. Jasper was content with modest winnings as long as he took pots away from my half brother. But that wasn't the worst of it for Jack. Rowdy Favor, once sobered up and healing well enough from his badly cut hand, forgot all about his confrontation with Jasper. It turned out he had done plenty of herd work with black cowboys both back in Texas and on the trails north to the Kansas cow towns of Abilene and Hays City.

"It don't matter none that I was all in for the Confederacy," Rowdy told Jasper over dinner at Coates Steakhouse, while Jack and I listened from across the table. "Those colored boys knew I never owned a slave. They were right by my side from the get-go, engaged in Indian fighting, shooting, roping, dare-devil riding, reveling with doves of the roost, bending elbows, and other such pleasurable pastimes. You give me a fair shake and got sand just like them, except you're twice their size. You're a big man, Jasper Washington, too big for Kansas. You'd fit right well in Texas."

"A right fine speech, Rowdy," said Jasper, applauding by striking his steak knife against his fork. "But I'm no cowboy. I'm a full-grown man who eats cows." He took a big bite of his steak. Rowdy laughed, and I joined in. Jack didn't. "I showed I can lick any man in the states of Kentucky, Missouri, and Kansas." He waved the knife and then pointed it at the crooked nose of Jack, who recoiled so hard he half fell out of his chair. Rowdy laughed harder while Jasper took his time chewing. "Perhaps someday I'll work up the nerve to head south and take on all you Tex-asses."

Rowdy roared with delight and gave Jasper a slap on the back.

"We might have to call out the Texas Rangers to stop a full-grown man as big and bad as you," Rowdy finally said.

"Ain't it enough that he's making fun of your Texas?" said Jack, who had never once set foot in the state. "You don't *need* to go along with it."

"You rather I talk about *your* Kentucky, Jack?" Jasper asked.

"Just don't say anything bad. It's your Kentucky, too, you know."

"I disown it. Kentucky never did like a free and free-spirited black man who won't back down."

"I thought you were half-bear, half-panther," Jack said, pointing his fork at Jasper but then quickly lowering it to stir the beans on his plate. "I heard you make that boast often enough. You act like you enjoy being some sort of dangerous animal."

Jasper growled like a bear who wanted to resume his eating. He took a smaller bite and didn't speak again until he had finished chewing. "And you, Little Jack, must be half-drunk and half-crazy daring to say something disrespectful nearly direct to my face," Jasper said matter-of-factly. "Isn't your usual way to talk behind a man's back, and sneak attack, and that sort of thing?"

Those words gave Jack pause for thought, but just for a moment. "I wanted to stop you from killing my friend from Texas. I'm half your size. What else could I do but hit you with a bottle? I could have shot you and nobody would have condemned me for that."

"You didn't have to use a whiskey bottle that was full, Jack," said Rowdy. He couldn't help but laugh at his own joke. Nobody else did. "I was out of line that night. It wasn't the first time and won't be the last. But Jasper wasn't about to kill me."

Jack let his fork fall onto the beans and pushed his plate away as if his friend had insulted him. "He might have. He's done it before. Springfield, 1865. He used his animal strength to squeeze one Joe Riggs, a decent gambler, to death in seconds. They would have hung Jasper Washington for murder down there, except he busted out of jail and ran. He can't go back or he'd face the rope. That's why he's not there now with his master. Wild Bill Hickok had to leave him . . ."

"That's enough, Jack," I interrupted. "You're completely out of line. Jasper came to my rescue that day at the school in Springfield. Joe Riggs might have been a decent gambler, but he was far from a decent human being. He was trying to shoot me dead. Jasper wasn't guilty of murder or even manslaughter."

"It was a half bear, half panther who did the slaughtering. But it was a man who was slaughtered." Jack's chair scraped against the floor as he pushed back from the table. "Now, Mr. Joe Riggs was no friend of mine. In fact, he threatened me a time or two. But he wasn't really ever going to shoot me over cards."

"That missing piece of your earlobe says differently."

"That's nothing. And he wasn't actually gunning for you,

Brother. Jasper didn't need to kill Riggs any more than his master needed to kill Dave Tutt."

I had lost my appetite. I pushed my plate aside and shook my head. Jack's recollections were as twisted as a two-headed snake. He must have been more than half-drunk to keep talking that way in front of Jasper Washington, who, to his credit, only smiled and said, "Would you remind me, Zach, to never do anything crazy like that again?"

"I don't think what you did to Joe Riggs was crazy at all," I said. "You saved my life, Jasper."

"I wasn't talking about that. I meant my crazy decision to include your brother when I asked Rowdy Favor and you to join me for Kansas City steaks and good conversation."

"Half brother," was all I managed to say.

CHAPTER TWENTY-FOUR:
HICKOK RETURNS

Rumors of Hickok's death filtered into the City of Kansas in the early months of 1873, and various newspapers reported them as fact. The most alarming report said that two Texas friends of the late Phil Coe caught up to Wild Bill in a saloon outside Fort Dodge and shot him six times, including once in the center of the forehead, the bullet piercing his brain. Most of the people I ran into expressed alarm, like I did, at the revenge killing of the frontier legend. Crooked Nose Jack, on the other hand, thought it justice belatedly served, and Rowdy Favor didn't disagree, since he thought Hickok should pay for unspecified crimes against Texas and the rest of the Confederacy, though Rowdy did regret never meeting up with the "Evil Yankee and personally separating him from his legend." At all of this talk and reaction, Jasper Washington either shrugged like an uncaring soul or smiled like a holy man who knew not only that God existed but also where God was currently hanging his hat, namely Springfield, Missouri.

"Wild Bill wouldn't leave Springfield and go to Fort Dodge without me," Jasper explained when he visited me at the City of Kansas's Elmwood Cemetery, where I had landed a job thanks to my previous experience as an assistant groundskeeper at the cemetery in Lexington, Kentucky. "And, even if he did, how could *any* two men put six bullets in him without themselves getting even a scratch. Nobody could shoot Wild Bill's brains out unless he was tied to a wagon wheel, and there were no wagons in that Fort Dodge saloon. Some folks just want to bury the man. And it sells newspapers!"

Jasper looked me so hard in the eye that I felt guilty and squirmed. I was holding a gravedigger's shovel, but I certainly didn't wish to bury a frontier legend, or anyone else, really. But death was a part of life, and it was my job. "I'm happy Mr. Hickok is in Springfield," I said. "That is to say, I'm happy he's alive and that the papers have it wrong."

"He'll be back before long, and you and everyone else will be able to see for yourselves that it ain't so easy killing Wild Bill Hickok, even without me standing guard. I will feel some better when he's in my sights again, though. We'll gamble here in the big city for a time more, I suspect, and then head west again. A new town was born near Fort Dodge, and the railroad arrived there last September. Dodge City is up and coming in the cattle trade—mark my word. There'll be plenty of opportunities for picking up the cards and laying down the law out that way."

"So, you aim to go out to where Mr. Hickok was *not* shot six times by two men?"

"Rumors don't come true any more than dreams do, Zach. Anyway, Wild Bill was a born gambler and town tamer who has proved to be a terror to evildoers. He'll be fine keeping his back to a wall when possible and, when not possible, having me watching his back. Dodge City is our kind of town. You'd be welcome to come along with Bill and me, of course, preferably without your brother and that Rowdy friend. The Texan is likable enough, but a little of him goes a mighty long way."

"I appreciate you inviting me to come along when you go, Jasper. But I must say, it's not as easy as you might think turning your back on kin, even if they aren't necessarily of the decent sort. Besides, I'm not so sure I want to revisit the wilder parts of the state of Kansas. I got my fill in Abilene and Ellsworth. I've become kind of settled and comfortable in the City of

Kansas, and I have steady work here at Elmwood."

"That's one way of looking at it, if you're an old man. You aren't that, Zach! Of course, if you stick to this dead-end job at the cemetery, you'll be old before your time."

I leaned hard against my shovel, as if it were a walking stick or a crutch. "It's not so bad here," I insisted. "People keep dying in the City of Kansas, naturally, but not at a rate I can't handle. And it's a decent place as far as cemeteries go. There's no looking down on anyone here. What I mean is, we're all underground together."

"I don't follow you, Zach."

"Well, I'm sure you've observed how most Negroes live in a certain part of the City of Kansas, stick to their own kind, and don't fraternize with white men, let alone white women."

"Me being the big exception, of course."

"Yes, very big. My point is, it's different here at Elmwood Cemetery. We allow men of color to be buried in any available plot of any section."

"Is that right? That's mighty big of you. But you best not try to bury me yet, Zach. This big bad black bastard still has plenty of carousing to do!"

I tried to explain that there was no man alive I'd less rather bury than him, but the right words didn't come out. I felt my white skin reddening, and I sighed to try to ease the tingling sensation. Jasper was sympathetic and gave me an enormous, friendly embrace, but it still hurt a little, for sometimes he didn't know his own strength.

Later that March Hickok himself confirmed that he was alive and well in Springfield by writing a couple of letters from there, not to Jasper, but to the editors of two St. Louis newspapers that had published accounts of his being gunned down in a saloon at Fort Dodge. "Wishing to correct an error in your paper of the 12th, I will state that no Texan has, nor *ever will* corral William," he wrote in the first letter. His second letter was much longer: "I wish to call your attention to an article published in your paper of the 19th in regard to my having been killed by Texans. You say when I was murdered it was fulfilling a prophecy that all men of my kind should die with their boots on. Now I would like to know the man that prophesies how men shall die, or classes of men, so that the public may know who is right and who is wrong. I never have insulted man or woman in my life, but if you knew what a wholesome regard I have for damn liars and rascals, they would be liable to keep out of my way." He added, "N. B. Ned Buntline of the *New York Weekly* has been trying to murder me with his pen for years; having failed, he is now, so I am told, trying to have it done by some Texans, but he has signally failed so far."

I was naturally curious as to why Wild Bill Hickok could write to newspapers about being alive but had never taken the time to pen a letter from Springfield to Jasper Washington in the City of Kansas. When I asked Jasper about it, he reluctantly admitted, since he wasn't a "damn liar," that he and Wild Bill had quarreled about the trip to Springfield. Jasper couldn't go back there because of the murder charge against him, and he didn't want Hickok to go alone because of the danger from Dave Tutt's old friends. Jasper then quoted Wild Bill's last speech to him before departing the City of Kansas: "Tutt's old friends know how game I am. They won't start any trouble. Besides, I have more friends there than that damn Southern gambler ever did, and I want to see them. A man gets mighty tired of seeing the same old face day after day, especially when that face is as ugly as a mud fence. No offense, Jasper, but you've been hanging around me more than a wife would. But don't worry, I'm *not* abandoning you. I'll return to Kansas when I've had my fill of Springfield. You know the old proverb 'Absence makes the heart grow fonder'? Well, maybe that's why

I'm bound for Springfield right now and is also the reason that, in time, I'll want to head back up this way."

I told him I understood and that I was sure one quarrel and separation couldn't do permanent damage to their friendship. I added that I looked forward to seeing the great lawman again even if he had apparently given up on being a lawman. Crooked Nose Jack felt just the opposite, telling me: "I don't regret any day in which I don't lay eyes on Hickok. I'm not saying I wish he were dead, maybe just laid up in bed nursing a head wound for the next two dozen years."

After hearing what Hickok wrote in those letters to the newspapers, Rowdy Favor took off his hat and began swatting the first spring flies with it. "I'm hoping Hickok returns real soon," he said. "I wouldn't mind being the first Texan to corral that vainglorious Yankee varmint."

In fact, Wild Bill Hickok did soon return to the City of Kansas. He shook hands with Jasper, a conciliatory act; with me, because I was there; and with Rowdy Favor, who squeezed too hard while announcing he was a true Texan. Little Jack elected to keep his hands in his pockets and to keep his distance, as if afraid Hickok might strike him or at least look upon him with disdain. Truth was, Hickok merely squinted at my half brother and didn't seem to recognize him. It was like old times for Wild Bill and Jasper, drinking, eating, and gambling together on Battle Row, the disreputable six-block district on Main Street between Second Street and Missouri Avenue. But it didn't last more than a week. Things soured fast after that.

What brought it on was Wild Bill's streak of bad luck at the card tables that made him short tempered, and Jasper's good fortunes at the same tables, which made him act superior to Hickok and all the other white players. Wild Bill was forced to borrow money from Jasper and then couldn't pay him back. Jasper held on to Hickok's pocket watch much as Dave Tutt had done in Springfield back in '65. This one, though, was more special—it being specially engraved and given to him by his friends in Abilene in recognition of his service as city marshal. Jasper meant the seizure as a private joke between two tough men who knew each other well, but it backfired. Wild Bill wasn't going to fight his friend over the watch, but he wasn't going to ask for it back or even be seen in the company of his onetime deputy. Hickok walked the streets and back alleys alone and sulking with pockets empty. Me being an early-to-bed, early-to-rise gravedigger, I witnessed almost none of this, but Jack did, and he was delighted. "Wouldn't it be grand if those two blowhards fought tooth and nail to the death and ended up in Elmwood Cemetery," he whispered to me one day while I was at work and he was killing time by loitering among the gravestones. "You could bury them together, Brother. That would serve them right."

A greater problem developed that affected Wild Bill, Jasper, Crooked Nose Jack, and every other gambler in the City of Kansas. A new administration was intent on cleaning up the open wagering activity on Battle Row by conducting periodic raids and arresting men who disregarded the new city anti-gambling ordinances. Jasper kept playing—and winning—underground games. His luck held, and nobody ever arrested him, though his size and skin color made him more conspicuous than a whale in a waterhole. But in mid-April, Jack was arrested for disorderly conduct at the Marble Hall saloon when a fight broke out, not over cards or drinks, but over the meaning of the Kentucky hoe cake that came with the fifty-cent meal of calf brains, corned beef, and cabbage. One gambler contended that Kentucky hoe cake was slave food, as the Negroes cooked them out in the cotton fields. Jack objected to being accused of liking slave food, and one thing led to another, in no small part because Rowdy Favor saw that his friend was overmatched and took a poke at the other gambler. In the end, only the floored Jack was shown the inside of a jail cell because the other gambler was the brother-in-law of the mayor and because Rowdy had gone to the Marble Hall kitchen to get a second helping of hoe cake. That very evening, Hickok was arrested for "vagrancy" and landed in the next cell.

"Bless my stars—how far the great marshal has fallen!" Jack dared say, no doubt because he had been drinking more than a little.

"Maybe so, but I won't stay down long," replied Hickok as he pressed against the iron bars that separated him from Jack. He certainly recognized the man in the next cell by face and voice if not by name. "And you can't fall any lower than where you've always been, mister, worming your way through the dirt."

I know for a fact that Jasper, despite their recent differences, intended to pay Hickok's fine so the famous lawman wouldn't have to spend one night on the wrong side of the bars. And I was considering paying Jack's bail in another day or two. But somebody got there first—Rowdy Favor, with the last of the money from the Christmas Eve robbery of the D. W. Powers & Co. Bank in Ellsworth. It was no surprise that the Texan bailed out his friend Jack, but it wasn't clear at first why he did the same for a man he had only recently met. Not only that, but he invited Wild Bill to join him that very night for a drink at the Faro Number Three, the gambling joint Rowdy liked best because faro, not poker, was his game. Crooked Nose Jack went along with all this, not because he wanted to be Hickok's friend or have *his* best friend become Hickok's friend. He went simply because Rowdy had promised to "corral William," as two other Texans had reportedly done in a Fort Dodge saloon but hadn't actually done because the newspaper report proved terribly false. Jack assumed that "corralling" did not necessarily mean shooting six times, once in the middle of the forehead. He would settle for Hickok's humiliation.

"I'm still not sure why you paid my fine, Mister . . . eh?" Wild Bill said after the second round of drinks, this one bought by Jack.

"Mr. Favor," said Rowdy. "But you can call me Tex."

"And you can call me Kentuck," said Jack. "I was bred in Kentucky."

"I'm from Illinois," said Hickok. "I reckon you can call me Ill."

All three men began a round of laughter, but even while they were doing so, Wild Bill pressed his back against the bar so he could keep an eye on the other two. The only other customers were on the far side of the room at the only faro table in operation. Hickok scowled as he scanned the room, his eyes twitching and turning pinkish. Since Hickok was temporarily broke, Rowdy also bought the third round.

"I wanted to get a closer look at the man who killed Dave Tutt and hates Texans," said Rowdy. "The man whom Buntline can't kill off in those outrageous lying books of his. The man who is supposed to be the greatest lawman the West has ever known, but who is actually a vagrant."

"I'm no vagrant. I've just had a run of bad luck."

"Sure. And you're getting old. It shows in your eyes."

"My eyes? Yes, my eyes." Hickok wiped both eyes with the backs of his hands.

While Wild Bill's hands were raised, Rowdy reached inside Hickok's coat and yanked out both Navy Colts without any trouble. Rowdy took three steps back but kept both six-shooters leveled at Wild Bill's waist. "Can you see me now?" the Texan asked, as he took another two steps back. "How about now?"

"Good enough, Tex." Hickok was blinking fast but otherwise showing no nervousness. "You aim to shoot me or just test my vision?"

"I aim to make you dance. I got you corralled, Yankee. Now dance before I shoot you in your heels."

"This has gone far enough. Don't push your luck."

"My luck? Your luck has run out, dandy man, less'n you dance pronto."

Instead of dancing, Hickok turned slightly to the side to address Jack. "So, you've pretended to be friendly to get me to let my guard down—the two of you. This must be your idea, Mister . . . McCall isn't it? The bad McCall. Out of jail but still worming yourself in the dirt, eh?"

"I didn't know, I swear I didn't," Little Jack said, acting as frightened as if Wild Bill were still armed. "Tell him, Rowdy, I had nothing to do with this, right?"

"It's my show," said Rowdy.

"It appears to have worked," Wild Bill said. "So, what now?"

"I already told you, damnit," Rowdy shouted, which finally caused the faro players across the room to look away from their game. "Dance, Hickok, dance."

Rowdy fired one shot, the slug striking the floor between Hickok's feet, neither of which raised off the floor. The Texan was determined to humiliate Hickok, but before he could fire again, Wild Bill grabbed Little Jack around the neck with one arm and in the same swift motion pulled my half brother in front of himself, essentially turning Jack into a human shield. A second shot immediately followed, and Jack collapsed into Hickok's arms. Wild Bill held him tight until Rowdy dropped both Colts and raced past the faro players, all of whom were now out of their seats, and out the saloon's back door. He then slowly let go of Jack, who slid down onto his knees before dropping to all fours and finally planting his face on the floor with his rear end in the air, blood beginning to soak through the seat of his pants.

Apparently Rowdy Favor didn't stop running. Maybe he

thought he had killed his Kentucky friend, or maybe he knew the law would be after him for the shooting. Most likely, though, he feared Wild Bill Hickok would pick up those two Colts and enact swift revenge.

Crooked Nose Jack acted as if he were dying or at least had been beaten severely by Fat Jack, but the bullet fragment that lodged in his fleshy backside caused only minimal damage and was easily extracted by one of the city doctors. After Jack got the medical attention he needed, I became his nurse for a week and a half as he mostly lay in bed . . . on his stomach, of course. I did owe him. I kept my job at the cemetery, too. I had an understanding boss. He even told me that if my half brother ended up dying, he'd give him a plot in Elmwood at half price.

During this brotherly time together, Jack told me the story of the shooting and tried to convince me he was nothing more than an innocent bystander. He also tried to convince me—as well as himself, I suspect—that Rowdy Favor had never been such a great friend, that Texans were as unpredictable and ready to stampede as their longhorn cattle, and that life would be far more peaceful without Rowdy around. All the days Jack lay there, the slug extracted from his right buttock rested in a jar on the bedside table. He planned on saving it for reasons not quite clear to me at the time. Later, I realized he wanted to have it to remind him what Wild Bill Hickok had done to him at the Faro Number Three in the City of Kansas, Missouri, on April 15, 1873. Later still, I came to realize he really needed no reminder.

Chapter Twenty-Five: Call of the East

Jasper Washington tried to patch things up with Wild Bill Hickok, starting the process by returning his "Marshal Abilene Kansas" watch. Hickok stared at it for a long time as if trying to recognize the face. He didn't say a word. Finally, he pocketed the watch, nodded solemnly, and walked away as if he had important business elsewhere. Jasper started to give chase but halted, maybe because I was standing right there, and he didn't want to appear like some kind of weakling, not that I would ever have thought that.

"J. B. Hickok can go to hell!" Jasper said, his arms crossed, the muscles in his forearms twitching.

"You don't mean that," I said. "He'll come around."

"Where's he going to go, then? The gambling's bad, the money's short, and he has no prospects. I tell you, Zach, Bill's at a loss, has no direction."

"Sounds like Crooked Nose Jack. He's been that way since he got shot in the behind."

"Don't mention Wild Bill and your maddening brother in the same breath."

"Did I do that? Sorry."

"Bill can't see the road ahead. His eyesight is declining as he ages. Of course, even with perfect vision a man can't always see someone sneaking up behind him or how enemies feign friendship to get an advantage. That's why Bill needs me more than ever. But he doesn't realize that. His thinking has become weaker than his eyes."

I thought Hickok had been thinking just fine when he used Jack as a shield from the gun-crazy Rowdy Favor. But I didn't say so. I nodded my head and pursed my lips at the same time.

"The man has me plumb worried," Jasper said.

"I doubt anyone would make the same mistake and arrest Mr. Hickok for vagrancy again."

"He needs to get his self-respect back, and it won't happen here. Bill and I need to get out of the City of Kansas and get into Dodge."

"You're still thinking about Fort Dodge?"

"Dodge City, five miles from the fort. I've been reading about it. It's become a shipping center for buffalo hides, but the cowboys and cows will be coming if I know anything about the state of Kansas. A dozen well-developed murderers walk around unmolested and doing what they please. Some Southern boys lynched a black storeowner the other day. It's a good week when only two men get killed. There are no sheriffs, no constables, no law at all. What Dodge City desperately needs is a town tamer. Who better to step in as marshal than Wild Bill Hickok with me as his deputy, just like old times?"

"It sounds . . . eh . . . dangerous. I thought you wanted to keep him out of danger."

"I'll stick close and do my damned best to watch his back in Dodge. That's better than him walking aimlessly without me on the streets of the City of Kansas."

"But what about his eyesight? Shouldn't a peace officer have good vision? I mean, what if someone challenges him the way Little Dave Tutt did at the town square in Springfield and they face off at one hundred yards? Would Mr. Hickok even be able to see his target?"

"Look, Zach, you might not understand this, being more mild than wild and as cautious as a schoolmarm walking through Battle Row. But sometimes a man can't run or hide. Sometimes a man must stand up for what he believes in, to live up to his purpose in this world."

I must have been taken aback and a little vexed for being compared to a schoolmarm, for I snapped at Jasper: "I'm *no* Wild Child, but I'm *not* that cautious! I ventured out to the frontier with you, didn't I? I'm a gravedigger, aren't I? A lot of people are afraid of ghosts. Not me."

"I apologize. But those ghosts don't carry Colt's revolvers, do they? Anyway, I'm talking about Wild Bill Hickok, not Mild Zach McCall."

"All right, then, but how are you so sure what Wild Bill Hickok's purpose is in this world?" I asked, though I was thinking more about my own purpose in the world. "Maybe he doesn't think risking his life needlessly and going to an early grave is necessarily the best thing for him."

"You don't know Bill the way I do, Zach. He'd agree wholeheartedly with me when I say: *It's far better to be shot down as a marshal than to bite the dust as a vagrant.*"

I didn't argue the point. I was just glad I was neither Wild Bill Hickok, whose celebrity status and reputation as a shootist made him a target for any fame-seeking gunman, nor Jasper Washington, whose bear-like size and coal-colored skin made him a target for any man opposed to Reconstruction. I was pretty much out of touch with both of them for the rest of the spring and into the summer. They came and they went, sometimes together but not always. Neither of them ever left the City of Kansas for more than a couple days, though. I suspect Jasper kept winning enough in the mostly "underground" poker games to stake his friend and keep him from returning to vagrancy.

Crooked Nose Jack was mostly out of touch with them as well. After finally recovering from his buttock wound, he wanted to avoid both of them and played faro instead of sitting in on the few poker games available to him. "The rules are easy, the company is better, and the odds of winning are much higher than poker," he told me. He did well at his new favorite gambling game. Although I never bothered to learn the rules, I suspected, knowing him so well, that he found a way to cheat. My suspicions were confirmed in late July when lawmen arrested him for using distraction techniques, sleight of hand, and a simple tool called a "horsehair copper" to change his bets on the sly. "How else can I hold my own against dealers using gaffed dealing boxes, stacked decks, and shaved cards to give the bank the advantage?" he asked when I visited him behind bars. I shrugged and walked out but returned the next day to pay his considerable fine.

I have no idea how close Wild Bill came to taking Jasper up on his suggestion that they head West and try their luck at enforcing the law, playing poker or both in Dodge City, Kansas. I just know they never got around to it and that Hickok got a more appealing offer that summer when a celebrity more than his equal showed up in the City of Kansas—Buffalo Bill Cody. Like his old friend Wild Bill, Buffalo Bill was a sometime scout and a heroic figure in some of Ned Buntline's breathless dime novels. Now he fancied himself an entertainer first, and he had come to the Missouri city specifically to recruit Hickok to join his company for a series of acting engagements in the East. I heard the details later from Jasper, who by then had sunk into funereal gloominess.

Wild Bill, with the aid of Jasper, was no longer behaving like a vagrant when the nattily dressed Buffalo Bill caught up with him on Main Street. But Hickok still wasn't his old self. His clothes were the worse for wear, his drinking was excessive, his tired eyes strained to see even in bright light, his self-doubt was out of character, his gambling losses were mounting, and his two guns seemed to be collecting rust. To the thirty-six-year-old Wild Bill, standing on a stage reciting lines might have seemed as uninviting as standing on the street facing off with a trigger-happy lout, but he listened hard when Buffalo Bill began talking money. Without even risking his life, he'd be earning a hundred dollars a week facing an audience and playing himself as a member of Cody's cast. As a risk-taking marshal in Abilene, he'd made just one hundred fifty dollars a month. Dodge City officials weren't likely to match that.

"You're a lawman, not a thespian," Jasper told Wild Bill. "You want tough, honest work, *not* fraudulent play."

"Says you," replied Hickok. "But who are you?"

"I'm Wash—your deputy, your protector, your benefactor, your friend."

"Off and on. Buffalo Bill says the world needs a hero. When I team up with him, that'll give the world two heroes on the same stage, three if you count the third scout in the company, Texas Jack Omohundro, and I do. And I haven't even mentioned the beautiful Italian actress who'll play Texas Jack's Indian wife, Pale Dove. Giuseppina Morlacchi is her name. She introduced the can-can to the American stage."

"You can't do it, Wild Bill. It'll be a disaster. They'll laugh at you. You can't act."

"I can act like myself better than anyone. Anyway, what makes you think you can be my number one critic?"

"I earned that right. I've been with you all these many years."

"Buffalo Bill says I have a presence. That means I impress people with my manner and appearance even when I'm just standing still."

"I know what it means, but for your presence to be meaningful, you have to be present in rough-and-tumble Dodge City, not namby-pamby New York City."

When it seemed inevitable that Wild Bill Hickok would be

joining Cody's play *Scouts of the Plains* in September, Jasper tried to land a part. Buffalo Bill denied him, saying he already had his full cast, including three famous scouts, three bonny lasses, the splendid Pale Dove, four Comanche and Kiowa warriors, a renegade horse thief, and a song-and-dance man to play "Nick Blunder." The play did not call for a freed slave or any other colored man, certainly not a muscular man killer who just might steal the spotlight from one of the stars.

"But I got presence, too," Jasper insisted. "And I talk good. My voice shall be heard!"

"Not this time," Cody said, shaking his head hard enough to cause his long hair to dance at his shoulders. "I'm sorry, Mr. Washington. You aren't what the audience wants."

"The audience or you, Mr. Cody?"

"The people want to see scout Wild Bill Hickok with his scout friends, Texas Jack and myself. You aren't a scout."

"Maybe not, but I could play one. And I *am* Wild Bill's closest friend."

"Perhaps you have been. But I was his good friend long before he met you, my friend. In any case, this isn't strictly a re-creation of reality. The play is the thing, and *Scouts of the Plains* is in good part made-up fun. You would be out of place."

"Hey, I know how to have fun. Just watch and listen." Jasper pulled Buffalo Bill's hair as if he were a schoolboy pestering a girl, told him he wasn't nearly as pretty as Wild Bill, and laughed deeply and without restraint while doing a circular, knee-slapping dance.

"Look, if I should stage *Uncle Tom's Cabin* in a future season, I very well might call on you, Mr. Washington. I also have an idea for another moral drama I'd entitle *Judge Lynch and His Law*. I can see you with a noose around your bull neck and cursing the unreconstructed rebels who are perpetuating this vile injustice against your person."

"That's not to my liking in any season, Mr. Cody."

Jasper could have traveled East with the company as a laborer who would carry the ladies' luggage, tend to the horses, change scenery when needed, fetch food and drinks, and control any disruptive behavior by unruly men in the audience. But he had too much pride to go in any capacity except as at least a minor actor or as Wild Bill Hickok's right-hand man. "See you later, Jasper," Wild Bill said, with no more warmth than he used to show his poker-playing acquaintances or the drunks he put behind bars during his marshaling days. "I'll be in hog heaven with Cody. Take care of your own self, you hear."

And so, before Jasper knew it, he and Wild Bill were separated again, now farther apart geographically and otherwise than they had been in the eight years since Jasper left Kentucky to visit the Yankee scout in Springfield, Missouri. I had never seen Jasper so down in the mouth or his massive shoulders droop so low. One September midday I left work to buy him a Kansas City steak at the Delmonico Hotel in the hopes of cheering him up. All he did was pick at the meat on his plate, pick his teeth, moan about the plummeting gambling opportunities in the city, and mutter about how he didn't have a friend left in the whole world even though I was sitting right across the table from him. It was almost a relief to get back to work among the dead at Elwood Cemetery.

Jasper couldn't bring himself to go alone to Dodge City in search of new opportunities. Several times he asked me indirectly to accompany him, but I was earning wages, living comfortably enough for my tastes, and feeling reasonably safe in the City of Kansas. The adventurous spirit that had caused me to serve General John Hunt Morgan during the war and afterward leave Kentucky for the West with Jasper Washington might not have left me entirely, but it had buried itself at least as deep as a regulation grave.

During this time, Crooked Nose Jack was as disappointed as Jasper over the anti-gambling sentiment that had overtaken the city, and he himself got the notion to head to Dodge. My mischievous suggestion that he and Jasper set out together for the new frontier did not go over well with either man. "I'd just as soon walk to the gallows with the devil," said Crooked Nose Jack. "So, Zach, you want to shed yourself of me as much as Bill did," said Jasper. "Now I know. Why not come right out with it and tell me to go to hell."

I apologized to Jasper but not to my half brother, for in this instance blood just didn't seem thicker than water. Jack would probably have argued that point because he couldn't bear to go anywhere again without me, even if he never admitted it. I was his safety net if things went wrong in his gambling endeavors, since he knew I would always find a steady, honest job that could at least support the two of us and that, despite his questionable behavior and beliefs (stealing, cheating, holding Jasper and Wild Bill and most of the North in contempt), I would never desert him.

But then the whole picture changed for Jack, Jasper, and me in October 1873. Three things happened—to be more precise, three letters happened, all within two weeks of each other, and it was as if Fate were doing the writing. The first letter was addressed to "Wild Bill's friend Jasper" from Colonel Cody and sent to General Delivery, City of Kansas:

Sir Jasper—I hope this communication reaches you, as I don't recall if you have a surname, and I am uncertain as to whether you can read. I will attempt to be brief. I am worried about Wild Bill. In our act, we three scouts sit at a campfire telling tales of our adventures on the Plains while passing around a bottle I filled with iced tea. Bill spit out the tea and demanded real whiskey. That got some laughs.

But now he demands whiskey during the performance, and before and after as well. He ignores or forgets his lines, stammers, and fails to project his voice. People laugh at him all the time, whether in Williamsport, Pennsylvania, or New York City. Mostly he stands there on stage and takes it, but on occasion his anger boils over. Once he shot out a spotlight, which showed fine marksmanship but frightened half the audience. In Titusville, Pennsylvania, he dealt with five roughs by knocking the leader down with one punch and then using a stiff chair to lay out the other four on the floor. Part of me wanted to applaud him, but at the same time we don't want to kill the critics.

In scenes with Pale Dove, he often grows fonder of the heroine than the script stipulates. This is unsettling to Giuseppina Morlacchi, who married Texas Jack last August. In scenes where he is supposed to 'kill' Comanches by firing blanks over their heads, he discharges his pistols close to their feet, causing them to dance and jump instead of fall and die and on occasion inflicting powder burns. As you can imagine, this makes him extremely unpopular with our Indian performers. I could go on but it's nearly show-time in Port Jervis, New York, that is if Bill can manage to break away from his poker game and get here on time. In a nutshell, Jasper, although the money is still flowing in, Bill's heart is not in what he calls 'staged foolishness,' and he keeps threatening to quit. Bill has no idea I am writing what I'm afraid has turned into a missive. But I know he misses your presence and that in the past in such places as Abilene, Kansas, you have steered him in the right direction. I thus request you, if it is within your means, to join Bill and the rest of our troupe while we are touring Pennsylvania and New York and as far north as Portland, Maine. Our upcoming schedule, as I now know it, is attached. I appreciate your consideration in this important matter, sir, and hope to see you soon. I believe I can make such a trip profitable for you. And as sure as my name is Buffalo Bill, I am certain your very presence will benefit immeasurably our beloved friend and reluctant thespian Wild Bill Hickok.

The second letter had first gone to Springfield, Missouri, before being forwarded to Abilene and then Ellsworth in Kansas and finally catching up with Crooked Nose Jack McCall in the City of Kansas, Missouri. It was sent by the oldest of his three sisters in Louisville, Kentucky.

Dear Brother—

You are harder to track down in Missouri than Jesse James. Do you plan to distance yourself from our family forever? All we know is that you went West to follow Father's illegitimate Wild Child. Mother believes that deplorable man raised in a bawdyhouse has been a most dreadful influence on your path in life. She hopes you are rid of him by now. I do, too. I remember how he invited himself into our Louisville home during the war and did nothing at all except eat our food and become an abominable leech. Some of us have missed you here in the gateway to the South. All of us have been quite sick off and on with Fever and Ague, and Mother has been terribly troubled by Biliousness that lasts and lasts. Speaking of lasting and sickness, the McCall marriage has NOT lasted. Last month, Father was consuming most of the whiskey he was supposed to sell and announced in our Living room that he was Sick and Tired of All of Us and was leaving. He did NOT say where he was going at first, but Mother got him to admit he was bound for Boonesborough and certain harlots at the very same bawdyhouse where the

Wild Child had been born and raised like some sort of filthy animal.

Needless to say, Mother and my Sisters hate Father now. I cannot hate him, for I continue to go to the Christ Church Cathedral every Sunday and have found NO hate in the Bible. Yet, I shall never forgive him for being so MEAN. It all started, I believe, when he beat you with his fists and broke your poor nose. Of course, you were often MEAN yourself, to me especially. But now that I am twenty years old, I can forgive you. Anyway, Father has gone off to live out his mean life in sin, and there is NO man of the house in Louisville. Mother needs you. I just know it. I do, too. Have you no love for us? Have you no money for us? With Father gone forever, Mother beside herself, and everyone getting sicker than a cur, none of us can live as we were once accustomed. We may have to sell our wonderful old home unless . . . I'll leave it at that. But, tell me, Jack, isn't it time you did your duty and returned, for you must know that in the McCall family only you can be the PRODIGAL SON?

—Your loving sister, Emily

The third letter was sent to me care of the Elwood Cemetery. It was from Belle Bragg, who explained in some detail how she located me. She said she was now the owner of the Daniel's Den, having purchased it from Angus Doyle, who had gone to Elmira, New York, home to a military prison where more than 12,000 Confederate soldiers were held during the Civil War and where 2,973 of them were buried by John W. Jones, a onetime escaped slave who became the cemetery caretaker. Feeling at home in the northern city, Doyle had become co-owner of Elmira's historic Teall's Tavern with the brother of the former prison commandant who had hired Jones. The two tavern owners had gone up to Rochester, New York, that fall specifically to see Wild Bill Hickok perform and had ended up buying him drinks and talking about the past. In the course of their conversation, the names Washington and McCall both came up. Hickok told Doyle that his friend Jasper Washington, whom he dearly missed, was one of the people who had helped John Jones pass through Kentucky during his escape from slavery. He also told Doyle that he knew of two McCalls living in the City of Kansas, one a tinhorn gambler, the other a digger of graves just like Mr. Jones. Doyle in turn brought the news about me to Belle when he returned to Boonesborough to close out the sale of the Daniel's Den to his enterprising former horizontal worker.

After that long explanation, Belle finally revealed the reason she had sent me the letter: "Fat Jack is here doing poorly. His spirits have been dashed. Blame the whiskey. Blame me. No matter. What matters to me, and I'm sure matters to you, is that your daddy is our patient now, lying near insensate on my bed. You know where we are. Come quick."

I naturally wished she had gone into more detail about this serious matter, since it *certainly did matter* to me. But there wasn't time to write her back to request elaboration. I immediately apologized to my generous employer and quit my job at Elmwood. I told Crooked Nose Jack that I was catching the next train east to see our dying father. Jack said he would catch the same train, not only to see Fat Jack die but also to support his mother and sisters and preserve the family name. I packed quickly and said my goodbye to only one person—Jasper Washington. He said no need for that. He would also be taking the "McCall Express," but not to revisit Kentucky. "I must answer the call of Buffalo Bill Cody," Jasper explained. "The show won't go on unless I save Wild Bill Hickok from himself."

Chapter Twenty-Six:
Back in the Den

Because it sounded as if Fat Jack McCall was near death, it was urgent that I get there as soon as possible. Crooked Nose Jack felt otherwise and wasn't shy about saying so on the train. He sniffed and snorted and ran his fingers over his crooked nose most of the way to Kentucky, insisting that it was no skin off his nose if our father died.

"You're the Bastard McCall, yet he always liked you best," Jack muttered. "I knew how mean he was even before Mother admitted it. He whipped me regular and he—"

"I know, I know. Daddy beat you, punched you, and left you with a disjointed nose. But I understand you didn't always act like a good egg. I recall how you got him jailed by the Yankee authorities in Louisville for harboring a Rebel—me!"

"I didn't let them get you, did I? Anyway, that's beside the point. A father shouldn't turn his back on his only son . . . you know, legitimate son. And now he's turned his back on my dear mother and sisters."

"Dear? I recall how you had your problems with them, too."

"My mother never whipped me or struck me with a full fist, just a little slap now and then. She never was straight-out mean."

"Hannah McCall was close to it with me. She didn't want me to even catch my breath in your Louisville attic. And when Fat Jack told her I could remain for a while, she walloped the back of his head with a skillet. My impression was it wasn't the first time."

"No point talking ill of my mother just because you never knew *your* whoring mother."

"Only *you* can say bad things about your mother. So sorry."

"Mother wants me and needs me. Emily said so in her letter. Father wants only harlots and needs only whiskey. You call him a daddy, I call him a mean, whiskey-soaked libertine. He can go to hell."

I felt like rearranging Jack's nose again, but I closed my eyes, took several deep breaths, and tried a different approach. After all, we were in the same train car. "Maybe he will, maybe he won't. Same goes for you and me. What matters now is, he is dying, and this is my chance to say goodbye and your chance to make amends with the old man."

"If he was a halfway tolerable man, he would be dying in his marriage bed at home in Louisville instead of with those dirty creatures at that hellhole in Boonesborough."

"Dirty creatures? Most of them bathed regular. They taught me plenty about cleanliness and raised me to . . . to *not* hate my mother and *not disrespect* my father. Belle Bragg was always real decent and—"

"You knew nothing better. She was nice with me, too, when I was there, but she's paid to be nice, being a harlot and everything."

"She's not! She now owns the business, which is mostly a tavern, and—"

"Make all the excuses for her you want. I ain't going to set foot in the Daniel's Den. I'm bound for Louisville. I've been away too long."

"Suit yourself. What do you say, Jasper? I know you've been listening."

"I'd rather listen to the wheels rolling and the whistle blowing," said Jasper, who was filling up an entire seat across from us.

"If you were a McCall, would you go see your mother or your father?"

"My pappy was a strapping field slave who was worked to death when I was but a babe. My mama was a free unmarried woman who wanted to free him and marry him but never got the chance. She never told me his name. After he died, she met an upright freeman named Homer Washington, and she had no objections when he put a silver band on her finger and vowed to treat little Jasper—that was me, believe it or not—like his own son. Homer had his own small Kentucky dirt farm, and once he brought her and me there, he named it 'Paradise.' They educated me in the ways of the world the best they could. I left soon enough to find *more* independence, but I knew where they were and that whenever I went back, they'd be there together. They encouraged me to attend Berea College in 1857. They had sure enough found their Paradise, but they wanted more for me. It stayed that way right up to the day they died, which—and not by coincidence—was on the same day. Got the cholera in '61 from white townsfolk."

I had heard Jasper previously mention his time at the college, but he had never before explained why he happened to be born a bastard like me. Of course, I had never asked.

"Yeah, blame *us*," said Crooked Nose Jack. "It's all bunkum as far as I'm concerned. There ain't no paradise, least not here on this Earth."

"I admit it's a rare thing for us colored folk. My advice to you, Little Jack McCall, is to go see your pappy, and maybe you both can say you're sorry. You can always see your mama later."

"Did I ask you for your advice? You and me don't see eye to eye on a lot of things."

"That's for damn sure. Must be because I'm so much bigger than you."

Jack's face had reddened, and he leaned forward on the passenger seat we shared with both his hands in tight balls. When the train whistle blew, however, he wisely unclenched and sat back. That Jasper was a few heads taller and more than one hundred pounds heavier was not something anyone could dispute.

"What do you say, Jack?" I asked. "Jasper is saying what I'm saying. You come to Boonesborough with me, and then we'll both head up to Louisville together."

"Maybe. But what about him?" Little Jack pointed an angry if shaky finger at Jasper. "I don't know why he's on this train with us. But I don't want him with me wherever I go in Kentucky. I just don't!"

"Don't fear, Little Jack. At St. Louis we'll be parting ways. I'm railroading my way to Buffalo, New York, hoping to catch Wild Bill there. I aim to save him. I sincerely hope you find your pappy in good health, Zach. As for you, Jack, it doesn't truly matter to me if you see your pappy or your mama or neither because, frankly, when it comes to you and your future, I don't give a damn."

"That's plain enough," replied Jack. "You know I feel exactly the same about you. I'll be glad to see you go. And I sincerely hope I am rid of you and Wild Bill Hickok forever." He crossed his arms and closed his eyes as if that would make Jasper disappear sooner.

None of us said a word the rest of the way to St. Louis. There, Jasper gave me an embrace that didn't cause any bodily pain but made my eyes tear up anyway. He said, "See you later, Wild Child." I said, "See you later, Wash." I'm not sure either of us believed we ever would. Crooked Nose Jack held his tongue but turned his back on Jasper.

Jack and I then proceeded to East St. Louis, Illinois, in a railcar on a ferry since the bridge across the Mississippi was still under construction. We were indeed headed for the Daniel's

Den first, though Jack acted as if it had been his idea all along. "I'll give the old reprobate a chance to atone for his sins before he meets his Maker," he said. "As soon we get him planted, we'll hightail it up to Louisville to take care of my family business." Our last stretch on the rails was on the Kentucky Central Railroad line to Lexington, and from there—since my savings had about run out—we walked the eighteen miles to Boonesborough.

The Daniel's Den had a fresh coat of blue paint and a fancy new wooden sign with the name of the establishment carved on it along with the outline of a whiskey bottle and a surprisingly detailed drawing of a raccoon cap, such as the kind Daniel Boone wore (at least in several portraits), hanging on a peg, such as the kind found in each upstairs bedroom. The tavern downstairs seemed smaller, but the bar and the tables were the same. Serving drinks in place of the former owner Angus Doyle was a tall and broad barmaid who filled out her dress so much that she spilled out on top. She looked like someone I might have known in reduced size in the old days, but her name (Minnie Mary) didn't ring a bell, and she didn't recognize my face, let alone the face of Crooked Nose Jack.

"We're the McCall brothers," said Jack, who elected to stand so close to Minnie Mary that the tip of his crooked nose penetrated her grand cleavage. "We got business here."

"Most men do," she said, allowing him to have his long close-up sniff of her flowery perfume before taking a step back. "McCall . . . McCall? You wouldn't happen to be related to a Fat Jack McCall, would you?"

"We would. Why so surprised? Don't you think we look like him . . . at least one of us?"

"I suppose you both do a little. But he's old and ill and doesn't look like himself. I hope you two aren't too close to him."

"Naw, only his sons. I'm Little Jack. We know he's old and sick."

"We're not too late, are we?" I asked.

"Too late? I didn't even know you were coming or that Fat Jack had two sons. Nobody told me, but then Madam Bragg never tells me a blessed thing. Only orders me to show myself off to the customers, but under no circumstances to leave my post at the bar and venture upstairs."

Crooked Nose Jack grinned and nudged me with his elbow. "You saying Belle Bragg is *mean*, Minnie Mary?" he asked as he jabbed me with his sharp elbow.

"No, I wouldn't say that, boys. I've had altogether worse bosses. What can I get you?"

"Whiskey, your best," Jack said.

"Nothing," I said at the same time.

She moved down the bar, reached behind it, and produced a bottle that she held under the nose of Crooked Nose Jack. "Might do you both some good."

"You know, Minnie, you'd be more than half right. Seeing him again might go down easier after I let some of this stuff burn my gullet."

"He hasn't already died, has he?" I was growing impatient and had already taken a couple of steps toward the familiar staircase.

"Not that I know of, but nobody tells me . . ."

"Which room?" I said.

"I don't know if it's my place to say. You say you are his sons and everything, but . . . maybe you should ask Madam Bragg first. She is the boss, and—"

"Which room?"

"Same room as her, I reckon. But maybe I should go see . . ."

"Just stick to the bar like you're supposed to, miss. I know the way."

I darted to the stairs and soon had my hand on the black oak banister.

"We both know the way, Minnie," Jack said. "But don't worry your pretty big head, I'll be back. I'll need more service after seeing him."

My half brother ran to catch up.

At the top of the stairs I confronted the familiar yellow door with the red plaque. But the plaque no longer said *Madam Raccoon* on it. In tall bold letters, it read, *Belle Bragg, Proprietor.* For the first time since leaving the City of Kansas I wondered if her husband, Robert "Raccoon" Gentry, was still alive and preaching. I knocked softly just once but didn't wait for an answer. I barged right in, confident I couldn't possibly be interrupting an act of intimacy.

Belle Bragg sat stiffly on her Red Room bed, dressed in full mourning attire, including a black cap and veil. Next to her lay Fat Jack McCall, looking strikingly slight beneath a much too colorful woven blanket; only his pale face was exposed, and it was thin, positively skeletal. She saw us and shot off the bed as if bitten by a snake. She parted a veil to see us better, and we saw her better, too. What hair I could see was silver. She had gained wrinkles about her eyes and lost the pink glow to her cheeks, but a couple of tears glistened in the narrow beam of light that passed through an opening in the dark curtains of the south-facing window and touched her like a gleam of hope.

"You came!" she said, opening her arms.

Crooked Nose Jack advanced faster, and she hugged him first. But she hugged me longer, so long in fact that I temporarily forgot who she was and why I was there and felt the stirrings of long-absent ardor. As we hugged—and as I admittedly rubbed against her some, first with my chest, then with my belly and all the way down to my feet—Jack moved past us to the edge of the bed, stared at our daddy, and let out a loud *ugh* that instantly cooled my inappropriate ardor.

"I thought he was dead," the legitimate son said. "What the hell is wrong with him?"

The senior McCall wasn't talking and was only staring out, as if he were looking through foggy windowpanes, as if he couldn't see us at all. Belle explained that he had come to her red faced and frisky two months ago after being, as he put it, "driven from my family home by horrible Hannah and three daughters who had turned against me in my time of weakness because they are all younger but no prettier versions of her." He had left the Louisville house in less than perfect health but had seemingly made a full recovery while enjoying what he called "Paradise in the Den." After two weeks, though, despite her best efforts, he had relapsed and begun to be plagued by a rash of miseries—persistent hoarseness and coughing, night sweats, trouble swallowing, belly pain, vomiting, swelling under the arm, lumps on his groin, blood in his stool. Whatever ailed him was deep inside him. Doctors had come to the Den and treated his misery with diet, bloodletting, and laxatives. One physician, from Louisville of all places, made the diagnosis of cancer. He said in some cases it could be treated with surgery, but that in this case the disease was spread everywhere, and even if it wasn't, he had no idea where to begin to cut.

If that wasn't bad enough, a second disaster had occurred two weeks before Crooked Nose Jack and I arrived. Fat Jack had become fed up with both the bedpan and his dry throat. He had slipped out of bed while Belle, suddenly more nurse than proprietor, was attending to another patient. His intent was twofold—to go to the outhouse and rid himself of bloody vomit and bloody stools and then go to the bar and sweet-talk Minnie Mary into handing over the last two bottles of the best whiskey, which he had brought to the Daniel's Den himself. He hadn't even managed to get down the stairs, at least not upright.

When he stumbled, he reached for the black oak banister but couldn't find it, and the tumble to the bottom broke his neck. In his paralytic state he could not move anything in his lower body, or his arms. Moving his head had gone from difficult to impossible. Mostly he just stared out, but sometimes he rolled his eyes with a sort of passion. His mouth still worked for eating and drinking and even sometimes for speaking, although not lately.

"So, which will do him in first, the cancer or the broken body?" Crooked Nose Jack asked.

"You can only be done in *once*," I said because I was irritated and couldn't get any better words out of my own mouth.

"In any case I'm afraid he doesn't have long, though that isn't necessarily a bad thing, considering . . . considering everything," said Belle Bragg. "I wrote the letter to you as soon as he fell down the stairs. He has somehow hung on, proving himself to be quite the fighter." She touched my arm, and it recoiled as if stung by a bee.

"Can he hear us?" I whispered.

"I'm quite sure he can. But we can speak freely. He asked me *not* to hide anything from him in one of his last lucid sentences."

"It doesn't look like he sees me," said Crooked Nose Jack.

"His vision seems to come and go."

"Can you see me now, Father!" Jack shouted. "It's me, your son, your legitimate son. I'm just back from the West. I wanted to . . . you know, visit with you before you die."

"Little Jack!" I shouted. "What a thing to say."

"Well, like Belle said, we don't want to hide anything from him."

I brushed past my half brother and carefully sat on the bed so I wasn't touching our father. "Hello, Daddy," I said. "Zach McCall here. You know, the bastard."

Fat Jack, now thin paralytic Jack, said nothing, but a half

smile formed on his lips. He closed his eyes, but the half smile stayed there.

"He needs to sleep," Belle said. "You can talk to him later, Zach."

"Me, too," said Crooked Nose Jack, and then he addressed his father. "There's a few things I might want to say to you. Like, what's this I hear about you deserting Mother and our Louisville home two months ago to come here."

"You!" Fat Jack managed to get out the one word. His eyes were still closed.

"Yes, it's me, Little Jack. You recognize my voice. You said 'you.' If you got something to say to me, say it, old man, before you stop talking altogether."

Fat Jack's eyes opened, just long enough to roll them once before they shut again.

"What the hell is that supposed to mean?" Crooked Nose Jack asked.

"You first," our father answered.

"I don't understand. I am your *first* child, that's true. As you might recall, I have three younger sisters—Emily, Catherine, and Sarah. You also saw fit to leave them behind in Louisville. I must clarify something. When it comes to sons, I'm actually your second. Like Zach over there said, he's *your* bastard first."

Fat Jack was able to add a third word: "You deserted first."

It was true that in 1865 Crooked Nose Jack had left home to join me at the Daniel's Den and then had followed Jasper Washington and me to find adventure in the West. But my half brother wasn't buying that, not even from a dying man. "It wasn't desertion, goddamn it!" he shouted, a little too close to a man who was dying but could still hear well enough. "I just went off to make my way in the world and seek my fortune. Sons have been doing that for centuries, and nobody calls it desertion! Anyway, right after I say goodbye to you, I'm going back home to see the wife and daughters you *did desert* for this . . . this . . ."

I pulled Crooked Nose Jack away from the bed, and the woman in question, Belle Bragg, helped. Our father's mouth was wide open, but the only things coming out were snorts and rattles.

"He's sleeping," Belle insisted, tugging both my half brother and me farther away from the bed. "That's certainly enough conversation for now. It doesn't seem to be helping."

"Nothing can help him," Jack concluded.

"Is there anything more we can do for him?" I asked, once the three of us were huddled as far as we could get from the bed without leaving the room.

"We can pray," she said, clasping her hands together.

"You pray?" Jack said. "I mean, you don't strike me as the type. I don't believe in it myself. It never works."

"You can't pray to fill an inside straight," I blurted out, having heard Jasper Washington use that expression a time or two without fully understanding what made a straight inside or outside.

"What do you pray for, Brother—a day without rain at the graveyard?"

"Stop it, you two," said Belle. "Truth is, most of the praying for your father has been done by Robert, bless his heart."

"You mean Preacher Raccoon, the man who taught me to read, the man you . . . you eventually married?" I said.

"Yes, my dear husband."

"I wasn't sure if he was . . . you know, still . . . you know, what with my father coming here."

"Robert has always been understanding about Fat Jack. Even before Fat Jack got here, I changed the sign on the Red Room door. He agreed with me after I bought the establishment from Angus Doyle and became the proprietor, it didn't sound dignified for me to continue calling myself Madam Raccoon."

"Don't tell me Preacher Raccoon . . . eh, your husband still goes out riding the circuit?"

"I'm afraid not. He's a sick old man, very sick. He's the other patient in my sick ward. He does all his praying right here now."

"Where?" Jack said. "Under the bed?"

It turned out the preacher was in the small, adjacent Blue Room that had been mine as a boy and had been used by Crooked Nose Jack when he first came to Daniel's Den in search of me. Belle Bragg led us in there as if entering a church during a sermon. The first thing I noticed were three cans of peaches, two opened and one with a spoon handle sticking out. Somehow it was comforting that he hadn't lost his taste for those. The preacher, whose long beard had turned white, was lying in bed on his back, both legs churning and one hand, the right, pressing to his frail chest a book, but I could tell it wasn't the Bible. The preacher had introduced me to some fine books at an early age, and though now I mostly only read newspapers, I wondered if the title was familiar. I took a step closer, then froze. He had kicked off all of his covers, but his bare legs, veiny and scaly, were still flapping like two pickerel that had freed themselves from hooks only to find themselves on dry land. He had removed his white nightshirt and was waving it over his head like a white flag.

"As a man is born, so shall he depart—naked!" he said, his whole gaunt head trembling faster with each word.

The sight of her husband's exposed body made Belle Bragg blush like a schoolgirl, and she quickly pulled the blankets back up to hide the nakedness. "Shame on you, Coony," she said. "You'll catch cold."

"Only after I'm dead, honey child," he said, dropping the nightshirt over his face.

I had never heard him call her that before.

"Now, Robert, that's no way to talk and so unlike you." She pulled the nightshirt away from his eyes and then stared at it as if unsure whether to try putting it on him or not. Finally, she just draped it over her arm and smiled at him. He didn't smile back. He seemed to be looking at me, so I moved in closer in case his eyesight was bad.

"Hello, sir. It's Zach. I'm back."

"Ah, the Wild Child. Did Belle ever tell you—I am a bastard, too?"

"No, sir. I never thought of you as one."

"I wasn't much over one year old when my young mother placed me in the Protestant Orphan Asylum—that is to say, left me at the doorstep next to the orphanage. My young father knew her for only one night before vanishing. He consumed intoxicating spirits to excess, and I later read in the newspapers that in his middle age he became a 'holy' man—that is to say, two sober men shot him full of holes, ten holes in all, with Samuel Colt's five-shot .36-caliber Paterson revolvers."

"What for?" Crooked Nose Jack asked.

"For committing adultery with both their wives while under the influence."

"Of whiskey?"

"No, the father I never knew was reportedly sober when he fornicated. He was drunk the rest of the time. Always he was under the influence of the Devil. That's why I became a preacher . . . to fight Satan."

"Whatever's wrong with him, it hasn't affected his mouth—he's still a talker!" Jack said to Belle as he also moved closer to the bed to peer at the dark circles around the preacher's eyes. Her husband resembled a raccoon more than ever, but even Jack wasn't rude enough to mention it. "So," he said, now talking directly to the preacher. "What's wrong with you, anyway?"

"I'm dying."

"All right, but from what?"

"I can't explain myself, I'm afraid, sir. Because I'm not myself, you see."

His words sounded vaguely familiar, but I couldn't place them until I read the title of the book he had pressed to his heart—*Alice's Adventures in Wonderland & Through the Looking-Glass*. The words were from Alice herself. I had read the book during my temporary late wartime residence in the McCall attic in Louisville. That other copy must have belonged to one of Little Jack's sisters.

"He's nearly blind," Belle said. "It is Coony's favorite book, well, second favorite. I read it to him over and over."

I felt a pang of remorse. When I was a boy, Belle had read me the story "The Little Match Girl," who is barefoot and shivering and beaten by her father and who ends up burning her bundle of matches and freezing to death. I think Belle was trying to show me that I really didn't have it so bad at the Daniel's Den without a real mother and with a father who only came around when selling whiskey to Angus Doyle. But I had seized the book out of her hands, flung it across the room, and declared that I hated stories about girls, even if they died at the end.

"That's nice," I said now.

"I remember when my mother gave that Alice book to Emily," said Jack. "I couldn't get through it. I couldn't stand it. I never liked reading about dumb animals, especially ones that talked. It didn't seem at all real, a girl having all those adventures while I'd never had a single one, not until I went West, anyway."

"I forgive you," said the preacher, pressing a bony finger into Jack's belly, who jerked back as if the finger were a Bowie knife. "Likely God will, too, though the Lord does forgive in mysterious ways."

"You must be out of your mind. I'm Little Jack McCall. The

man you want to forgive is lying in the next room, likely even worse off than you. He's Fat Jack McCall. I'm his son, and a son can't be held accountable for his father's sinful actions."

"You left here like an escaped convict. You stole fifty dollars from Belle and bottles of whiskey from the bar. You gave me a severe blow to the head with the Daniel's Den sign. You stole my horse and carriage that I relied on in my work as a circuit preacher. You stole the first Bible Belle ever gave me, my most prized possession in the world."

"That was a long time ago. I near forgot."

"Some men can do that."

"But not you, eh? Anyway, your head seems fine now, far better than the rest of you. I took some whiskey that day, so what! My father would bring plenty more. And what was a mere fifty dollars to Belle? We all know she could get that back in half a night. As for your rig, I couldn't very well have gone off on foot, could I? I'd give it back to you if I could. But we had to get rid of the rig. My brother was in on it, too, but a colored man is the most to blame. He was bigger than us and as audacious as hell—a born killer, no doubt under the influence of Satan, just like your father and mine. You'll be happy to know we finally ditched the big black bastard in St. Louis."

"And my first Bible from Belle? What became of that?"

"Never saw it. I didn't know it was even in the rig, *if* it was. I'd swear to that on a stack of . . . Anyway, I'd swear to it. Why in the hell would I, chasing after my bastard brother and his big black bastard friend like I was, want to take a Bible along!"

"Why, indeed. But know it or not, the Bible went West with you in my buggy."

"I saw it," I said. "It was in the buggy parked in front of a boardinghouse Jasper and I stayed at in Hickman, Kentucky, right near the Mississippi River. I wondered what you'd be doing way out there, Preacher Raccoon, sir. But it wasn't you, of course. It was Little Jack. I brought the Bible into the boardinghouse. I saw Belle's writing, how she called you the kindest man she ever knew. She said something about bastards being a blessing just the same as other children. I didn't know at the time that you were a bastard, too, sir. I knew it was a special gift from her to you. I'm sorry."

"You have no call to be sorry, my son," the preacher said.

"But I do. It meant something to me, not to Jack. Yet I left it behind in the boardinghouse room the three of us shared, and I don't think I even missed it when we crossed the Mississippi and moved on to Springfield, Missouri. Maybe the Bible is still in Hickman. I'm thinking the housekeeper there picked it up and kept it. She seemed like a God-fearing woman. But, of course, I don't know for sure. So, I'm sorry. Very sorry."

Preacher Raccoon reached out, and I sort of bowed so he could pat me on the head. He missed, but his hand landed on my left shoulder and gave a slight but earnest squeeze. At that point, Belle reached under the bed and pulled out three Bibles. She opened each one in turn to show me how she had signed the trio in the same way: *To the Kindest Man I Ever Knew.*

"I don't have much imagination," she explained. "For a while there I kept giving him the same gift each Christmas. But being such a kind man, Coony gave his heartfelt thanks each time without ever questioning why in the name of God I kept repeating myself."

"Out of love, honey child," said the preacher. "God's and your own. So, you see, Zach my boy, there is not the slightest thing for you to be sorry for. I have no shortage of Bibles from my loving wife."

Crooked Nose Jack threw his hands in the air, then crossed his arms at his chest and tapped his foot. "And I suppose you think I have something to be sorry for? But let me tell you, if I hadn't done what I done, I'd never have gone West and . . . and become a man, an independent gambling man, if you must know. And there's nothing wrong with that, no matter what your Bible says."

"Off the top of my head I can't think of anything said directly about gambling, Little Jack, but you're certainly welcome to *borrow* a Bible and look for yourself."

"No thanks, preacher."

"Well, then . . ." *Alice's Adventures in Wonderland* slid off his beard but stayed on the bed as he picked up one of the three Bibles and patted it as one might a baby. "It's time for me to pray. I can't do so on my knees anymore, but God doesn't object. I'll pray for you, gambling man."

"No need. I do just fine at the poker table without your help."

Belle Bragg and I gasped simultaneously. I thought if my half brother was doing so fine, he should pay Belle back her fifty dollars, but said nothing. That could wait till later. Belle sighed and told us her husband needed his rest and that we boys could talk to him later.

"Sure," Crooked Nose Jack said. "My stomach's talking anyway. Isn't anyone going to offer me some food? I have my eye on those peaches."

"No," snapped Belle. "Those are Coony's peaches. But come downstairs. We'll find you both something to eat while he gets some rest." She tried to take the Bible out of her husband's hand as if that might make him rest better, but he clutched it to his chest, and she gave up. The old guy still seemed to have surprising strength when needed.

As we filed out, Preacher Raccoon called out, not to me or his wife but to Crooked Nose Jack. "One thing I do know, gambling man, and my sense of duty compels me to share it with you. The Good Book is quite direct when it states that love of money is the root of all evil."

"Tell it to honey child."

CHAPTER TWENTY-SEVEN:
GOODBYE IN BOONESBOROUGH

I suppose a son is fortunate when fate allows him to return home in time to see and even talk to a dying father. I certainly was glad to get back to the Daniel's Den and exchange a few words with Fat Jack McCall on his deathbed in the Red Room. Almost all those words were on the day Crooked Nose Jack and I arrived. When I went to visit him the next morning, his eyes popped open, and he stared right through me as if I was made of the same thin fabric the working girls wore. I greeted him with *good morning*, though it was anything but that. He didn't even try to reply. Nor did he nod or blink. "I guess even you don't drink whiskey this early, and I'm not much of a drinking man anytime anymore," I told him, "but nothing I'd rather do this instant than share a bottle and a few toasts to life, liberty, and the pursuit of happiness wherever one can find it." Nothing—no words, no nod of the heavy head, no rolling of the eyes, not the slightest movement. And then his ears suddenly twitched, or I thought they did, and I felt a twinge of hope.

"You feel any pain?" I asked him, my nose now practically touching his. "Would whiskey help? Can I do anything at all for you? Can Little Jack do anything? I can wake him and bring him to you. A good time for all father and son wounds to heal, eh? If you can hear me, Daddy, blink . . . one eye will do." His stare was blank, and it stayed that way for ten minutes until his eyelids shut, loudly it seemed to me. In my mind I saw a young pale-skinned lady, perhaps the mother I never knew, desperately closing shutters to keep out an unforgiving west wind. And then Belle Bragg walked in, wrapped in a substantial cotton night dress and carrying some kind of foul-smelling brown liquid in a cup with a tarnished silver spoon.

"I put a touch of honey in it, honey," she said, which made me wonder if she ever called her husband "honey," too. I knew the preacher had addressed her as "honey child." The situation at the Den was confusing, all right, but there was nothing confusing about death and dying.

Belle was all business after that. Her clear intent was to see if Fat Jack could swallow and get down any nourishment. Twice she got a spoonful on his lips, more on his chin. On the third try she got some in his mouth, but he spit most of it out.

"By the great horn spoon!" Fat Jack blurted. "No more shit!"

Startled by these words, Belle dropped the cup and teaspoon, and the remainder of the brown liquid spilled like blood onto Fat Jack's blankets. Crooked Nose Jack entered the Red Room at that point, trying to scratch his belly and rub an eye at the same time.

"What did he say? Did he ask for me?"

"Nope," I said. "He said, 'No more shit.' "

"Oh." Little Jack brushed past Belle and me and leaned over the bed to peer into Fat Jack's dull eyes. "Can't you even see me at all? I rushed to be here this morning just in case. I thought you might want to ask my forgiveness or something . . . like the preacher done last night. You know, the preacher in the next room, the legal husband of your mistress."

Fat Jack's mouth hung open, plump lips still. But I couldn't keep quiet. "Preacher Raccoon didn't ask for your forgiveness, Little Jack," I said, a bit too harshly. "He said he *forgave you.*"

"It doesn't matter. Fat Jack can't talk."

"He did talk," Belle said, "about a spoon made from horn."

"I mean he can't talk and make sense."

Belle picked up the empty cup from the bed and the tarnished silver spoon off the floor. "I've been in and out all night, and he hadn't said a single word. And then this morning . . . Amazing."

"He ain't talking now. I don't believe he can even see me." Little Jack raised his arms as if totally exasperated and stepped back from the bed. "He can't do a damn thing. He . . ."

"He might be able to hear you if you would only . . ."

"No, I won't forgive him, wouldn't do so even if he could ask for it. He acted mean to me and Mother all his life and would act mean again if he could move as much as a pinky. I'm going back to bed."

Belle and I watched the legitimate son walk out, and then we made brief eye contact to confirm our understanding that we could no more stop my half brother from being himself than stop the earth from spinning on its axis. After that we spent most of the morning silently staring at Fat Jack, who stared back at nothing.

For three more days, Fat Jack was the same—not eating, not speaking, not showing any sign he recognized us or where he was. Belle talked to him about good bourbon whiskey, passionflowers, the "animalistic" aroma of musk perfume, phases of the moon, her recent discovery that there were sunrises as well as sunsets, and me, his illegitimate son. I talked to him about the distant past only—the kindness showed to young me by Preacher Raccoon, the coercion of me by Angus Doyle, the happy times when Fat Jack's whiskey-selling road trips brought him to the Daniel's Den, my visions of the mother I never knew, and the love of my substitute mother, Belle.

Five or six times a day, when I could think of nothing else to say, I simply said, "Hi, Daddy," as casually as any son might do after his father returns home from a working day. Not even his ears twitched anymore; I had no idea whether he was hearing us or not. But on the fourth morning, while I sat still half-asleep on the edge of his bed, two words arose from deep inside him or maybe from somewhere outside of him. "Hi, Zach!" he said, and it sounded so cheerful, I never would have imagined those would be his last words on this earth, and that he would die at midnight while not only Belle and I but also the enfeebled Preacher Raccoon hovered over him. At the time of Fat Jack's death rattle, Little Jack was elsewhere but not sleeping. He had begun to rendezvous each night in the Green Room with the working girl from downstairs, the barmaid Minnie Mary.

I shed more than a few tears for Fat Jack, though he had been only a part-time father. Dry-eyed Little Jack expressed displeasure that Fat Jack had not saved that unexpected last greeting for his *real son,* but otherwise showed no concern that they hadn't reconciled their differences or even talked while Fat Jack still could. He did write his mother in Louisville with news of a death that he hoped "won't be too sad for you." He added a few details—that her husband had expired with a broken neck and many cancerous internal organs, without a word but clearly suffering terribly. He asked if she wanted him to bring up the corpse for burial in the McCall plot in Louisville but said in any case he would be taking his leave of Boonesborough damn soon to join his family during their time of need. She promptly replied in a short letter: *We have no plot. It was over before it was over. He wasn't planning to return while alive, so I don't want him back dead. Do as you like with his remains. Hope to see you soon, my only son.*

We buried Fat Jack, though the early December ground was hard, in the tiny cemetery just beyond the red maples behind the Daniel's Den back fence. At least two working ladies and three customers (two of them anonymous) had markers there already. I dug most of the new grave myself. Little Jack threw the last couple shovelfuls of dirt onto the head-end of the pine box and commented, "I reckon I'm the *only* Jack now." Preacher Raccoon made it downstairs with the help of myself and four working girls and stepped outside for the first time in a month. He held one of his Bibles as he spoke at the graveside, but he said the verses from memory instead of reading them, and he added some words of his own. I listened without hearing much, and remembering less. He said something about *My Father's* house having many unoccupied rooms and asked the late father of Zach and Jack McCall to prepare a place for him, since he would be joining the deceased soon enough, and also to reserve a larger room for the two sons—"the blessed former Wild Child who mourns and walks uprightly as one of God's children, and the cross-eyed estranged one who pursues the dishonorable desires of youth, for he knows not yet the pathway to Heaven."

Preacher Raccoon's words irritated my half brother, who also told me that even though he was now the only Jack, he still preferred being called "Little Jack," to continue to honor the memory of the late "Little Dave" Tutt. "Oh, and I'm not answering to Crooked Nose Jack again," he added. "That nickname dies with Fat Jack. Understand, Brother?"

I might have nodded my head, but just barely. It irritated me that my half brother was thinking more about Little Dave Tutt and himself than Fat Jack McCall at the time of our daddy's demise. I suppose I understood him not wanting to be labeled "Crooked Nose" anymore, but at least I never referred to him as "Cross-eyed Jack." His mind worked differently than mine. I thought he would now rush up to Louisville to be with his mother and three sisters. I was mistaken.

He put the trip north on hold indefinitely, and maybe it shouldn't have surprised me. It was more than his mind at work. Minnie Mary, with her biting tongue, long loose black hair, abundant bosom, and willingness to defy convention not only caught Little Jack's fancy but also had him dancing to her every passing whim. Just so he could be near her and at least buy her a few things, he went to work in the tavern and kitchen parts of the Daniel's Den. Belle Bragg was just as demanding a boss as Angus Doyle, only her demands came with honeyed words and a full understanding of what a man was capable of doing when he was madly in love but believed it was as perishable as a pear.

What I did day after day was read to Preacher Racoon every book in the house (yes, including the Bible, although more often he recited verses from memory at random times), stock his bedside table with canned peaches, manage his medicines and bedpan, and keep his dear wife company during the preacher's long stretches of peaceful sleep that occurred during the day and somewhat less so at night. The nature of people being what it is, I must add that while my relationship with Belle was *not* strictly like mother and son, it definitely was *not* like a young woman (for she was at least forty-five) and a young man (for I was honorable and would turn twenty-nine in the spring)—*not* during those dying days or even after her husband finally succumbed to his illness. He voiced his very last words on the first of January 1874: "I am full."

Free from the responsibility of dealing with the two dying men, I sat around or lay around (alone) in a torpid state for several weeks before Belle, who kept her sorrow as concealed as a schoolmarm's petticoats, told me to stop mourning and start acting like I was still alive. She put me to work. She didn't need a handyman, since Little Jack fulfilled that job beyond her expectations and certainly mine. She tested me out at other things, but in short order I proved to be an incompetent accountant, a feeble protector of the working ladies, a careless cook, and awkward and unhappy pouring drinks. Following in my father's footsteps as a whiskey seller was out of the question, but Belle thought getting out of the house would do me good. Encouraged by her, I found that Preacher Raccoon's old clothes fit me just fine, and I liked the feel of any of his three Bibles in my hand. The war was long over, but Kentucky wasn't adjusting well to black men running around free and equal, and lynching was widespread. (I was glad Jasper Washington wasn't around to see it.) "People need to hear God's word as much as ever," insisted Belle. "Not everyone can get to a church, so we got to bring God's word to them. That can't be done here in the Den. And it can't be done by me or by my girls or by Little Jack. It's up to you, Zach McCall, to go out amongst them; you got the calling."

I only heard the calling from her, but she reminded me that I owed her late husband that much. I began to try out the preaching circuit, following a shorter route than the real preacher used to take. Not that I was exactly a fake. I overcame my diffidence to a degree and read the words just fine, projecting my voice as if it belonged to somebody else, perhaps Preacher Raccoon himself. Belle would have let me use her fine buggy, but I was happy riding around on a horse that answered to "Hope" and plugged along at my kind of speed. I found enough people willing to listen to me to feel darn near righteous. It didn't matter to me that most of those people were dark skinned and half of them couldn't read. Once I had warmed up to the task, I was wishing Jasper Washington *was* there to see me, even if some of the folks who used to listen to Preacher Raccoon started calling me Preacher Kit or Preacher Cub, which happen to be two names for baby raccoons.

In early March I was still sensibly spreading the Word on horseback when there occurred a mix-up at home about matters of the heart that really wasn't my fault. Minnie Mary, Crooked Nose Jack's paramour, started to take an interest in my person because, as she told me, she wanted to be touched by a man who had been touched by the Lord the way her daddy had been back in North Carolina. I didn't ask questions about her late daddy or anything else. I simply told her I had *not* been touched by our Heavenly Father, and I didn't want to touch her. I admit I perhaps wasn't forceful enough in my wish to remain an untainted preacher.

One evening I was in bed in my old room (the small blue one adjacent to the Red Room) trying to read Genesis aloud using a deeper voice than usual, when she showed up out of the blue in her corsets and drawers she made clear had a split crotch. I was insisting she respect Little Jack, God, the late Preacher Raccoon, and me (in about that order) when she hurled the Bible off the bed. It struck the chest of my half brother, who had just come upstairs to see *his girl.* I immediately sprang off the bed, picked the Bible off the floor, and hurried from the room before Little Jack could so much as close his gaping mouth. I saddled up Hope and rode hard out to a small settlement where I knew two colored families were always ready to pray with me and share their food. I suspect I needed them more than they needed me, but they never treated me like a beggar.

I stayed for nearly a week. When I finally got back home, Belle Bragg said everyone had been worried sick about me. But everyone seemed perfectly well. It was business as usual at the Daniel's Den, except that the "little lovers"—Little Jack and Minnie Mary—went about their work and their renewed romance without seeming to notice I had returned.

I didn't let that bother me. In fact, I felt fortunate. I prayed for the couple at night and by day continued to go out and care for the people I had met on my preaching circuit like a shepherd tending his flock. I was proud to welcome both black sheep and white sheep into the fold. I told myself we all profited, spiritually speaking, even though, I can admit now, I never completely stopped asking myself, "Am I pulling the wool over their eyes?" Toward the end of the month a long letter arrived from Jasper

Washington, and I was so deeply involved in my work that I somehow expected him to praise me for helping *his* people in our home state. Of course, that was wishful thinking on my part. I hadn't sent him a letter about what I was doing because I had no idea where to write him. All I knew was that Cody's troupe was moving about the Northeast, a long way from Kentucky. It's funny, though, how a person—at least me—can get his expectations raised about something when the chances of it happening are slimmer than Minnie Mary's waist in a tight-laced corset. All right, I admit it: I could never completely erase certain visions of her from my mind.

Anyway, Jasper Washington didn't even ask how I was or what I was up to, and he seemed to have forgotten that the reason I had gone to the Daniel's Den was to see about my ill father. All he talked about was how the acting bug had about done in Wild Bill Hickok. By the time Jasper had caught up to the troupe, Wild Bill was missing his life on the Great Plains something awful. As a man alone on the frontier he had faced off with wild cowboys and wild Indians, faced down the likes of Dave Tutt and Phil Coe on the street, and faced formidable odds and opponents at the poker table. How seriously could he take performing in front of an audience of shopkeepers and genteel ladies? It was all well and good for his fellow actor scouts Buffalo Bill and Texas Jack, but then they were naturals who could ad-lib under the bright lights while he got tongue tied and alternated between being bored and embarrassed. What's more, those theater lights, especially the powerful spotlights, made his eyes burn like the devil. Jasper's letter closed this way:

> Buffalo Bill wanted me there to convince Wild Bill the show must go on. In fact, I got Wild Bill to agree that the show must go on, but with one important proviso—he

himself wouldn't play any part in it. At the Rochester Opera House several days ago, he took off his buckskin outfit and packed it in, bidding farewell to Cody and company, and taking off with me to the largest, most important so-called civilized spot in the country—New York City. You ask, but wasn't that going in the wrong direction? The short answer is yes, but Bill got the notion he must go where the most money was—believing he'd make a killing there doing the thing he loves most in the whole world, gambling—and where Agnes Thatcher Lake happened to be. You might remember that tightrope-walking lion tamer from when she caught Bill's eye back in Abilene? Well, he was dying to see the old gal again.

I knew my man was out of his element, but I also realized he needed to get Eastern gambling and lovemaking out of his system. Besides, I wanted to test the poker waters there myself. Did I do all right? You bet—I more than broke even. But, as I suspected, those New York sharps about cleaned Bill out of all his stage earnings. Fortunately, I caught a couple of them using marked cards, and after I showed them the error of their ways with a slight feat of strength and a casual reference to Wild Bill's prowess with a pistol, the pair restored Bill's chips and then some. Still, there was another problem. Bill kept misreading his cards and those of the other players, not because he is that bad a card player, but because his sight has diminished some. As for his lovemaking, I reckon that went better than his cards, but in the end the two lovebirds agreed to separate. She wanted Bill to stay and help her run her circus, but Bill told her putting on a circus sounded as fake and foolish as putting on a play and, besides, General Phil Sheridan had requested he drop everything to come scout for the army out of Fort Laramie. I'm not convinced Bill actually got such a message from the general, but I was elated to hear he was ready to put unhealthy, overpeopled New York City and the rest of the East in our dust. Agnes is really too old for him anyway and so preoccupied with her own business she'd never be able to devote herself to him fully. I'm proud to say I remain totally devoted to Bill, who needs me more than ever, what with his eyes being the way they are. Who knows, maybe the clear, crisp Western air will do his eyes some good.

In any case, Bill and I leave for Cheyenne, Wyoming Territory, real soon. It's our ticket to new adventure, new opportunity. Bill's not ready for the rocking chair yet. Maybe someday we'll see you out there in Cheyenne if you can manage it. I'd like that because you're the best damn Southern boy I ever did meet. Do try to leave you-know-who in Kentucky, though. Neither Bill nor I have any use for that wayward lad you call a half brother, but you already knew that.

—Your black bastard brother, Wash

Naturally, I didn't show Jasper Washington's letter to Crooked Nose Jack, who was already in an agitated state. He had become discontented with his duties in the kitchen and the tavern ("It amounts to doing women's work and slave work"), indignant at Belle Bragg's perceived treatment of him and me ("she degrades me despite my hard, honest work and elevates you to the rank of holy man, even though you never had any religion"), aggrieved at how Minnie Mary was now treating him ("like I was just another of those forlorn upstairs customers"), and nearly ashamed at having selfishly neglected to return to Louisville, first because he couldn't bear to leave the soft side of the love of his life for one hour and lately because he was desperately trying to win back the suddenly heartless barmaid.

For a while, Jack blamed me for everything—for making him

come to Boonesborough to see Fat Jack, mean and unforgiving to the end; for making him look bad in the eyes of Belle, Minnie Mary, and God by assuming the faux preacher role; for supposedly luring Minnie Mary to my bed and turning her against him; for not helping him with clean-up and other chores in the kitchen and tavern; and for never acting like a good older brother by offering to go with him to Louisville to help out the female McCalls. But then one day in early April, he suddenly announced, "I forgive you, Brother." His troubles had always been of his own making, of course, but I thanked him anyway since I felt even a faux preacher should show generosity.

The next thing I knew we were sitting on the Daniel's Den back porch, and he was suggesting it might be time at last for him to go to Louisville. One of his sisters had written, asking what in heaven's name had happened to him and wondering if he had "caught" whatever Father had and also died. More importantly, she stated without elaboration that their mother was suffering from dropsy.

"I'm sure it is horrible," he said. "First she loses my father and now this. She does have my sisters, if they haven't drowned in their own tears. They've always been such crybabies. I assume they must have grown up some after all these years. Would it help anything if I went back to all that at this particular time? Would I be able to stand it? Should I go, or should I stay?"

"You should go, Little Jack," I said, as a good older brother would surely advise. "It could be severe."

"Maybe it is, maybe it isn't. All three sisters are prone to exaggeration as well as excessive crying."

"Even if it isn't severe, you should go."

"I feel funny about the whole thing."

"Funny?"

"I've been in Kentucky all this time without going up there. What excuse can I give her?"

"Maybe you won't need one. Go. It's not too late."

"You think our mother is dying from this dropsy thing?"

"*Your* mother, Jack. I don't know. But why take any chances. Go."

"Minnie Mary won't care. She wants to be with other men. She made that damn clear, damn her. As soon as I go, I bet she'll . . . well, damn, damn, damn."

"I won't damn her, but I won't . . . that is to say, I will keep my eye on her if you want. You do know I don't have any interest in her at all . . ."

"It don't matter. Not anymore."

"I wouldn't say it, if it wasn't true, Little Jack."

"Drop it, Wild Child. I already told you I forgive you. You were raised among her kind."

I elected not to say anything, not wanting to start an argument. I just wanted him to leave.

"Belle Bragg won't miss me, but you can bet your bottom dollar she'll miss my cooking and slave labor."

"I'll try to help out a little more around here, Jack. I'll cut back on my circuit riding if need be."

"No, you won't."

"I can. I don't need to preach so regular."

"No doubt. Anyway, it don't matter. You're coming with me."

"That's not in my plans."

"Change your plans. These are dire times. I need your support. I came here for you when our father was dying, now you got to come to Louisville for me when Mother is dying."

"Maybe it's not so bad. I mean, your sister didn't say it was severe, right?"

"Come to think of it, Brother, Emily wouldn't have written me if it wasn't severe. You said I should go, and I'm saying you should come with me. We got to stick together like we always did."

Not always, I thought but said nothing. I sighed and began thinking about all the people I saw while on my preaching circuit. Sometimes their faces lit up when I took Bible in hand and started reading; sometimes they looked blank. I was due to ride out again the next day. I had gotten into a routine. I liked my borrowed horse, Hope.

"You think you are really *that* needed," he said, as if reading my mind. "You've been a stable boy, a swamper, a part-time jailer, and a gravedigger. How does that qualify you to be a preacher?"

"I don't know," I admitted. "I guess some of Preacher Raccoon rubbed off on me."

"It ain't that hard reading a Bible you know."

"No, but understanding it takes a little work. I'm not saying I'm a great preacher or even a good one, but I . . ."

"So, how about being a good brother for a change. I don't want to face Mother alone. I can't do it. How can I look her in the face? What can I possibly say? You do so much better around the dying."

"I barely know your mother. You remember during the war when I was in your attic and she . . . but forget about that. I just don't know if I can get away and . . ."

"Of course, you can. You can read to her from one of Preacher Raccoon's old Bibles."

"But you just said I wasn't a real preacher . . ."

"That is, unless you think Belle Bragg will miss you too much and won't approve of you taking off again and leaving her behind to groom some other young man for preaching."

"What? It's not like that. She knows I won't be preaching around these parts forever. I know it, too. I can read with an honest voice, but it's true what you said. No matter how long I stay, I may never feel like an actual genuine living preacher. From time to time, I've even talked to Belle about leaving the

Den. She has always encouraged me to listen to my heart and to go forth in this big wide-open country, to be independent, fearless, and . . . well, a man, and not necessarily a holy one. In any case, I never meant to come back to Boonesborough for life, you know."

"I know, *only* for death. Look, Brother, any way you look at the state of things in this place, it's time for me to go and it's time for you to go. Minnie Mary and Belle don't need either of us around. What say you? Don't be a bad egg. Be a good brother. Come with me to Louisville. Where else have you to go?"

I scratched my head for the longest time. Little Jack waited for an answer with unusual patience.

"I'm not sure," I finally said, as I leaned against the porch railing and, facing dead west, stared out through the bare branches of the red maple trees. "I've given some recent thought to starting over somewhere, somewhere out there." I pointed like some great explorer of the past or at least a brave pioneer. My finger began to shake a little.

"The woods?"

"The plains."

"Back to Kansas, you mean?"

"Or maybe closer to the mountains."

"What mountains?"

"I don't know, but I believe they got some out in Wyoming Territory. You ever hear of Cheyenne?"

CHAPTER TWENTY-EIGHT:
THE CALL OF CHEYENNE

I had visions of Cheyenne in my head, more specifically of Jasper Washington and me seated in the best restaurant in town sharing a medium-rare sirloin steak and good talk, as well as congenial laughter over those strange, hard-to-believe "old days" when Wild Bill Hickok actually fancied himself an actor and me a preacher. Funny, but in none of these visions was either Wild Bill or Crooked Nose Jack present, and in none of them was it clear what my occupation might be. That my sights were set on Cheyenne pleased Belle Bragg because she had wisely detected that, despite my commendable efforts and outward appearance, my heart and soul were not totally engaged in the preaching profession. She never did believe it when Minnie Mary announced her pregnancy and then indicated she was uncertain which of the two McCall boys was the father. Belle did, however, think I really needed to find the right woman for me (whatever kind that might be) and that I was more likely to find her out West than in the Daniel's Den.

"I'll miss you, Zach," Belle told me. "You've been more than like a son to me."

"And you've been more than like a mother to me," I said.

"God knows I miss Preacher Raccoon and Fat Jack. Such different men, but both meant so much to me, just as you do. You know that don't you, dear Zach?"

"Yet you want me to go?"

"I'd hate for you to miss out on all that life has to offer, and all that life has to offer can't be found at my place. We're hanging on here at the Den, but Boonesborough is on its last legs. You left this nest once; now it's time to fly away again. As a present, the least I can do is give you Hope."

But first there was Louisville. Crooked Nose Jack couldn't leave the Daniel's Den fast enough after Minnie Mary made her startling announcement and even brought in a doctor from out of town to confirm that she was pregnant. Although we never discussed the matter as we rode north together on the strong back of Belle's gift, Hope the horse, I'm sure Jack knew the baby-to-be couldn't possibly be mine. That didn't make things any easier for him. He no more wished to be a father than he did a dead man. He sagged in the saddle until we got five miles away from the Den, at which point he sat up straight and yelled, "Can't this damn nag move any faster?" He dug his heels in both the horse and me. It was smooth riding the rest of the way to Louisville, but nothing went smoothly once we were there dealing with the four female McCalls and especially the man who had moved in with them, Hector Browning.

When I say moved in, I mean that in the strongest terms. He was a New Yorker who had arrived in Louisville during Reconstruction and become a leading banker in the community. Emily, the oldest, fairest, and dandiest of Little Jack's three sisters, now wore Hector's gold wedding ring, and the couple shared the master bedroom of the McCall home, now more often referred to as the Browning home. Emily had not mentioned Hector in her letter to her brother; the new husband must have moved in and taken over faster than any conquering army. He had purchased the two-story (plus attic) house from the widow Hannah McCall so the financially strapped family didn't have to sell it to an outsider and so she would have a familiar place to lay her bonnet for the rest of her born days.

Unclear to me was anything Hector had in common with

Emily, except money—he was a banker and a speculator who never tired of making it, and she was a docile young woman who never tired of spending it. Emily's sisters, Catherine and Sarah, weren't twins, of course, but they looked so similar in their utter pale plainness and long-sleeved, high-neckline dresses that I constantly called one by the other's name. The pair might have been jealous, perturbed, and feeling diminished, but they kept their complaints to themselves. They could keep their small rooms, receive modest allowances from their breadwinner brother-in-law, and not have to fend for themselves until they secured husbands of their own. Jack, though, suggested they were both destined to become old maids.

Things were worse for widow Hannah McCall. She had made herself into a devout teetotaler while living with a hard-drinking, whiskey-selling husband who had taken most of his ardor on the road, and when Fat Jack left her it confirmed her belief that hard drink was the "devil's invention." But soon after his death, she realized the devil had invented plenty of equally evil things— including sober, pipe-smoking Hector Browning, an advocate of the temperance movement yet totally drunk on power, possessions, and command and with no use at all for a sick mother-in-law. He had relegated her and her dropsy to the attic as if she were a leper. She sat up day and night in the very bed where I had lingered and been ministered to by Little Jack near the end of the Civil War. She found it difficult to lie on either side, and when she lay on her back, she could hardly breathe at all. Her heart wasn't pumping right. Her pulse was feeble, her countenance pale, her lips livid, her belly swollen and soft. On our first visit to the attic, Jack only touched her thinning hair once before turning away in disgust. "She couldn't look more like a ghost if you put a white sheet over her head," he told me. Emily told Jack that physicians had come and gone and treated their mother's symptoms in a wide variety of ways—among them, mercury, purple foxglove, lungwort, snake oil, bloodletting, hydropathy, and draining excess fluid. These healers were all men, and all had different ideas about what dropsy was and how to treat it. What none could do was cure her.

What I did was pray for Hannah McCall. I had left Preacher Raccoon's three Bibles back at the Den since Belle had given them to him, but I tried to recite some biblical verses from memory to ease Hannah's pain. It wasn't much, but it caused her to briefly apologize for having treated me unkindly during my wartime residence in the attic, and it was far more than her son did. For the next three days, Jack made only short, irregular visits to the attic because he claimed his mother had nothing but a cold stare for him, and he could tell she was silently passing harsh judgment on him and hating him for running away from home in 1865, for not coming to see her sooner, and for looking too much like her late husband. Hector Browning had assigned us to a guest room with one bed, which Jack had never slept in before, and he woke me up each night with pre-dawn screams.

"You feel badly about everything," I suggested on our fourth day in Louisville. "I understand."

"Everything here sickens me," Little Jack replied, "especially Hector Browning. He was originally a New England Yankee, you know."

On our fifth day visiting the attic I was fumbling with the right words to say to Hannah McCall, and Jack was rummaging through an old trunk full of boys' and men's clothing when the patient broke her usual silence by shouting, "At least I outlived the bastard!" I immediately thought of myself, but I was still very much alive. She meant Fat Jack, of course, but had nothing more to say about him.

When Little Jack and I descended the attic stairs five minutes later, he grew loud: "It's too much to bear. She looks like she's already dead, and I'd swear those words she spoke came from beyond the grave. Your praying obviously isn't helping her none. No big surprise! She gets worse every day. Your Lord above must delight in eyeballing *our* pain. This house is hell, and that attic is the top level. How can a fellow even breathe? It is only a matter of time before . . ." He couldn't finish his rant. He clutched his stomach with both hands and raced down the rest of the stairs, trying to get outside to vomit. He made it, but only barely. He retched all over the doormat just as Hector Browning approached the front door, strutting with the help of a duck-head decorative walking stick, while Emily, weighted down by two hat boxes, followed five ungainly steps behind.

Hector Browning was revolted by the sight in front of him, as much by Little Jack himself as by the vomited matter. It had been that way since we first rode Hope across *his* immaculate front yard. His every gesture and unspoken word indicated he was permitting Emily's no-account brother and his unworthy bastard accomplice to sponge off him only so long as Mrs. McCall lived. The process, however, was taking too long, not only for him but also for Little Jack.

At noontime one gloomy day in early April, Hector surprised everyone by leaving his bank and showing up at his house, not to enjoy a meal with the family but to censure Little Jack. He called him into the Browning library, full of thick, dust-free books and antique swords and pistols, and I followed along. The owner took the best chair and told us to sit. Little Jack elected to remain standing, so I did, too, in a corner next to a case of firearms. The owner spent a minute putting tobacco in his pipe. But then he placed it carefully on a side table next to a fancy ashtray that depicted a colorfully dressed maiden wandering through a bright bluegrass meadow. He must have felt the pipe was too much of a distraction. While speaking his mind, he cradled his walking stick and fidgeted with it as if cleaning a rifle.

"I have extended my hospitality to you because you were once a legitimate member of this household," he told my half brother, while illegitimate me stood by unnoticed or ignored. "Has my generosity been reciprocated? Not at all. You have simply taken advantage of it. Have you uttered a single word of thanks? Not one. You have eaten my food, made messes everywhere, treated my wife like a servant, awakened memories of things best forgotten, and brought whiskey to your room and even the attic, though you know I forbid the use or presence of alcohol in this household in deference to your unfortunate mother. In short, you have been unscrupulous."

Little Jack crossed his arms and snorted. "That's a high-falutin' word from a big bug, the biggest toad in the puddle," he finally said.

"If you're trying to get me in a pucker by calling me a toad, it simply won't work. I've been called a lot worse by piddling little people."

"You can go piddle on yourself."

Little Jack stepped back when Hector Browning rose from his chair. Seeing what effect his movement had on his brother-in-law seemed to give Hector encouragement, and he made short thrusts with his walking stick as if fencing. Little Jack took another step back and held his stomach as if he had been nicked.

"Em warned me you were a saucebox," Hector said, but he pulled back the walking stick and tapped the rug with it. "I took you in but will not allow myself to be taken in. Since I became a banker, I haven't given anyone a good thrashing, and I won't start now, so you can stop shaking like a bigtooth aspen leaf. But I'll have to ask you to leave my home."

"You don't have to ask me twice. I'd already decided: we're leaving."

"We?"

"That's right. Me and my brother."

"Brother? Oh, right." Hector Browning glanced over to the corner for the first time, and I nodded to show him I was alive.

"We've both had a hankering to absquatulate," continued Jack. "Put that big word in your pipe and smoke it, Mr. Banker!" Little Jack snorted, showed his back to Hector Browning, and then stomped toward the library door. "Come, Brother," he said, waving me along. "It's time to absquatulate."

The next morning when Little Jack and I went up to the attic, his mother was sitting up in bed as usual, but her eyes were closed. I put my ear close to her face to make sure she was still breathing. We waited for half a minute until she gasped as if some dream had agitated her.

"It's best her eyes aren't open," Little Jack said. "Let's get the hell out of here."

"I'll pray for your full recovery, Mrs. McCall," I stupidly said. "I'll pray for all of us."

Downstairs, all was quiet. The homeowner had gone off for an early breakfast meeting with other Louisville bigwigs. Catherine and Sarah were still asleep. "It ain't beauty sleep," said Little Jack, who saw no point in awakening either of them. In the kitchen we drank coffee and stuffed ourselves with biscuits for the road. Emily showed up in her nightclothes and laid her head on the breakfast table and began to weep. Little Jack shook his head and told her to stop it, even as I patted Emily on her sharp shoulder blades and tried to recall a biblical passage that dealt with saying farewell.

"You just got here," she said.

"We stayed too long," Little Jack replied. "That son of a bitch husband of yours isn't going to ride roughshod over me one day longer."

"You can't go. Mother wouldn't want you to just suddenly

leave after she waited so long for you to return."

"She's past caring. Hospitable Hector asked us to leave yesterday, and we're leaving."

"He told me what he said. There was a misunderstanding. He asked you to leave his library, not the house."

"It doesn't matter. I'm sick of the guest room. I'm sick of the attic. I'm sick of everything and everybody in this entire house. So long, Sis. Hope all your hats, jewelry, and such keep you happy."

"Oh, Jack, where would you go?"

"Where? Anywhere."

"That's the trouble," she said, abruptly raising her head, which caused my hand to fly off her back. "You have nowhere to go. You can't be just a wanderer, and you certainly can't want to go back to Boonesborough with *him*?" She pointed at me, and for the first time I took full note of what appeared to be a diamond wedding ring.

"*Him* is my brother, Sis. And he's not going back there either. The West is wide open for the McCall brothers. Nothing is written in limestone, but we are bound for Cheyenne. That's way out in Wyoming Territory. Ain't that right, Brother?"

He was right about it being in Wyoming Territory. The "we" didn't sound right.

"Tell her, Wild Child," Little Jack shouted as he stood up.

"I really do have to go, half sister," I said, but I stayed seated. My intention was to go to Cheyenne, meet up with Jasper Washington, and, without thinking through any specifics, somehow make something of myself or at least be myself far from the shadows and ghosts in Kentucky. Crooked Nose Jack hadn't been part of my vision. I had figured one way or another we'd part ways in Louisville in due time. But what could I do? I couldn't order my half brother to stay behind with his dying mother and crying sisters. And I couldn't tell him I wanted to be alone.

"We're leaving now," Jack said.

"You bet," I said, finally standing up.

Emily stared at me with big red, wet eyes, then laid her head back down on the breakfast table. I knew she wasn't crying about me going, as I had never been a part of her life. But I wasn't so sure she was crying about Jack going either. Maybe she was crying over her mother in the attic and the fact that soon Hector Browning would be the only man in the house again.

Crooked Nose Jack and I scurried down the street to where Hope was stabled and told the liveryman that Hector Browning was paying the bill for boarding the horse. We could have caught a train out of the Louisville station, but we were both far less eager to say goodbye to Hope than we were to banker Browning and the surviving female McCalls. So, we rode the sixty miles up to Vernon, Indiana, where we (me tearfully) bid farewell to Hope, sold the gift horse for a good price, and then hopped on the next westbound.

Jack and I spoke up a storm as we traveled by rail west and further west, but only because talking helped him *not* think. We spoke of many things—the landscape and wildlife we passed, the clouds and the wind, smoke and fire, hostile Indians and reservation Indians, outlaws and lawmen, poker and faro, whiskey and women (of the saloon variety only), love (brotherly only), his hate (of most everything east of the Mississippi), soon-to-be-explored Cheyenne and frontier cities whose names we didn't yet know, our present adventure and the bright future (him finding fortune and fame, me finding a decent way to make a living and a measure of happiness). Things we made a point of *not* discussing were family or death (we both knew Hannah McCall might die even before we reached the

Mississippi), Minnie Mary or Belle Bragg, goodbyes or see you laters, the past (at least not anything that took place in Kentucky), or exactly why, despite our differences in character and views, we were still sticking together. I thought plenty about Jasper Washington and Wild Bill Hickok as we steamed across Nebraska, but I kept those thoughts to myself, knowing how my half brother held both those fine men in such low regard.

It turned out Cheyenne wasn't exactly in the mountains, but I could see a range about thirty or forty miles away, which was close enough for me. Being a railroad hub, Cheyenne had its share of hustle and bustle, but when we arrived in the afternoon, we couldn't help but remark how surprisingly quiet it seemed. We learned from the train conductor that things had been vastly different when it was a hell-on-wheels, end-of-track rail town in 1867 and for a number of years after that when it proved a magnet for professional gamblers, bunco artists, prostitutes, dance hall queens, roughs, road agents, and killers. At the depot, a convivial if unofficial town promoter greeted us like a couple of local boys come home even though we had never previously set foot in Cheyenne.

"Welcome, strangers, welcome," he said, doffing his bowler and then running a toil-hardened hand through thinning hair slick with bear grease. "Had a good trip?"

"Passable," Little Jack and I said at the same time.

"Friends, I presume. Know each other like a book, I'd wager if I was a betting man."

"I don't read much," Jack said. "I do bet. We're brothers."

"Wonderful, wonderful. Brothers from where?"

"From different mothers, same father."

He seemed to back up a step but at the same time moved his head forward for a closer look. "I meant what neck of the woods, or possibly what throat of the prairie."

He chuckled at his amiable wit, so I smiled. Jack snorted.

"Kentucky," I said.

"Glad to meet you Kentucky boys. I hail from the Green Mountain State. You might know it better as Vermont. Name's Greeley, like that newspaperman from New York who told us all to go west when we were young. Well, I wasn't all that young, but I come west anyhow. Landed hereabouts in '67, two months ahead of the railroad. I was green all right when I got here, and hardly a mountain of a man, as you can plainly see. Who'd have thought I'd last this long?"

He resumed chuckling, and he only stopped again when I told him our last name.

"The McCall brothers, eh? Answering the call of the West, eh? I reckon asking a man where he's from isn't a smart thing to do out here in man's country. But I can't help myself. I'm just naturally a friendly fellow. You can call me Chester, boys. Everyone does. Anyone in this fair city will tell you what a square deal you'll always get from Chester Greeley, long-time resident, though of course Cheyenne hasn't been around all that long. I'm in the hardware business. Hired by Charles Boettcher in '71 after his brother Herman had gone off to start a second store in Colorado. A couple years ago Charles also left for Colorado to start a third store. So, boys, guess who was left in charge of Boettcher and Company Hardware right here in Cheyenne? That's right. You might say that I am *'and Company.'* Everyone in town knows me now, at least all those who've ever purchased tools, nails, tins, or utensils. You'll know Chester Greeley, too, if you stick around for any length of time at all."

"We might and we might not," Jack said. "Your town looks pretty dead."

"We were as overflowing with sin as Abilene in the bad old days," said the hardware store man, raising his thick eyebrows at the memory. "We became known as the 'Magic City of the Plains,' if you call all that disorderly conduct magical. I figure that nickname helped us be named territorial capital. We've settled down plenty in the last couple years. The hardware business is going great guns. You see, respectable businessmen like me stayed on while the old roughs and cardsharps left one way or another, and most newcomers of their ilk have just been passing through. You two are lucky to be visiting our fair city at this juncture in our existence."

"That remains to be seen, mister," Jack said. "Must still be poker palaces around."

"Not on this side of town. I didn't catch your first name?"

"Didn't throw it."

"He's Little Jack, I'm plain Zach," I said.

"Excellent," said Chester Greeley. "I'd love to chat with you gentlemen all day, but the time has come for me to head back to my 'we got everything you need' store. Customers in need of everything await. Stop by Boettcher Hardware any old time, and we'll chew the fat some more. Until we meet again, gentlemen."

"Hold on, sir," I said. "You must have pretty good lawmen hereabouts."

"I'll say, stranger, starting with the best law and order man in the West."

"Mr. Hickok?"

"What? You must be talking about the gambler known as Wild Bill. I heard he was recently charged with causing an affray in the Gold Room, beat two men to the floor with a cane. Nasty business. Sheriff Carr probably made the arrest. That's who I'm talking about—town-taming Laramie County Sheriff T. Jeff Carr."

"Oh," I said. I had never seen Wild Bill use a cane before, for walking or for fighting. "But Mr. Hickok is still around?"

"Not in jail anymore."

"I meant, is he here in Cheyenne?"

"Don't rightly know. I believe I read somewhere that he was out in the wilds guiding a dozen English lords and noblemen on a hunting expedition."

"Accompanied by a large black man, perhaps?"

"I wouldn't know. But I doubt any of their manservants are coloreds. Why do you ask?"

"Never mind that," said Little Jack. "Tell me more about this Gold Room. It sounds enticing."

"It's the gambling concession in Jim Allen's Variety Hall and Saloon. I don't gamble myself."

"Gambling as in poker?"

"I suppose. I must be going. Business can't wait forever."

"Show us the way to the Gold Room, mister, and I'll give you two bits."

The hardware clerk pursed his slight lips and scowled at Jack but still tipped his bowler hat before turning away. "I happen to be headed in the opposite direction," he explained, high stepping away from us like a deer with its white tail up.

Crooked Nose Jack and I spent our first night in the Union Pacific Hotel next to the depot, but the next day we took room and board for a dollar a day at Dyer's Hotel. Jack found the Gold Room on his own, and he took to that gambling hall right away when he discovered a game of stud. He won enough big pots to stick to it day after day, night after night. He even became a dealer that somebody nicknamed "Jack of Hearts," apparently because the previously named Jack of Clubs was a lot luckier in cards than with a certain pair of buxom redheads. The only thing Jack had to say to me about the two ladies in question was that they were twins originally from a feuding family in Pikeville, Kentucky, but that the two of them stacked together couldn't add up to one Minnie Mary.

Jack had only a little more to say about Wild Bill Hickok and Jasper Washington. Wild Bill had indeed made his presence felt in the Gold Room with his cane, pistols, and daring raises, but he hadn't been seen there in weeks, and neither had "Bill's Big Boy." Even next to Hickok, Jasper had stood out because of his size and because he had been the first colored man to frequent the establishment since former slave turned prominent businessman Barney Ford temporarily folded his hand in Cheyenne and left for Denver in 1871. I had no call to visit the Gold Room myself, at least not until Jasper returned.

That was fine with Crooked Nose Jack—not having Hickok and Washington around, having me around but not at his place of business. He had found what he was looking for, even if it was a stretch to call the Gold Room a poker palace. I soon also found what I was looking for in Cheyenne—a job. The day it happened didn't start out so well. I visited a couple of churches in town to pray (not necessarily for myself, but it turned out that way in both churches) and in between had been told at the 17th Street stable that not even a good man experienced with horses was needed. I skipped my noontime meal and was on Eddy Street with my head lowered, following directions to the cemetery to see if a good man was needed there, when I bumped into the only Cheyenne businessman who wasn't a stranger— Chester Greeley.

His friendliness to two strangers at the depot hadn't been an act. He remembered who I was and proved even friendlier on our second meeting. He brought me to the hardware store, which was still named Boettcher and Company and still carried the Boettcher brothers' slogan, "Hard Goods. Hard Ware. Hard Cash." We got to talking in between his waiting on customers, for he was a talker, and I let it out that I was hunting for employment. He asked what my last job was, and I told him the truth: I'd been a novice circuit preacher in Madison County, Kentucky. Just like that, he said he had an opening and that he strongly believed if I could sell backwater folks on the good

Lord, I could surely sell frontier folks on the lesser but still essential things his store had to offer. I didn't have to sell him on me; he said he was a good judge of character and that he knew when he met the two McCall brothers at the depot, Cheyenne would be getting one good man. At first, I failed to be enthusiastic because I wasn't certain he was actually offering me a job and because I had doubts about my ability to sell anything.

"You won't be serving the Lord, but you'll be serving churchgoing Chester Greeley and a bunch of God-fearing people," he said, with an arm wrapped around my shoulders. "And Charles Boettcher spoke the God's honest truth when he told me: 'Hardware is one of the best businesses there is. Axes and hammers don't go out of style like so many other things.' So, Zach my boy, I'll go Charles one better and tell you straight out: Hardware is the *best* goddamned business in Cheyenne today."

"Sold!" I shouted, which drew the stares of a couple of Chester's customers.

CHAPTER TWENTY-NINE: CHEYENNE DAYS

Life in Cheyenne became one of routine for me and Crooked Nose Jack, but they were different routines, of course. We kept paying for our room at the Dyer's Hotel one month in advance. I slept eight hours every night; my roommate slept by day, though a couple of days each week he didn't sleep at all, at least not in our room. I ate my two-egg breakfast right in the hotel the same time every morning and then took my daily constitutional to the cemetery (strictly because it made me feel more alive) before starting my long workday at usually busy Boettcher and Company Hardware (I didn't really have to sell anyone on anything; people came in with specific needs) and then enjoying an evening meal and endless conversation with my never-silent boss, Chester Greeley. Although neither of us gambled or was much of a drinking man, once a week we went to the Gold Room so Chester could sit before a larger listening audience.

For several months the Gold Room remained Jack's favorite place to play poker because he rarely had consecutive losing nights there. But he got around for a change of pace, rotating among a variety of theater and gambling saloons, billiard parlors, and private game rooms. When the soldiers from nearby Fort D. A. Russell came to town seeking opportunities to indulge in dissipation, he weeded out the card players among them and usually ended up taking their week's pay and then buying them drinks. While poker was Jack's game of choice, he bucked the tiger every other afternoon because he loved to beat certain faro dealers at *their* game. Rarely did he even acknowl-edge Chester and me on our Gold Room night because, as he complained to me on several occasions, Chester prattled worse than a preacher. Being a former preacher of sorts, I might have taken offense, but I let it pass since I didn't feel up to an argu-ment.

One September night in the Gold Room, however, Little Jack interrupted us at our crowded corner table, and his whiskey-loosened tongue went right to work. Chester had been telling me and three respectable merchants all he knew about Colonel Custer's recent expedition to the Black Hills of Dakota Terri-tory that confirmed there was gold in those hills. Little Jack sat in my chair while I was still in it, so I stood up. He pulled the chair closer to Chester and got right into the sober hardware man's jolly, naturally pink-cheeked face. "I never trust a man who won't let you buy him a drink," he said loudly enough for customers to hear far beyond our table. "It figures any teetotaler must be a self-righteous bastard. What's more, show me a man who won't gamble at any game, and I'll show you an imbecile."

It was hard to tell whether he was addressing me or Chester or both of us. I took offense this time. Sure, I was a bastard as a matter of fact, but I wasn't a self-righteous one. And Chester, from a solid Vermont family, wasn't any kind of bastard. Little Jack's calling me an imbecile was at best a case of the pot call-ing the kettle black. As for my boss and my friend, he was smarter than a bull whip and sharper than a Boettcher ax. That very evening before Custer and gold came up, he had said countless interesting things about recently invented barb wire, the stars in the sky, his family, tea-drinking New England ladies he had known, railroad history, homesteading, Sioux chiefs including Sitting Bull, American presidents from George Washington to U. S. Grant, and the importance of good fellow-ship.

"That'll be enough," I told my half brother. "You best find another table."

"This is *my* house," he replied, still staring hard at Chester. "I can sit anywhere I damn please in *my* house."

"And when did you buy the Gold Room, stranger?" the hardware man asked.

"We ain't strangers, you long-winded sidewinder."

"That's right, friend. I almost forgot. We met at the depot. You're welcome to pull up another chair."

"I got me this chair, and don't call me friend."

"That's Zach's chair."

"Must not be if I'm in it."

"Take my chair. I'll fetch another one for Zach."

"I don't want your niminy-piminy, self-righteous chair, you imbecile."

"That'll be enough," I repeated a little louder. I yanked away Jack's chair, and it worked even better than I anticipated. He slid right off the seat, and his backside crashed to the floor. He was more stunned than hurt but finally stood up, rubbing his backside. The three merchants laughed as if they were watching a circus clown's routine. I was in no mood to laugh, and neither was Chester. My knees wobbled, so I reclaimed my chair. My heart was pounding, and when I tried to take a full breath I gasped. I had never struck my half brother in my life, but whatever I had just done made me feel excited and sort of good. Meanwhile, Chester Greeley, who believed acts of kindness would be reciprocated, reached down to Little Jack and helped him to his feet.

Jack kept rubbing himself while staring blankly at Chester. But when the merchants provided another round of laughter, he spun completely around. Perhaps he thought I had joined them, but I was just sitting in the chair trying to breathe normally. I saw the bulge in his vest where he now carried his derringer. He didn't go for his weapon, and I was relieved, right up until he yelled, "Bastard McCall" and threw a roundhouse punch. The effort caused him to lose his balance, and he fell on top of me, causing both of us to fall backward along with the disputed chair. The back of my head struck something hard twice—a spittoon, I later learned, and then the floor—and I saw an array of twinkling lights that made me think I was gazing at the night sky with Chester. It didn't last. Everything went dark.

When I opened my eyes some time later, I was lying on a card table and looking up into a somewhat nebulous dark face. My head was throbbing, in back, in front, and on both sides, but I smiled anyway as the face peering at me became clearer. Jasper Washington was back in my life. And Crooked Nose Jack would be out of it for a while in jail. A fellow was supposed to watch out for his brother—Jack had said those very words to me more than once. But after what happened in the Gold Room, I didn't want to see Crooked Nose Jack (no apology from him would change that, not that he was ever one to apologize for anything), and he didn't want to see me (because he must have felt ashamed of his violent, unbrotherly actions, or so I imagined).

Jasper filled me in on what I had missed that night in the Gold Room, including Crooked Nose Jack's lunatic behavior. Even with my senses already benumbed, my half brother had kicked me repeatedly about the shoulders, neck, and head. That got the merchant trio to stop laughing, but they continued to watch as if the drubbing was part of the clever clown act. Chester Greeley, though, saw the true nature of the violent act and screamed for somebody to make him (meaning Jack) stop. But nobody did, so Chester went against his passive nature and launched himself into the fray. Good intentions were not enough. He tripped over the upside-down spittoon and never quite reached my assailant.

There's no telling how long my brother would have kept kicking me if Jasper hadn't at that moment followed Wild Bill Hickok and another buckskin-clad man into the Gold Room and spotted me on the floor. Instantly, Jasper rushed past the other two men and with just one hand grabbed Little Jack by the back of his shirt and lifted him off me. For a few moments he held my half brother high in the air and considered tossing him out the back door like a bucket of dirty water. But then his other large hand came into play as if it had a mind of its own, and Jasper gave Little Jack a squeeze to remember, breaking two of his ribs before letting go. My protector then scooped me up and carried me to a table, which he wiped clear of cards, chips, money, and whiskey glasses with one hand before gently placing me on top.

Neither Sheriff Jeff Carr, the city marshal, nor any other lawman showed up in timely fashion, so Wild Bill dragged aching Little Jack out of the Gold Room and all the way to the city jail. The man who had entered the Gold Room with Wild Bill and Jasper nodded approvingly as he watched Hickok make his citizen's arrest. Sporting hand-tailored fringed buckskins, a fine linen shirt, flowing blond hair, and mustache, he looked every bit like a shorter version of Wild Bill. He positioned himself in the middle of the saloon, hitched up his large silver belt buckle, and made an announcement loud enough for everyone in the Gold Room to hear (except me, of course, as I was still unconscious):"Yes, folks, your patron saint, the preeminent pistoleer of the plains, has returned. Riffraff, cheats, and bullies beware! And now that *our* Wild Bill has matters well in hand, I bid you a good evening, gentlemen. It's bath time!"

I didn't understand at first why Jasper's recounting of events included so much about that other man in buckskins, who was considered a colorful character in Cheyenne because he insisted on a nightly soak in a tub of hot water with a wooden back scrubber and a bar of lavender-scented soap (the last item available at Boettcher and Company Hardware). But I figured it out soon enough. The man, widely known as Colorado Charlie Utter, had long been in the freighting business and never wanted to smell like a mule or other beast of burden. I could relate to that from my previous stable work. Colorado Charlie had met Wild Bill in Hays, Kansas, in the late '60s, and they had enjoyed each other's company before going their separate ways. They had renewed their friendship during the past year and, before I arrived in Cheyenne, had become well-known in the Gold Room—Hickok because of his gun-handling reputation and handsome poker face and Utter for being not only colorful and friendly but also sufficiently hardened to deal with any trouble that might arise.

"I swear those two are closer than two bullets in an over-under double-barreled derringer," Jasper commented during one of our bench talks on the raised boardwalk in front of the Underwood Boarding House on Eddy Street, where I'd moved to get away from Little Jack in the Dyer's Hotel.

I was surprised to detect dark lines around Jasper's eyes that I hadn't previously noticed. "You mean as close as Mr. Hickok and Mr. Cody?" I asked, but my own words made me squirm. Jasper himself fit into the equation somewhere. I didn't want to offend him.

"Closer," he said, more subdued than usual. "There's no acting going on between Wild Bill and Colorado Charlie. They are as natural together as the earth and the moon, the king of hearts and the king of diamonds, boots and spurs, pork and beans . . . and like that."

Concerned, I studied Jasper's face more closely, and just like that the wrinkles on his forehead deepened, and the corners of his mouth turned downward. "But not like you and Mr. Hickok, right?" I said. "Wherever Bill goes, you go, except when he went

343

East to act, but you did join him there later and brought him back to where he belongs—the West. When I see you two I can't help but think of that old phrase 'as alike as two peas in a pod.' "

"Sure enough—a white pea and a black pea."

"Mr. Hickok always seemed fair about such matters, being from an abolitionist family and all."

"True, but no fairer than you, and you're a white Kentuckian who fought for slavery."

"I'm not exactly sure why I served the South for a time, but it never was for that."

"I believe you. You were young and didn't know any better. Right now, I'd say you're near color blind, and Bill is going blind, hopefully not too damned fast. Don't let the secret out, not even to your brother. He's liable to take advantage of Bill's predicament and talk someone into trying to assassinate him."

"Crooked Nose Jack would never . . ." I caught myself and shut up. Trying to defend my half brother had become a bad habit over the years. And right now, I was still mad as hell at him for jumping me in the Gold Room. Too much whiskey didn't excuse all bad behavior.

Jasper dragged his bulk off the bench and slowly paced in front of me with shoulders slumped. Occasionally he muttered something I couldn't make out. I had always looked up to him as a self-confident and proud man whom I could turn to for advice or help. He had saved my life in Springfield from Joe Riggs's smoking gun, and he may have saved my life again in Cheyenne from Jack McCall's vicious kicks. But now his eyes were glazed over with a muddy film and his tight fists were like cannonballs, dragging his arms and upper body down. I doubted I could help him with anything unless he walked into Boettcher and Company Hardware wanting to buy a hammer and nails. But I asked what was wrong, which was the least a friend should do.

"Haven't felt this god-awful since that time in Ohio when I lost the bout to Victor the tame bear," he admitted. "It's like I've lost a brother, though I never had a brother. Of course, that might be a blessing, because if I had a brother like *your* brother, I'd *want* to lose him."

"Half brother," I corrected, but I couldn't disagree with his sentiment.

"It's more like I just saw my best friend fall off a cliff. No! It's more like my best friend pushed me off a cliff. Not exactly, though, because then I'd be dead and not give a damn about what I'm talking about."

He wasn't making himself particularly clear, though I knew the man he considered his best friend wasn't me. But it was all right to be his friend; I didn't have to be the best. I certainly wouldn't try to push him anywhere, let alone off a cliff—and not just because of his great bulk. I felt I should do something, though, so I sprang off the bench and followed him back and forth for a while before I patted his broad back, perhaps too softly for him to even feel my hand. He just kept pacing as if I wasn't at his heels.

"It's Wild Bill Hickok, you're talking about, right?" I finally asked. "That's what's wrong, isn't it?"

"Nothing wrong with Bill except his eyes. It's Colorado Charlie who's the problem."

"You don't like Mr. Utter?"

"An utterly magnificent soul—that's what Bill calls him. Of course, Charlie isn't that—no man is—but what does Bill care what I think anymore."

"What's wrong with Mr. Utter? I know he must smell nice, bathing every night like he does. I like a good bath, too. So do you."

"He's just fine and dandy, too fine and dandy. You've heard that imitation is the sincerest form of flattery?"

I couldn't remember where I'd heard it. I thought maybe I'd read it in the Bible during my circuit preaching days. "Sure." I said. "And Mr. Utter imitates Mr. Hickok?"

"Imitates him and worships him. Colorado Charlie moved into Bill's life like a locust, stepped right over me, which you'd think would be hard to do considering my size. But Bill let it happen, sort of pushed me aside and embraced that diminutive clinging lookalike."

"You sure you're not reading too much into it, Jasper? Mr. Hickok must know that nobody could replace you after all those years of you sticking by him like . . ."

"Colorado Charlie has managed it. As you recall, I always said Bill needed me to watch his back and such. Want to know what happens now when Bill walks up to a bar or sits down at a poker table? Charlie is a short distance behind him, or fronting him if Bill has his back against a wall as he is wont to do. Charlie has two pistols, too, you know, and he's constantly on the alert in case of attack from enemies looking for a chance to get the drop on Bill. That's what I used to do, but all I had going for me was my brute strength; I never was much on carrying a firearm, let alone a pair. So, you see, Bill doesn't need me. He's got Charlie."

Jasper stopped pacing at the edge of the raised boardwalk and looked down at the street as if he wished he were on a cliff and wanted to jump. I tried to pat him on the back again. He felt my hand this time, and it so startled him that he did jump. He landed on both feet, hard enough to make miniature craters in Eddy Street. No harm done to him, though. In fact, he began laughing so hard that he had to hold his stomach. I was puzzled.

"I'm like an old wrinkled wife thrown over by her husband for a dance hall girl," he finally said. "How you think I'd look in a black mourning dress?"

"Peculiar. Like a bear in short pants. But it isn't that bad, is it, Jasper? You still have a good friend right here, you know?"

"That goes without saying. Nice to know you got my back, friend."

For the rest of 1874 and into the next year, Jasper Washington spent more time with me and my other friend, Chester Greeley, than he did with Wild Bill Hickok, although on occasion Jasper and Wild Bill would find themselves in the same poker game (with Charlie Utter positioned close by, of course). Having no wish to associate with either Hickok or Washington, let alone possibly losing money to them, Little Jack stopped showing up in the Gold Room. I suppose he found enough good luck gambling in other establishments to at least keep his room in the Dyer's Hotel, keep his belly full, and keep company now and then with disreputable ladies. We still weren't talking, but his name seemed to pop up frequently during my daily conversations with Jasper, Chester, and the respectable citizens who patronized Boettcher and Company Hardware.

Jasper still kept an eye, or at least the corner of an eye, on Wild Bill, and told me he thought Hickok was filling himself with whiskey too often. Even when he came up a loser at the poker table, admirers—including his greatest admirer, Charlie Utter—were ready to buy him drinks. Not everyone admired him, though. The editor of the *Cheyenne Daily Leader*, for one, said Wild Bill had a reputation as a brave, scrupulous man, but "wine and women have ruined his constitution and impaired his faculties," and he had showed himself to be "a very tame and worthless loafer and bummer."

According to Jasper, Wild Bill and Charlie sometimes wandered the streets at night, singing to the moon and stars and telling each other stories about their adventurous pasts but even more so about the fabulous riches in gold coming out of the Black Hills. On one occasion, Wild Bill was staggering in front of the Dyer's Hotel and accidentally knocked heads with an equally intoxicated Little Jack coming home from the opposite direction. Wild Bill automatically apologized but then tried to take it back when his hazy eyes cleared long enough to recognize the face of the other fellow.

"It's you—what's-his-name!" he shouted. "You trying to start something again, you cowardly cur?"

"You once arrested me illegally," Little Jack said. "Now I'm going to have you arrested for assault with a deadly weapon."

"What weapon, my head?" said Hickok, even as he pulled out both his six-shooters with a smoothness that belied his condition.

Little Jack reportedly shrieked at that point. Charlie Utter, only half-drunk, stepped between the two men, but Little Jack was already backing up. Five steps back, he fell, picked himself off the boardwalk with some difficulty, and then ran steady enough to the law. Nothing came of it immediately, though Wild Bill later was arrested, not for assault but on a charge of vagrancy. Charlie Utter bailed his friend out of jail immediately, so Little Jack couldn't have gotten too much satisfaction out of his "revenge."

At least one other time, back in the City of Kansas, Wild Bill had landed in jail for "vagrancy," but it didn't mean much. During his lawman days, he'd arrested his share of men on the same charge when they were drunk and somewhat disorderly but hadn't committed any definite crime. After his short jail time in Cheyenne, Hickok didn't change his ways. A month later, Sheriff Carr noticed the former lawman relieving himself in front of the Dyer's Hotel and shouted to him, "Bill, I guess I'll have to run you out of town." Hickok finished his business at his own pace and then looked plenty sober when he coolly replied, "Jeff Carr, when I go, you'll go with me." Charlie Utter quickly led his friend away, and that was the end of that. The sheriff never bothered Wild Bill again in Cheyenne, although the city marshal would list him as a vagrant in hopes of running him out of the city. Meanwhile, Wild Bill kept talking about wanting to leave Cheyenne, not with Jeff Carr, but with Charlie Utter. The two friends heard gold calling out to them from the wild country 270 miles to the north. Charlie told anyone he met in the Gold Room: "Hurrah for the Black Hillers! This rush is going to be a lallapaloozer."

Still, they stayed. It might have been because the military had declared the Black Hills off limits to white prospectors and because the Sioux Indians, who considered the place not only *theirs* but also sacred, were angry enough to kill intruders. Jasper suggested other reasons Wild Bill preferred to remain in Cheyenne: He needed blue-lensed glasses to see the cards in front of him as well as the stars in the sky; he could buy a pick and a shovel easy enough at the hardware store but the thought of spending long hours using them was demoralizing; he was enjoying the easy and relatively safe life in Cheyenne at an age (thirty-eight) when risky adventure wasn't quite so appealing; and he was regularly exchanging letters with his circus lady, Agnes Lake.

"I'm glad Bill's making his home in Cheyenne," Jasper told me. "I want him to be safe. He would likely need me up there, even with Colorado Charlie at his side, but I'm not ready to leave Cheyenne to get my hands dirty in Sioux country. The allure of gold is mighty powerful for most, but not for me. Digging is too much like picking for my taste. How 'bout you, Zach?"

"Never been a picker and I don't see myself being a digger," I replied.

"Not a gambler, either. What would you say you are, Zach?"

"I'm a hardware clerk, and I like my work. I'm a law-abiding citizen. Nobody calls me a vagrant, and nobody wants to shoot me. I sleep well in my room at the Underwood Boarding House. I eat well. I don't have myself a lady friend at this point in time, but I'm not going to find one in the Black Hills, either. I do have a couple of real good friends you might know of who keep things lively enough for me. And I do have my half brother. We haven't been talking for some time, but that can't last forever. Like Crooked Nose Jack used to say, no matter what we'll always be family. He'll say it again. For better or worse, that's the way it is. I haven't totally given up on him. Maybe I'm a little too hopeful, but I see better days ahead for Jack and more of the same for me."

CHAPTER THIRTY:
CHEYENNE NIGHTS

Better days were slow in coming. At least, as far as I knew, Crooked Nose Jack McCall and Wild Bill Hickok managed *not* to run into each other again in 1875. In some ways Cheyenne was becoming more civilized in that respectable types kept moving in while undesirables kept moving out, often with a nudge from city and county peace officers. Wild Bill was an old town tamer, of course, and Jack usually tried to stay away from openly instigating trouble (his attack on me the previous year being a most notable exception), but I had a feeling neither of them particularly welcomed that kind of progress. That was probably the only thing the two men had in common, besides a passion for poker. Gamblers weren't getting any respect. In June, Wild Bill faced another charge of vagrancy and needed another bailout from Charlie Utter. The city marshal's "vagrant list" also included the name Jack McCall, and my half brother landed in jail twice that summer—once on the vague vagrancy charge and once for brawling, not with another man but with a fallen angel who called herself Silver Dollar Sally.

Jasper Washington saw it as his duty as my friend to report the arrests, both times late at night when I was already dreaming in my narrow little bed at the Underwood Boarding House. The first time, I didn't even get out of bed. The second time I stirred because Jasper said Jack was on his jail cot bleeding like a stuck pig. Silver Dollar Sally apparently had gotten the best of it in an alley (sitting on Jack's belly, clutching his small bankroll in one hand while punching his face with the other) when a patrolling deputy marshal pulled them apart. After a half-hour debate with myself, I decided to visit the jailhouse, as much to get a look at this Silver Dollar Sally as to see about my half brother. I was disappointed to find that Sally wasn't even being held, and Little Jack was holding a nearly bloodless towel over his already crooked nose.

"What happened to you?" I asked from the right side of the bars, hoping for more details than Jasper had provided.

"What do you care?" Little Jack snapped. "You up and abandoned me last time I got into a fight."

"Your last fight was with me. And, as I *don't* recall, since I was unconscious but later learned *and felt,* you spent a good deal of time kicking my head as if it were a tin can."

"All right. All right. That was a long time ago."

"Some things a man just can't forget. But I'm glad you're not bleeding too much."

"A man can hurt without blood showing. I can't forget what a mean father I had, yet certain people liked him." He paused to glare at me before continuing. "So, I get mean *once* in my life and people hate me." He pointed accusingly at me and accidentally dropped the towel. His nose looked as crooked as ever but no worse. I saw a little dried blood below his left nostril.

I could have given him a long list of mean things he had done in his life, but it was too late to argue. I assumed he had angered the fallen angel by getting too rough with her or perhaps failing to pay her sufficiently for her services.

"Who was the girl?" I asked, which only made him glare again. "Jasper told me it was a girl."

"To hell with Jasper Washington. The black bastard should mind his own bloody business."

"Hey, he's my best friend."

"That's your problem."

"All right then, let's talk about your problem. Doesn't appear the girl hurt you too terribly much."

"Girl! She was an amazon, as old as the hills, bigger than them, too—a mountain of a whore. You remember how large Minnie Mary was—of course you do. Well, Silver Dollar Sally is twice her size and twice as faithless."

"Why then did you . . . you know, take up with her."

"I couldn't see her so well in that dark alley at first. She didn't look nearly so large peering at me from behind the outhouse. And by the time she got ahold of me, it was too late. I closed my eyes and pretended she was Minnie Mary. She didn't care who I was as long as I paid. And then she tried to rob me and played rough when I protested. I reckon I shouldn't have expected anything less from a fat whore with a name like Silver Dollar Sally."

I couldn't work up sufficient sympathy to please him or enough for me to want to stay for a minute longer. "See you later," I said on my way out, and I didn't look back or even flinch when I heard him curse from his cell.

The jailer said he had permission from the marshal to release the prisoner should anyone pay the thirty-five dollars. "That's a high price for getting beat up," I said.

"The marshal's office will keep only twenty-five dollars. That's the usual fine. The other ten goes to Sally."

"I see. Maybe we should call her Ten-Dollar Sally."

"You got the thirty-five dollars to get your brother out or not?"

"Maybe. If not, I can always get an advance on my salary from Mr. Greeley. It's something to think about, anyway. Have a nice night, mister. I was once a jailer myself. I might be back in a day or two."

I did return in three days with twenty-five dollars from my savings and a ten-dollar contribution from Jasper Washington, who told me—whether from personal experience or not, I didn't ask—that Silver Dollar Sally was worth every penny of it. I'm pretty sure Jasper did it for me, too, since I believed my half brother had learned his lesson and been punished enough by the fallen angel and the law. Maybe I thought Little Jack would show some gratitude and try to patch up his relationship with me, and maybe even with Jasper. I was wrong. He didn't immediately thank either of us for his "rescue" from jail. He went right back to avoiding any face-to-face encounters with either Jasper or me and, of course, refrained from encounters of any kind with big-fisted Sally.

I managed to stay friends with my employer, Chester Greeley, even though I had my bad days at the hardware store. Too frequently I forgot my old Bible readings about treating others the way you want to be treated and acted rude to those customers who complained about Boettcher prices or my own listless service. I suppose my mind wandered excessively. Sometimes images of women popped into my head for no reason at all. For instance, I saw my mother stuck and starving to death in snowy Donner Pass; Belle Bragg reflecting in front of the Red Room mirror at the Daniel's Den; Hannah McCall coughing and gasping in the Louisville attic; Minnie Mary, in a state of undress, throwing herself at me in places she had never been; and Silver Dollar Sally, whom I had never even seen in real life, coming at me in some Cheyenne alleyway where I had never ventured.

Chester and I continued our social visits at the Gold Room, but more like twice a month instead of every week. Almost always Wild Bill Hickok would be there, doing some gambling, but more talking and drinking, with Charlie Utter keeping watch. Wild Bill had a knack for getting everyone's attention—and most of his drinks bought for him—just by opening his mouth. His stories captivated his beguiled and often besotted audience. Sometimes he spoke of his scouting and gunfighting days, recounting all those times he had responded brilliantly to threats by killing in honorable self-defense as many as forty-five men, presumably some Indians and some Rebels but mentioning by name only David McCanles, Little Dave Tutt, Bill Mulvey, Samuel Strahun, and Philip Coe. He understandably kept to himself the accidental shooting of Mike Williams during the Abilene shootout with Coe. More often, Hickok delivered thrilling tales about leading small expeditions north and finding tons of gold and silver and even diamonds while fighting off hostile Sioux warriors and Black Hills bandits. Truth was, he and his pal Charlie Utter's expedition to Deadwood was still only in the lengthy planning stage. I was impressed, though, with what I heard. Hickok might have been a lousy actor, but he was one fabulous storyteller. His stories would have done dime novelist Ned Buntline proud.

Jasper Washington would sometimes sit down with Chester and me but never for long. He would roll his eyes at Wild Bill's words and then say it was time to get rolling—which meant either finding a poker game in back or leaving the Gold Room to gamble in a "quieter" saloon. In mid-summer, a big change came over Jasper. He stopped worrying about where Wild Bill and Colorado Charlie were or what they were planning together and also stopped sitting with me on the bench in front of the Underwood Boarding House to relate his worries or anything else on his mind. What happened was that Jasper found a new best friend. Barney Ford was back in town.

Ford, the son of a Virginia plantation owner and a slave woman, had been one of the most prominent Cheyenne restaurant and hotel owners in the boom years after the railroad arrived. When a fire destroyed his hotel in 1870, he reestablished himself in Denver, where he became one of the wealthiest men in Colorado. But he never forgot the potential of Wyoming's territorial capital, and he and his riches had returned to open the grandest commercial establishment in Cheyenne—his Inter-Ocean Hotel. Jasper had never been a slave or been associated with a plantation anywhere, but he was raised in Kentucky and, of course, knew full well about the obstacles any black man faced in the South, the North, and even the West. Barney Ford was a rich, respected independent businessman whose light-black skin coloring was no drawback when it came to rubbing elbows with the white moneyed men. Jasper was a professional gambler who had won more than his share of pots and had gained a small measure of respect (never having been arrested for vagrancy) despite his overwhelming size and blackness—or maybe, in some cases, because of it. No matter their differences in social status, Barney and Jasper became joined in the collective Cheyenne mind even more than Wild Bill and Colorado Charlie.

"We're the two peas in the pod you mentioned earlier, but we're both black peas," Jasper said to me just before he started forgetting about me. "We got a bond I can't expect you to understand, Zach. It's more than brother and brother, certainly more than brother and half brother. Barney and I get on 'like a house on fire' . . . make that a hotel."

The Inter-Ocean Hotel, to be precise. The three-story building offered lodging for 150 people, including Jasper at nominal cost because of his connection with the owner, and two fine dining rooms. The main dining room boasted of "meals at all hours—fresh oysters, fish, and game our specialty" and could seat 180, including Barney and Jasper most every evening. There was also a small ladies' dining room, presumably for respectable women who wanted to gossip freely among themselves or who didn't want to be stared at either by couples wondering why they were eating alone or by men with appetites for more than fancy food.

Also on the premises was a billiard hall, where Jasper became as handy with a cue stick as he already was with a deck of cards, and a gentlemen's club, which catered to leading citizens and dignitaries but didn't officially exclude anyone, certainly not Jasper. In fact, his friendship with the owner was so well known that many of those white moneyed men wanted to rub Jasper's massive elbows. Some high-stakes gambling took place there, and Jasper, no doubt using Barney Ford's money, sat in on one of those games. I don't know how many other so-called professional gamblers frequented the gentlemen's club, but I heard Crooked Nose Jack only went twice (and never got into an actual game) mainly because Jasper made him feel unwelcome.

Meanwhile, Wild Bill Hickok and Charlie Utter apparently remained fixtures in the Gold Room. The long-haired pals reportedly did visit the Inter-Ocean's exceptional barber shop for hair and mustache trimming on at least one occasion. Chester Greeley closely inspected everything in the Inter-Ocean from the dining room silverware to the door hinges and declared it the finest hotel between St. Louis and San Francisco, though I doubt he would have had time to visit many of the others. As for me, I felt out of my element in both dining rooms, and it was worse in the gentlemen's club the lone time Barney and Jasper invited me. I couldn't shoot straight on a billiard table, so I avoided that room, and I couldn't afford to take a bedroom in the Inter-Ocean Hotel even had I wished to move out of the Underwood Boarding House, which I did not.

Not wishing my already thinning hair to grow half as long as Hickok's or Utter's, I visited the Inter-Ocean barbershop myself one day in late summer. The place had gold-plated fixtures and a silver chandelier, and even as the barber, dressed in spotless white with a bowtie, did his careful snipping, a helper swept my hair off the otherwise clean floor. It was a little too much for my simple tastes, but the musky substance the barber smeared in my hair did call to nose memory a similar odor at the Daniel's Den. While waiting my turn in the chair, I read an item of interest about Wild Bill in the *Cheyenne Leader.* The writer said that while City Marshal J. N. Slaughter denied ever telling Hickok to leave town, the newspaper could prove that on several occasions both city and county officials had ordered Wild Bill out of Cheyenne. The *Leader* then asked a closing question: "By the way, was the Marshal afraid of Wild Bill?" I concluded that even if Marshal Slaughter wasn't afraid of this older, poor-vision version of Wild Bill, he might have had second thoughts about getting tough when Charlie Utter was standing by like the bodyguard of a king or president.

In October none other than President Ulysses S. Grant, no doubt with a bodyguard or two, stopped in Cheyenne. Twice earlier in the year the president had made failed attempts to buy mining rights in the Black Hills from the Sioux Indians. I reckon he was still trying, because at that time the army was under orders to enforce the Sioux claim to those gold-rich hills by turning back would-be prospectors. I caught a glimpse of Grant's beard when a crowd of important and unimportant people gathered at the train depot to greet him, and then I saw his backside briefly when the presidential party climbed into a carriage for the short ride to the Inter-Ocean Hotel. That was enough for me, and I wasn't invited for dinner anyway, but I heard that when he dined on an exquisitely prepared meal of oysters, fish, and game in the dining room he was personally served by Barney Ford and a waiter-for-the-night, Jasper Washington.

President Grant left Cheyenne soon enough, but the Inter-Ocean continued to be the place to go, especially at night, for the cream of Cheyenne society and no doubt some of the dregs of Cheyenne society as well. Barney Ford, though, wasn't making Cheyenne his home base. Earlier, he had established his first Inter-Ocean Hotel in Denver, and he went back there to explore new business and political opportunities and to engage in civic affairs. Jasper Washington went with him by invitation.

"How could I turn Barney down?" Jasper said to me when he returned to our Underwood Boarding House bench for a last visit. "He's the preeminent businessman in all of Denver, and he's the same color as me, more or less. Think of all the opportunities I'll have for advancement and prosperity serving under a great man like that!"

"Oysters, champagne, four-poster beds, feather pillows, gold pocket watches, silver chandeliers, mahogany tables and chairs, red velvet curtains, fine ladies in pearl earrings and diamond necklaces, servants at your beck and call." I crossed my legs and arms and frowned, not particularly liking the picture I was trying to create of the rich, easy life.

"Not your idea of advancement, Zach? But then, you never were a slave."

"Neither were you."

"That's right, but lots of your folks wanted me to be one. I'm a gambler, and Denver is a big city, full of gaming opportunities. They'll be high-stakes poker now any time I want it. How can you beat that?"

"By not losing, I suppose."

"And there's a billiard hall at his hotel down there, too. Poker and billiards, and whatever else Barney offers me. How can I not go with the great man?"

"I'm sure there'll be something else, Jasper. Mr. Ford might require you to do some work. You've always told me you hate the idea of working for somebody else."

"Look, I am not exactly sure what I'll be doing for Barney, but I won't be waiting tables the way I did for President Grant's party or carrying other people's luggage or . . ." Jasper stopped talking suddenly and nudged me on the shoulder a little too hard for the comfort of either of us. "Damn, you're confusing me, boy," he said, rising off the bench. He began to pace the boardwalk but soon halted and threw both massive arms in the air. "Truth is, I do not know what I want to advance to in Denver, but who doesn't like prosperity? Why do you think all those wannabe miners are lining up to head up to the Black Hills? The whole world rushes for gold, whether it be in California, Nevada, Idaho, Montana, Colorado, or Dakota."

"I'm not rushing anywhere."

"Your work that fulfilling? You a hardware man for life, Zach?"

I suppose I started squirming on the bench. I was doing more daydreaming than ever at work, paying less attention to customers. Mostly in my day-to-day life I just liked the idea of resting, but sometimes I got restless. "I won't be there forever," I insisted.

"That's right, so why not come to Denver with Barney and me? We're pals, and I'm sure he wouldn't mind if his pal brought along another pal."

I was touched he was calling me a pal after he'd all but forgotten about me for several months. For the next half a minute I tried to imagine what the women in Denver looked like. I figured there must be more of them, anyway.

"You considering it?" Jasper asked.

"I don't want to wait on tables or carry luggage either," I said. "And I don't play poker or billiards."

"I know I've asked you this before, but what exactly do you want, Zach McCall?"

That was a big question, too big for me to contemplate at that moment or most other moments. "To stay, I reckon. I'm still hoping for happier days with my half brother, I reckon."

Jasper didn't press the issue. He told me to write him a letter now and then care of the Inter-Ocean Hotel of Denver. We both wished each other well. I'm pretty sure we were both wondering if we were making the right decision, because he started to walk away but came back.

"If you ever change your mind about leaving Cheyenne, you know where I'll be, at least for a while," he said. "Anyway, I'm going to give it a try. If things don't work out, I can always return. I'm not saying they won't work out, but if they don't and I got to leave, Barney will understand. We're pals."

"Yes, I know."

"Would you do me a favor while I'm away and keep an eye on him—and let me know right away if he gets into any kind of trouble?"

"What? Really? If that's what you want. I didn't know you cared that much about my half brother. Little Jack hasn't always been that nice to you, and—"

"To hell with him! Wild Bill is who I'm talking about. When I'm down in Colorado, I'm not going to suddenly stop caring about Bill and stop worrying about him, even if he does have Colorado Charlie hanging around up here. So, keep an eye out, will you?"

"I'll do what I can. Want me to keep an eye on Mr. Utter, too?

"To hell with him. And to hell with you for even suggesting that. Not that I expect the devil to ever let you into hell, preacher, not with your clean reputation and clear conscience. See you later."

It was sad to see Jasper go, of course, but I hadn't been seeing much of him lately anyway. As the rest of 1875 played out, I never missed a day of work, though I can't say I was getting better at my job or even staying the same. The notion of being a hardware man for life was weighing on my mind, as was the disturbing concept of me being settled down but not settled down with anyone but myself. After work I did try to keep my eye out for Wild Bill Hickok, mostly at the Gold Room, where I now sometimes went without the company of Chester Greeley. I also kept an eye out for Crooked Nose Jack—that is to say, I checked regularly to make sure he wasn't back in jail, and once in a while I stopped by the Dyer's Hotel to ask the desk clerk about him. I never found out much, but at least I knew Jack never got too far behind on his rent, though now he was paying on a weekly instead of monthly basis.

The United States' centennial year arrived before I knew it. I hadn't been looking forward to it, since the new year didn't promise anything but more of the same. But I got a hint that something just might be different about 1876 in early February, when Jack startled me by showing up at the Underwood Boarding House one night not only to look me over but also to tell me what was on his mind. Something was weighing heavily on it. In a word, that thing was gold.

"I got to go," he said. "By that, I mean *we* got to go. White men are swarming to gold country like locusts now that the army has all but stopped trying to keep them out. And let me tell you, those Black Hillers are finding the right stuff, mostly at a new camp called Deadwood Gulch."

"That name sounds a little bit . . . well, frightening," I said.

"Everywhere frightens you, Brother—Springfield, Hays City, Abilene, City of Kansas, Louisville."

"That's not true. I kind of felt safe in Boonesborough."

"Don't mention that place to me. It's dead, dead, dead. In fact, as far as I'm concerned, so is Louisville and the rest of Kentucky."

"Have you heard from the family?"

"The dropsy did kill Mother, if that's what you're asking. Not that you ever really cared."

"I'm sorry. We're both orphans now."

"But you remain the only bastard, Zach."

I didn't take offense. I smiled, and then he smiled. "Emily

wrote me about Mother."

"How is she and your other two sisters?"

"She didn't say. And she didn't mention her husband. No doubt Hector Browning continues to rule the household. No matter to me. They all may as well be dead. But not Deadwood, Dakota Territory. It happens to be a lively spot right now. We ought to rush up there, Brother, before all that gold gets claimed by folks no more deserving of riches than us."

Instead of imagining Deadwood, my mind wandered back to Scripture. The Bible, as I recalled, had quite a bit to say about gold, both good and bad. Jerusalem streets were said to be made of pure gold, and Abraham, blessed by God, possessed plenty of it. On the other hand, children of Israel weren't supposed to worship a golden calf, and Christian women were admonished for wearing gold and told to adorn themselves instead with interior virtues.

"You figuring what all that gold will mean, Brother?" Jack asked. "I'll tell you what it means. Nobody would dare keep me out of a high-stakes poker game or that high-falutin' gentlemen's club ever again. Hell, I might even buy the whole Inter-Ocean from that cocky colored man. And you could purchase the Underwood Boarding House and then rent out rooms only to pious people so you could feel completely safe in your room. And think of all those genteel ladies who'll be flocking to the McCall brothers when we start to shine like gold in their pretty eyes. We'd cast aside without a second thought all the Minnie Marys and Silver Dollar Sallys in the deceitful world or else buy an entire bordello for our own amusement—and I'm not talking about the Daniel's Den!"

"You have some imagination, Little Jack. And nice of you to include me in your imagination, but . . ."

"The gold has been confirmed. It's as real as the shovels and picks you're selling every day. You want to work there your entire life, Brother? Hell, with all that gold we collect, you can buy your own bloody hardware store."

"I'm sure it involves more than just collecting nuggets off the ground."

"All right, so you got to dig a little. I'm willing to get my hands dirty for the right cause, in this case the perfect cause. You can't be against the idea of getting rich. Bags of gold buy a lot of happiness, Brother. It'll be you and me together again. I can already see the headline in the *Cheyenne Leader:* 'BO-NANZA YEAR FOR McCALL BROTHERS—THEY STRIKE IT RICH IN DEADWOOD'."

"I never knew you to read any newspaper, Little Jack."

"Never been a newspaper that wrote anything about me before. What do you say, Zach? Tell me our next adventure will be in Deadwood Gulch. And tell me real soon. I'd hate to miss out on all that gold."

"I'll think on it," I said. "Nice of you to . . . eh, think of me. But I better get some sleep now. Tomorrow, I have to . . ."

"I know, go to work. Work, work, work. If you got to work why not do something that pays off. Say to hell with the hardware. Say to hell with growing old poor. Let's be Black Hillers, Brother. There's gold in them hills!"

"So I've heard."

CHAPTER THIRTY-ONE:
SO LONG, CHEYENNE

I did not get back to Crooked Nose Jack about his Black Hills dream because I not only had no wish to go there but also had no faith that the two of us could reach there alive even if we didn't kill each other en route. Between Cheyenne and Deadwood Gulch were almost three hundred miles of rugged wintry country, countless incensed Sioux, road agents eager to pick up gold the easy way, and false trails leading in all directions.

He returned to the Underwood Boarding House two weeks after his first visit to appeal to me again, emphasizing the importance of brothers sticking together and looking out for each other. I told him I could best look out for him right there in Cheyenne and that if he ever wanted to just have a talk, a good place to do so was the bench in front of the boarding house. Jack admitted that poker had not been going well for him lately, and he couldn't get his name off the city marshal's vagrant list. He had sold his derringer and a pair of boots to stay in games, couldn't afford a horse, could pay his rent but only by limiting himself to one or two meals a day, had been left out in the cold by poker-playing acquaintances, couldn't find one woman in town willing to touch a man with empty pockets, and didn't have a single friend in Wyoming Territory except me. I'm not sure if he thought detailing his misery in Cheyenne would somehow change my reluctance about leaving with him. It didn't, though I tried to show him what little sympathy I could spare.

"That's tough," I said. "I can lend you a few bucks, but that's about all I can do."

"You can do more. You could ask Greeley for the loan of a couple of horses and all the equipment two prospectors would need."

"Chester's my friend, but he's also my boss. He might give me a few days' time off from work, but *not* weeks or months, and he has no horses to spare and no tools free for the taking."

"We could simply go into the store in the middle of the night and take what we need. When we come back to Cheyenne rich, we'll pay him back with interest."

"You don't really think I'd do anything like that? I make an honest dollar there, and that's all I expect or want."

"You speak of a few dollars. I'm speaking about thousands of dollars in gold."

"Sorry, Little Jack, it won't work. It's impossible."

"I'll go myself then, damn it!" he shouted as he stormed off down Eddy Street. "I don't need you or anyone else to help me get rich."

But, as expected, he stayed in Cheyenne rather than become a brave, solitary Black Hiller. Meanwhile, Wild Bill Hickok and Charlie Utter, despite all their talk and planning, hadn't gone for the gold either. I learned from one of my visits to the Gold Room for observation that Wild Bill had more than gold and Colorado Charlie on his mind. Wild Bill wasn't even there, but Utter was, filling in for his pal as the night's primary storyteller. But he also said something that wasn't a story and that explained why he was there alone. Her name was Agnes Lake, and she and James (as she called him, using the first name he was born with) had required privacy that evening.

Mrs. Lake (as Wild Bill was still calling her at the time, at least publicly) still had a circus to run back East, but she had taken a break in Cheyenne, certainly not to enjoy its mid-winter weather. She apparently was there to visit and stay with businessman Sylvester Moyer and his family, but that would be like saying people went to a circus to see the large canvas tent rather than the daring equestrians and wire walkers performing inside. It became clear from Colorado Charlie's tongue flapping in the Gold Room that Agnes Lake, no longer content with sweet words by mail, had traveled far and wide to find out exactly what James Butler Hickok's intentions were toward her.

It didn't take her long to find out, presumably before Charlie Utter did, and not long before I and the rest of Cheyenne did. The *Leader* broke the news in its March 7, 1876, edition that two days earlier, at the residence of S. L. Moyer, the Rev. W. F. Warren had married Mrs. Agnes Thatcher Lake of Cincinnati "to James Butler Hickok, WILD BILL, of this city." The Moyers, of course, witnessed the ceremony. Where Charlie Utter was at the time, I do not know, and I don't know his reaction to this commentary from the March 8 *Cheyenne Daily Sun:* " 'Wild Bill,' of Western fame, has conquered numerous Indians, outlaws, bears, and buffaloes, but a charming widow has stolen the magic wand. The scepter has departed, and he is as meek and gentle as a lamb. In other words, he has shuffled off the coils of bachelorhood."

I did my duty and wrote Jasper Washington with the news in case the Denver newspapers had somehow failed to report the event. I told him it all came about without any warning (thus no earlier letters about Bill and Agnes) and that I would have congratulated Mr. and Mrs. Hickok, but they took off by train right away to honeymoon in St. Louis and then continue on to the bride's hometown. I added that Charlie Utter had not gone to Cincinnati with them, which I thought Jasper might like to hear, and also mentioned the six words the Rev. Warren said when I visited him at the Methodist Church in hopes of learning more details: "I don't think they meant it."

"Let's hope they meant it," Crooked Nose Jack said when I also told him about the reverend's words. "I truly like the idea of a Mild Bill being supported by his old lady in Cincinnati. I have a mind to celebrate. May we never see the return of Wild Bill Hickok."

He'd said such things before, of course. As for me, I didn't care that much whether I saw Wild Bill Hickok again or not, but I did favor him returning to Cheyenne because that might eventually cause Jasper Washington to also come back. I did wish the newly married man happiness in his marriage, but it also made me dwell on my own bachelorhood. Where was the loving woman—younger, older, didn't matter a lick—in my life? Where was my Agnes?

Two weeks later, Jack reported a Hickok sighting in Cheyenne. Wild Bill was seen huddled with Charlie Utter outside the Gold Room talking intently without drinks or an audience. Jack watched them from across the street for a while, but there was no sign of Agnes. Since he wasn't talking to those two men, he made some inquiries at the Moyer home and learned that everything was fine with the Hickoks. As difficult as it was to be apart again so soon, it would all be for the good. She would rejoin her husband in Cheyenne in the fall after she concluded her circus business and he had taken a party to the Black Hills and built up a nest egg—golden eggs, of course. This information excited Crooked Nose Jack.

"You know something, Brother," he said. "We can join his party."

"But you said you hate Mr. Hickok."

"I can overlook our differences. I've been asking around and started reading the papers. It wouldn't be safe for me and you going up there on our own. Those Sioux are serious about taking scalps. We need a large party, no matter whose party it is.

No doubt Colorado Charlie would be in it. He and Hickok would sure come in handy should the Sioux make trouble for us."

"I'm not going out of my way to find trouble with Indians or anyone else."

"It's not out of our way to go find gold. And we will find it, Brother. If not in the hills, then me at the Deadwood poker tables. It'll be easy pickings separating those diggers from their pokes. We can't let this opportunity pass us by."

His optimism didn't rub off on me. "You keep saying *we*. I never said I wanted to go. And I still don't. And who says Mr. Hickok would even want you to be in his party?"

"You could put in a good word for me."

"I'm not that close to Mr. Hickok anymore, probably never was. He only knows me because Jasper Washington was my friend."

"I remember. Only one thing to do now—get word out to Washington. If he joins Hickok's party, you'll want to join, and then we'll both be Black Hillers for real."

"Jasper is in Denver."

"You write him letters, don't you? I never told you this before, Brother, but that Jasper Washington isn't half bad for a colored man who doesn't always mind his own business."

I told myself *don't do it*, but I did. I wrote Jasper a letter about the Black Hills party, even suggested he might like to join up if life wasn't going as well as he imagined working for Barney Ford at Denver's Inter-Ocean Hotel. I don't know if I was that desperate to see Jasper again or had reached the point of wanting to break out of my safe but dreary routine of working, eating, trying to sleep, and only dreaming about women, Agnes Thatcher Lake Hickok unexpectedly included.

I didn't get a return letter from Jasper, but that was just as well. Wild Bill soon departed Cheyenne again, and so did

Colorado Charlie, but not to the Black Hills. Utter went to Colorado to visit family, and Hickok went to St. Louis to raise enough adventurers to form a Black Hills expedition. Little Jack wondered if we should go to St. Louis ourselves to make sure we weren't left out but then decided Hickok and company would have to take the train our way at some point because the best route to the Black Hills was through Cheyenne. And so at least once a day, Little Jack went to the depot to see if Hickok and his company of adventurers had arrived. I went back to my daily routine, and it didn't get any better.

Charlie Utter returned first from his Colorado trip and was all business. Little Jack had his eye out for him, too, and soon learned of Utter's grand plans that included organizing a transportation line to carry freight and passengers between Cheyenne and the Black Hills and a Pony Express mail delivery service between Fort Laramie and Deadwood. Little Jack went right up to Charlie and humbled himself, possibly even apologized about past behavior, to try to get in Utter's good graces. It must not have worked that well because Little Jack came to me with complaints about Charlie's disparaging remarks and suggested I better write to Jasper Washington again in Denver.

"The son of a bitch wants to start a stage line to gold country," Little Jack said. "Not sure when that will be or how much passage will cost. Our best bet is still to join Hickok's party, and I know you won't join unless Washington does. So, get him here. He's always liked adventure. I give him that much. Hickok and company should be back any day now and raring to head for the hills."

"Jasper didn't answer my other letter," I said. "He must be content in Denver."

"How can that be? The gold rush is long over in Colorado. It's up here now. Mention the Hickok expedition and the poker possibilities, too. Colored folks ain't no different in that regard—they're as likely to catch the gold bug as the rest of us."

Because my heart still wasn't into exploring the gold country, I put off writing another letter to Jasper Washington. It didn't matter because he came back anyway in late May. He had grown tired of his assistant manager job at the Denver Inter-Ocean, which mostly consisted of overseeing the porters and the clean-up crew and saying "yes, sir" to the manager. Even worse, he seldom saw Barney Ford, who still liked to spend time with his long-time wife, Julia, and the rest of the time was immersed in overseeing all his business interests, church work, community building, campaigning for the education of freedmen and freed-women, and doing all he could to ensure that when Colorado became a state in a couple of months, its constitution would grant black men and other minorities the right to vote.

"That's one hell of a busy black man, doing all kinds of good, and not just to benefit himself and Julia," Jasper told me when he was back with me on the bench in front of the Underwood Boarding House. "Too much for me, Zach. He gave me a big steady job with a generous salary, but that was too much for me, too. I didn't have much opportunity to play poker, and I wasn't getting any respect since I was blacker than anyone else on the payroll, and everyone thought I only had the job because Barney either owed me a favor or I had intimidated him. I know one thing, Zach, no matter how well off a man might appear to be on the outside, he carries a deep hurt inside unless he feels free and joyous in his heart."

I wasn't feeling free and joyous myself, but it was wonderful to have my friend in Cheyenne again. "So, you quit your job down there," I said, with perhaps too much joy in my voice.

"No. I got to give Barney credit. He recognized my discontent and knew I was missing my friends and old poker haunts in Cheyenne. He sent me here on a mission—to find out why the

Cheyenne Inter-Ocean started losing money and then to do something about it if I could. So here I am. On the way over, I saw Charlie Utter walking into the Salida Bath House by himself. Where's Wild Bill?"

I explained to him about Wild Bill being in St. Louis organizing an expedition to the Black Hills. I was surprised when Jasper only shrugged and said, "No matter. I best get over to the Inter-Ocean and down to business. Barney is counting on me." He made no mention of gold or the Black Hills, which was fine with me.

The situation soon changed, though. In June Wild Bill Hickok arrived at the Cheyenne depot without any volunteers for his expedition. I wasn't certain what went wrong. Maybe he just couldn't get enough people to go with him because he had a reputation for shooting men, not leading them anywhere. Maybe trying to get a hundred men to join together in a common pursuit became too frustrating. Or maybe the men he wanted had enlisted in another expedition. The Black Hills had become a prime destination. It was just as well Hickok's expedition had been abandoned, because his pal Charlie Utter and other partners were busy putting together a wagon train that would roll north to Fort Laramie and then continue on to Deadwood. The word I heard at the hardware store was, it really didn't matter to Wild Bill that he wouldn't be in charge. That Colorado Charlie would be leading this group of adventurers was just dandy.

Meanwhile, things hadn't worked out at the Cheyenne Inter-Ocean for Jasper Washington. He had been a little too aggressive in trimming the fat from operations there. He had wanted to cut back on the oysters and other delicacies that arrived from the East by train, eliminate the ladies' dining room, increase the price of rooms for double occupancies, and make guests pay extra to step foot in the billiard room. The existing management in Cheyenne took exception to his high-handedness, and the top three men, backed for their protection by four porters and a beefy chef, dared say that directly to Jasper's face. The ensuing argument progressed beyond words. Jasper squeezed two porters until they were limp and, while relieving the chef of his butcher knife, accidentally sliced the man's left cheek and broke his right arm. The management trio escaped unscathed and, as they retreated into their office, told Jasper they would report him immediately to Barney Ford in Denver.

"Are you worried about your job?" I asked Jasper.

"No," he said, and he smiled so wide I didn't think he had enough face to contain it. "I'm not waiting to hear what Barney says. Maybe he'll want to bring me back to Denver or maybe he'll want to dismiss me. It won't matter. This time I sure did quit. And I sure am joyous about it."

"Because you're free to play more poker?"

"Maybe. But mostly because I'm free to leave the Inter-Ocean and Cheyenne behind."

"Oh. You'll go back to Denver and . . ."

"Hell, no. And don't look so gloomy. When he saw me, Wild Bill couldn't have been any gladder had I been his dear old mother from Illinois. He let me in on his immediate plans, and they're damn good plans. I finally jawed with Colorado Charlie, too. The three of us are cut from the same sturdy cloth. That's right. I'm throwing in with Wild Bill and Charlie."

"You mean you're going to be a Black Hiller?"

"A black Black Hiller, to be exact. You ready to leave the dull life of a storekeeper?"

"You mean you want me to be part of the expedition?"

"You could be useful to the party. Everyone knows what a hard worker you are. Besides, an old friend is the best kind of friend. I brought you out West, and I've always felt sort of responsible for you. You too can be joyous, pal."

"Funny, but Little Jack guessed you'd want to go for the gold just like he does."

"Man alive! Why bring him into the conversation?"

"Can't be helped. He also guessed if you wanted to go, then I'd want to go, and he could come along to be with me."

"Did he now? I didn't bring him West; he followed us. Hasn't he caused you—and me, too—enough aggravation? Isn't there some way to get one McCall without the other?"

"There has been. I'm not so sure now. He has his heart set on being a Black Hiller, and nobody wants to go it alone. He'd be alone if he stayed in Cheyenne. I reckon when you get right down to it, Jasper, I'd hate to leave him behind no matter what he's done in the past."

"You never learn, do you? Still, if you're willing to quit your own work and join us in this adventure, who am I to say your brother can't be a member of the traveling party?"

Only a *half brother*, I thought. But I didn't say it this time. Instead, I thanked Jasper. Not that I was overcome by joyousness. I wouldn't need to say goodbye to Little Jack, but it would be even harder telling Chester Greeley I was leaving the hardware store to risk my life traveling through Sioux country to a remote location where I'd be looking for riches that I wasn't sure I really needed or even wanted. Chester had given me my good, steady job and befriended me. Cheyenne had a future, and I could be a part of it. What if things didn't pan out in Deadwood, for not only me but also Little Jack, Jasper, Wild Bill, and Colorado Charlie?

"Having your usual second thoughts about doing something?" Jasper asked.

"I've already had those. I'm on my third or fourth thoughts now."

The party was to leave Cheyenne on June 27. I put off telling Chester Greeley what I was doing until June 24, but he already knew. He had heard rumors for weeks, and then Little Jack had taken it upon himself to tell my boss directly, to make sure I got all the money I was due and maybe even extra money or prospecting tools as a going-away present.

"I'm sorry I didn't let you know sooner," I said. "You're the best boss I ever had."

"And you were of value to Boettcher and Company, Zach. More than that, too, of course. A true friend, you listened to my ramblings after hours in your free time. I won't try to talk you out of this. You still have youth on your side. Sometimes a young man must go West. And sometimes a young man must go North. I wish you all the luck in the world, and whatever else it takes up there besides luck."

"Thank you, Mr. Greeley—Chester. Have you ever considered trying your luck in the Black Hills?"

"Old men stay put. Besides, if I left, who could I leave in charge of the store? Boettcher and Company has always been like a little gold mine to me."

"I'll miss you and the hardware . . . well, mostly you."

"Be off with you now. Take this hickory shovel with my compliments and my good wishes. Notice I tied a yellow ribbon to the handle for good luck."

"Thanks. It should come in handy since I imagined a lot of digging will take place in Deadwood."

"May you dig *only* for gold, never for a grave."

Those words coming out of good old Chester Greeley's mouth stunned me. He was one of those people whose constant good cheer and optimism made you almost believe when in his company that illnesses and death weren't in his future, your future, or anybody's future.

Perhaps he saw my face turn pale because he quickly added something more soothing: "What I meant to say, Zach, is that I hope you find what you are looking for—that is to say, I'm certain your adventure will be rewarding, one way or another. And remember this: you can come back to Cheyenne afterward if you wish and know that my door, at least during store hours, will always be open to you."

CHAPTER THIRTY-TWO:
HEADING FOR THE HILLS

We left Cheyenne on schedule. Out in front was Charlie Utter driving a fully loaded wagon pulled by four massive horses familiar with the road to Fort Laramie. Wild Bill Hickok rode alongside him on a long-eared mule he called Grey Nell, his idea of a little joke since he once owned the talented horse Black Nell, who climbed onto saloon tables and got written up in the newspapers. Jasper Washington drove his own loaded two-horse wagon, all easily paid for because of his earnings working for Barney Ford. I sat beside him while Little Jack, who had no say in the matter, rode in back with the food and mining supplies. Jasper and I sang over and over for miles the one verse from the hymn "I Will Follow Thee" I remembered from a powerful-voiced farmer during my circuit preaching days:

> Though the road be rough and thorny,
> Trackless as the foaming sea;
> Thou hast trod this way before me,
> And I'll gladly follow Thee.

The "Thee" was intended to be the Savior, of course, who was to be followed on the road to salvation, I suppose. But now for Jasper it meant following Colorado Charlie on the road to Deadwood gold. And it would have been impolite for me not to join in. Finally, he got tired of that one verse and deepened his already deep voice to sing "Song of the Free," about a man fleeing slavery in Tennessee all the way up to Canada via the Underground Railroad. It had been composed to the tune of "Oh! Susanna," which got me confused. While Jasper would be singing "I'm on my way to Canada," I'd be singing, "Well, I come from Alabama." He tired of that real soon. "We're both from Kentucky, so let's both shut up," he said.

A few nights out, camped under the stars, I was lying awake thinking about how vast the universe was, even when compared to the wide-open American West, when I heard Wild Bill Hickok, a few bedrolls over, talking in his sleep. The only words I made out were, "Oh, Agnes, I will *not* forsake you, my darling." He then began snoring like a freight train rolling past at full throttle. But it wasn't so loud I couldn't hear Jack. Awake or asleep, he was hiccupping, which he hadn't done much of when I was sharing rooms with him. He suddenly interrupted himself by shouting, "For pity's sake, Minnie Mary, quit painting your tonsils!" During his waking hours he usually avoided mentioning her name, but night dreams were impossible to control.

That's all I heard from my half brother, though his words got me thinking of soiled doves—mostly how through my boyhood in Kentucky I had lived amongst them but as a man in the wide-open West had largely kept my distance from them. I couldn't explain it to myself, and that kept me awake. I was eventually able to get my mind back on the universe, but that didn't help. My eyes stayed wide open as I contemplated how mankind, even the Wild Bill Hickok kind of man, didn't amount to much when you stared up at the big Western sky at night instead of dreaming and talking in your sleep.

We pushed on early the next morning and had gone about six miles when Wild Bill realized he didn't have his cane and was much distressed. He had stuck it in the ground at his head when laying out his bedroll the previous night and had forgotten to reclaim it after Jasper Washington brought him his morning coffee. Hickok didn't truly rely on his cane, but it was all Charlie Utter could do to keep his friend from returning to the camp site.

"When you're rich you can buy a gold-headed cane, Bill," said Colorado Utter. "But none of us can get rich unless we get to Deadwood."

"That's not the point," Wild Bill said, rubbing his eyes as if there were tears in them. There weren't, but he was clearly having some kind of eye pain.

He never said what the point was, but Jasper suggested it was because Wild Bill, with his vision problems, aches, and pains, was already feeling old at thirty-nine and believed he needed *that* cane as much as his pair of six-shooters. Regardless, Wild Bill rode Grey Nell out ahead of Utter's wagon, and even from Jasper's wagon I could hear Hickok scolding either the mule or himself.

"He'll get over it," Jasper said, nudging me with his elbow to make sure I was still awake but nearly knocking me off the seat. "Bill replaced his beloved .36-caliber Colt Navy cap and ball pistols with two Colt .38-caliber cartridge six-shooters. I have no doubt he can replace his cane, too."

We reached Fort Laramie on June 30 and were joined by many other wagons, all bound for the Black Hills. At the army's suggestion, we waited for still more wagons so we'd enjoy further protection should our paths cross with hostile Sioux, who were now at war with American soldiers. Word reached the fort that over in Montana Territory, Sioux warriors and their Cheyenne allies had wiped out most of Lt. Col. George Custer's 7th Cavalry command along the Little Bighorn River. Wild Bill Hickok and Colorado Charlie weren't exactly shaking in their boots, but they agreed to delay our departure a few days. Some sixty or more men—mostly prospectors but also gamblers and whiskey peddlers—joined us for the last part of our journey.

Crooked Nose Jack was more interested in the dozen female travelers who were prostitutes and camp followers and whose names alone elicited a certain agitation, if not anticipation—Sizzling Kate, Big Dollie, Dirty Emma, Madame Mustache, and especially the redhead Tid Bit.

"Man alive!" he said to me. "Don't that Tid Bit have class, and there's no excess to her, unlike others of her sort." He introduced himself to her as "the well-known Cheyenne gambler Big Jack McCall" and said nothing about having me along. Apparently the "Big" replacing the "Little" didn't work because she took a shine to the actually big Jasper Washington and his sizable bankroll. When my half brother saw this lady of easy virtue clinging lovingly to Jasper's arms with her feet not even touching the ground, he backed away. He was getting a free ride in the back of Jasper's wagon, so he didn't want to start anything, he told me, but of course he wouldn't dare start anything with Jasper anyway.

"I'd have quit Tid Bit soon enough," Jack said. "I don't need her."

Crooked Nose Jack found himself a substitute—or thought he did—in one Martha Jane Cannary, known far and wide as "Calamity Jane." I'm not sure why she had that nickname, but I suspect it was because trouble and distress followed her like ominous drifting clouds. We didn't see her at first because she was locked in the fort's guardhouse for being drunk and disorderly—not unusual behavior for her. She emerged looking worn out and soiled but not much like a dove. For one thing, she wore tattered buckskins and alternated between appearing fierce and mockingly amused. She swore at the guard who let her out and spat tobacco at his feet. She then went looking for whiskey. She had apparently done some actual scouting for the U.S. Army, but none of the soldiers was willing to buy her a drink. Wild Bill Hickok and Charlie Utter, though, shared some of the whiskey they had brought along in a five-gallon keg. When Colorado Charlie excused himself to go bathe in the Laramie River, Calamity Jane tagged along. Nobody had offered Crooked Nose Jack a drink, but he had enjoyed watching Calamity drink, and now he followed them to the river, not to wash but to observe some more.

When Jack returned an hour later, he happily reported to me that Colorado Charlie and Calamity Jane had bathed in different parts of the river and separated by a reasonable amount of sagebrush. "She don't want Utter, and Utter don't want her," he concluded. "You know, I don't mind a little grit on a body, but I got to tell you when I saw her wash it off and emerge from the river all cleaned up and sober, I knew she was the one I'd been looking for all this time."

When next I saw Calamity, I agreed she didn't look half bad, at least when I compared her to Big Dolly and Dirty Emma. Her fierceness had apparently washed off with the grit.

"Hands off, Brother," Little Jack said to me. "I saw her first."

I had been hands-off most of my life, but I guess he was remembering how Minnie Mary had suddenly showed an interest in me once I had remodeled myself—at least temporarily—into a traveling preacher. "Of course," I said. "She's all yours."

But she wasn't, of course. This became much clearer once we left Fort Laramie, and our now much larger wagon train, with about one hundred optimistic travelers, was rolling again toward the Black Hills. Charlie Utter told me flat out that Calamity had washed so thoroughly in the Laramie River because she was drawn to Wild Bill Hickok as if he were made of gold. He added that it hardly discouraged her when he told her Wild Bill had been married for four months and was sending love and a thousand kisses in letters to his dear wife, Agnes. Hickok believed a drink or two a day (and another couple in the evening) made travel more tolerable, and he allowed Calamity

Jane to wet her whistle with the boys. But otherwise, and Colorado Charlie confirmed this, Wild Bill could do without the kind of trouble Calamity might bring to a happily married man. Jack either didn't notice the way Calamity looked at Wild Bill or else chose to ignore it. He continued to believe he could win her over, even without money, since she was so "big-hearted," and his heart—or so he claimed—was "beating like a Sioux war drum."

When we reached Sage Creek on July 7, we ran into cavalry-men on high alert because of what the northern Plains Indians had done to the 7th Cavalry. Scouting for them was none other than Buffalo Bill Cody, who had stepped away from show business at least temporarily. Cody and Hickok, his old friend and onetime fellow actor, broke away from everybody else to converse privately. I could only imagine what they were talking about—scouting, the Sioux, the late Colonel Custer, the stage, wives (Agnes and Luisa, who had married Buffalo Bill in 1866), camp followers (such as Calamity Jane), Deadwood, gold, whiskey, celebrity, dime novelist Ned Buntline, guns, eyes, growing old, meeting again somewhere down the road. Actually, they might not have talked about all those things because they had only two hours together before it was time for the soldiers and their trusty scout to move on.

"There goes a real buckskin man of the West in the wrong direction," Calamity Jane commented as she watched Mr. Cody ride away. "I adore his small pointed beard and full mustache and the waving abundance of his long hair. Whether on stage or in the wilds, that man performs!"

I happened to be standing close enough to Calamity at the time to smell whiskey on her breath and her overall earthy scent, so I felt I should say something. "I didn't know you knew Buffalo Bill."

"All of us famous scouts know each other," she said matter-of-factly. "I knew him all to pieces as soon as I caught sight of him."

"I never even got to shake his hand. He was pretty busy with Mr. Hickok."

"Too bad, but you have the pleasure of knowing Wild Bill, mister. He's the Bill for me. He is similarly clad, has the same beard, mustache, and beautiful hair tumbling at his shoulders as Buffalo Bill, but Wild Bill's shoulders are broader, his waist narrower, his well-poised head higher, his body freer in every motion, his every muscle more perfectly defined, his hind end a greater delight to look upon. He must be the finest figure of a buckskin man in all creation, loaded with dash-fire. Listen to me, would you? I'm carrying on like all possessed. Sorry to bend your ear like this, mister. I acknowledge the corn; I'm a wee bit drunk."

"I understand. He's a nice guy. They say his draw with both hands is as fast as greased lightning, and I can vouch for that. I've known him since before he shot Dave Tutt in Springfield, Missouri. Met him through Mr. Washington, another nice guy."

"That would be the dark, handsome giant—the one Tid Bit craves more than a little. What about you, mister? You a nice guy?"

"Just a guy. I'm not known or anything. Everyone knows about Mr. Hickock, of course, but nobody knows about me. Still, he has been most generous to me and . . . Sorry. I guess I'm carrying on some myself."

"And you haven't touched a drop from Wild Bill's five-gallon keg. Now I remember who you are. You're another McCall, brother of Big Jack McCall."

"Zach McCall, correct, older half brother of Little Jack McCall."

"Makes more sense, him being small the way he is. Seems to me he's little all over except for his large crooked nose. You then must be the big McCall."

"I wouldn't go that far. There's no Big McCall, never has been. Our father was Fat Jack McCall."

"Yeah, Jack said he was an orphan like me. Of course, I've been one longer than him, ever since I was eleven as far as I can recollect. I was born in Princeton, Missouri, on May 1, 1852. I'm twenty-four years old, but some say I look a mite older on account of I've lived a life of daring, hardship, and danger."

"You look just fine to me, miss," I said. "I mean, who wouldn't think that?"

"Way out here on the lonely, untamed frontier not many, I suppose—'ceptin' Wild Bill. It seems he's head over heels in love with some damned refined, dainty young thing back in civilized high society."

"Actually, Agnes Hickok is ten years older than him, was a popular circus performer, and last I heard runs the whole circus."

"Is that a fact? Well now, that's a little better. Circus performing ain't like scouting for real on the Plains, but it's pleasing to know Bill ain't put off by females with a rugged side." Calamity Jane threw a hip at me and knocked me off balance. I staggered but held my ground. "Sorry 'bout that, mister. Believe it or not, I can also be as tender as Florence Nightingale."

"I believe it. I believe most people have at least two sides to them."

"That right? Well, I'd settle for either of Wild Bill's sides. But never mind about him now. He shares his whiskey with us mere mortals, but he's kind of a Godlike figure, out of our touch and full understanding. Hope that doesn't sound too blasphemous."

"Not at all. My preaching days are long over, miss . . ."

"Call me Jane. I like you, Zach McCall. You're real polite even if I'm not what you'd call a lady or like any females you've been around. On the other paw—and let me be honest with you, because that's the only damn way I can be in mixed company—your crooked-nosed brother is a foul-mouthed, liver-lilied hobbledehoy who should keep his bone box shut more often than not."

"Little Jack's not all bad, and I know he likes you a whole lot. But I appreciate your honesty, miss . . . eh, Jane."

And just like that, Calamity Jane wrapped her arms around me and gave a powerful squeeze—not a Jasper Washington squeeze, of course, because it caused no immediate damage, but still was a real eye-opener. And while pressed against me in full body embrace, she rubbed her sinuous lips against mine, and I got a slight taste of the alcohol she had consumed that day. I surprised myself by closing my eyes and enjoying it.

I forgot the two of us were *not* alone until I heard some vigorous clapping behind me. I separated from Calamity Jane with some difficulty and spun around, certain my face was redder than that of any Sioux warrior lurking out there. Jasper Washington winked at me and kept a steady clap going. Calamity put her hands on her hips, stamped one leg at Jasper, and tried to put on her fierce face, but then she started laughing.

"Our caravan is moving again, children," Jasper said. He gave one last hard clap, looking like a man trying to kill a mosquito. "Best find your respective wagons."

I was already in motion before he finished. "Yes, sir," I said, on the run, convinced my face was now flushed with excitement rather than embarrassment. I was considerably relieved that Crooked Nose Jack hadn't witnessed Calamity's ardent kiss.

CHAPTER THIRTY-THREE:
DECISIONS IN DEADWOOD

Our large party reached the boomtown of Deadwood on July
12. We hadn't seen a single Sioux, hostile or not, along the way,
but nobody was complaining. In the gulch, we saw mostly tents
and shanties, but more substantial two-story wood buildings
were scattered about, and others were under construction. The
rutted, dried-mud street was packed with men, not necessarily
rushing anywhere but all looking busy. Some paused to hail our
arrival. Charlie Utter stood up on the lead wagon and bowed.
Nobody seemed to take notice when Wild Bill Hickok slid off
his mule and dusted off his buckskins. But when a man with a
beard to his belly recognized Calamity Jane from one of her
previous haunts, he shouted her name, and it drew applause.
Five prospectors emerged from a tent saloon with mugs of beer
in each hand, and after one of them handed a mug to Calamity,
they gave her a welcoming toast, and she toasted to their good
health and fortune. Calamity downed a second beer and then
blew kisses—first in the direction of Wild Bill (no doubt about
that) and then to where Little Jack and I were standing (at me,
I suspected, but I hoped my half brother thought otherwise).

"I bid all my manly traveling companions farewell," she said.
"Come on, gals. Let's go a-prospecting."

Calamity Jane waved Big Dolly, Dirty Emma, and the others
along, and the female newcomers marched down Main Street
through a gauntlet of ogling men with arms stretched out to pat
backs and heads or else grasp whatever flesh they could reach.

Only Tid Bit lingered with the wagons, because she had taken hold of Jasper Washington and was squeezing him for all she was worth. Eventually, Jasper sent the last of the soiled doves into the heart of Deadwood, and he, Jack, and I returned to the Washington wagon and followed the tracks of the Utter and Hickock wagon to Whitewood Creek, where we all made camp.

It didn't take long for the five of us to join in the whirlwind that was life in Deadwood. For the first two days, Wild Bill Hickok, Charlie Utter, and Jasper Washington sized up the placer mining possibilities and found them extremely limited. Crooked Nose Jack and I ventured out together just once, and we were rudely run off a half-dozen claims, mainly because the chip my half brother carried on his shoulder was made of fool's gold. Thousands of prospectors had come before us "looking for color," and the earliest and luckiest ones found pieces of gold mixed in with the rocks and soil in Deadwood and Whitewood creeks. But by the time we got there in the summer of 1876, miners had staked claims to all the land along the creeks. Some of the later arrivals—and people continued to flock there into the fall—began looking in the hills for the hard-rock deposits that were the source of the placer gold below. That involved much hard work that might never pay off. None of us five had ever mined before, and none of us would ever start in earnest. The picks and shovels and other tools we brought along would mostly stay in the wagons.

Fortunately, a boom town offered other ways of making money, if not getting rich particularly fast. Charlie Utter, for instance, went to work with several partners setting up an express delivery service between Deadwood and Cheyenne. It figured to be lucrative, since they planned to charge twenty-five cents a letter, and a hired rider figured to deliver as many as two thousand letters on each forty-eight-hour trip. I wanted some kind of job if I wasn't going to be a prospector, but I never went so far as to ask Colorado Charlie how much pay the riders would get. I had experience feeding stabled horses and shoveling their manure, but riding hard and fast in dangerous country was not my idea of a decent job even had I been capable of doing it. Besides, he never asked, having only seen me travel from Cheyenne to Deadwood seated in a wagon next to burly driver Jasper Washington.

What I did instead was look over the town each day with the idea of landing a position in a store or stable. The sights and sounds and smells were both appalling and fascinating. Everything was louder and dirtier and generally less civilized than in Cheyenne. Dirt, dust, and wood smoke clung to my clothes and invaded my nostrils. I started to understand Colorado Charlie's wish to take a bath each night, but I doubted there was even one bathtub in the entire encampment. With my every step I worried about accidentally bumping into someone who might take exception to the path I was taking.

Even without entering the saloons and such I witnessed at least four fights of various lengths break out in three days among seemingly sober residents. I had no idea if these men were fighting over gold, the high price of goods, or just to have enough space to walk freely down the street. Bystanders like me stopped to watch the flying fists, kicking, and eye-gouging, but other folks hurried about their business as if violence were nothing to bother with when there was money to be made. I didn't see a single badge-wearer during my excursions into town, or for that matter anyone attempt to break up a fight. I developed a bad feeling in the pit of my stomach, and a kind of caution grew from the inside out about taking the wrong job or even staying around in Deadwood long enough to become a working man.

Crooked Nose Jack moaned over the fact he wouldn't be able to walk along a stream and scoop up gold nuggets, but he got over his disappointment fast enough, for he could walk through town and find an endless string of gaming tables, saloons, and dance halls. He preferred the faro banks and poker games set up in tents because he determined that was where the bad and inexperienced players went while the cleverest dealers and professional players practiced their craft in the more permanent-looking establishments. One of the latter was Nuttall and Mann's No. 10 Saloon on Main Street, and that's where Wild Bill Hickok made his headquarters in part because he was welcomed by owner Carl Mann and was practically worshipped by one-time Kansas acquaintance Harry Young who tended bar there. Jasper Washington also did some gambling there when he got the urge, but mostly he picked up his old habit of watching Wild Bill's back, even if Hickok always tried to sit with his back against the wall.

I had seen for myself what a lawless town Deadwood was, and Jack reported stepping behind one of the tent saloons and stumbling over the bodies of two men he had seen bucking the tiger earlier in the night. One had been clubbed to death, the other stabbed in the back—both murdered for their meager faro winnings. Whether Wild Bill Hickok was taking precautions for any possible danger, imagined himself becoming a lawman again, or simply enjoyed doing it, I don't know, but each morning at our camp he would draw both his six-shooters at once and fire simultaneously at tin cans or small branches. His eyes might have been troubling him, but at twenty-five paces with the sun at his back, he didn't miss a target.

Wild Bill had more reason than most to worry about his safety. Men recognized him (although sometimes Colorado Charlie was mistaken for him) or else heard about him being in town and sought him out. Most just wanted to gaze at the man who had shot Dave Tutt and however many other men, had tamed Abilene (a town once nearly as unruly as Deadwood), had scouted for the late Colonel Custer, and had been written up not only in newspapers but also dime novels. Any one of them, though, might be a gunman with a grudge against the former lawman or a rogue with a revolver who might go to any extreme to ensure Wild Bill never pinned on a badge to clean up Deadwood as he had those towns in Kansas. We all heard rumors that testy individuals were in town wanting to do Hickok harm.

On one occasion it wasn't just rumor. Half a dozen armed cowboys from Montana Territory made public insults and threats against Wild Bill at the Cricket Saloon. Drunk or not, they stated Hickok would be dead before the sun went down. Jack happened to be in there scouting for untutored card players. He didn't mind that kind of talk, although he swore he didn't encourage it even after those Montana boys bought him a drink. Not finding anyone in the Cricket who wanted to play poker instead of drink whiskey, Jack moved on toward the next saloon. Along the way he bumped into me and laughingly threatened to punch me in the nose for impeding his progress. I laughed, too, until he told me what the Montana cowboys were saying.

"It's just talk, Brother, pure reverie," Jack said. "I've engaged in it myself. That is, I've at least thought about putting Wild Bill in his place a time or two."

"I know," I said.

"Thinking ain't doing, Zach. Gotta go."

"Where to?"

"To wherever I can find me a game. Too many damn fools running around here loaded down by pouches full of gold. Somebody's got to take some of it from them. I feel it's my duty."

"Well, good luck, I guess."

"What about you? You still acting like a damn fool running around looking for employment?"

"I'm not running exactly. But I better go, too. Wild Bill will want to know about this."

"That way he can mosey over to the Cricket, pull on them, empty his six-shooters, and kill all six. That'd get him more renown than he got killing Little Dave Tutt, eh?"

"I'm against all killing as a rule, unless it can't be helped."

"And I guess Hickok can't help himself now and then. He's a killer."

I didn't feel I had time to argue, so I turned away from him and began to run.

"Of course," he shouted after me, "should one of those cowboys get lucky and put another hole in Hickok's pretty face, I'm liable to buy a round for everybody in the Cricket."

I kept going, weaving through the Main Street crowd till I got to the No. 10 saloon. I broke the news to him as I breathlessly approached his poker table. Wild Bill peered at me for some time before leaning back on his stool and letting the back of his head rest against the wall. Then he looked at the other players, one by one, smiling at each, as unruffled as his legend. "As long as they stay in the Cricket, and I sit tight in No. 10, I'll be as safe as a babe in his mother's arms," he said, sounding half-amused, half-detached. He went back to studying the poker hand he held close to his nose. "I'll check to you," he said to the man on his left, and the game continued without further interruption from me.

Jasper Washington wasn't playing, though, and he took my news more seriously. He put an arm around me and guided me out the No. 10 door. "I best see what the Cricket cowboys are all about, Zach," he said. We didn't rush there, but Jasper told me if I saw one of the blowhards coming toward us to let him know. I couldn't help but notice how townsfolk quickly cleared a path for the large, self-confident black man as if he were a two-thousand-pound bull buffalo.

At the Cricket, Jasper didn't hesitate even though he wasn't carrying a gun. He walked right up to the bar, where at least five of the Montana cowboys were still drinking but now talking about the late Colonel Custer, fat cows, mavericks, and livestock brand registration in their home territory. I tried to hide behind Jasper's bulk, but he insisted on buying us drinks and then clinked his glass against mine while toasting "the greatest lawman who ever set foot on the Great Plains, Wild Bill Hickok." That, of course, got the cowboys' undivided attention. They wanted to know who the hell he thought he was to interrupt their conversation.

"Just a messenger," Jasper said.

"From Hickok?" the tallest of them asked.

"No. From the great beyond."

"Beyond Deadwood?"

"Beyond your understanding. But let me make things perfectly clear. I wish you to understand that unless you stop your threats against Wild Bill, there will shortly be a handful of cheap funerals in Deadwood."

"Sounds like a threat. Is that coming from Hickok or you, or the great beyond?"

"Look, Wild Bill came to this town to live in peace, not to court notoriety."

"Hell of a town to come to for peace and quiet. You must not be looking for peace and quiet yourself, coming in here like this and shooting your mouth off about—"

"Best you worry about your own mouths. I'm telling you Wild Bill doesn't want trouble, and I don't want him to have trouble. Understood?"

"You're a big one, all right, but there are six of us. And you ain't even heeled."

"I only count five of you. If you insist on *not* hearing me, you are welcome to put your pistols on the bar, and I'll teach you all a lesson, one by one, in pairs or whatever."

The tall cowboy seemed to be considering that challenge when the sixth cowboy, the one Jasper didn't see, approached him from behind carrying a raised stool as a weapon. I saw what was happening, called out to Jasper, and at the same time splashed my full glass of whiskey in the attacker's face. The man immediately dropped the stool to the floor, and one of its legs broke. While he rubbed the sting from his eyes, Jasper grabbed him, lifted him higher than the stool had been, squeezed him, and set him down none too gently on the stool, which caused another of its legs to break. The tall cowboy and the other four stood frozen with their backs to the bar, apparently all too surprised to act immediately. Given a little more time, one or more of them might have thrown punches or flashed six-shooters, endangering not only Jasper but also me, the whiskey-tosser. But they didn't get the time. Wild Bill himself had entered the Cricket and had both six-shooters out, ready for old-time action.

No, Hickok didn't enhance his legend by firing a shot. He kept both deadly weapons pointed at the Montana cowboys as he instructed both Jasper and me to leave the saloon. We did so (me quickly, Jasper as if it was his own idea), and only then did Wild Bill back out himself with six-shooters still raised. No cowboy drew a pistol or did anything else except pick the failed attacker off the floor. And all the other Cricket customers just watched. Once the three of us were out on the street, we heard from inside the saloon vigorous claps for what we had done and mocking comments directed at the Montana six.

"Tell me, Jasper, who is protecting whom from the Deadwood desperados?" Wild Bill asked as we strolled back to Saloon No. 10.

"You did all right for an ancient former marshal," said Jasper. "But Zach and I had things under control back there."

I thought he must be joking, but I wasn't sure.

"I was fretting so much about you two, I folded a pair of aces and a pair of eights—a winning hand. I knew I better get a move on to keep you out of something you couldn't handle. It's plumb foolish to go about this town unarmed no matter how big and mighty your arms happen to be." Wild Bill gave Jasper a friendly poke on his right bicep for emphasis, not that anyone could possibly have wondered whose arms he was talking about.

Having nearly regained my composure from the unsettling incident in the Cricket Saloon, I was able to speak, asking Wild Bill something I had wondered about ever since he shot Tutt in Springfield. "Where'd you get all that nerve, Mr. Hickok? There were six of them."

"My guns were already out, theirs were not."

"But there were other times when that wasn't the case. Men were shooting at you."

"When a man believes the bullet isn't molded that is going to kill him, what in hell has he got to be afraid of?"

"And that's what you believe?"

"Perhaps not as much as I once did, young man. Even Wild Bill Hickok can have his doubts now and again about what the future might hold. Don't let this get around, but a man slows down as the years start to show on his face, and he makes plans to settle down with the right woman, the one he intends to take care of till the end of their days."

"Some of us have never been fast to begin with," I admitted, "nor have we come close to finding the right woman or even the wrong one."

"Don't underrate yourself. I liked the way you threw the whiskey in that cowboy's face. He would have broken the stool over Wash's head. You showed mettle I hadn't seen in you before, Zach McCall."

I was pleased he remembered my name, and just like that I

decided to do as he said and not underrate myself. "I couldn't let that cowboy do my best friend Jasper that way. Without a gun handy, I had to think of something fast, so I quickly . . ." I stopped talking as soon as Wild Bill stopped walking. It was no use going on in that same self-congratulatory vein. When he looked me straight in the face with his unblinking blue eyes, I knew I couldn't go on pretending to be something I wasn't— namely, a brave man like him. "Truth is, Mr. Hickok, I was ready to run out of that saloon like a frightened hare until you showed up with your pistols drawn."

"Never run from a gun is the advice I give to any human being. Bullets travel faster than you can. Besides, if you're going to get shot, better it be to the front than the back. It looks better."

"If you're dead," said Jasper, "you won't care how it looks. I'm going to take my chances without a gun. How many men are mean enough to gun down an unarmed man, even if he's as black as me?"

Hickok put one long arm around Jasper and another around me, and we continued down the street like some kind of three-headed mythical beast. People scattered to get out of our way. Wild Bill didn't speak again until we neared the No. 10 Saloon. He let go of us and lined us up facing him as if we were two school children—the strongest, biggest kid in class and little timid me. Then he addressed Jasper's earlier question. "I'm willing to bet, whether you are black, white, brown, yellow, or purple, you won't have to look far in Deadwood to find a man mean enough to do that."

CHAPTER THIRTY-FOUR:
DEADWOOD DESTINY

August 1, 1876. That is a date I shall never forget. No, it has nothing to do with Wild Bill Hickok—well, very little. Wild Bill had completely given up on the idea of mining and had all but squashed the rumor that he might become Deadwood's marshal. Even though he lost at poker more times than he won, he kept returning to Mann's No. 10 every day to get out of the sun, drink a little, chat with bartender Harry Young, tell sometimes true stories to the saloon crowd, and jaw with friend Jasper Washington. Yes, Jasper was there most days, too, because, as he put it, "There doesn't seem to be enough room for a big black miner to get a fair shake in the Black Hills." The truth was, as I saw it, Jasper saw no point aggravating his feet or breaking his back on the well-trodden ground when he could sit in the shade watching over Wild Bill and rake in money to boot.

Whether playing in the same card game as his best friend or at an adjacent table, Jasper won regularly, enough so that he could be most generous to me. At Whitewood Creek he shared his fresh game and other food and allowed me to share his tent while Wild Bill and Colorado Charlie slept nearby in separate tents because Utter preferred to sleep, groom, and dress in his own neatly organized place. The four of us all enjoyed bathing in the creek, although Utter could also afford to visit the new Deadwood bathhouse regularly. Crooked Nose Jack had moved into town and found a more suitable place, although I doubted he was making a comfortable living gambling. Various reports and rumors indicated he had become a petticoat pensioner and was living in the same shack as the prostitute Tid Bit, who had been immediately dismissed from our camp by Jasper. "There was too much room for a big black gambler in that nymph du prairie's presumed passion," Jasper told me. "I had no wish to take on a female dependent."

Apparently, once she had been rejected by the big man, the little redhead had gone back to Little Jack. I wasn't certain, because my half brother had broken off contact with those who had brought him to Deadwood. He didn't want to work for Charlie Utter or anyone else, he didn't want to play poker with Wild Bill Hickok, he didn't want anything at all to do with Jasper Washington, and he didn't have any immediate need to call me "brother."

Thanks to Jasper's generosity, I no longer felt that I *must* find work. Besides eating, bathing, and sleeping well, I did little but daydream and amble, usually seeking out remote areas where there couldn't possibly be gold and thus were no people. I did go into the heart of Deadwood on occasion, not looking for work anymore but for companionship, albeit the kind that comes without a price (certainly a rarity in Deadwood).

This act of what might be called desperation came about, at least indirectly, because of things Wild Bill Hickok was saying. Jasper said that his best friend admitted to missing his wife each morning when he woke up and each night when he lay in his bedroll waiting for sleep to come. And once in late July, when Hickok couldn't sleep at all, he came into the tent I shared with Jasper, and I heard him giving Jasper an explanation. "Damn it, Wash, I miss Agnes so much I feel like a lone wolf howling at the moon, 'cept I can't howl or I'll wake up Charlie in the next tent, and that old cuss needs his beauty sleep. Will I ever see Agnes again? This isn't the first night I've asked myself that same damn question. You see, I feel my days are numbered; my sun is sinking fast. Something tells me I shall never leave these hills alive; somebody is going to kill me. Thing is, I don't know who it is or why he is going to do it. You know better than anyone, Wash. I have killed many men in my day, but I never killed a man yet but what it was kill or get killed with me. Charlie's busy with business. But I still have three trusty friends who stick real close and whom I can count on to protect me: two are my six-shooters, and the other is you, Wash. I want to tell Agnes how I feel, but I haven't written her yet on account of I don't wish her to be worrying herself sick over me."

"My advice to you, Bill, is not to worry and get some sleep," Jasper replied.

"Easy for you to say," Wild Bill said, shifting his weight in the darkness. "You keep winning at cards and sleeping like a breast-fed baby. What have you got to worry about?"

"You for one thing, Bill. But that doesn't interfere with my days or ruin my nights."

"Don't know where I'd be without you and Charlie, and right now just you, since Charlie is snoring like a bear still holed up from winter."

"Go ahead and write Agnes about your worries. A woman likes a strong man, but not one who believes he is immortal. And above all else, a woman will appreciate your honesty."

"Like your honesty with that fallen angel who couldn't keep her hands off you? I heard you tell her you didn't love her one lick and that she was no more welcome in camp than a claim-jumper—this despite the fact you don't have a gold claim or another woman who claims you."

"True, Tid Bit didn't appreciate my honesty, but it did the job. Haven't seen her since. The big difference is, I didn't even like her much, but you love your Agnes."

I was wide awake at that point, and I couldn't help but express an opinion. "You're a lucky man, Mr. Hickok, having that kind of great love for some woman who loves you right back to the same degree."

"Not some woman," Wild Bill said. "My wife."

"I'm sorry, Mr. Hickok. That's who I meant."

"No need to apologize. Maybe you're right, young man. Instead of worrying, I should feel lucky to have Agnes waiting for me. You ever been married?"

Jasper answered for me: "Zach isn't so young, only eight years younger than you, Bill. At the rate he's going, he's liable to be a lifetime bachelor."

"Like you, Wash?" Hickok said.

"You bet. But some of us don't mind. Not much freedom in marriage."

"Too late to be talking about freedom. I feel better now, anyway. I'm ready to head back to my own slumber tent."

And so he went. After that I couldn't sleep.

Nor could I sleep for two more nights. You see, I wasn't like Jasper Washington in that respect. I did *not* wish to remain a bachelor my entire life. On the third night, the last day of July, I got to sleep, but Jasper woke me up. In his hand he held the draft of a letter Wild Bill was writing to Agnes. Wild Bill had wanted his friend to look it over with any suggestions about content and corrections in his grammar.

"What he's said so far worries me," Jasper told me. "He plans to send it off tomorrow with one of Charlie Utter's riders. I know I told him to be honest about his feelings with Agnes, but this can't help. Why he has to be *this* afraid is beyond me."

"Huh? You saying Wild Bill's sun is still sinking?"

"If it hasn't already sunk."

"Somebody threatened to kill him?"

"Not that I know of. Have you heard anything?"

"No, but I don't hear much."

"Well, listen to this, Zach." Jasper proceeded to read me what was in the letter so far: " 'Agnes Darling, if such should be we never meet again, while firing my last shot, I will gently breathe the name of my wife—Agnes—and with wishes even for my enemies I will make the plunge and try to swim to the other shore.' "

"That doesn't sound too good. I mean, it *does* sound good, too. It kind of makes my eyes watery. I'm not sure I fully understand, though. Make the plunge? Into Whitewood Creek? How well does Wild Bill swim?"

"Look, if that's not plain enough, last night I heard him say straight out to Charlie Utter, 'Charlie, I feel this is going to be my last camp, and I won't leave it alive.' If there was another threat against him, I would have heard about it. Bill must have had a presentiment."

"You going to suggest he *not* send it off, or at least do a rewrite?"

"I don't know. I do know I'm going to have to keep a close watch on the old boy the next few days."

I wasn't sure how Jasper could watch Hickok any closer, but I didn't argue the point.

"I've been mostly worried about his eyes," Jasper continued. "Now I'm worried about his head." Jasper folded the letter and slapped it against his own head. "Anyway, Zach, sorry to wake you. Sleep well."

And I did. I fell asleep again in an instant and dreamed the rest of the night about female figures, although their faces weren't clear. I woke up fully rested, yet restless, at dawn. I had this overwhelming feeling—though only thirty-one years old—that time was running out on me, too. In other words, I wasn't thinking about Wild Bill at all, only myself. On that day, August 1, 1876, I didn't wish to be without the companionship of *some* woman.

I grabbed a stale biscuit for breakfast and ran instead of

walked to town. I went to a number of saloons and makeshift dance halls. Of course, all the women who frequented those places weren't up and about yet. I felt unwelcome in the Cricket Saloon, so I walked around out back and found a fully clothed woman sleeping sitting up with her back to a tree. I recognized both her face and body and sat down next to her. I swear I was just sitting there with my hands to myself when she reached out and grabbed me. I'm certain I didn't respond, but I couldn't bring myself to break free and stand up, either.

"Oh Bill, dearest Bill," she said, her left arm active but her eyes still closed. "You've come to me at last."

"It's not Bill," I whispered because I wasn't sure I wanted to wake her. "It's only Zach, Zach McCall."

"Goddamn, Bill!" she said, throwing her left leg clear over my raised knee. "You drive me wild!"

After Calamity Jane had moved her sleepy self onto my lap, she opened her eyes, and they immediately widened, but then they suddenly narrowed as if she were angry. She couldn't have been too angry, though, because she planted her lips against mine. Whether I tasted any whiskey on her lips or inside her mouth, I can't remember, because what happened next was that we stayed locked at the lips as we slid away from the tree and stretched out on the hard ground, pressed together like two marked face cards. All this and more led to our retiring (yet remaining active) indoors for the sake of modesty and privacy—mine, that is, for Calamity didn't care about such matters.

"It'll be over in two shakes of a lamb's tail," she said, but I put my foot down, and she did not protest too much. She dragged me around a corner of empty whiskey bottles and broken boxes to a small, dilapidated building that seemed to be trembling on a downward slope. Hand in hand, we plunged inside. Considering the rush and the brevity of our amorous congress on the only bed in that one-room shack, Calamity called it a "brush," although Crooked Nose Jack had several other names for it when he threw open the humble door and carried an altogether naked Tid Bit inside.

It turned out to be Tid Bit's working residence. Calamity Jane had taken the liberty of using it without asking, though I am certain it wasn't the first time. Tid Bit only laughed and continued to do so even after Jack unceremoniously tossed her aside on an unused blanket. It was Jack who took violent exception to our presence. He showed previously hidden strength by lifting me off Calamity, savagely kicking the side of her face in the undertaking, and then hurling me on top of Tid Bit as if he were an angry God taking his wrath out on wretched sinners.

The fallen angel didn't even try to push me off, but I got off anyway. It wasn't easy because my trousers were bunched at my ankles. As I struggled to keep my balance while yanking at my trousers, I saw how small her naked body looked. I apologized to her as if I had bumped into her on crowded Main Street.

"How dare you!" Little Jack shouted. I thought he was talking to me, but he had dropped to his knees beside the bed and was leaning over Calamity Jane as if he intended to strangle her or at least give her a vigorous shaking. "He's my brother!" he screamed in her face.

"That who he was? Poor man." She spat in his face, which seemed to take the starch out of him, and while he was wiping his eyes, she raised up and threw her entire body into a punch. It missed Jack's crooked nose but connected with his jaw. It must have packed even more punch than Silver Dollar Sally's fist back in Cheyenne. He tumbled onto his side and lay perfectly still. It looked as if he would be out for a while, so Calamity Jane wiped blood off her right ear and then casually put her buckskin pants and shirt back on. Tid Bit partially covered herself with the blanket and lay on her side, paying me no mind but staring at her motionless lover.

"I'm sorry," I said to both women as I buttoned my trousers. "I don't know what got into him."

"He's a son of a bitch," Calamity said.

"She wouldn't have him," said Tid Bit as if that explained everything.

"You saying he's *not* a son of a bitch, Bit?"

"I ain't saying that exactly, Calamity. All I'm saying is, I'm not as particular. A gal like me can't afford to be. Even a son of a bitch can do some things good, can show his worth."

"Far as I'm concerned, the son of a bitch is worthless." Calamity looked at me and patted her belly. "But his brother ain't. Now I got my head on straight. You're Zach. I come with you from Fort Laramie."

"That's right, eh . . . ma'am."

"You look like you might be thinking of leaving, Zach. What's your all-fired hurry?"

"I . . . eh, got to go. I . . . eh . . . need to see Mr. Hickok about something?"

"Don't we all. What's your business with Wild . . ." She cut off his name halfway through. I could tell she was thinking of Wild Bill Hickok now, not me. I didn't actually have any business with Hickok, but I was glad I had brought his name into the shack, even if it meant telling a fib. "Yup, you better go," Calamity said. "I'm no longer in good humor."

"I'm sorry," I said again. I started toward the door but stopped to look at Tid Bit. She was biting a strand of red hair and still staring at Little Jack as if he were a wolf caught in a trap and she wasn't sure whether to release him or shoot him. "I'm sure he'll be all right," I told her.

"Sure," she said. "We'll all be all right. Forever."

She didn't sound sincere, but I didn't blame her. "Nice to meet you," I said. I gave her a quick wave and then Calamity a longer one as I went out the door like a traveling salesman taking his leave.

It wasn't even noon yet, but I wanted nothing more to do with Deadwood that day. I took the long way back to Whitewood Creek, trying to figure out my state of mind as I trudged up and down hills. I kept painting an almost tragic picture of what had occurred overall in the one-room shack, yet every dozen steps I would recall the feel of Calamity and nearly burst with delight. I found nobody at our camp and had mixed feelings about that. Jasper, Wild Bill, and Colorado Charlie didn't need to hear about what had happened to me, but I had a hankering to tell somebody. I settled for talking to the trout. I ran to my favorite bathing area in the creek, stripped, and plunged in. I washed myself thoroughly as I told the unseen fish everything. Afterward, I tried to see how long I could keep my head underwater—something I hadn't done since I was a boy fascinated by the Kentucky River and the miracle of being alive. It wasn't nearly as long as I expected.

I stayed around camp all day wondering about my future, actually about what would happen in the next day or two. I figured Little Jack would be mad at the world for at least forty-eight hours. I figured some other things out, too. Having Tid Bit wasn't enough for him. She wasn't his first choice in Deadwood, and, anyway, she had only taken up with him because Jasper Washington didn't want her. The one Little Jack really wanted was Calamity Jane. He knew she wanted Wild Bill Hickok, but that didn't discourage him since he also knew Wild Bill Hickok only wanted his beloved wife back in Cincinnati. But seeing me with Calamity Jane on that narrow bed had no doubt shocked my half brother and upset his balance. It must have seemed as if he'd been stabbed in the back or at least punched in the jaw, which was in fact what Calamity had given him. He'd be mad at her, of course, but no doubt madder at me. I'd already told him once I wasn't interested in Calamity Jane. Would I tell him again? At the moment I didn't see how I could do that. Had it been just a *brush* between Calamity and me? I couldn't say for sure, but that afternoon alone at the campsite amid all my thinking about the *wants* of other people, I started to *want* Calamity Jane again. I busied myself in a wood-gathering frenzy to start the evening fire, but my desire refused to burn itself out, so I sought out the steepest hill around and climbed it three times in a row to exhaust myself.

During the evening meal of rabbit stew, Jasper Washington asked me if I wanted to do something different for a change that night—accompany him and Wild Bill to the No. 10 Saloon.

"You know I don't play poker," I told him.

"Sure, I know that. All of Deadwood knows that by now. I thought you might like to observe a true professional in action."

"You talking about yourself or Mr. Hickok?"

"All right, two true professionals. Anyway, there's more going on at the No. 10 than poker. Harry Young serves up the best drinks in town, plus there is often good conversation among agreeable white men, and the occasional appearance of a fine-looking woman in a dress or Calamity Jane."

I began to choke as if a rabbit bone had lodged in my throat. Jasper pounded me on the back until I could speak, albeit with a sore back. "Can't," I whispered. "Too tired. Much too tired."

"From what?"

"I don't know. Thinking, I reckon."

"Is that what you do, think all day?"

"Not always. I made the fire. I . . . I'll find a job somewhere real soon. I promise."

"Work or don't work. It's all the same to me. But you are my friend, Zach, and I want my friends to have fun. You could find yourself a lady. There are one or two around, you know?"

"Could be I already found one," I blurted out. Embarrassed, I immediately went about poking a stray piece of burning wood back into the heart of the cookfire.

"Keeping secrets from your old pal, eh?"

"Not really. I just don't want to go back to town tonight."

"Sure. I understand, Zach. Those ladies can be awfully tiring."

CHAPTER THIRTY-FIVE:
DEATH IN DEADWOOD

I fell asleep on the night of August 1, 1876, recalling in detail the time I had spent that day with Calamity Jane, and my sleeping dreams continued in that same vein, although once her figure transformed into a cross between Minnie Mary and Tid Bit, and another time her face looked so much like Belle Bragg's that I woke up in a sweat. I was surprised to see Jasper Washington sitting on the only stool in our tent looking at me with amused curiosity. He still wore his frock coat and hat.

"Having a nightmare?" he asked.

"What? What time is it?"

"Not morning yet, Zach my man. I just got in from a long night at the No. 10. I figured you were dreaming about her."

"Who? Who says I was dreaming at all?"

"Of course, maybe it wasn't a nightmare. I was only thinking that if I happened to be dreaming about her, heaven help me, it would have to be a nightmare."

"It's too late and too early for riddles, Jasper. I don't know what you're talking about."

"I'm talking about her. Your brother was in the No. 10 tonight drinking too much, playing cards poorly, and telling sordid tales about you and Miss Calamity."

That got me to sit up. I wasn't sure whether to protest or deny or ask for more details. "You mean Little Jack?"

"You have some other brother?"

"No. And he's only a half brother."

"And it seems you are no longer half a man. Yes, it was Calamity, but a fellow has to start somewhere. Now, Jack didn't call you half of anything. He did use the words *betrayer* and *bastard* all night at the card table. In sum, he said, you were an insatiable monster."

"And you just sat there?"

"Sure. You can't argue with a man on a pain-killing spree. Besides, I was winning, and so was Wild Bill for a change."

"What was Little Jack doing there, anyway? He makes a point of avoiding you two."

"He'd been drinking steadily elsewhere. I figure he was lost and confused when he stumbled into the No. 10 saloon about ten o'clock. It cost him."

"He lost a lot?"

"We cleaned him out. Bill gave him money for breakfast, which is more than I would have done. I did give your brother, your half brother that is, some advice: *Don't play out of turn, don't bluff four hands in a row, don't fold and then tell everyone why you did, don't talk about your bad luck, and don't play at all if you can't afford to cover your losses.*"

"Little Jack must have been beside himself with anger."

"Sure. He called me the black bastard companion of that unbrotherly bastard betrayer—you. I shrugged it off. I had most of his money."

"What did he do then?"

"He took Bill's handout and left muttering. Oh, he did say one thing plenty clear before he was out the door. He shouted, 'I'll be getting my revenge soon enough.' "

"Really? He thinks he'll get enough money to play with you two again?"

"I didn't get the impression he meant revenge at the poker table. I could be wrong, but I believe he was thinking about you when he said it. You and Calamity together hit the boy hard."

"He's no boy. And I didn't hit him. Calamity did."

I didn't get back to sleep before the sun came up on August 2. I wasn't exactly worried about Crooked Nose Jack seeking revenge against me. I was bigger than him, and Calamity Jane had knocked him out with one punch. I wasn't sure if he had acquired a new firearm or not, but even if he did, I figured it would take far more than my one coupling with Calamity for him to blast me. After all, we were family. What kept me awake was wondering how I stood with that tough old gal, contemplating what I would say and do when we next met, and, yes, imagining future couplings.

I finally arose around noon, at the same time as Jasper Washington. Wild Bill Hickok entered our tent, pushed back his low-crowned black hat, and told us to put our boots on as he was taking us and Charlie Utter to town to buy us steaks. He was a generous man when he had poker winnings at his disposal. We followed him to Sluice Sam's Steakhouse at the corner of Main and Gold Streets. At that corner, the Reverend Henry Weston Smith often spoke out against demon spirits and unfettered greed, but on this day, he happened to be preaching against sexual immorality and fornication. It caught my attention, and I stopped in my tracks for a listen. Only a half-dozen other men had gathered around to hear his message, but that didn't matter. It seemed as if Preacher Smith was talking directly to me.

"To those of you who are unmarried, I say it is good to stay unmarried like me," he said, staring at me and into me as if he could see that one of my internal organs was rotten. "But if you cannot control yourself and can't keep yourself from being as promiscuous as the naked savages and wild buffalo, then I say to you, you had better marry quick, for the Good Book says it is better to marry than to burn with passion. You who sin sexually sin against your own bodies."

I don't know if it was what he was saying or the way he said it, but I was frozen, as if the very act of moving might be interpreted as a sin.

"Never before saw a body that attentive," said Wild Bill, who had paused at the door to the steakhouse. "You think the young man will learn something?"

"Naw," said Jasper. "He knows all about that kind of thing."

"You don't say. I never would have guessed it."

"He's not that young, Bill, and . . ."

Jasper stopped talking and winked at me. I thought for sure he'd say something about me and Calamity Jane, but he fooled me. "And he used to be a circuit preacher in Kentucky. Not only that, but he was born and raised in a bordello."

"Bless my soul!" said Charlie Utter. "His brother, too, no doubt."

"Actually, not," said Jasper. "They're half brothers and were raised separately."

"Figures," said Wild Bill. "I'm betting Jack McCall was raised in a southerly pigsty."

"Well, we cleaned Little Jack out just fine last night, didn't we, Bill?" said Jasper.

"Never mind him—them," said Utter. "I'm hungry enough to eat a bear."

"You betcha," said Wild Bill. "I best bless my belly before I bless my soul."

"Amen to that, Bill," said Jasper, and then he called out to me: "Come in when you're done being enraptured, Zach. We'll save you a seat."

I snapped out of it soon enough. Preacher Smith wasn't about to bless any part of me and certainly wasn't about to forgive me, so I went inside with my appetite for a rare steak undeterred. We all had our bellies filled just fine at Sluice Sam's and left eager for a post-meal walk. On the street Preacher Smith was done sermonizing against sin, and in that very spot I saw two men each tugging on a beefy arm of a buxom painted lady I recognized as Big Dollie, who'd come to Deadwood with us in the Utter-Hickok caravan. Across the way I saw a Chinese man lying on his back in the street, either dead drunk or just dead. Several men stepped around him, one right over him. I was relieved when the Chinese man finally raised a hand to slap at the flies buzzing about his face. My three companions didn't seem to pay attention to anything else happening on the street, or perhaps they were coolly taking it all in out of the corners of their eyes. They moved side-by-side-by-side like the Three Musketeers. I had to scuttle some to keep up with their matching long strides.

Colorado Charlie finally broke away. He was a working man, and he needed to finish arranging a race between his express service and a newly formed rival company to see who could deliver copies of the *Cheyenne Daily Leader* to Deadwood fastest. "See you later, Charlie," said Wild Bill, who had become a full-time playing man in Deadwood. He suggested he had started a hot streak the night before, so he patted his flat belly, threw his free arm around Jasper's broad back, and directed him toward the No. 10 Saloon. Jasper in turn swung a long arm back to catch my arm and pull me along, like a cowboy who'd lassoed a stray calf.

"Now, Zach, don't you be throwing a wet blanket on our rising spirits," Jasper said. "I don't know about you, but I'm sweating like a lay preacher in a sporting house. You got anything better to do than get out of the sun and allow your friends to buy you a drink?"

It occurred to me, even as I felt perspiration running down my forehead, that I could likely find Calamity Jane somewhere out of the sun and that I didn't need a drink first. But then I started thinking about Preacher Smith and my own long-ago preaching days in Kentucky, and I naturally had no wish to run into Crooked Nose Jack or Tid Bit or anyone else who might see me sweating too much.

"Nothing I need to do," I told Jasper. "Nothing at all."

A poker game was already in progress when we arrived at the No. 10. Owner Carl Mann was one of the players and said there was room for one more. And then he made it more specific, inviting Wild Bill Hickok to join them. Jasper tipped his hat and pulled out the empty stool for Hickok, about the only man he would defer to in Deadwood or anywhere. Wild Bill Hickok hesitated and then asked to switch places with one of the other players—the one who had the wall seat. That player, Charles Rich, shook his head and said he had staked a claim to the lucky seat. Hickok hesitated and looked as if he'd pass on sitting down for a while and go to the bar for a drink.

"Don't worry, Bill," Jasper said from the bar. "You can see the front door from there. I'll keep an eye on that little rear door."

"And I'll bring you a whiskey, Mr. Hickok," I said.

Hickok grudgingly sat. When I handed him his glass, his eyes narrowed, and he stared hard at me as if he couldn't quite place my face, even though I had come there with him. He rubbed his eyes with both fists and took another look. "You're not Harry Young," he said, smiling. "Thank you, young man."

"My pleasure, Mr. Hickok," I said. "Good luck."

The drink seemed to help some, but the famous old lawman couldn't sit easy in that seat. He asked to change stools a couple more times, in part because he did like his back against the wall but probably more so because he kept losing. He had been denied his usual seat, the one that had been so lucky for him the previous night. The other players kidded him about being as nervous as a young bride on her wedding night. When Captain William Massie won what might have been the biggest pot of the afternoon, Wild Bill should have stood up and quit. Jasper even offered to take his place. Instead, Hickok leaned back on his unlucky stool, patted his belly, and called to bartender Young requesting a loan.

"Never mind, Harry," Jasper said. "I got it."

Jasper gave the bartender fifty dollars, and Young brought Hickok that amount in chips.

"That'll do me," Wild Bill said. "The old duffer broke me on the last hand."

The game continued, more draw poker. It was Rich's deal, and he dealt fast. I watched Hickok pick up each of his cards without looking at them. Only when all five were in his hands did he slowly reveal each to his own tired eyes. His facial expression stayed much the same, but I saw his left eyebrow twitch. I'd been observing enough that day to believe that meant he thought he had a good hand. But, of course, he had thought that before and had mostly ended up losing to better hands.

"This is the hand that turns it around for him," I suggested in a rare show of optimism, perhaps brought on by the two glasses of whiskey I had drunk.

"Maybe we've been watching him too closely," Jasper said. "Let's let him alone for a bit and see if it changes his luck."

"All the time I've known you, I never knew you to be superstitious, Wash," I said.

"Well, I tell you, Zach. Nobody can sit at a poker table day in and day out and *not* be superstitious about something—where he sits, how he sits (I for one never cross my legs), what he wears, how tightly he holds his cards, how many times he glances at his cards or counts his chips, what he says to himself or the other players, how often he silently begs the poker gods to look out for him."

"I understand. When I worked at the stables, I never approached a horse straight toward his face, but toward his left shoulder if possible, and I always touched that shoulder or his neck rather than his face or nose. And I often silently prayed a horse wouldn't kick me."

"Something like that. Works pretty well with women, too. Come on, let's talk to Harry."

Jasper turned away from the poker table, wrapped an arm around me, and escorted me along the bar until we ware directly across from Harry Young, who was polishing glasses with a clean white towel. We literally had our bellies to the bar. Without a word, Harry poured fresh drinks. And as I downed my third glass of whiskey (two over my usual limit) I wondered if Fat Jack McCall was looking down from heaven and saying, "That's my bastard boy, a bastard man at last!"

"Say, Harry, I suppose you've seen your share of bar fights?" Jasper asked.

"I'd say I have," the bartender replied.

"But I bet you never saw a bear fight. I mean man vs. bear."

"Can't say that I have."

"Should you ever want to see one, tell your boss to bring in a bear from the hills, and I'm your man. It'll draw in the customers; you'd pack this place, and Carl Mann will raise your pay."

"You don't say."

"I am saying, Harry. Back in Ohio and thereabouts I used to wrestle a bear named Victor. Now his name is a bit misleading, because I almost always won out in those contests of strength, skill, and shrewdness."

Whether I needed to or not, I put down my glass and held onto the bar with both hands for support. I couldn't remember the last time I'd drunk so much. When Jasper raised his glass to drink, I peeked under his arm and couldn't quite register what I saw—my half brother standing a few paces behind Wild Bill Hickok, who was studying his hand after the card draw. In my inebriated state I thought Hickok looked like a monk hunched over an ancient manuscript. I had no idea if Crooked Nose Jack had come through the back door or the front door. But that was of no matter; he was there—if I could believe my eyes—and nobody but me seemed to be paying any attention to him.

I couldn't doubt my eyes when Little Jack pulled out a large-caliber six-shooter. I had never seen him with anything but a derringer in years, so I knew he meant business. And I was convinced his business was with me. *Why else has he come to this saloon on this day except to shoot me for carrying on with Calamity Jane behind his back?* Yes, that is what I asked myself, even as I pushed away from the bar and scrambled in the direction of the front door. I suppose fear came into play, but I am convinced the main reason I moved was so my friend Jasper Washington wouldn't be in the line of fire. I also didn't believe Little Jack could possibly be an accurate shot at that distance, especially if I was a moving target.

I had misread everything. When Little Jack fired that big pistol, the muzzle was against the back of Hickok's head. The bang came first, and then came those words that rang in my ears and sometimes still do: "Damn you, take that!"

Hickok's head jerked violently forward a moment before his body toppled from his stool. Jack, waving his weapon wildly, backed toward the rear door. "Come on, you sons of bitches!" he yelled. I froze when he said it. Most everyone else rushed past me for the front door to get away from the gunman. The big exception was the unarmed Jasper Washington, who charged Jack and surely would have squeezed him to death had he caught him. It wasn't to be. Jack snapped off at least three more shots, two misfires but one slug that pierced Jasper's side and caused the big man to stagger forward clutching his wound before dropping to his knees.

"You bastard!" shouted Jasper, who didn't get off his knees but refused to fall over onto his side.

I actually thought Jasper was addressing me. I went to him, but he jerked his head forward and pointed a bloody hand at the small rear door that Jack had just passed through. For a change I didn't think what to do next. I ran after him. I got outside in time to see Jack mount a horse and then tumble to the ground because the saddle cinch was loose. He picked himself off the dirt and started to dust himself off as if he had all the time in the world. When he saw me standing a few yards away staring at him, he opened his mouth to speak, but only one word came out: "Brother." He still held his smoking six-shooter, but instead of pointing it at me, he hurled it at me and ran.

I didn't react until the gun had flown harmlessly over my left shoulder and slammed against the back door of the No. 10. But when I heard the thump I went back into motion, chasing Jack down the street while seemingly a hundred voices cried out. I heard the accurate shouts of "Wild Bill is shot!" and "Wild Bill is dead!" but also the inaccurate shouts of "Wild Bill shot a man!" and "Wild Bill has killed again!"

Others also gave chase. Crooked Nose Jack was caught soon enough, but not by me. A couple of Deadwood citizens, mistaking me for the man who shot Hickok, tripped me up and began pounding me with their fists and kicking me with their boots. They were not particular where their blows landed. Soon they got word that the real killer had been caught trying to hide in a butcher shop. My assailants made sure I was alive but didn't try to help me to my feet or apologize. I never saw their faces or learned their identities.

No jail had yet been built in Deadwood, but once I learned that my half brother had been captured and was under guard, I didn't try to go see him. I had seen him shoot Wild Bill Hickok from behind and then Jasper Washington from the front. Crooked Nose Jack was beyond my help. I stumbled along back to Saloon No. 10, stopping every so often to catch my breath or wipe blood from my eyes. I found Harry Young, now scrubbing blood off the floor instead of tending bar. Wild Bill's body had been carted away. The bullet had done its damage to the back of his head, and he had bled out quickly, so while stretched out on the floor face up, he had looked like he was sleeping or just resting his eyes. It had taken six men to carry Jasper to the medical office of Dr. L. F. Babcock, who had just arrived in Deadwood the day before.

"He's more than likely going to survive," the bartender assured me. "He's in good hands. I heard the doc graduated from the Rush Medical College in Chicago. We haven't had a doctor in Deadwood till now. That Washington is one lucky fellow. He has a chance. Wild Bill never had one. By the way, what happened to you?"

"Nothing. I'm fine. I got to go see Jasper. Can you direct me to the doctor's office?" A pain shot through my hip where I'd been kicked a half-dozen times, and my old ankle war wounds were throbbing like they hadn't done in years. I would have dropped to my knees except Harry Young caught my arm.

"I'll do that," he said. "But you better sit awhile first." He led me to the table where the deadly poker game had been played and sat me down on the nearest stool which happened to be the last one ever occupied by Wild Bill. "Look at this," Young said, pointing to the five cards face up on the table. I leaned closer but didn't touch them.

"I see a queen, two eights, and two of the aces," I said.

"That was Wild Bill's last hand."

"I'm not a player, just an observer. That means two pairs, right? A pretty good hand, right?"

"Not bad, but not good enough. He drew one card. He needed another ace or eight to beat William Massie's flush. Instead he got that queen."

I didn't know what to say. I didn't see how it mattered much since Wild Bill's luck had already run out permanently.

CHAPTER THIRTY-SIX:
TRIAL AND TRIBULATION

The evening of the shooting of Wild Bill Hickok and Jasper Washington, most of the town was preoccupied with Hickok's corpse and the very much alive captured killer, Crooked Nose Jack. In Dr. D. F. Babcock's office, though, the doc was intent on doing all he could to make sure Jasper survived. I was the only other person in the room, so by default I became his assistant. Jasper had vomited blood, and I did the mopping up. The doc, a trained surgeon, probed the wound and showed me the entrance, a bullet hole two inches to the left of the spinal column and just below Jasper's last rib. There was no exit wound. He said he must operate and sent me to the restaurant next door to fetch a better table lamp and water. I wiped the sweat off Jasper's brow while Dr. Babcock boiled his instruments.

"Nothing too vital hit, right, Doc?" Jasper asked.

"I'll need to enter your abdominal cavity," the doctor said.

"No. No. Forget that. That's vital. I like to eat."

"Unless I take the bullet out and stop the bleeding, you don't figure to eat again, mister."

"That right? Well, maybe that's for the best. Wild Bill is dead, my best friend in the whole world gone. I let him down. It was my job to protect him. I never saw that cross-eyed son of a bitch until it was too late."

"For God's sake, don't refuse the doctor," I said. "It'll take more than my prayers."

"Well, thanks for praying for me anyway, Preacher McCall."

"Look, Jasper. It was my fault, too. I saw Little Jack standing there behind Mr. Hickok, but I thought he was gunning for me and . . . Anyway. You got to live. You got to show me the way. I don't have anyone else."

"They got him, right?"

"Yup. Little Jack is in custody."

"Good. I got a reason to live, at least long enough to see him hang."

"Then I best operate now," Dr. Babcock said. "If you concur, Mr. Washington, I'll give you the chloroform."

"That's real considerate of you, Doc. Just do your best. If that steak I had this afternoon at Sluice Sam's was my last supper, I can live with that."

Dr. Babcock proceeded, and I handed him the instruments he needed. I didn't see as much blood as I thought I would when he entered the cavity of the abdomen, but it was enough to make me unsteady on my feet. By constantly reminding myself that Jasper was the best friend I'd had since leaving Kentucky and, whenever possible, by diverting my gaze to the wall where the doc's Rush Medical College diploma hung only slightly askew, I managed to stay upright. The patient began vomiting blood again, and during the strain his stomach pushed partially out of the abdomen, but at the same time the bullet came completely out and fell into my hands. Next came sponging to get the area as dry as possible and who knows what else. My eyes were closed at that point. They reopened when the doctor said Jasper's pulse was growing weak. I tilted Jasper's enormous body as best I could so the doctor could give hypodermics of whiskey to his rectum. Finally, the doctor closed Jasper's abdomen with sutures of braided silk. It was during this closure that I couldn't stop myself from thinking too much about what was happening and fainted right next to the makeshift operating table.

The next day, August 3, was a busy one, what with the coroner's jury ruling—"J. B. Hickok came to his death from a wound resulting from a shot fired from a pistol in the hands of Jack McCall"—the trial and the funeral service at Charlie Utter's Whitewood Creek camp. I missed all of it. I had fallen asleep on an office stool during the night, and I was determined not to leave Jasper's side. He continued to lie on the operating table, but Dr. Babcock and I had managed to get a couple blankets under his body and head to make him more comfortable. Jasper woke up with great pain in the abdomen, so the doctor and I gave him saline purges. After his bowels moved ten times by my count, the patient felt considerably better. But taking food by the stomach was out of the question. I brought him crushed ice to suck, and that was it.

"Your stitches look fine, and your temperature isn't running but a degree over normal," the doctor reported in the afternoon.

"Mighty pleased to hear it. I feel like I'm getting my appetite back."

"Best not to think about food, Mr. Washington. For the next five days you'll be nourished by the rectum. You have a lot of healing to do." The doctor poked his belly, and Jasper grimaced.

"I believe you, Doc, but I don't see how you're going to get one of Sluice Sam's steaks in me."

"You just rest up, you hear? You won't feel up to going to a restaurant or anywhere else for a couple weeks. I'm going to do my sworn duty and treat the ladies in town right now. Your friend will keep an eye on you until I return."

"Ladies have been shot, too?"

"Of course not. They have their own difficulties. I am not a one-patient physician, you know."

Dr. Babcock patted me on the head, picked up his medical bag, and hurried out the door.

Jasper tried to sit up but felt the pain in his midsection and settled back down. He shook his head as he watched me read *The Black Hills Pioneer*. "What's it say?" he asked. "Wild Bill still above ground?"

"Says people can see him lying in repose out at the camp before he's buried," I said.

"I couldn't go even if I wanted to, and I don't. When I think back on Bill, I don't want to see him reposing. You should go, Zach. Don't mind me."

"Nothing I can do for Mr. Hickok. But maybe I can do something for you."

"What about your brother? It say anything in that paper about him hanging in the air?"

"Not yet. It's customary to have a trial first."

"Why don't you go find out. They might want you there. You're an eyewitness."

"I'm not going to go testify against him. Enough other people saw what he did. There can't be any doubt he ambushed Mr. Hickok from behind in cold blood. If they hang Crooked Nose Jack, I don't want to see that either. Nothing I can do for him. I'm here for you, at least until the doc returns. You need something, Jasper?"

"A bottle of whiskey, but you'll have to turn me over and pour it up my ass."

"Maybe I'll just read you some other news."

I started to read, because it beat thinking about the late Hickok and the soon-to-be-late Jack McCall. Jasper soon closed his eyes and fell asleep. I watched and listened to him. His breathing was peaceful and rhythmic. It soothed my head. The paper fell out of my hands; I didn't bother to pick it up. My eyes stayed open, but I slipped into sleep anyway.

The soiled dove Tid Bit woke me up. She was completely covered in a black dress fitting for a church-going woman. She wanted to see how Jasper Washington was doing. She ran her fingers gently over his warm cheeks and chin stubble, and only peeked down at where he was bandaged. I reassured her the patient would be all right but didn't go into any detail except to say the slug was out. Maybe she didn't believe me, because she asked to see it. I obliged. She nodded, said she didn't want to wake him, and started to walk out.

I called her back, sprang off my stool, and asked about Little Jack. With her back to me, her shoulders rose and fell heavily three times and then she let out a gush of air before slowly turning to face me.

"Calamity Jane is telling everyone she was the one who caught him—found him in Shurdy's butcher shop, grabbed a meat cleaver, and made him throw up his hands. That's a barefaced lie. I know exactly where she was at the time—in my tent fighting off the demons of a two-day spree."

"Oh. But he was caught."

"Yes, and there was lynch talk, but nothing came of it."

"So, there is a trial? I mean, a trial is the right thing to do no matter what . . ."

"He spoke at the miners' court on his own behalf down at the McDaniels' Theater," she said. "He said he had only a few words to say." She paused and studied my face. I suspected she was comparing my features to those of my half brother. "You want to hear what he said?"

"Of course, if you know."

"I wasn't there, but I know because I know most of the miners and the presiding judge, Willie Kuykendall, knows me."

"Go on."

"You won't like this, but this is what Jack told the court: 'Wild Bill killed my brother, and I killed him. Wild Bill threatened to kill me if I crossed his path. I am not sorry for what I have done. I would do the same thing once again.' "

I had to sit back down on the stool. "That's all a lie," I said. "How could he have killed his brother if *I'm* his brother?"

"You're only his half brother, Jack told me. I figured he had another brother, and Hickok killed *that* brother in Abilene or someplace like that."

"No. Little Jack only has three sisters, and as far as I know, none of them has ever been on this side of the Mississippi River. Didn't those miners and that judge know that I'm alive and almost well right here in Deadwood?"

"I reckon not. You two didn't act like brothers. And you don't really look like brothers. I wouldn't have known myself if Jack hadn't told me after he caught you giving Calamity Jane a tumble."

"Maybe I should tell them I'm alive. The court is still in session?"

"Both sides have called all their witnesses and made their closing statements. The jurors are now doing what jurors do, deliberating mostly. If I was you, I'd sit tight. You show up alive, and there goes Jack's entire defense. How could it be an act of brotherly vengeance if you aren't dead?"

"Are you saying if the jurors think it was brotherly vengeance, they won't hang Little Jack?"

"I don't know. I'm a female. What do I know about such proceedings? He had to say something. Everyone knows he did it. The thing is, if you show up, Jack won't have a fighting chance."

"Good," mumbled Jasper, with eyes still closed. I didn't know what to say. Crooked Nose Jack hadn't given Wild Bill Hickok a fighting chance. Of course, if he had, Jack certainly would have been the dead one. If vengeance was truly the motive, it would stem from Wild Bill's killing of Little Dave Tutt all those years ago in Springfield. Ever since that day, Crooked Nose Jack had carried a hatred—sometimes on the surface, sometimes deep within—for Wild Bill. No matter Little Jack's motive, the bigger question for me was, did I really want to see my half brother hang or at least to hear about his hanging? If Deadwood only had a jail, maybe they could lock him up awhile and take him to some place where there was a real judge and jury. No matter how hard I thought about it, I couldn't conceive of a not-guilty verdict even if I elected *not* to introduce myself to the court.

"You'd like me to just sit here, wouldn't you?" I asked her.

"All I'm saying is if he were my brother, I wouldn't help anyone get him hanged." She was curling a strand or two of red hair around her forefinger.

"You aren't his sister, that's for sure. But you are something to him and him to you. I mean . . ."

"I know what you mean. But me and Jack are done, whether they hang him or not."

Tid Bit left without another word. I paced in the office, keeping one eye on the sleeping Jasper and another on the door. Jasper didn't wake up until the early evening, about the same time Dr. Babcock returned with a basket of fried chicken and biscuits compliments of Al Swearengen and his working girls at the Cricket Saloon. The doctor could not offer the patient any, of course, which caused Jasper to snort and pound his belly so hard that I thought he'd break open his sutures. Dr. Babcock lifted Jasper's hands and laid them across the patient's chest.

"Don't go ruining my hard work, Mr. Washington," he said.

"Why'd you bring this here food, Doc?" Jasper asked. "You couldn't kill me directly, so you plan to torture me to death?"

"It was my payment for examining and treating the girls and not charging a fee. I couldn't refuse the basket."

"You were gone a long time, Doc. What were you doing while the chicken was cooking?"

"Trying to get word about the man who did the shooting. I went to McDaniels' Theater. A guard wouldn't let me in; he had orders to shoot anyone who interfered with the course of justice. I told him I was a doctor, but that didn't sway him. I was fortunate that a man came out with some news."

"A verdict has been reached?" I said as I rushed up to the doctor and accidentally bumped against Jasper's hip, the one on his wounded side.

"Never mind, never mind," Jasper said when I tried to apologize. "When's the hanging, Doc?"

"The jurors are again deliberating the particulars."

"What do you mean, again?" I asked.

"Mr. Hickok might be a well-known former lawman, but he is also reputed to be a man-killer. The jury has *not* been sympathetic toward him, not so far."

"Talk plain, Doc," Jasper said. "What the hell is going on?"

"I heard—this is second hand, of course—from the man who came out of McDaniels' that initially eleven jurors were for acquittal and only one for conviction. One of the men who voted for acquittal proposed that the accused be fined twenty dollars and released."

"What?" said Jasper. "And what did the others want—to give Jack a basket of chicken?"

"Look. Things can change. All I know for sure is that the deliberating has continued."

Jasper was so agitated that Dr. Babcock gave him a pill to help him go back to sleep. More pills were needed, though, because Jasper's wide-open eyes darkened with rage as he ranted about how Wild Bill deserved much better and Crooked Nose Jack deserved a quick noose. "Deadwood can't let that son of a bitch get away with murder," Jasper yelled. "Deadwood—hell, the entire frontier will never see the likes of Wild Bill again. If I could move my ass, I'd go hang the assassin myself."

"It's not over till it's over," I said, because I couldn't agree with him but couldn't disagree either.

The doctor had heard enough. He went to a corner of his office, cleared some medical books off a stool, sat down with the basket on his lap, and started in on the chicken.

"It's up to you and only you, Zach," Jasper said, with such urgency that I began to tremble. "You got to get your ass over to McDaniels' Theater, get past that guard, get in to wherever those twelve dumb men are deliberating, and tell them you are Zach McCall, and your half brother is a lying son of a bitch who can no longer use your death as his reason for back-shooting the greatest lawman the West has ever known."

I stood up, still shaking. "I don't know if I can do that, Jasper," I said, hardly believing my own words.

"Well, start knowing, Zach. You know Jack McCall doesn't deserve to walk the Deadwood streets a day longer or to ever sit down again at a poker table. It's your turn, brother or no brother, to do what a man's got to do."

"But . . ." I couldn't argue against his point. I turned to Dr. Babcock for guidance.

"The truth always counts for something," the doc said. "Take a drumstick and go!"

I left, but I didn't go directly to the theater. I went back to the No. 10 Saloon to help me go over in my mind exactly what I saw. But I couldn't get inside. The door was locked, and a handwritten sign posted on the front door said, GONE TO TRIAL. I leaned against a hitching post and nibbled at the drumstick. But I didn't have an appetite. A mongrel came around begging at a distance, and I threw the half-eaten drumstick as if it were a spear, hitting the dog right on the nose. The dog didn't mind. It carried the prize off to a safer distance.

"Why in tarnation did you do it, Little Jack!" I called out to the dark sky, where the first stars were already out, acting, as usual, as if nothing significant was going on below. I was think-

ing about him wounding Jasper as much as him killing Wild
Bill. "If you had to shoot someone, why didn't you just keep it
in the family and shoot me!" I meant it, too, at least at that moment. That part of the street was surprisingly uncongested.
What few people I saw were looking elsewhere. I dropped to my
knees on the spot and prayed for Jasper Washington's quick and
speedy recovery. Only after that did I proceed to McDaniels'
Theater.

When I got there, no guard was around to stop me from going inside, but there was no need to enter. The trial was over.
The men milling around outside were not happy. I spotted
several card-playing associates of the late Mr. Hickok. Harry
Young was there, too, and he confirmed that the jurors had
found Jack McCall not guilty.

"They say while he waited for a verdict, his feet were beating
like drums on the floor and his teeth were chattering. Judge
Kuykendall said the prisoner was a pitiable object of abject fear.
Even when the verdict was read, he was still shaking. I don't
think he believed it himself."

"It is hard to believe, Mr. Young," I said. I didn't know if I
was relieved or disappointed. As soon as I felt one way, I began
to feel I should *not* be feeling that way. Every emotion a man
could feel, I felt. Emotions were being shuffled inside my
confused head as if they were a deck of cards.

"It has been suggested that the jurors received bribes. That
wouldn't be so hard to do, especially with men who haven't
found their share of gold. There has always been an element,
criminal or otherwise, that has hated Hickok. It figured that
he'd be ambushed by a dirty cross-eyed little coward as
insignificant as a bug. Wild Bill deserved a better fate—a few
more friendly games of poker, a chance to reunite with his wife
and spend many years just rocking on a porch someplace far
more peaceful than Deadwood."

The bartender stamped his foot and then ground his boot into the street as if flattening a fat insect. I wasn't sure if he knew Little Jack and I had the same father.

"Where is he now?" I asked.

"He was buried this afternoon on that mountain over there, Ingleside."

"I . . . eh . . . meant Little . . . the man who shot him."

"He didn't stay around here long, left in a hurry. The lynch talk was starting again. I wouldn't be surprised if the dirty coward runs all the way to Cheyenne—better to face wild Indians and road agents along the way rather than Wild Bill's friends in Deadwood."

The best of those friends, Charlie Utter, stepped out of the crowd. "We won't lynch him, but he'll get what's due him," he said, more to me than to Harry Young. "There was no justice here today, but there will be justice at some other place and time. Mark my word. How do you feel about that, Mr. McCall? You glad your brother got off? Whose side are you on, anyway?"

Harry Young stared at me, turned away to scratch his head, and then stared again. Both looks were ones of shock.

"He's *only* my half brother. And I'm *not* siding with him. I'm all for justice."

"I see," Colorado Charlie said. "Missed you at Wild Bill's service today."

"I was busy with Dr. Babcock. Jasper Washington was badly wounded, you know."

"No, I didn't. What happened to him?"

"Little Jack shot him, too, in the No. 10. He could . . . you know, also die."

"In which case, your brother could be tried again for murder." Charlie Utter stood on his tippy-toes, and his face lit up as if he had just discovered a pocket of gold. But then he rubbed his head and put his weight back on the heels of his boots. "No damn good. The results would be no different. If he can get away with killing a celebrity lawman in cold blood, what matter is it to anyone that he also killed a colored man nobody has ever heard of."

"Jasper Washington is somebody. He was every bit as good a friend to Mr. Hickok as you are. And if he should die, it would be worse than . . . well, just as terrible. Crooked Nose Jack is responsible for that, too. I had better get back to him."

"Back to who?"

"Jasper, of course. Didn't you hear me? He could be dying."

"Not going to see your brother, then?"

"Half brother. No, sir. No matter what happens to Jasper, I don't want anything more to do with him."

"Jasper?"

"No! Little Jack."

"I would say that is wise. But if you do happen to see him—your brother, that is—tell him he'd better keep looking over his shoulder because Charlie Utter don't ever forget."

CHAPTER THIRTY-SEVEN:
THE TRIAL OF LIFE

It wasn't until three days after the assassination of Wild Bill Hickok that I finally left Dr. Babcock's office and went to Charlie Utter's camp. Jasper Washington was doing well enough with his ice packs and rectum feedings to want different clothes as well as one hundred dollars he had hidden in an old shoe for emergencies. He would be confined to the office for at least another week, and he wanted to pay for his food and the valuable medical service he was receiving. And I wanted a change of clothes myself as well as a thorough washing in Whitewood Creek. I was scouring my body with a brush and a bar of white Castile soap I borrowed from Colorado Charlie when Little Jack popped out from behind a bush but stayed low like a pocket gopher uneasy about showing itself above ground.

"It's me," he said, as if I couldn't see for myself. "I had a hell of a time finding you, Brother. I reckon you've been avoiding me since . . . since the shooting."

"There were two shootings and you did them both. Don't call me brother."

"Keep your voice down, Brother. If Utter finds me here, my goose is cooked. He and his friends would surely string me up in that old cottonwood across the creek."

"Don't call me brother! I hate you for what you did."

"I had to kill Hickok."

"To avenge my death, I heard. I can't believe you got away with it."

431

"He always looked down his nose at me at the bar, at the poker table, everywhere! It's been the same since Springfield. To him, I was dirt. You, too. He considered us McCalls nothing but Southern dirt. He could never even remember our names."

"You shot him in the back of the head for that? I'm ashamed at what you did. I'm ashamed at myself for not stopping you. No matter how hard I brush, I can't get all the Southern dirt off."

"All right. All right. Not so loud. We have nothing to be ashamed about. If I hadn't shot Hickok, he would have shot me sooner or later."

"I don't believe that. Anyway, he never would have shot you from behind."

"I wouldn't have had a chance facing him head on. The jurors understood that and—"

"Damn you. There's no excuse for what you did. And to top it off, you shot Jasper."

"The black bastard was charging me."

"He was unarmed."

"I saw those big arms of his coming toward me. He would have squeezed me to death. He's done that kind of thing before."

If I hadn't been stark naked, I might have charged Little Jack myself. I had to settle for punching the creek water—and I did it with such force that I splashed water in my own face and lost my balance.

"Looks to me like you're plain angry, angrier than you are ashamed about anything."

"Not about *anything* . . . about you and what you did. If Jasper doesn't fully recover, then I'll . . . well, there's no telling what I might do."

"Look, Zach. You've been plenty angry at me before. You got over it before, and you'll get over it again. I was angry as a black bear caught in a trap when you did Calamity Jane that way behind my back. But I got over it. In fact, right now I'd rather see a man-killing brown bear than Calamity. She acts like I killed her husband or something when Hickok didn't even care a mule's ass about her. She'd see me hanged in a second if she had her way. But don't think just because she hates me that it'll do you any good. Only thing on her mind is the dead Wild Bill. To have her again you'd need to grow a mustache, put on buckskins, and offer her a pot of gold."

"I haven't given Calamity Jane a single thought during this calamity you yourself created."

"That's good. Real good. We can't hold a grudge a second longer."

"You looked like you wanted to shoot me, too. Why didn't you? And why not do so now? I'm an easy target standing here naked in midstream."

"I didn't shoot you, did I? I won't ever do that. That's Civil War stuff, a brother shooting a brother. It doesn't happen nowadays. Brothers got to stick together. Okay, half brothers. But we have enough of the same McCall blood running through us to carry us through anything anyone throws at us, including Hickok's friends." Little Jack pounded his chest but then glanced around nervously. Finally, he dared crawl closer to the creek, as far as where my clothes lay in a pile.

"You got away with murder. What more do you want?"

"Your support. You want the hotheads to lynch me? Even Tid Bit has turned against me."

"I don't know what I want. My head's pretty hot right now, too. You'd better leave."

"Right. I want to leave Deadwood. Stick your head under the water, cool off, and come out. We'll leave together, as always."

"It's never been *always.* I'm not going anywhere with you, Little Jack. Those days are gone."

"What's keeping you here? You don't have work. And I

already told you, you don't have Calamity. We could go to Montana Territory. No. That's where Custer got it. Cheyenne wasn't really so bad. We're free men. We can go back to Wyoming Territory or wherever we want, as long as it's the West. I ain't ever going East again. Nothing for us back there."

I did stick my head under water for a long time. I panicked after a while and raised up abruptly, coughing from having gulped a mouthful of water. I shook myself off like a wet dog. My half brother was still there at water's edge, now crouched like a wild animal.

"You are on your own, Crooked Nose Jack. Go now."

"All right, I will. But the cheating Hickok and Washington teamed up and took everything I had the other night and . . ."

"Is that why you shot them? You thought they somehow cheated you and . . ."

"No, no. I already told you why I shot them—self-defense, self-protection."

"You can go to hell, Little Jack."

"I'll need some traveling money, Brother."

"Like you said, I don't work; I don't have any money . . ." I remembered that I had the hundred dollars in paper money that Jasper had asked me to fetch from his old shoe. It was in a pouch pinned to the inside of my blue flannel shirt. "Anyway, nothing for you. That jury gave you your life. Take it and get the hell out of Deadwood so you don't lose it again."

"You know something, Zach. You're acting just like Fat Jack McCall did—as mean as a rattlesnake. I won't stand for it!"

But Crooked Nose Jack did stand, and when he did, he had my grey-blue Kentucky jean trousers in his hands. He was going through the pockets. When he came up empty, he picked up my blue shirt, unbuttoned it, and turned it inside out.

"What are you doing!" I yelled. "Leave my clothes alone."

"You were holding out on me, Bastard McCall. I only wanted

ten dollars to buy me a mule. Now I can purchase a fine horse and ride to Cheyenne in style. Never expected this." He waved the currency and flicked the pin at me.

"Hey, that's not my money. It belongs to Jasper. I'm taking it to him."

"All the better. Looks like a hundred bucks. That big black bastard was as rotten as Hickok. See you later, Brother."

I plowed my way through the creek water, but by the time I reached the bank, Crooked Nose Jack was gone and so were my clothes. I just stood there dripping dry and getting madder all the time, as much at myself as him for having believed, or half-believed, for more than a decade in the West that he was capable of becoming a decent man. I finally looked up at the sky, maybe to ask the Lord what I should do now. At that very instant an aggressive cloud, black as Jasper, blotted out the sun.

Fortunately, I had other clothes and more of Jasper Washington's shoe reserves in my nearby tent. Once in town, I checked around and peppered people with questions. I didn't learn who had sold Little Jack a horse, but one observant gambler described having seen less than a half hour ago a rider with a bent nose, slightly crossed eyes, curling light hair, and florid complexion that he identified as "the scamp that shot the shoot-ist Hickok and got away with it." When I finally made it back to Dr. Babcock's office and sheepishly told Jasper what had happened, he patted me on the head as if I were the wounded man and told me everything would fix itself in time.

"You mean one day Crooked Nose Jack will get himself shot or otherwise killed and have to answer to God and be punished for the sins he committed on earth?" I asked.

"Hell, no," Jasper said. "You're thinking like a preacher again, Zach. It won't take nearly that long for justice to be served."

"Whatever happens to him, happens. I'll be happy enough just to *not* see him again and *not* think of him too much."

I did almost forget about my half brother for a while. Jasper's strong constitution allowed him to get back on his feet much more quickly than Dr. Babcock had anticipated. After the stitches came out, Jasper moved back in with me at Whitewood Creek camp to continue his recovery. I continued to do things for him. Charlie Utter, once he stopped blaming Jasper and pretty much the rest of Deadwood's population for Wild Bill's death, also provided assistance, telling me, "It's too late to help Bill, but at least I can help his right-hand man—and I know Bill would like that." In mid-August, all three of us left the camp and moved into town. Jasper bought a two-room log building from a miner who had found just enough gold to get out while the going was good. Jasper, telling me straight out he liked my company, allowed me to share it with him, while Colorado Charlie, intent as always upon having his own sleeping quarters, rented a well-built shack next to Salida's Bath House.

Not being able to sit at a poker table just yet, Jasper had about used up all his old shoe money. I decided I was done taking advantage of his generosity and finally got myself a job. It was a good one, too. I was back in the hardware store business, working for Seth Bullock and Sol Star at, as their wordy sign said, *Office of Star and Bullock, Auctioneers and Commission Merchants.* They had recently purchased a lot and set up a tent, but they were a bright, enterprising duo and figured to move into a sound wood structure before fall. They needed me to help because Bullock was busy with other things, serving on the Board of Health and Street Commission that ran the town and then becoming defacto county sheriff on August 21. He was a good man and a good lawman. Mr. Hickok would have approved.

While I rarely called to mind Crooked Nose Jack that month, a few other things bothered me. One of them was what happened to the Reverend Henry Weston Smith, whom I'd heard preaching against sin on the corner a time or two. This only minister in the Black Hills was not liked by many in Deadwood's rough crowd that represented the saloons and brothels, but when someone worried about his safety, he replied: "The Bible is my protection. It has never failed me yet." Well, it didn't fail him in Deadwood itself, but on August 20 he left a note on his cabin door, saying, "Gone to Crook City to preach, and if God is willing, will be back at three o'clock." God wasn't willing on that day. Reverend Smith was shot through the heart as he walked the ten miles to Crook City, and since he wasn't robbed, most folks figured the worst of the natural-born sinners or maybe Indians had done it.

I prayed often on his behalf after I heard the news—not that it would do any good for him now. I also considered trying to fill his shoes and become the next circuit preacher in the Black Hills. I got over that notion fairly quickly, though, telling myself I had just started at the hardware store and couldn't very well quit on Star and Bullock. Besides, the truth was, my name was McCall, and I knew I was better at selling lumber, lamps, furniture, and mining equipment than trying to sell people on the Creator, good will, and righteousness.

It also bothered me the one time I visited Calamity Jane, with two weeks' salary pinned under my shirt no less, to see how things stood between her and me. It wasn't just that I lacked female companionship in a woman-starved mining camp or that I was attracted to a woman who could dress, drink, shoot, swear, and spit like a man. I honestly believed I could see past her rough and rugged side and enjoy her softer, gentler side. And I indeed did see some of that milder side again when she spoke adoringly of the man she loved, Wild Bill Hickok, and how she would always retain his memory fresh in her bosom. But then the rough-and-rugged Calamity took over. Once she connected my face to a certain place (Tid Bit's shack) and I helped her recall my name, she drew a long-bladed knife and held it under my nose.

"You're the son of a bitch brother of that monstrous McCall, and you ain't even dead!" she screamed. "I'm betting you helped your goddamned kin escape this goddamned town before I could slit his goddamned throat. I can't get at him, but I can get at you. How'd he like it if I spilled your blood?"

"Don't know. I do know I wouldn't like it, Miss Jane. Sorry, I don't know your actual last name. I'm *not* like Jack McCall one bit. I'd swear on a stack of Bibles to that."

"I don't have time for any of your goddamn swearing," she said, but she put the knife away. "I won't kill you, and I won't cut you up too bad. But least I can do is punch you in the nose."

I flinched but held my ground. "And maybe I deserve it. I was Mr. Hickok's friend, too, you know."

'Friend? Hogwash. That's easy for you to say now. But let me tell you something, Jack McCall's brother. I was closer to Bill than I ever was to any man in all my born days. He was more than a friend. More than a lover. He was a goddamned God."

It didn't look like she was going to punch me, so I bowed my head and then tipped my hat. "Sorry to bother you, Miss Jane," I said as I retreated to the safety of the hardware store.

And so I went about my business, determined to show Star and Bullock that I was as honest and hard working as any man who ever set foot in gold country and to act the same way when they weren't looking. But I also read the out-of-town news-papers and heard the rumors at the store. Little Jack McCall was back in the news. He couldn't go off and live quietly in anonymity. In Julesburg, Colorado, and then in Laramie,

Wyoming Territory, he couldn't keep his mouth shut. He crowed about killing the celebrated Wild Bill Hickok and even boasted that earlier he had slapped the arrogant gunman in the face without consequence. He was either the biggest fool in the West or thought he was beyond the law or justice for Hickok's murder.

Apparently none other than Colorado Charlie had convinced the Wyoming authorities that Little Jack's trial had been illegal because Deadwood was on Indian land and not officially in a U.S. state or territory. My half brother was arrested in Laramie on August 29, taken to Cheyenne for a preliminary hearing and then transported to Yankton on the eastern end of Dakota Territory. On October 18 he was indicted for murder and pleaded not guilty. Not liking his chances for getting off a second time, he tried a November jailbreak that failed. He tried to make a deal with the prosecution, saying someone in Deadwood had paid him to assassinate Wild Bill. That also failed. His trial was set for December.

Jasper Washington had returned to the poker tables at the end of September and was once again winning more than his share of big pots. He was determined to take another long break, though, so he could testify against Little Jack. Star and Bullock, who were as good to me as Chester Greeley had been when I worked at the Boettcher and Company Hardware in Cheyenne, gave me all the time I needed to do what I had to do in Yankton. They said my job would be waiting for me whenever I got back. "I really don't have to go," I told them. "I didn't even go to his first trial. It's nearly four hundred miles to Yankton, and my half brother is out of my life. Whatever happens to him, happens to him. It's no concern of mine." They knew better. Little Jack had popped back into my head and refused to leave. I reluctantly made the exhausting trip with Jasper, crossing the prairie and creeks by horseback on the trail to Fort Pierre and then catching a Missouri River steamboat down to Yankton.

The second trial began in earnest at 10 a.m. on December 4 in U.S. District Court, Judge Peter C. Shannon presiding. Little Jack put on a bold front, showing no excitement or anxiety except when he saw Jasper and me sitting in the back of the courtroom. "You're late, friend," he called out, even though I had arrived with a minute to spare. He no doubt realized it was best not to call me brother, seeing as how he had previously contended that Hickok killed me. "No matter, old friend. You haven't missed much. The fireworks are still to come."

I did not tell anyone who I was. Jasper Washington wanted everyone to know who he was, even going so far as to show the jagged scar on his belly to one of the prosecutors. The prosecution, however, neither wanted nor needed a large, forbidding black man to testify. The No. 10 Saloon owner, Carl Mann, and Captain William Massie, two of the players present when Hickok was dealt his dead man's hand, were highly reliable eyewitnesses. Mann pointed the finger at Little Jack on the trial's first day, and Massie did so on the second. On the third day, December 6, the defense made its case, attorneys delivered their closing arguments, and the jury began deliberation at 7 p.m. We missed supper because Jasper insisted that we not go anywhere. He got angrier as each hour passed while I alternated between suppressing yawns and biting my lip. At last, near midnight, the jurors returned their verdict: guilty.

"About time!" Jasper shouted, patting his belly and then pounding his chest. "Justice at last! Justice! Justice! Justice!"

Judge Shannon waited for him to finish before pounding his gavel and suppressing what looked to be his own half smile and half yawn.

Sentencing wouldn't be for a month, and that disappointed Jasper all over again. He knew they would never let him into the jailhouse to see the prisoner but wanted me to go. "They can't say no to a family member," he insisted. "You can tell him exactly how you feel about him—that he is nothing more than a murdering, thieving no-account liar, and you hope he hangs slowly and painfully."

"I don't know exactly how I feel," I admitted. "He's done some horrible things, but he is my brother."

"Half brother," Jasper reminded me. "What do you want to tell him, then?"

"Nothing. There's nothing more to be said. I want to go, not to the jail, but back to Deadwood. I want to get back to work and back to . . . well, anything else. I've spent too much time thinking about him. He's guilty, and he'll pay for it."

Jasper protested a little but gave in for a change. We would catch the next steamboat headed upriver to Fort Pierre.

"But that judge better sentence him to hang," Jasper said. "And the execution better take place pronto, or I'll return looking for real justice!"

I wouldn't have wanted to go back to Yankton no matter what, and, as it turned out, there was no reason for Jasper to do any correcting of the law. On January 3, 1877, according to the newspapers, Little Jack appeared once more before Judge Shannon and in desperation claimed he had been so intoxicated on the afternoon of August 2, 1876, he didn't know what he was doing. The judge didn't buy it and sentenced the convicted killer to hanging on March 1. The defense attorneys said the territorial governor supported the claim McCall was drunk and even petitioned the president of the United States to issue a pardon. The government declined to interfere with the sentence of the court. The hanging went on as scheduled.

If the papers are to be believed, Crooked Nose Jack spent his last few nights eating and sleeping well and his last days talking to a Catholic priest and reading the Bible. There was no reason for him to confess about anything; everyone knew all about the worst things he had done. One newspaper based in Missouri (perhaps out of Springfield—I can't remember) quoted him as telling the priest: "You know what, Father, I got a brother who was born in Kentucky like me, and he's still alive. Not only that but he did some preaching for a spell back there and has never been guilty of a crime anywhere that I know of. I called him mean to his face, and I regret that. Someone called him Wild Child, but he never was that. Truth is, he acted pretty damn good to me through the years—if you'll pardon my language, Father—not anything like our *father*, who was a real bastard, let me tell you."

Crooked Nose Jack's last words, according to most accounts, were cried out when the trap door of the gallows sprang open: "Oh, God." He had disgraced the McCall name, not that it was ever held in high regard. I had to carry the name onward, of course, but I kept as anonymous as possible after leaving Deadwood in September 1879 when a fire damaged much of the business district. Before I left, I received a terse letter from none other than Minnie Mary that the Daniel's Den in Boonesborough had closed its doors after Belle Bragg died peacefully in bed. That saddened me, of course, and convinced me I had no reason to ever return to Kentucky.

I could have stayed on in Deadwood, I suppose, and the increasingly civilized residents in Deadwood rebuilt the place in brick and stone instead of lumber. But Jasper Washington was ready to move west again, this time to Montana Territory. Silver and copper had been discovered, and Butte had emerged as a bustling, growing city with plenty of opportunities for accomplished poker players to strike it rich and no doubt several decent hardware stores to boot. By then the Sioux had returned to the reservations in Dakota Territory so I wasn't too worried about making the journey. I had no idea what kind of law and order there was in Butte, but safety wasn't a big concern, not when I was with Jasper Washington, who had become like a brother to me and who I knew, whenever possible, would be watching my back.

ABOUT THE AUTHOR

Gregory J. Lalire majored in history at the University of New Mexico; worked for newspapers in New Mexico, Montana, New York, and Virginia; and has been editor of *Wild West* magazine since 1995. His fiction books include *The Red Sweater* (1982), *Captured: From the Frontier Diary of Infant Danny Duly* (2014), *Our Frontier Pastime: 1804-1815* (2019), and *Man from Montana* (2021). He was a Western Writers of America (WWA) Spur Finalist for his article "Custer's Art Stand" in the April 1994 *Wild West* and a WWA Stirrup Award winner in 2015 for his nonfiction article about baseball in the West. He lives in Lees-burg, Virginia.

The employees of Five Star Publishing hope you have enjoyed this book.

Our Five Star novels explore little-known chapters from America's history, stories told from unique perspectives that will entertain a broad range of readers.

Other Five Star books are available at your local library, bookstore, all major book distributors, and directly from Five Star/Gale.

Connect with Five Star Publishing

Website:
  gale.com/five-star

Facebook:
  facebook.com/FiveStarCengage

Twitter:
  twitter.com/FiveStarCengage

Email:
  FiveStar@cengage.com

For information about titles and placing orders:
  (800) 223-1244
  gale.orders@cengage.com

To share your comments, write to us:
  Five Star Publishing
  Attn: Publisher
  10 Water St., Suite 310
  Waterville, ME 04901